M000012437

Acclaim for *Blood Seed*

"In a book world replete with genre reads, *Blood Seed* offers something different: a potent mix of fantasy, romance, intrigue, and a believable protagonist whose current dilemma is just the beginning."
D. Donovan, Senior Reviewer, Midwest Book Review

"There is something mysterious about Sheft that draws Mariat toward him, and they eventually fall in love. But the author refused to create a predictable love story. *Blood Seed* has all the elements of a fantasy novel [but] does not let you swim in a shallow sea of fiction writing. A new approach to this genre. Five stars!"
Readers' Favorite

"A riveting, beautifully rendered piece with stunning depth…The protagonist, Sheft, is unique and strong enough to rise above the wounds that would have destroyed most people. A wonderful and original tale with a strong story/character arc for the series as a whole."
Lorin Oberweger, *award-winning author, poet, and independent book editor.*

"Fascinating concept, intriguing characters. *Blood Seed* is a beautifully crafted page-turner."
Bonnie Hearn Hill, *author of If Anything Should Happen, Severn House.*

Blood Seed

Coin of Rulve Book One

by Veronica Dale

Nika Press

Published by Nika Press

Macomb, MI

Copyright © 2016 by Nika Press
ISBN 13:978-0-9969521-0-1

*Thanks to my family and my novel critique group,
for walking with me through the long haul!*

Cover: Christa Holland, Paper and Sage
Map: Jaimie Trampus

Dear Reader...

Even though *Blood Seed* is the first of a series, it can be read and relished on its own. For many readers, that's all the information they might need. But for those who want to know more, read on.

Blood Seed is the start of a four-book journey. I've been on this journey—writing the Coin of Rulve series—since 2003, so I can offer a few tips about what to expect.

First, if you've never read a fantasy book before, don't be leery of trying this one. For many who reviewed or critiqued *Blood Seed* , it was their first experience with fantasy. And most of them were pleasantly surprised. There are no vampires, faeries, or superheroes in the Coin series. Nothing against these; they're just not there. But plenty of dark Shadows are.

The Shadow is psychologist Carl Jung's term for the part of ourselves that we regard as weak or bad, or a challenge we just can't deal with. This Shadow can be denied—and therefore gets projected into our horror stories or even onto other people or groups—or it can be met face-to-face.

Such self-acceptance takes tremendous courage, but Jung believed that those who meet the Shadow's challenge will find an inner light. In *Blood Seed*, the protagonist encounters the Shadow in several nightmarish forms.

Second, even though I have a background in pastoral

ministry, I'm not a preacher! As one reviewer wrote about my short story collection *Night Cruiser*, "The author never lets religion get in the way of her highly spiritual and deeply psychological message." Many books that make an impression on us are like that. They treat spirituality—not necessarily any particular religion—as an integral part of what makes us human.

Falling in love, longing for what we do not know, or struggling to believe in oneself despite the scorn of others can be a life-changing spiritual experience. All of these and more happen in *Blood Seed*.

In short, this book describes a "eucatastrophe," Tolkien's word for a tragic event that can be redeemed. His *Lord of the Rings* is a prime example of that, as are the New Testament Passion narratives.

So, take a chance with *Blood Seed* and walk the first step with me in the *Coin of Rulve* journey. I'd be grateful for your company!

P.S. A heads-up: Questions for Discussion are listed at the back of this book. You might find them helpful if you belong to a book club, would like to start one with a few friends, or just want to get clued into what might be happening at a deeper level in *Blood Seed*. If you're like me and want to be on the lookout for these questions as you read, take a glance at them before you begin.

Veronica ("Vernie") Dale
www.veronicadale.com

TABLE OF CONTENTS

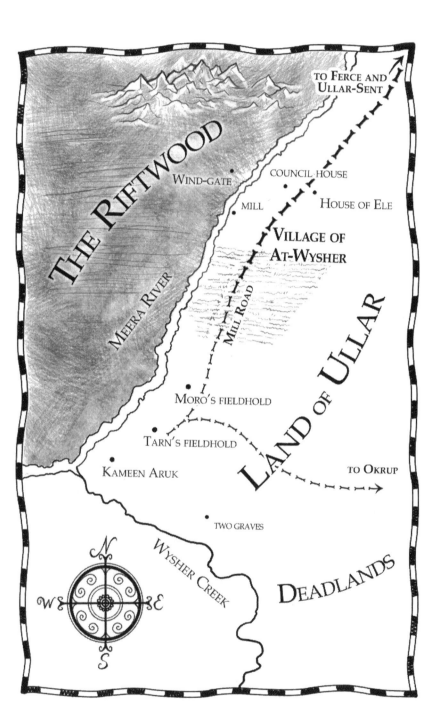

THE RIFTWOOD

TO FERCE AND
ULLAR-SENT

WIND-GATE

COUNCIL·HOUSE

MILL

HOUSE OF ELE

VILLAGE OF
AT-WYSHER

MEERA RIVER

MILL ROAD

LAND OF ULLAR

MORO'S FIELDHOLD

TARN'S FIELDHOLD

TO OKRUP

KAMEEN ARUK

TWO GRAVES

N

W

E

WYSHER CREEK

DEADLANDS

S

Every one of us carries the cross of the redeemer—not in the bright moments of our victories, but in the silence of our personal despair.
Joseph Campbell, *The Hero with a Thousand Faces*

Blessed is the one who is alone and chosen.
Gospel of Thomas

Blood Seed

Coin of Rulve Book One

Chapter 1

Night Beetles

Sheft lay rigid on his mat in the loft. Only last night his beloved had slept here, but she never would again. Only hours ago, he thought he knew who he was, but had been wrong. And now he could no longer push aside the fear that flickered through his veins. It was the month of Hawk, and the dark of the moon. What he might have to do tomorrow night terrified him.

The low roof beam, from which dangled bunches of herbs and the ghostly white knobs of dried onions, stretched into the shadows. The tendriled shapes hung down like roots, and turned slowly in the air.

No one ever spoke about the Rites, and he had no idea what happened there. But one thing he did know. If the hostility all around him broke his concentration, if he couldn't summon his power to stop it, then tomorrow night he would come face to face with the entity he most feared.

(Twelve years earlier, in the month of Seed)

I've got to hurry, Sheft thought as he grabbed a bag of seed and the spade from the barn. It would be dark soon, and no one ever stayed out after dark. He glanced at the Riftwood, looming only two fields away. Already the

3

claws of its ancient trees seemed to be reaching up to catch and devour the setting sun.

The rest of his chores were done, but even though he'd never get all the peas planted before sunset, he could at least make enough of a start to satisfy his father.

He'd just turned six, and Father had decreed him old enough to handle the spade, but it felt a lot heavier and more awkward than he'd expected. He slung the bag of seeds over his shoulder and, dragging the spade behind him, headed toward the kitchen garden.

He couldn't help but look at the Riftwood again. Every twilight, when the forest cast its long shadow over the fields, his father barred the door, his mother drew the curtains, and outside their house their whole fieldhold lay uneasy under the night.

He had just reached the star-nut tree when soft cries of distress stopped him. They came from the nest up there, from the two mewlet babies that had been born on his birthday, just a few days ago on the sixth of Seed. He hadn't told his father about the little creatures, even though he was supposed to. They used their surprisingly human-looking hands to steal from orchards and kitchen gardens and then escaped by swinging through the trees, balancing their bodies with their long tails. Farmers killed any they could catch.

It sounded like the mewlets needed help.

Setting the bag and spade aside, he climbed up to the third big branch. A pair of big eyes looked at him. They belonged to the father mewlet, who sat in a nest made of twigs and old leaves and held one of the babies on his lap.

His own father, Tarn, never held him on his lap. Only his mother did—sometimes.

The mother mewlet had disappeared two days ago, probably taken by a hawk. In other animal families, her

4

absence meant the babies would die. But this wasn't always the case for mewlets. In emergency situations, the father could feed the babies from a wound he scratched into his chest. He was doing that right now for one of them.

Not much bigger than Sheft's outspread hand, the baby mewlet clutched at her father's fur with tiny pink fingers and made gratified grunts and murmurs as she sucked. Her much smaller brother—Sheft had named him Squeak—crawled around, making soft squeaks, his eyes never leaving his father's chest.

When the first baby was finished, the father would sometimes open another wound with his sharp, brown claw, but sometimes he seemed just too drained. Then Squeak would make those hungry mewing sounds that pulled at Sheft's heart.

They were like the cries he sometimes heard carried by the wind. They came from far away, from across the river, from people who sounded hurt and lost. They seemed to be looking in his direction, crying out to him, and he always wanted to rush off and help them. But the sound came from across the Meera River, from out of the dangerous Riftwood.

"I know you're hungry," he said to Squeak, "but I'll keep you company while you wait your turn." He sat back against the trunk of the tree and watched the father feed his bigger baby. The mewlet was a good father, giving his very blood to his child. Maybe one day he'd be a father like that.

The wind made golden shade-dapples pass over the branches, and a feeling of peace settled over him. From up here, the sun didn't seem so low, and the dark further off. He sighed in contentment, but worry still squirmed in the back of his mind. His mother would call him in any minute now, and he hadn't even started digging a row for the peas.

He was about to shimmy down the tree when a startling blur of feathers and claws swooped down on the nest. A hawk. The father mewlet leaped to his feet, the baby clinging to him, and fought furiously while Squeak clutched at the tossing branch.

"No!" Sheft cried. He crawled toward the nest, the branch dangerously dipping, but it was already too late. Squeak couldn't hold on. He tumbled down, just as the hawk took off with his father and sister in its claws.

Sheft half-slid, half-jumped down the tree, his chest so full of pain he could hardly breathe. Squeak lay on the ground and Sheft fell to his knees beside him. The baby was trembling. As gently as he could, Sheft scooped him up and held him against his shirt. He seemed to weigh almost nothing. "Are you all right? Are you hurt?"

The baby mewed weakly and began to root against Sheft's chest.

"I don't think I can feed you."

The big eyes looked up at him; the little mouth made hopeful sucking motions.

Its father and mother were gone, and Squeak had nobody left. "I'll try," he said.

He put the baby down, pulled off his shirt, and grabbed his father's awl out of his pants pocket. He'd used it a few hours earlier to inscribe the letter T onto the skin above his knee. He'd hoped that would get rid of the loneliness, the longing for a brother, for someone his own age who would play with him during the day and sleep with him at night, back to back. Somehow, the T stood for this person. Drawing it hadn't helped though. He felt just as lonely as ever.

Now, as he had seen the father mewlet do, he cut his

chest with the awl. It hurt a little, but he forgot about that as he swept Squeak to the wound. He cupped him in both hands, feeling the fragile bones under the tautly stretched fur. The warm little mouth began sucking, and the baby sighed in satisfaction.

It felt odd at first, but Sheft closed his eyes and let the baby pull nourishment out of him. A pleasant sensation seeped through his body and wrapped like a warm, furry animal around his heart. *I'm sort of being a good father already*, he thought.

The little body at his chest tensed, and Sheft looked down. The baby had stopped sucking. Its face twisted in pain.

"Oh no," Sheft whispered. "Did something break inside you when you fell?"

The big eyes fluttered as a spasm shook it.

"Don't die," he pleaded. With one finger he rubbed the bare little stomach and then the side of its face.

"Please don't die."

But it did.

Squeak lay still, the light gone from his once-bright eyes. Sheft rocked him as tears spilled down his cheeks. He tried to warm the tiny body between his hands, but it still turned cold. An ache swelled inside him, so big it hurt his ribs. He squeezed his eyes shut, until finally it passed.

There was one last thing he could do. Getting onto his knees, he leaned over to scoop a shallow depression in the ground. He laid the little mewlet into its final nest and covered it with a blanket of last year's leaves.

Tears blurred his vision, so it took him a minute to notice that blood dripped from his chest. It was making a dark, moist spot on the ground. The earth was stirring on that spot. He sat back on his heels and watched as a mat of tiny bubbles formed.

He'd bled before, but never so much that his blood dripped onto the ground. It hadn't happened even this afternoon, when he drew the T. Sheft stared in astonishment as the bubbles hardened into seeds. All by themselves, they burrowed into the earth and then, making soft crickly sounds, little plants pushed their heads up. They swelled with green and spread out their baby leaves. Were they real? He touched them. They felt soft under his hand, just like the little mewlet's fur.

His blood was doing this. It was bringing something fresh and green out of the soil—like farmers did with their seeds, like his father did in the fields. Joy bloomed from the very center of his body. Squeak had died, but this patch of soil lived. Father would be amazed and proud.

Almost breathless with excitement, he dried the chest wound with a handful of grass, pulled his shirt back on, and ran the short distance to the barn, where his father was repairing one of the paper-making screens.

"Father, come see!"

Tapping the screen back into its frame with his hammer, his father did not look up. "I've seen enough pea-furrows in my life."

"It's something better than that! Come on."

Frowning, his father threw the hammer down and followed him to the spot.

"Look what I did!" Sheft exclaimed. "I bled on the ground and grew these plants."

His father shoved him roughly aside, his eyes wide and staring. "What is this? You were supposed to plant peas, not invent stories." He grabbed the spade and speared at the newborn plants. He chopped the delicate seed-heads from the stems, twisted the roots into the soil. Some of the leaves still poked out of the ground, and he stomped on them as if they were a pile of night-beetles, fat and hard to kill.

Hot tears blurred Sheft's vision, and the place beneath his ribs hurt, as if something rooted there was being viciously wrenched out. *I'm sorry!* he wailed in his heart. *I'm sorry!* But he didn't know for what, and his father didn't seem to hear.

His face red, Tarn turned to look down at him. It was as if he looked at something inhuman, as if he saw in his own son one of the creatures that lurked in the Riftwood. "By Ele's eyes," he barked, "I'd hoped for a boy who'd help me fight the dark, and instead I got one who invents tales about it."

Father dragged him into the house. "Get up to bed," he ordered.

Mama turned away from the hearth at their abrupt entrance, but said nothing.

Sheft climbed the ladder to his loft and crawled onto his straw mattress. The cut on his chest stung, and beneath him his parents spoke in angry, hissing voices. He couldn't make out the words, but knew they were arguing about whatever it was he had done.

It grew dark, and the voices petered out. All was silent below. To his right, a knothole in the floorboard glowed from the fire lit room beneath. He rolled onto his stomach and peered through it.

His mother, alone now, moved about. Her form disappeared from view as she headed toward the hearth. A gurgle and clink told him she had added water to the stew and covered the pot for the night. He was hungry, but there was nothing for it but to lie back and cover himself up.

The little owl that lived under the eaves gave out its sad hoot.

Or was it the owl? Maybe it was the baby mewlet.

Sheft bolted upright. Could Squeak still be alive under the leaves?

But he was too afraid to go out and see. It was night, and the Riftwood was much too close. All the tales he had heard about what lived inside the old forest jumped into his head. Tales of wraiths and voras, of luniku moths that laid their eggs in your ears, of a snake-brown stream that was never seen twice in the same place. But what scared him the most was the thing that crept out of the tales and into their everyday lives: the black mist.

On certain nights, it gathered itself out of the darkness under the great trees and found its way across the Meera River. It crawled over fields and sniffed around houses, trying to find a way inside. Sometimes it rose from the root cellar beneath your house, or seeped up through the floorboards, taking monstrous shape next to your bed.

They called it the Groper, because it had no eyes.

Sometimes it changed into the beetle-man, and then its name was Wask. Wask was a flesh-eater, and it could see.

Uneasy, he pulled the blanket up to his chin. What if Squeak were all alone in the dark, weak and shivering in the cold? He needed help. Now, before it was too late.

"Come with me," he whispered to the boy whose name began with T.

Sheft wrapped the blanket around his shoulders and crawled through the black rectangular opening in the floor. Halfway down the ladder he stopped and glanced at the door to his parents' room. It was closed, and he heard nothing beyond it. The fire in the hearth was banked for the night.

"Shhh," he whispered.

He padded to the door and reached up to lift the bar. The hinges creaked, but after a moment, satisfied his parents had not heard, he slipped outside.

Frigid air struck his face and he blinked against the glaring brightness of a full moon hanging just above a cloud bank. It cast shadows everywhere, in a confusing welter of stark black and white. Nothing looked familiar.

He shivered and drew the blanket closer around him. Over the fields and across the Meera, the Riftwood rose up like a big, ever-threatening storm. The barn seemed far off. He thought of his warm bed, but the call he'd heard pulled him forward.

The ground felt damp and cold under his bare feet, and he was afraid he would step into icy pools that had not existed during the day, but which seemed to have formed during the night. But they were only moon-shadows, lying motionless because there was no wind. Nothing moved. No night-beetles stealthily pulled themselves out of the earth.

He turned the corner of the house and crept after his long shadow, keeping his eyes fixed on the base of the big, silent star-nut tree.

What was that? He stopped to listen, but heard nothing but his own heart thumping.

"Maybe we should go back," he whispered.

But he couldn't. Not until he was sure about Squeak.

The leaf-covered spot lay not far ahead. When he got there, a quick investigation told him the baby mewlet was still safely dead. He exhaled his relief.

Suddenly a warning jangled in his head. Something was coming over the fields. He felt it, a chill on his arms. He heard it, a rustling in the night. And then he saw it. From the crooked, rectangular shadow of the barn, a black ground-mist was emerging. It poured silently into the moonlight like a rivulet of poison. His stomach clenched.

Don't be afraid. Don't be afraid. The Groper had no eyes. If he didn't make a sound, if he didn't breathe or move a single muscle, it wouldn't know he was there. He stood perfectly still, trying to keep his shadow from trembling on the moonlit ground.

Like a monstrous hand, the leading edge of the mist crawled toward him. Barely two strides away, it halted, and lifted three long, foggy fingers. Like sensitive feelers, they turned from side to side. Then, as if it had detected something, the hand rustled through the dead leaves to the spot where he had bled. The fingers hunched over it and scrabbled eagerly at the soil.

As if it were eating.

Sheft's heart pounded so loudly the mist must have heard. The fingers reared up, pointed directly at him, and stiffened.

An icy knot formed beneath his ribs. It clenched tighter and tighter, crystallizing into his abdomen and spreading through his entire body. He froze.

With heart-sinking inevitability, the moon slid into a cloud bank. Encased in ice, he couldn't see, couldn't move, couldn't swallow. *Don't be afraid. Don't be afraid.*

Leaves rustled.

With startling suddenness the moonlight rolled back. The misty appendages, like a three-headed snake poised to strike, stood only inches away from his bare foot. His toes tingled, about to be touched.

The strange ice that had formed inside him seeped into his head. It numbed his thoughts, froze the back of his throat.

Don't breathe. Stay very, very still. Ice gripped him, yet his hands were sweating.

The Groper hissed, like a long slow chill. There was something here it didn't like.

The fingers drew back; then slowly, one by one, withdrew into the body of the mist. As silently as it had come, it flowed backward, into the shadow of the barn. The blackness there momentarily increased with its presence, then ebbed away.

It was gone. He took a deep, tremulous breath.

A faint chittering sound pulled his eyes to the ground. The spot where he had bled teemed with night-beetles as big as acorns, their busy brown shells glinting in the moonlight. Something cold crawled over his foot. A beetle. Its horny mouth parts clicked and its antennae whisked back and forth. Wildly, he shook it off and ran.

Back in his bed, he shivered beneath his blanket and rubbed his foot over the place where the beetle had crawled. The strange ice inside him took a long time to thaw.

He dreamed the beetle-man crept after him as he ran in terror through moon-touched dream-fields. His own footsteps followed him, and they were packed with roots; and just when he thought he was safe in the loft, the beetle-man rose from the black rectangle beside his bed, chittering.

CHAPTER 2

HIDDEN AND IN THE DARK

The voices of his parents awakened him in the morning. They must have been standing at the bottom of the ladder because he heard them clearly.

"I'll be taking Sheft into the village today," his father said.

Sheft's heart jumped in excitement. He'd never been to At-Wysher; Mama always said he wasn't old enough.

"The villagers won't like it," his mother answered.

"That is regrettable, but they'll have to get used to his appearance."

Sheft's excitement winked out. What was wrong with his appearance? Wavy reflections in a window or shadowy images in a bucket of water never showed him much, and he never thought about what he looked like. Maybe he was ugly.

With that thought, the memory of last night flooded back. A part of him wanted to tell his mother about it, but another part didn't. Sometimes it seemed he had two mothers, and he was afraid of the second one. That one would watch him with cold, appraising eyes, would call him "S'eft." That one would stand in the vegetable garden for long periods of time, the wind blowing her skirt, and search the skies above the Riftwood.

That one might slap him if she heard about the

mewlets, or knew he left the house at night, or thought he was making it up about the Groper. He didn't want to tell that one about the blood and the mist and the beetles.

But then there was his real mother. When she returned, he'd feel forgiven. She would read to him in the evenings from the red book of tales while he sat on her lap on the nodding chair. Twining a lock of his hair around her finger, she would laugh call him her little hayseed.

Hoping he'd find his real mother, Sheft rolled off his mat. He felt strange: light-headed and so shaky he could hardly put on his shoes. What was wrong with him? Clutching the rails to steady himself, he climbed down the ladder. At the bottom he turned to look at his mother. Backlit against the window, she stared down at him. Her face was a rayed shadow, like a storm cloud blocking the sun, and he knew he couldn't tell her anything.

After breakfast, Father hitched Padiky to the wagon and they headed into At-Wysher. His stomach fluttered as they rumbled down ruts and then onto the Mill Road, where people were working in the common fields. They straightened up to watch him pass, and their eyes were like hard, dark stones.

It was even worse in the village. The man who loaded their wagon with bags of seed gave him sour looks. Then they took his mother's frying pan to Rom the smith, so the cracked handle could be repaired. Sheft offered a shy smile to Rom's son Gwin, a big boy who worked the bellows; but Gwin only made a face at him. Tarn stopped at another shop to pick up a pair of leather boots and left him waiting in the wagon. A man walking by spat at his feet. Why were they treating him like this? Tears burned the back of his eyes, but he blinked them away.

Tarn had just climbed up on the seat next to him

when an old lady with straggly grey hair approached. His father nodded curtly to her. "Priestess."

Her sharp look raked over Sheft's hair, bored into his eyes, and then cut to Tarn. "How dare you," she hissed. "How dare you parade your sin before Ele's people!"

His father placed the boots behind him in the wagon. By the way his lips tightened, Sheft knew he was angry, but when he spoke his voice was calm. "My wife and this child are no sin. I married Riah in the Temple of Ul in a perfectly legal manner."

"Your so-called wife is a foreigner, likely a harlot from the streets. You consorted with a heathen in Ullar-Sent and this"—she jerked her pointy chin at Sheft—"is the misbegotten result! What you did is against Ele's express command."

"As interpreted by you. The time is past when the priestess of Ele can dictate who people can marry. This is an old argument, Parduka, and the council majority agrees with me."

"You mean Dorik and his ilk. They are not devout. They trample upon our traditions. But some of the elders still follow the way of truth. I warned your father not to allow you to go to Ullar-Sent. I told him you would return full of pagan notions. But no, he would not listen, and you came home with godless foreigners and an outlandish craft."

Tarn stiffened. "If you are referring to my paper-making business, that is a respectable occupation that allows scholarship to be disseminated and ignorance dissipated. And more of both, I am sure you agree, needs to be done in this town."

She grasped the edge of Tarn's seat like a hawk clutching a branch. "It is the goddess who must be obeyed, not scholars. It is she who must be pleased, for she is our only protection against Wask. I will not see the people of At-Wysher endangered."

"Nor will I. Good day." Tarn flicked the reins, and Padiky moved on.

"I will be watching," she called after them. "With Ele's eyes, I will be watching."

The old lady's stare burned on the back of Sheft's neck, but he dared not turn. One glance at his father's rigid face told him he should ask no questions. He only wanted to go home.

His father, however, announced, "I'm thirsty. We'll get something to drink at Cloor's."

They approached the door to the alehouse. Above the entrance hung a row of tiny, shriveled heads, mewlet heads. Sheft hung back, but his father dragged him inside. Everyone in the crowded room fell silent when they entered, and he walked through a tunnel of stares as Tarn steered him toward a long table in front of the hearth. There was room on the bench for only one person, so he sat stiffly on his father's knee, and soon a tankard appeared. Tarn took a long drink, and slowly the men turned away and conversations resumed. Glances continued to flick toward Sheft, but no one said anything to him.

A man with a fat stomach resumed speaking. "...and I never heard a thing. Ele knows the hairs on the back of my head stood straight up when I saw it in the morning. One of my prize calves, crawling with night-beetles."

"Last night, you say?" another man asked.

"Yep. The night of the full moon."

Sheft froze. It was a night he wanted to forget.

The second man frowned. "That's when Lola's baby died."

"So?" Tarn remarked, lighting his pipe. "The child was born sickly, Blinor."

"True," Blinor went on, "but I saw something last night too. Mist creeping out of the river and curling around my mill. I watched it from the window at the back of my house, but I didn't say nothing to the wife."

A big lump formed in Sheft's throat, hard to swallow down. The mist hadn't gone away, hadn't returned to the Riftwood. It had gone into the village.

"You gotta get them Holy Guards from Parduka," a third man advised. "Them fabric tubes filled with soil blessed by Ele. Lay 'em agin' the door cracks, Delo, and nuthin'll creep in at night."

"I *had* Holy Guards," the fat man named Delo protested, "but it got in anyway."

A cackle issued from someone sitting on the chair nearest the fire. "Hee, hee, hee! That's our Groper, all right." An old man turned to look at them, and one of his eyes stared from behind a milky white film. "But he's come out a little early, I'd say."

"It ain't time for the Rites," the miller muttered in agreement. "Not for months yet."

The old man grinned in a way Sheft didn't like. "Wask's been getting restless. For years he's been getting more and more restless." He stared pointedly at Sheft. "Ever since foreigners come into town."

Tarn put his tankard down with a thump and met the old man's gaze. "What foreigners, Pogreb? I don't see any foreigners here. Mist comes off the river and a sickly child dies, and you start harping about foreigners again?"

A man with a long nose nodded. "I wouldn't mind a few foreigners. What's wrong with new customers?"

"They don't fit in," Pogreb said darkly. "They don't understand about the Rites."

The Rites. Sheft didn't know what they were, only that he'd find out when he was old enough. The word hung over the room like a shadow. Year after year, the morning after the Rites, he'd glimpsed a long cut on his father's arm.

The man on the other side of Tarn was Dorik, who'd come to their house from time to time on council business. He was the Holdman, the head of the council of elders. Now he stood up and jabbed a finger at Pogreb. "Something bothers you, Pogreb, bring it up at the next council meeting. Meanwhile,"—he grinned and looked around—"drinks are on me."

Enthusiastic cheers greeted this remark, and in the midst of them Sheft caught the glint of Dorik's eye as it briefly met Tarn's, as if something unpleasant had been avoided. In the bustle of mugs being lifted and refilled, no one looked his way as Pogreb got out of his chair, hobbled around the table, and bent to stare into Sheft's face. One dark eye surveyed him, but the other, barely visible under the mucus-like film, seemed as cold and dead as a ghost's.

"Our Groper is looking for something," he hissed. He bared his yellow teeth in a ghastly smile. "Hee, hee, hee! What do you think it wants?"

Sheft shrank back against his father's chest and, with another cackle, Pogreb shuffled away.

Farther up the table, the miller pulled out a knife and began showing it to those around him. "Got it at the last market-fair in Ferce," he said. "See these here swirls on the hilt? Gives it a better grip." He passed the dagger around so the men could feel its weight. Some tried it out with slashing motions in the air.

At the sight of it, Sheft stiffened. It reminded him of his father's awl, and what he had done with it, and what happened after that. The room seemed to darken. He saw only the dagger, as if it flashed against a black background. The sharp blade stalked closer, getting larger, until it glittered on the table in front of him. It felt as if the point were pressing against his stomach.

"Pick it up," Tarn ordered.

Sheft hid his face against his father's shirt.

Tarn twisted him around. "I said, pick it up." He put his big hand over Sheft's and made him grasp the hilt.

Fear made him squeeze his eyes shut. Laughter rippled around him.

With a muttered oath, Tarn took his hand away and the blade passed on.

All the way home, his father stared fixedly at the road and said not a word to him.

When they got back, he hid in the barn until his father went into the fields and his mother was busy in the kitchen garden, then he darted inside the house. He had to see why the villagers glared at him, why they spit at him. Feeling guilty, he crept into his parents' bedroom, pulled out the box under the bed, and took out the mirror his mother kept there. It was a precious thing, not for children to touch, but he did it anyway. He looked into it.

He had never seen such a face. His parents and the villagers all had beautiful brown eyes, not these frightening silver eyes that stared out like a fish's. Everyone else had rich chestnut hair that gleamed in the sun, not these pale, straw-colored strands that fell over his forehead. Is this why his mother called him her little hayseed? Was this really him?

He touched his hair, his eyes, and the hand in the mirror did the same. This was what the priestess saw, what Pogreb saw: the sin, the misbegotten thing.

A chill ran through him. He was all wrong on the outside. That meant there was something even worse on the inside, an ugly thing that leaked through: blood so disgusting it drew the beetle-man. He thrust the mirror back in the box and shoved it under the bed. There it should stay, hidden and in the dark.

He ran out of the bedroom and into a suddenly frightening world. Sharp-toothed knives grinned at him from the kitchen table. Outside, an ax bit into a log in the woodpile. Rakes hanging on the wall in the barn displayed their claws. Until today, he had never noticed the sharp objects all around him; but now he knew that every one of these blades could, with a single careless slip, make him bleed.

And bleeding on the ground summoned the mist. Last night it had lured the Groper out of the Riftwood and into people's barns and mills. A calf had died, and then a little baby.

In the following days, Sheft tried to convince himself that his encounter with Wask had been a nightmare. Soon it became one, coming night after night. Under the trailing roots in his loft, his dreams crawled with horrors.

One morning in Greenmist, after a particularly bad night, he sat at the kitchen table and stared unseeing at the breakfast bowl before him. His father, who never spoke to him at meals, or much at any other time, had already finished and gone out.

"Is something troubling you, Sheft?" His mother came to sit beside him on the bench.

He looked up at her, then nodded. She was his real mother, and he wanted to cling to her.

"Tell me."

It was hard to find the words, hard to tell her about the nightmares. Root-like tendrils crawled out of the ground, twined around his legs, and searched for a cut they could creep into. Sometimes a knife flashed out of the dark and slashed his arm. Black blood flowed out, but it was clotted with roots. They pulled him down to the soil where beetles swarmed, rushing into his nose and mouth until he woke up gasping.

He must not ask what he was in agony to ask, but a desperate need to be reassured pushed him beyond caution. "What's wrong with me, Mama?" he cried. "Am I bad?"

She said nothing, and he at last found the courage to look up at her. To his dismay, he found he'd questioned the wrong mother. Her face was pale and her eyes wide. She was afraid. Whether of him or for him seemed equally terrible.

"I don't know what you are," she hissed. "Tell me how I should know, S'eft."

It felt like black water closing over his head.

"And yet…" A thoughtful look came over her face, and he grasped at her words as if he were drowning. "You were put into the hands of Rulve from birth. Surely, Rulve can protect you."

Rulve. The name hung in the air like a light. "Who is Rulve, Mama? Why does he have to protect me?"

At first he thought she would not answer, for her look grew distant. "Rulve is the One Who Summons," she said. "The Creator who calls us."

She was drifting away from him, and he had to get her back. "Tell me about him," he urged.

It worked; she looked down at him. "Here in the land of Ullar," she went on, "most people worship Ul the Lawgiver. But in At-Wysher, the villagers bow down before a stone they call Ele. Rulve is different from such gods and goddesses. Rulve isn't a man or a woman, but a spirit: the great mystery that is both he and she. He is our father; she is our mother. He made all things, and she loves everything she made. He teaches us and she heals us. Where I was born, we speak to Rulve heart to heart."

"Where is this place?"

"In a village far away, where I grew up. People come to be with Rulve in a great hall. A round window takes up most of the western wall. This window is made of jade, so when the sun shines through it, the whole place glows with a forest light."

Her voice grew soft and dreamy. Now she was his real mother again, telling him a story. Sheft settled into her warmth to listen, and she put her arm around him.

"Two open hands are carved into the bottom of the circle, big enough for a grown man to lie in. These are Rulve's hands, which uphold the world."

Her voice was like healoil, applied to an open wound.

"In this hall they hold a ceremony for certain newborn babies. Afterward, the infants are bundled up and laid to sleep in Rulve's great, green hands. And you know what?" She tipped his chin up to look at him, and her eyes were gentle. "They sleep untroubled through the night. So when they get older and have a nightmare, they remember how peacefully they slept in the hands of Rulve, and are not afraid."

"I wish I could sleep there."

His mother smiled at him. "Those who lie in those great palms can look up at the circle and read the words inscribed far above: 'My life is in your hands.' Some of the wise people believe this is what we should say to Rulve, but others say this is what Rulve says to us."

He pulled away to look up at her. "That Rulve's life is in our hands? How can that be?"

"Because she has no hands, no heart, but ours. He has ordained the world that way: that God and people need each other."

He didn't understand, but leaned against her once more. "We should go visit this place."

"It's very far away. But Rulve lives here too, and so every night you can think about sleeping in his hands." She smiled down at him and ruffled his hair. "But now, little hayseed, I think you have chores to do."

He gave her a quick hug and dashed out. It wasn't until later that he realized she had not answered either of his burning questions: what was wrong with him, and why did Rulve have to protect him?

But he put these questions aside, and every night thought about sleeping in Rulve's hands. Most of the time that worked, and the bad dreams came less often.

Except, in the middle of Acorn, he had a terrible one. It started with the tolling of a bell, much bigger than their dinner bell, and the sound caused his spirikai to clench with tension. The bell called him urgently, persistently, even worse than the voices. It thrummed in his head, in his whole body. A shadow dimmed the sun and descended upon him. He tried to run, but a huge claw twined around his waist and pinned his arms to his sides. Powerful bat-wings beat above his head. His feet left the ground.

"No!" he screamed. "No!"

His mother woke him, only her head and shoulders visible in the opening on the floor. His heart was pounding, and the T above his knee, although long healed, stung fiercely.

"Be silent!" she hissed. "You'll wake Tarn."

"Wings," he cried. "They were taking me away!" Away from everything he knew, from everything that could keep him safe.

"Don't be such a baby." She pointed to a moth beating against the window. "That's all it was. Now go to sleep."

She disappeared down the ladder. The dream still

vivid in his mind, Sheft rolled off his mattress and shooed the moth outside. The rest of the night, he fought to pull away from the tatters of a dream that felt as real as anything he had ever experienced.

Gradually, the horror of the nightmare of wings faded. The event itself seemed real; but, in some unaccountable way, he remembered it, felt it, as if it had happened to someone else. Maybe, the odd thought struck him, it happened to his imaginary friend: the boy whose name began with T. The dream left a residual feeling of desolation, as if it had permanently turned down a once-bright lantern in his mind.

He took on more and more work in the fieldhold, but when his chores were finished, he roamed the deadlands, a wilderness of purple lupines and yellow strawflowers that rolled league upon league to the east. He followed the long gullies filled with buttonbush and low trees, watched birds bring insects to their nestlings, or coaxed a mantis onto his hand, careful not to hurt its fragile arms. When he had to go into the village with his father, he never forgot what he looked like and as much as possible kept his silver gaze on the ground.

Time passed, and many moons shone through the window of his loft. They lingered on a sleeping boy of twelve, moved over the pale hair of a fifteen-year-old, and left in darkness a young man who was now eighteen.

CHAPTER 3

BLOOD IN THE WHEAT

It was late summer, in the month of Redstar, and Sheft and his only friend Etane headed down the track to the common field. They were old enough now to cut wheat there, and today would be their first time. Etane jaunted along, his sickle over his shoulder, his eyes lit with anticipation. But Sheft faced a situation much darker, and he flicked away images of steel points and curved blades. He had partially overcome his fear of sharp object—taking up wood-carving had helped—but they still made him uneasy.

"You'll be fine," Etane said. "Just take your usual spot on the very edge of the field. That way you'll have—"

"Blades swinging at me from only one side. I know, Etane. It's not like I haven't cut wheat before." But not in the common field, and not as the target of a dozen hostile stares.

"You don't have to be here," Etane said. "You could've stayed home."

No I couldn't, Sheft thought. Even though village elders and their sons weren't required to participate in the common harvests, he was determined not to excuse himself. If he were ever to hold his head up in the village, he couldn't hide behind his father's status nor indulge his own fears.

He shared none of this with Etane, only said, "It would cause too much resentment if the sons of elders never showed up. And you can't fool me with that 'poor me' attitude. You've been looking forward to this for weeks. It gives you a chance to show off your muscles to the girls."

"Darn right. Give 'em something to brighten their day."

Ever since that time at Cloor's, Sheft had always been wary around hoes, sickles and scythes. He noted where they lay in the field lest he step on one, always removed them carefully from their hooks in the barn, and hung them up the same way. He stacked them with the wooden handles facing him in the cart so he could pull them out without leaning over the lethal metal. He filed away rough edges on the wagon seat, pounded nails flat, and took on even more arduous tasks to avoid chopping wood.

Certainly, over the years, there had been minor accidents, but he'd learned to use the power of ice to prevent his blood from falling to the ground. He was far from certain, however, that he could summon ice with so many villagers watching.

It took effort to constrict his solar plexus, the spot just beneath his ribs that his mother called his spirikai. It took concentration to pull the inner knot so tight that what he had come to know as ice would race to the cut and freeze his blood. And then he'd have to deal with the inevitable reaction afterward.

With this secret fear heavy in his chest, he arrived with Etane at the common field. It lay between the road and the Meera River to the west and pasture to the east and had been planted last fall with winter wheat. Now it swayed with ripe seed-heads ready to be cut. Gwin, the blacksmith's son, gave Sheft a murderous glance as he passed him in the field, but said nothing.

Dreading the moment when sickles would start swinging all around him, he stood tensely. At the headman's whistle, it began. The reapers sliced the stalks about two hands below the ripe grain-heads, leaving the rest to be cut the next day for straw. Behind them, young women and boys gathered up the grain, bound it, and loaded it into the wagons. One them was hitched to Surilla, the big mare that belonged to Etane's father, Moro.

Etane worked the swath next to him, with Gwin and the others beyond. It was hard, wrist-straining work, and the day was hot. The men soon removed their shirts, and Sheft tied his around his waist by the sleeves. As he cut, wheat chaff flew everywhere and stuck to his sweaty face and chest. He grew thirsty as the morning passed, but none of the village girls who went about with jugs of water came near him, so he had to go to the wagon to get a drink for himself. This made him fall behind the other reapers when he returned to work. Some of the younger boys, including Gwin's half-brother Oris, soon grew tired of gathering and ran about, shrieking, at their games. All this movement and noise, plus the pressure to catch up with the others, made it harder for him to concentrate.

Just before noon, he stopped to wipe the sweat out of his eyes and stretch his back. Heat shimmered over the next field where a flock of small birds wheeled and issued piping cries. They flashed white as they all turned together, as if they were gesturing to him, and flew toward the Riftwood. A sense of unreality filtered over him, a shiver of portent. Time slowed, and the sounds around him fell into silence. He raised his eyes to the haze beyond the Meera River.

A wind was gathering, from an unseen source between earth and sky. It was the great wind that tossed the seas and stirred up the clouds. It came, shaking the trees of the primeval Riftwood and surging across the Meera River. The fields of wheat bowed before its passage as it swept toward him. Panicked, he threw up a hand to ward it off.

It whirled around him, but it was more than wind. It was a vast being who heard the cries of a suffering people, a compassionate force that felt the slow dying of their land. Heavy with pain it could not relieve, it sighed and diminished itself into a breeze. It curled around him, breathed on him, and brushed over his hair like a bird-wing. "S'eft," it whispered. "Please come. Come as soon as you can."

He dropped his hand. His whole being reached out, and he leaned into the breeze. *I want to come. I will.*

For several heartbeats the yearning filled him, the compassion pulled at him, then it all drained away.

He took a breath. What just happened?

An inner warning jangled. Still half-wrapped in the gauze of the vision, he blinked. A series of glints were rushing toward him, a metal object flashing in the sun. A sickle spun through the air—*whish-whish-whish*—heading toward his chest. The grin of its blade sprang up huge before him. He lunged out, caught the handle, and in its downward arc the blade nicked his upper arm. Drops of red sprang out, hung motionless in the sun, then sank into the wheat stubble.

Blood welled on his arm, and a nightmare leaped into reality.

Immediately he squeezed his eyes closed, clenched his hands. *Stop bleeding, stop bleeding!* He bore down on the inner knot, almost blacking out with the effort, and constricted his spirikai. Out of its intricate coils, ice rushed into his veins, up his chest, across his shoulders, down his arms. He shoved it into the wound and froze it. But he had summoned too much and now stood encased. He couldn't move his fingers, couldn't even feel them. It was exactly as it had been that night when he was a six-year-old standing inches away from the Groper, frozen with fear. His eyes flew open. The glistening red was retreating into the cut. Even as he stared, it disappeared.

Then everything was happening at once and too fast. Etane was shouting, and Gwin was shouting back. "An accident! The damn thing slipped out of my hands!"

Nearby cutters straightened up and craned their necks to see what was going on. Sheft looked down at the sickle he so impossibly caught. His blood stained the blade. Numb, he wiped it clean on the sweat-cloth at his belt and then dropped it with a clang next to his own. Now ice-reaction was spreading through him, making him light-headed, fuzzing his thoughts, fumbling his fingers as he bound up his arm with the sweat-cloth.

The drops. The flying red drops. Some must have soaked into the ground. His stomach turned over.

He kicked the sickles aside, and his eyes darted over the soil. There—oh God—an area writhing with roots. With incredible swiftness green stems whipped up. They burst open and spewed out leaves. Horrified, he did just what his father had done that day in Seed: stomped on them, ground them under his heel. There, another one, and another. Frantic, he obliterated them too and looked for more. Grotesque, impossible, they grew from his blood, had their roots in his veins, marked him as something inhuman.

"The hayseed's havin' a fit!" a voice exclaimed. "By Ele's eyes, the foreigner's havin' a fit!"

He drew a deep shuddering breath, and everywhere people were rushing toward him, exclaiming and questioning.

"What happened?"

"He *caught* it?"

"That's impossible!"

"It could have killed him!"

A muttered "Too bad it didn't," followed by laughter.

Etane grabbed his arm. "Are you all right?"

Sheft forced words through cold lips. "Yes. A graze. It's fine." Maintaining the ice in his arm, he retrieved the sickle and ran his eyes across the base of the pale stalks. He could see no greenery. Back by the wagons, the bell jangled for the noon meal and the workers drifted away. He straightened.

Etane looked at him intently. "Are you sure you're all right?"

Sheft nodded, his heart thudding. Ice had done its work, but now came the aftermath.

"Let's take a look," Etane said.

He reached for the sweat-cloth, but Sheft pulled away. He didn't want Etane to see there'd be more blood on the outside, where he wiped his sickle, than on the inside. "I said it's all right."

"That was no accident. Gwin's been reaping for years now, and sickles don't just fly out of his hands."

"He'd say it's hot," Sheft said, through chattering teeth. "He'd say his hands were sweating."

"Are you shivering?" Etane asked incredulously.

"It's just reaction. It'll stop."

"Come on then. Let's get something to eat."

"I think I'll just—just find a spot in the shade."

Etane moved off. First glancing around to make sure everyone had gone to the wagons, Sheft knelt on knees that barely held him up and once more searched the ground. The sun seemed too bright and the stalks shimmered before his eyes, but he found no more of the plants pushing through the soil. He climbed unsteadily to his feet and headed for the shade of the nearest tree.

Etane joined him there. "I brought you this."

"Thanks." Sheft gulped down the water, but the sight of the bread and cheese made him feel slightly sick.

Etane wolfed down his lunch, then looked up as two village girls called to him. With a sheepish grin at Sheft, he went.

Under a haze of ice reaction, Sheft watched the girls flirt with Etane. All smiles and dimples, they tossed their long hair and cast bright glances at him.

No young woman ever looked at him like that. Still trembling inside, he rested his arms on his drawn-up knees and stared at the ground.

The confidence he had built up over the years was gone. For over a decade, ever since he discovered his power of ice, he'd practiced summoning it. It started when he learned that the Groper was seldom seen in the dead of winter because the creature seemed to be repelled by extreme cold. Then he remembered his icy terror on the night he'd first encountered it, remembered how his half-physical, half-mental reaction had produced the ice that had saved his life. He'd learned a way to re-create it.

At first, the necessity of re-living the terror of that night and the effort of constricting his spirikai resulted in pounding headaches and constant nightmares. But it stopped the bleeding. He became skilled in the use of ice, and no drop of his blood ever reached the ground. He thought he'd succeeded, thought he'd never bleed again, thought he'd avoid making a spectacle of himself in front of others.

But he'd been wrong.

The sound of the headman's whistle got everyone to their feet. The reapers stood, stretched, and headed toward their swaths. He took several deep breaths, trying to dispel the light-headedness; but before he could stand, Gwin sauntered over with Voy, snatching up his sickle on the way. Gwin's muscular arms hung in arcs at his sides. Two lines between his eyebrows gave him a concerned look, as if he recognized a painful problem and regretted the measures needed to solve it.

Voy stood beside him like an inseparable shadow; slyness, as opposed to Gwin's intelligence, glinted in his ferret's eyes. "Too bad," he said, "you got hurt today. Too bad if it happens again."

As it had happened before.

After that first disastrous visit to the village when he was six, Sheft had become determined to find a friend. He'd asked his father to drop him off at a low place just south of the village, where children often gathered to play by the mill. Watching his father's wagon disappear down the road, he hoped Tarn would remember to pick him up on his way back from the council meeting.

Six or seven children stopped their games and stared as he scrambled down the embankment. As he came closer, one of them yelped and ran off. It must be his eyes, he thought, his horrible fish's eyes, so he averted them. "Can I play with you?"

"If you can keep up with us, straw-head," one boy answered. He ran off, and the crowd of children followed.

Sheft did keep up. He climbed the tree even higher than they did, walked the log without falling off, and was winning the race beside the river. Until he slipped and skinned his knee.

Instantly the warning screamed in his mind, and the ground reared up before him. Terrified he'd be unable to stop the blood from falling and the disgusting roots sprouting, he pulled the spirikai knot too tight and summoned too much ice. Half-blind, he stiffened with cold, while the other children gaped at him.

"Look!" one shouted. "A demon's got him!"

"He's listening to it talk."

Two older boys, who had been throwing stones at a dead tree, ambled up. "So you're the witch-boy," the biggest one said. Sheft recognized him as Gwin, the blacksmith's son. He had straight-across eyebrows, a thick neck, and stood with his hands on his hips.

Shivering with ice-reaction, Sheft got to his feet. "I'm not a witch-boy! I don't even know what that is."

"It's a freak with dead-fish eyes," the second boy jeered. His name was Voy, and he reminded Sheft of a sleek and dangerous ferret. "A foreigner with haystack-hair."

Sheft's face burned, and he lowered his eyes.

"Afraid of us, hayseed?" Gwin asked, thrusting his face into Sheft's.

He flinched at the name, his mother's name for him, and Gwin must have seen that. "Hayseed! Hayseed!" he shouted, and then pushed him.

Sheft tottered a few steps backward and the others caught on, shouting the name and pushing him back and forth, until finally he stumbled and fell.

"He doesn't even know how to cry," Voy remarked, looking down on him.

Gwin threw a stone. It hit Sheft on the side of his mouth, and he immediately covered the spot with his hand and squeezed his eyes shut.

"Now he does," Gwin said, and they all ran off, laughing.

But he wasn't crying. He clenched himself in ice. His mouth hurt, and his heart hurt, but he wouldn't bleed.

When his father came with the wagon, he immediately saw the raw spot. "I don't approve of brawling. If your opponent is smaller, you are a bully; if larger, a fool."

Years had passed, and now a bully was staring fixedly at him and thumbing the blade of his sickle. "You should go away, freak," Gwin said. "Leave town."

As Gwin well knew, only criminals or irresponsible malcontents left home, or those who were cast out. Sheft got to his feet, his arm stinging and his patience thin. Gwin had always been bigger than him, and still was, but now they were about the same height. "I'm not going anywhere," Sheft said.

Gwin's eyes hardened. "Too bad, piss-head. Accidents happen to foreigners who don't belong here."

"I belong here as much as you do. My grandfather was council Holdman."

"And your mother was a whore in Ullar-Sent."

Sheft lunged at him, but Voy grabbed his bandaged arm. "You're lookin' awful pale, hayseed," he drawled. "Can't stand the sight of blood?"

Sheft threw his hand off and addressed Gwin. "Get away from me. And take your shadow with you."

"With pleasure. But if that little cut bothers you so much, I'm wondering how you'll manage the Rites." Gwin showed his teeth. "It'll be your first time, won't it?"

"And barely three months away," Voy remarked. "Lots of time to think about it. You gotta handle the knife just right, you know. I'm bettin' you won't. I'm bettin' you'll have one of your fits instead."

Gwin leaned into Sheft's face. "There'll be twenty of us watching that night. Watching every move you make."

"Is that so?" Sheft deliberately lifted his gaze, and hiding none of the anger he felt, glared directly into his eyes.

Gwin took an involuntary step backward. For the first time, from only inches away, the silver eyes bored into him. They were profoundly alien. They showed no familiar brown depths, no reflection of himself, only a metallic surface he could never fathom. These eyes couldn't possibly see the way a normal person saw. They were filmed, diseased. His gorge rose at the sight of them.

Gwin raised his fists, eager to bloody the foreign face, tear out handfuls of the piss-colored hair. Parduka was right. Aberrations like this weren't human. They were like something spawned in the Riftwood, like something that formed in the depths of one of its foul and stinking ponds.

The gaze glinted with slivers of ice. A chill ran down Gwin's back. The hayseed was possessed by a demon. He had seen it himself, years ago, when the foreigner suddenly turned rigid and the eel-eyes stared. There was danger here. More than he had realized, more than anyone realized. Under this albino veneer, a malevolent power was growing among them.

For the good of the entire village, this thing must be destroyed.

He swallowed to make sure of his voice. "Just watch yourself, hayseed," he said. "Someone might mistake that head of yours for the wheat, and one day cut it off."

"Big talk when you can't even keep hold of a sickle."

With one last glare, Gwin turned and motioned for Voy to follow him to the field. But all the way he felt those eel eyes on the back of his head.

★

The harvest resumed, and the satisfaction Sheft felt when Gwin backed away from him quickly dwindled away. There'd been something other than hate in Gwin's eyes: The blacksmith's son had looked at him as if he sensed black roots instead of veins inside him, as if his blood were dirt.

As if he knew the truth.

CHAPTER 4

DRAWING THE CURTAIN

The sun was lowering when the headman whistled the end of the work day. The men clapped each other on the shoulder and headed down the road to Cloor's. Not invited, his head still feeling hollow from ice-reaction, Sheft trudged home. He found no one there, and after burning his makeshift bandage and scraping out leftovers from the pot for dinner, he headed out to the Meera.

By day, he managed to hide what he was and endure. But he dreaded the nights. No matter how tired from fieldwork, he'd put off going to bed by carving deadfall maple or ash in front of the hearth. He made spoons, a miniature heron, a bowl; but when his head nodded and the knife fell from his hands, when he was forced to seek his mattress, the dream of the knife came again and again.

Now, after all this time, and in the form of a sickle, another blade had flashed out of the dark and into his life. Was it was only a matter of time before it happened again?

No. He kicked a stone into the river. He would increase his wariness, redouble his efforts, and it would never happen again.

The ripples from the stone disappeared and the brown water at his feet slid by in glints and murmurs.

The vision from this morning, eclipsed by so many tumbling events, shimmered in his mind.

Please come, as soon as you can. The call resonated, deep in his heart.

But come where? To do what? He strained to listen, but heard only the buzz of cicadas, the drone of a fly.

The toll of a far off bell.

Dreamed or remembered, distant, then suddenly, urgently, very near, it clamored in his head: *come heal the wound of a distant land, the suffering of an anguished people.* His spirikai swelled with the desire to assuage, to pour oil over, to heal, but the call came through the Riftwood—the domain of Wask who wanted his blood. If there was a bridge across the Meera, it went only one way. Wask's way. Shadows from the great trees had already crossed the river and were reaching toward his feet. He stepped back.

Yet even as he stood there, the Riftwood's powerful beauty pulled at him. Clouds of butterflies fluttered in a shaft of sun between the trees, their wings glowing with turquoise iridescence. The forest displayed shades of green he had no name for, textures of bark he could almost feel from here, and scents of leaf and loam that brought the forest vividly to mind even when he closed his eyes. Yes, the primeval forest ate the sun and stars and harbored creatures with no names or many; but it also exuded the aura of another world, vast and timeless.

With an effort, he turned away from it all, away from the beauty, the evil, and the pain.

Away from a call he wouldn't answer, from someone he couldn't be.

Late that night, a black mist seeped out of the Riftwood and coiled across the slow-moving surface of the river. It came to the solitary black boulder, and its long, wispy fingers explored the depression on top. Finding nothing but a few dead insects, it flicked them angrily away and moved on. Raising its leading edge slightly off the ground, it put out its senses. It detected a faint smell—once savored, long remembered. It groped its way over the fields and found a certain spot. Excited, it tore into the ground, but there was barely enough blood to taste, and it wanted more. The mist flowed up the empty Mill Road and poured silently into the village.

Fire-lit windows cast rectangles of light here and there on the ground, shadowed by people moving about inside, and these the mist avoided. As if the residents within sensed something, the rectangles disappeared as shutters closed.

Parduka lay in a restless sleep in her room adjoining the silent hall of worship. In his house across the Mill Road, Dorik, the village Holdman, also tossed and turned.

Sheft's arm throbbed, and he dreamed of the darkened wheat field. The stalks shook and the ground chittered, alive with unseen beetles.

He started awake, his head filled with the nightmare. Pre-dawn light seeped through his window. He dressed, seized the spade and sickle out of the barn, and rushed down the road as the red-gold sun was rising from the deadlands. No one would be working in the common field until the morning dew had dried. His arm still stung, but he wasn't surprised. Using ice not only brought on the dreaded reaction, but also slowed down the normal healing process and increased, rather than alleviated, the pain.

He waded through the damp straw, searching for the place where the sickle had grazed him. There was no mistaking the spot. He looked down at a ragged circle where night-beetles had chewed every stalk down to the bare earth.

Wask had emerged and once more found his blood.

The feeling he was not alone made him cut his eyes to the Riftwood. He saw nothing but the shadowy recesses between the trees. Yet a presence seemed to hover there, radiating the blind determination of hostile roots. A chill of panic ran down his back.

As quickly as he could, he cut the damp stalks and hid the bare soil before any of the others saw it. But no one appeared. The Mill Road lay eerily quiet. Only hours ago, in the night, something malicious had traversed it.

When he got home, his mother said the reaping had been canceled for the day, and Tarn had been called to an emergency meeting of the elders. Dorik's son-in-law had been found dead behind the Council House. And beetles had been at the corpse.

A sick feeling rose in his throat. Like a cancer, his terror of the Groper had grown from fear of bleeding to a fear of sharp objects, and then swelled into the disgusting image of his polluted blood packed with roots. Now things had gotten far worse: now his whole being cringed from the thought that his cursed blood might be connected to a young man's death.

His mother looked up from the dishpan. "What's wrong? You didn't even know the man."

"I didn't, but I know Dorik, and this would be the third death in his family this year." Etane had told him the whole story. The Holdman's son-in-law lost his wife and baby during childbirth a few months ago and then he turned to drink. He'd passed out once behind the smith's and another time in the alley between Cloor's and the butcher shop.

Riah turned back to her work. "The son-in-law was probably drunk again. Maybe stumbled and hit his head on that outcrop of rock behind the Council House."

A terrible thing, he thought. But an accident. The fact that he had failed, that he had allowed his blood to reach the ground, had nothing to do with what happened in the village. It had nothing to do with that baby dying all those years ago. It had been a twin, and one of twins was usually born sickly. It was Ele's punishment for promiscuity because everyone knew twins had different fathers.

He spent the rest of the day out in the barn, making sure the next batch of paper had dried, carefully peeling the sheets off the screens, then cutting them to size. It was twilight when Tarn came home and reported on the Council's decision.

"The elders took their good old time about it, Riah, but they eventually ruled that the death was caused by drunkenness and not by Wask."

Putting new logs on the fire, Sheft drew a silent breath of relief while Tarn retrieved his pipe from the shelf, filled it, and tamped down the leaf with his thumb. He sat in his nodding chair, and soon aromatic smoke coiled around his head.

"The priestess was there," he went on, "screeching about restoring the Rites." He shook his head. "Anyway, we put an end to that. Dorik's faction prevailed, but only by my vote. Those against us are angry. They say the ruling was based not on facts but on the Holdman's power to avert scandal."

"Scandal?" Riah asked.

"Women's gossip." He waved it away. "The important thing is the priestess insisted that Ele was punishing Dorik—that the goddess allowed his family to be struck by the Groper because his 'religious laxity' was corrupting the council."

"Wasn't he punished enough by losing his daughter and grandchild?"

"Must I spell it out? Ele despises foreigners. Any tolerance the council shows to them, even if they have lived here all their lives, is part of the 'religious laxity' Parduka sees everywhere. The priestess looks for any excuse to weaken my reputation on the council because my vote is the deciding one against her."

It had gotten dark, so Sheft lit the lantern and placed it on the table.

"That is why," Tarn added with a grim look at him, "your behavior must be impeccable, Sheft. No more causing trouble in the common field."

Incredulity flooded him. "I didn't cause—"

"I'm in no mood for backtalk. Just fit in for once."

Swallowing his anger, Sheft closed the kitchen window for the night. His shadow lay outside, framed in light on the ground. For some reason, the sight made him deeply uneasy. He pushed the feeling aside and drew the curtain shut.

As he did so, something his father had said came back to him. He turned to look at him. "What did the priestess mean by 'restoring the Rites'?"

Tarn sucked on his pipe, leaned back, and blew out smoke. "It doesn't matter. The council would never allow it."

CHAPTER 5

CALLED FORTH

The next day, Sheft's whole life changed.

A morning downpour had postponed the harvest again, but by early afternoon, the sun shone bright through the chinks in Moro's barn. Sheft was helping Etane repair a partition in Surilla's stall when he heard Ane's joyful shout. He rushed to the doorway and saw Moro helping his daughter out of the wagon and Ane, leaning on the cane she used now, hobbling toward them.

After all these years, their daughter Mariat had come home.

Etane rushed forward to greet his little sister, but Sheft hung back, reluctant to intrude on the family reunion. Mariat was no longer the little girl he remembered. She was a young woman, radiant and slender. Her long brown hair swung about her as she turned from father to mother to brother and back again in a dance of kisses and hugs. Her beauty filled his eyes and heart.

Finally, entwined in an embrace that included the four of them, Ane looked up and saw him. "Come, Sheft," she said, opening up their family circle and extending a hand. "Give our dear Mariat a welcome hug."

Painfully conscious of what he looked like, of the pollution that ran in his veins, he wanted to draw back, to stay in the shadows. But Mariat's dazzling grace tugged at him and the curve of her cheek, the shape of her body, pulled him forward. Inwardly pleading for her tolerance, gambling on her kindness, he came out from the doorway. He could not lower his gaze as he knew he should. For one aching, heart-stopping moment, he looked full into her soft brown eyes.

Weariness dragged at Mariat's body and soul. The trip home had been a long one, over cart-jolting roads—very like, she thought, her aunt's slow journey through sickness and into death. She had accompanied her aunt every step of the way, ever since she'd gone to stay with her when she'd been eleven years old. So much of her time had been spent behind shuttered windows, in a small cottage that smelled, in spite of her best efforts, like urine and medicine. Now she was heart-worn and longed for air and sun.

Then Ane called Sheft forth, and he came out of the dimness of the barn like a tentative light. He wore a loose shirt with sleeves rolled up, and strands of his wheat-colored hair fell over his forehead. He was tall, sun-browned, male. Vivid memories sprang up from when she was a little girl, and they twined disconcertingly with how he looked now. She remembered his warm hand enclosing hers, the nearness of his cheek as he bent down to listen to her, the feel of his hard shoulders as she rode him piggy-back.

A shaft of acute emotion pierced her. Unexpected, intense, it ripped from her heart to her abdomen and down. She felt a blush creep up her face.

But then the sunlight reached his eyes. They gazed full at her. A chill swept through her, and she stiffened. She remembered them as a shining grey, not this startling, metallic silver.

He flinched and looked down.

She had hurt him. With a pang of compassion, she saw the sensitivity in his mouth, the vulnerability in his jaw and throat, and realized that deep inside, he was already wounded. But there was something more, the same trait her aunt had manifested during her final illness: endurance in the face of unrelenting pain. She was not prepared for her urge to heal it, not prepared for this bruised strength, not prepared for her longing that he take her into his arms.

With averted heads, barely touching, they embraced as Ane had requested.

Mumbling some excuse, Sheft escaped as soon as he could to the banks of the Meera. He shouldn't have looked at her like that. He should have kept his eyes on the ground, where he wouldn't have seen her revulsion. His spirikai twisted inside him, trying to make ice, but with an effort of will he stopped it. *I'm not hurt*, he told himself, *not bleeding*. He stood with his hands clenched, not seeing anything, until the threat of ice receded.

Early the next morning, the wheat harvest resumed. He could have avoided it, but to defy Gwin, he went. A bastion of hard stares followed him as he stationed himself in his row and set to work. He tried to ignore the hostility that hung over the field, tried to ignore how his skin prickled at the sight of sharp and swinging blades. How long, he wondered, before this re-doubled wariness would whittle him away?

After a while, the cutters rested, and the gatherers came into the field. One of them was Mariat.

He watched her, laughing and talking with the others as she made her way closer to his row, until she finally took a place at the end of it. She would be gathering the grain behind him. She had not glanced at him, probably didn't even notice he was there, but she would be near him for much of the day.

It was, he now noticed, a beautiful late summer morning. The grain smelled like fresh baked bread, and the sun felt warm on his shoulders. Bits of straw and the shouts and calls of children floated in the air. Even Gwin's little brother Oris seemed content to stay back by the wagons where he belonged. Surilla's services were again being put to use, and Moro was grinning in anticipation of receiving an extra grain-share in payment.

The headman whistled and the cutters returned to their work. Sheft bent to his task, and Mariat's presence at his back felt as tangible as a hand laid on him. When she left his row to help the other women tote baskets of food off the wagons, it was as if the sun had gone behind a cloud.

The noon bell rang, and along with the others, Sheft flung down his sickle, wiped his forehead, and got in line for his meal. It smelled delicious, and turned out to be sausage and yellow cheese, still warm and wrapped in dark bread. With Etane being occupied with a pert young lady from the village, Sheft found shade under a tree at the edge of the field while Gwin and his cronies settled nearby.

As he ate, he watched Mariat move among the workers with a cup and a jug. Amidst welcome-homes and glad-you-are-backs, she poured with slim-wristed charm and open warmth. Like everyone, she wore a belted tunic over trousers, but these did little to hide the curves beneath.

He couldn't help looking at her. Apparently neither could several other young men sitting in the shade, especially Gwin, whose head turned to follow Mariat's

progress through the field. Time after time Sheft tore his
gaze away from her, only to find himself staring again. She
bent to pour a drink for someone in the next row, and a
tendril of her hair came loose from however it was tied in
back. It brushed against her cheek, which was as delicate as
a flower petal. It would feel soft against the back of his fingers.

Mariat must have felt his gaze. She straightened and
returned it, and the brown flash of her eyes made his
breath come short, and the soft curves at the corners of
her mouth melted his heart. As she looked at him, her
smile faded away.

He ordered himself to look down, hide the alien silver,
not make the same mistake twice. But her eyes held him,
skewered him through and through, and he waited helplessly for that lift of the upper lip, the pinched nostrils,
the look of repugnance that would rip him apart.

They never materialized.

Instead, her eyes softened and warmed for him in a
way he could hardly believe. She simply looked at him
and let him look at her. Her whole body said something
he desperately needed to hear, and with a surge of desire
he longed to answer.

But when she came to sit beside him, he couldn't
think of anything to say. He moved to make room for
her in the shade, thinking himself a tongue-tied fool.

She handed him a brimming cup of tea. "We had this
cooling in the Meera all morning. Good thing, now that
it's gotten so warm. It's got honey in it too."

A short blade of wheat had gotten caught in the
strands of her shining brown hair and stuck straight up
from behind her ear. Perhaps another man, here in his
place, would reach out and remove it for her, but he
could not. He took the cup, discovered he was thirsty,
and drank it down. "Thank you."

"My brother says you and he had some problems with wasps while I was gone."

Sitting here with Mariat, he felt himself smiling at a memory from last summer. "We thought the smoke-pot we were using had done the job, but I guess it was too windy. All the wasps swarmed out and made a—well, a bee-line—right for us. We wound up rolling and yelling in the squash patch. Your mother had to use up a whole jar of bee-balm on us. We were lumpy-looking for days." A glad thought, which to Sheft was strange and new, jumped suddenly into his mind. Mariat remembered something Etane had said about him. She had thought—at least once—about him.

Mariat searched his face. "Well, you don't look lumpy now. As a matter of fact, you look"—she colored and glanced away—"fine."

He swallowed. "So do you." For a moment they sat in silence. "I hear from Etane," he finally said, "that you took up bee-keeping when you were at your aunt's."

"I did. I brought some of her hives home with me and now we have our own honey."

"Do you ever get stung?"

"Actually, no. Honeybees are quite gentle and won't sting if you come among them quietly. I only have to make sure that my sleeves and pant legs are tied shut." She grinned sheepishly. "I figured this out after a bee once got into my shirt and buzzed around in there—"

He found himself imagining this must have been heaven for the bee, but resolutely put the thought aside as Mariat went on. "—smacking at my shirt like an idiot, but even then I wasn't stung. Later on I learned how to think calm thoughts at them. You know what I mean, Sheft?"

He breathed in the way she said his name as if it were a fragile scent.

Perhaps she noticed, for her cheek turned even pinker. "You showed me how, remember, when we used to catch frogs by the river. Think reassuring thoughts, you said; move slowly, and foop! you've got one!" Smiling at the memory, Mariat settled back against the tree trunk, and they both looked out at the sunny field. Crickets trilled contentedly, and bees droned in the asters blooming nearby, but after a while he noticed that sadness had crept into her eyes.

"I'm sorry about your aunt," he said.

Mariat glanced down at her hands in her lap. "She often told me she'd seen many summers and lived a full life. At the end, I could comfort her a little with those stories about Rulve your mother used to read to us. We prayed together. My aunt said she wanted to die in Rulve's hands, and I think she did."

To die in Rulve's hands. A passing breeze rustled the leaves above his head, like a lingering caress. An ineffable feeling, part longing and part dread, washed through him. He blinked it away.

"...and all that time," Mariat was saying, "I'd been caring for my aunt, and now I worry about my mother. Ane has some pretty bad days."

"When she can't get into the garden anymore, you know she must be hurting." Sometimes, when he looked into Ane's pain-creased face, he thought he could feel what she felt: a multi-pronged jab in his abdomen.

Mariat reached out to pick a deep blue aster and twirled the stem. "That's a beautiful cane you carved for her."

"Thank you."

"I like the squash-leaves twining around it, and those little ladybugs hiding there."

Sheft's heart skipped a beat. To notice the two tiny

insects she must have looked closely at what he had made. "I thought they'd be better than squash-beetles." Of course they would; what an idiotic thing to say.

She laughed. "That's true. The cane is so well done you must have carved other things too."

"A few." To put off going to bed, to avoid the nightmares as long as he could.

The tip of her long and lovely finger touched the aster's yellow center. "Maybe one day, if you have time, you could bring Riah's book of tales to read to my mother. She loves stories, and I think they would make her feel better." A shadow passed over her face, as if she needed to hear stories too.

"I'll come tomorrow," he said, then inwardly winced for sounding so eager.

Mariat refilled his cup and shot a teasing glance at him. "Did you know my auntie saw you when you first came here?"

"You mean here, to At-Wysher?"

"Yes. My uncle was alive then, and both of them came out here to visit. Auntie saw your family drive by in Tarn's wagon. She told me it was full of those blue-flowering plants your father makes paper out of, and a foreign lady was holding a baby. That must've been you. Auntie said you were about eight months old, and still as bald as a peach."

He leaned back and laughed out loud. Fleetingly, he wondered if he had ever done such a thing before. "You should talk. Until you were, let's see, about five, your hair grew straight out all over your head. You looked like a little wild thistle."

Making a face at him, Mariat stood. He realized that someone had been calling her.

It was Gwin, motioning her over to his group.

"Mistress Mari," he called, smiling. "We're dying of thirst here."

Mariat signaled she would be right there and then turned back to Sheft. She reached down to take something out of his hair. It was a wheat stalk.

"This was sticking straight up behind your ear, straw-head," she said with a grin, and then ran off.

CHAPTER 6

THE GREEN CLOAK

During the month of Harvest, after chores were done, Sheft often strode through the sunny fields to Moro's house, the red book of tales under his arm. Most of the time he was invited to stay for dinner, which Mariat prepared because Ane could do little now but rest in her chair by the hearth. These meals were merry events, and as they spent time together, it began to dawn on him that Mariat saw him very differently from the way he saw himself. She rescued him from roots and ice and gave him a vision of normalcy and acceptance. Even when he said little, he felt he was talking more than ever in his life.

Their family circle warmed him, and while talk wreathed around him he tried to describe to himself the color of Mariat's eyes. They were the same complicated shade as a piece of polished oak, like the velvet brown in a sunflower's center, like the soft burnt umber in the wings of a wren. Sometimes, gazing at them when she wasn't looking, he decided there was no word for how beautiful they were.

After one of these meals, the five of them were still sitting around the table, their dinner long finished, when Mariat turned to him, her eyes bright with excitement.

Meera-brown, he decided, because of all the glints in them.

"Sheft, I'm going to sell my extra honey at the market-fair in Ferce. You should come there with Etane and me!"

He lowered his gaze, and a chunk of the happiness he had been feeling dropped away. His reception in At-Wysher was bad enough, but the residents of a strange town might react even worse. "I've got to help Tarn get the rest of the paper-mash pounded and dried," he said. "Before the frost."

They'd already gathered the last batch of the airy, blue-flowered plants from the south field, stripped away the leaves, and dumped the stems into a water-filled trough to soak. After the fibers from the stems rose to the top, Tarn had wrung them out until they were almost dry and carefully spread the mash over the fabric screens, making sure the pulp was even to the very edges. Now the pulp had to be pounded with special wooden mallets to break down the fibers and make them stick together.

"I guess I can help with the pounding," Etane said with a grimace.

Sheft smiled to himself. At first, when they'd been boys, Etane had been eager to help with that, but soon discovered that pounding was a long and boring task that made his arms ache.

"Except," Etane added with an obviously fake look of regret, "your father probably wouldn't let me near his screens."

Sheft's smile faded away. He remembered the first time Tarn had peeled a dried sheet off a screen. It was beautiful, as soft and pliable as the finest leather, and so thin he could see the shadow of his father's hand behind it. As an eight-year-old, he'd wanted very much to do this part, but he tore the sheet the first time he tried, and it had been two years before Tarn let him try again.

"Probably not," agreed Sheft.

"Well, the weather's still fairly warm," Mariat said. "Maybe the sheets will dry early."

"Maybe."

Something must have occurred to her because her whole face lit up. "I've been thinking—"

"Uh-oh," Etane interrupted. "It's always bad when she thinks."

Mariat smacked him on the leg with her spoon. "I've been thinking about your carvings, Sheft. Etane says you have a whole box of them in your barn, and if Mama's cane is any indication, they're beautiful. Let me and Etane take them to the fair. We'll set them out next to my honey pots, and I bet they'd go for a good price."

She was amazing, always bringing new brightness into his life. But something he made, that people would spend coppers on? "I don't think they'd be good enough to sell."

"Nonsense," Ane said. "Let us women be the judges of that."

"There's not enough in the box to bother with." Now it was his turn to get smacked by Mariat's spoon—but he noticed the blow was a gentle tap compared to what Etane got.

"Then get busy, Sheft. The fair's at the end of Acorn, and you only have a few weeks."

A cold thought—that the Rites would take place shortly after that—he pushed out of his mind.

"Now that's settled," Ane said, "I want you to see the beautiful cloak my sister left me. Show him, Mariat."

Mariat took it from one of the pegs beside the door. The cloak was a truly sumptuous garment—long and hooded and made of thick, green wool.

"The Okrup villagers gave this to my sister," Ane said,

"in gratitude for all the medicines she made for them over the years." She stroked the lining with hands that trembled almost imperceptibly. "After I no longer need it, daughter, it shall be yours."

"Not for a long time yet," Moro said, reaching for the last slice of bread.

Ane passed the cloak to Sheft for his inspection. The green wool felt soft in his hands, but as he held it, the room seemed to darken. As had happened in the wheat field, sounds around him drained away. A picture flashed into his mind: new grass blanketing a quiet grave. He was clutching the folds tight in his fist and eased his grip.

"As long as I'm up," a voice said. "Anyone want more tea?"

From far away, he heard himself say, "No thank you." He didn't want to look at the cloak anymore and draped it over the back of his chair. What was wrong with him? It felt as if some other place and time had edged into the room.

Mariat's hand touched his shoulder and her hair brushed against his cheek. She was bending close to him and her eyes were soft with concern. "Are you all right, Sheft?"

"Yes." He put his hand over hers. "Yes, fine."

Ane was trying to push herself up from the table, so Etane jumped to her side, helped her to her chair by the fire, and got her settled in.

"Sheft," she said, "before you have to leave, read me the story about the creek."

Pleased that she asked, but still feeling strangely distanced, he retrieved the red book of tales that he had placed on the mantle, and sat cross-legged on the carpet at her feet. He found the place and read.

"*Once in a land far to the south, there was a small creek that ran over rocks and through fields until it came upon a vast desert. It tried to cross, but found that its waters merely sank into the sand. The creek swirled about, looking for a way through, but could not find one. Just as it was about to give up and become a quagmire, the sun spoke.*

'*You can only save your life if you lose it.*'

The creek trusted the sun and stilled itself. It slowly dried up as the sun drew its water high into the air, until it was a cloud. The wind blew the cloud over the desert. There the cloud emptied itself in joy, and fell over the land as rain, and under it the desert bloomed."

As he read the tale of trust and sacrifice, his throat unaccountably filled with so much emotion his voice came near to cracking. The story, luminous yet full of pain, impaled him on a sweet-sharp point. As he finished reading, it seemed that a gentle hand pulled the blade out of him, and released the life that watered the thirsty ground.

As if in a dream, he saw Ane lean back with a contented sigh. Mariat covered her with the cloak, a cloak as green as a desert in bloom. A clear thought broke over him: one day it would cover his body.

"It's getting on towards twilight," Moro's voice said. "Time you be leaving us, Sheft."

CHAPTER 7

A LONG-AWAITED MESSENGER

The next morning, Sheft dragged the box of his woodcarvings out from under the angle of the eaves in his loft and examined the household items inside. They were serviceable enough, but too plain. He decided to add a leaf design on the spoon handles and on the matching bowl. There'd probably be lots of children at the fair, so he'd make a few toys—little animals with features painted on. They could be set on wheels and pulled along with a string.

He liked this last idea, so as the evenings grew longer, he carved several mice with round noses, ducks with open beaks, and then a smiling bee for Mariat. In the meantime, the path to Moro's fieldhold became well-worn.

His world was much brighter now, but his mother seemed to be living in an increasingly dreary one. She didn't search the skies anymore and hardly ever spoke. After chores one day he told her he was going to Moro's house to take Mariat the bee he had finished. Riah sat at the kitchen table, her eyes distant.

"Invite her for dinner," she said, much to Sheft's surprise. "I will make rabbit stew."

Their family dinners were desultory affairs, and he wasn't sure he wanted to subject Mariat to that, but he didn't have the heart to discourage his mother's effort to break her somber silence. "We'll help you chop carrots," he said, not too confident that the dinner would actually appear.

"No need." She moved her hand into a spot of sun on the table and stared at it. "It's a beautiful day."

With Mariat's bee in hand, he set out over the fields. A warm west wind tossed the hay, which was ripe and waiting to be cut. Perhaps tomorrow, if the weather cooperated. He scanned the sky and saw a few high, thin clouds coming over the Riftwood. Among them soared a falcon. One of truly enormous size, which he remembered having seen before.

It had been on a hot summer day when he was six. He'd gone down to where a little creek called the Wysher tumbled down from the southern hills and joined the Meera in its shallow, stately course. A thin boy about his own age—one he'd seen at the play-place by the mill— was splashing around a small sandbank that had formed where the creek met the river.

This was Sheft's favorite spot because he could stand with one foot in the cold Wysher water and the other in the warmer Meera. Now someone else had found it.

The intruder looked up and saw him. His eyes widened, and then he waved his arms in a curious way.

Puzzled, Sheft did nothing.

"Eel eyes!" the boy shouted.

"Cow eyes!" Sheft retaliated.

"Pee head!"

"Dung hair!"

Frowning, the boy pinched his lower lip between his thumb and forefinger. "Hey, wait a minute. You can see."

"What? Of course I can see."

"Well, don't look right at me like that. Your eyes are creepy."

"All right." Sheft lowered his gaze.

"Gwin said eyes like yours can't see, except maybe shadows. Just like babies can't really see until their eyes turn brown."

"That's not true. I can see as good as anybody and maybe better."

"Prove it."

Sheft looked around, then in the sky above the Riftwood. "Do you see that bird way up there?"

The boy shaded his eyes and squinted. "You mean that little speck? It's a sparrow."

"No, it's a giant falcon, and it's higher than you think. Can't you see the grey and white stripes under the tail?"

"You're just making that up."

"I am not! Once it flew over our barn, and I saw it up close. Its wings are big, way bigger than this." He spread his arms wide.

The other thought a moment. "You know, that would be big enough to carry off my little sister. Then I wouldn't have to watch her anymore."

"Are you supposed to be watching her now?"

"I guess," the boy said, looking around. "She was here a minute ago. Oh, there she is."

A little girl, maybe three years old, had just launched a leaf into the water nearby. She straightened and stared at him.

Sheft tensed and averted his eyes. He didn't want her to burst into tears or run away.

She did neither. After the first long, unblinking appraisal of him, she turned back to her play, as if he were a normal person.

"That's Mariat," the boy said, "and I'm Etane. Let's sit in the water."

They stripped down to their small-cloths and settled down in the shallows. Minnows soon appeared and began picking bubbles off their legs. Sheft tried and failed to catch one, then lowered an arm into the water to see if they'd come to it too. Etane searched among stones for water-bugs, occasionally calling to his sister to take something or other out of her mouth.

"Why," Etane suddenly asked him, "are you so ugly?"

Sheft scooped up some pebbles and pretended to study them. "I don't know."

"Pro'ly because you're a foreigner." Etane thought for a moment. "Do demons really talk to you?"

"What's a demon?"

"I'm not exactly sure. Something bad, from how Gwin talks."

"Maybe you shouldn't listen to him so much."

Mariat came wading up, clutching a wet, silver-colored stone. "Lookit," she said to Sheft, holding it up to her eye. "Pretty eye. Like you's."

Etane guffawed. "He's got fish-eyes, Mariat. Ugly!"

The little girl didn't know any better, Sheft thought, but still he was pleased. She wandered off, and he lay back on his elbows in the water. He looked past Etane and idly scanned the edge of the Riftwood across the river. He caught sight of something, and his heart lurched. From out of the brush, a face covered with dead leaves grinned at him. It was Wask, emerging from his nightmares and into broad daylight. He sat up with a splash.

"Hey!" Etane grinned and splashed back.

The face resolved into a tangle of leaves and shadows.

Relief washed over him and Sheft found himself in the middle of a water-fight. It ended only when Mariat, who had been splashing with gusto, stumbled up to her waist in a hole, panicked, and had to be rescued. After things settled down, he and Etane sat in the water again while Mariat brought handfuls of sand and dumped them over Sheft's foot. Etane glanced at him with a dark I-have-a-secret look. "You want to hear something my dad told me?"

He wasn't sure he wanted to hear anything scary—his dreams were scary enough—but he couldn't help but ask, "What?"

"Something that happened last spring. You know, that time when the Groper came out?"

Across the river, dark tree branches stirred in the breeze, like the feelers of giant, blind insects trying to detect his blood. He knew. But he could never tell Etane about it.

The other boy continued his story. "Well, a few days after that, there must've been a rain up north, and something got washed down the Wind-gate." That was a usually dry, boulder-filled gully that came out of the Riftwood just past the village. Etane leaned toward him, his eyes big.

"And that something was *bones*."

"Bones!"

"That's what Gwin and Voy found. Bones, my Dad said, of a 'squat, man-like creature.'"

Could these creatures, Sheft wondered, have something to do with the far-off cries he heard? Maybe—the idea rasped over his spirikai—these creatures were hurting people. "Do you ever hear, uh, voices coming from there?" He nodded toward the Riftwood.

"*Human* voices?"

"Well, yes."

"Where've you been?" Etane asked incredulously. "Humans don't live in the Riftwood."

"Oh. Yeah. I guess they wouldn't."

"You don't really hear voices, do you?" Etane drew back from him and wrinkled his nose. "Are you crazy or something?"

"I'm not anything! I was just asking." It was time to change the subject, so he said the first thing that came into his head: "I hate emptying the night-pot."

"I do too. My mother always fusses when I spill any, even a little."

They continued to discuss chores they particularly disliked until Etane suddenly jumped to his feet. "I've got to show you something. My dad likes to play Double-sides, and he won this most amazing horse. C'mon and see."

Their route to his house took them past a lone black boulder that stood between the river and the edge of the fields. It was called The Palm, but Tarn said it had another, older name—the K'meen Arûk. The rock was about as high as a man's waist, one stride long, and relatively flat. Nothing grew around it, and not even snakes would sun themselves on it. There was a depression on top where rainwater collected. As the water dried up, it left behind a reddish, foul-smelling slime. The three of them gave it wide berth.

"My dad told me that rock is the palm of the Groper's hand," Etane said. "A long time ago, the priestess used to put eyes in there."

"Eyes!" Sheft wondered if he had heard aright.

"People's eyes," Etane said with relish, "for the mist to eat. On certain nights the Groper still comes here, looking for eyes. Even though we have the Rites."

An uneasy feeling coiled through his spirikai. "What are these Rites?"

"I'm not sure. We won't find out 'til we're eighteen."

Mariat, who had been holding her brother's hand as they walked, now took Sheft's. In spite of the foreboding that had settled over him, her little hand in his gave him a warm feeling. Someone had come to him, in trust, for protection.

When they got to Etane's house, a large man whose shirt bulged over his stomach was standing outside the barn, brushing down the biggest horse Sheft had ever seen. As they approached, the man turned to stare at him. Sheft tensed and lowered his eyes.

"We made a new friend, Dad," Etane announced, and Mariat pulled Sheft forward. "See hosie," she explained.

Sheft glanced up to see the man's grin. "Well, new friend. I'm Moro. This here 'hosie' is Surilla. Not the prettiest girl around, but a stronger plow-horse than any of the villagers own." He ran his hand over the mare's sleek brown neck. "This one's actually going to earn us a few coppers. I'm going to rent her out for plowing. It's time someone gives Delo's ox a little competition." He scratched his round chin and then told them a curious thing.

"This mare can be guided with three magic words. If you want her to go left, you say *eechareeva*. Right is *as*, and forward is *ista*. Now isn't that a marvel!" He set both boys on Surilla's back—Mariat was too little—and let them try it out.

Sheft was amazed. The mare was a wonderful beast and brought to his mind the mighty steeds pictured in the red book of tales. After Etane's mother Ane made them lunch and had settled Mariat down for her nap, Sheft decided to show the book to Etane, even though he knew he shouldn't. Books were valuable objects, so Riah kept it out of his reach on the mantle. It had a strange name: the *Tajemnika*. This meant, his mother said, "Regarding the Heart."

Back at Sheft's house, he dragged a chair over to the fireplace. First wiping his hands on his pants—fortunately so, for they left a grimy stain—he climbed up, retrieved the heavy book, and took it to the kitchen table. It was bound in thick, red leather, and contained not only stories, but also pictures. Etane's mouth fell open in awe at the sight of them.

One showed a man standing with his back to a field in which children played among lacy-leaved flowers. The man looked sad, and the scene behind him was drawn in faint lines, as if the man were remembering a happier time, long gone. Could this man be one of those people whose cries the wind brought?

The next page was covered by a complicated picture of many parts, done, amazingly, in colors. But it was a terrible picture. At the bottom a village was engulfed in red and yellow flames, and was surrounded by short, boar-men with bows and arrows. Above this were blue wavy lines meant to be a river, and then big wooden gates of a fortress built into a cliff. Dark green ivy climbed all over the walls, but on top of the cliff grew rows and rows of strange plants that bristled with prickly leaves and stems. Their flowers were evil-looking—purple and hairy and far too big—and spiders crouched among them. At the top of the page stood a crowned man, and people knelt before him. Sheft looked closely at the man's face, and a chill ran down his arms.

He had no eyes.

A shadow fell over the book. Sheft looked up to see his mother standing in the doorway.

"Uh," Etane said quickly, "*he* took the book down. I never touched it!"

"But first I wiped my hands!"

His mother sat down across from them and, to his

relief, Sheft saw she was his real mother, and not angry. "Some of these stories are not for children to read," she said. "They're written in Widjar and tell about another place and a tragic time."

Etane told her about the magic words that Surilla obeyed, and they turned out to be Widjar too. Seeing his mother's good mood, Sheft asked her to read them a story, and she agreed. Etane grinned, his eyes shining with expectancy, and the two boys gathered close around Riah.

And so he heard the story of Remeld of the Dark Hand, and it filled his head and heart. The tale was laid out before him, about a knight with golden hair, brother to the king. The king's new wife had been abducted by Dol the Sorcerer and imprisoned in his tunnels, and Remeld rode to her aid. After many hardships, he led her out, leaving behind in trade his own right hand.

Now, years later and on his way to Moro's house with Mariat's carved bee under his arm, he found it strange that the memory of a story heard so long ago could still stir something in his spirikai.

Sheft had been gone for some time before Riah managed to gather up the energy to start dinner. They rarely had guests for dinner, so different from how it had been when she was growing up. She missed eating in the community dining room, the passionate conversations, the feeling of unity that arose when people endured hardships together. They'd all been immersed in a cause that gave their lives meaning, and she'd never felt alone. Except for that one terrible time when... She shook her head to rid herself of the memory.

Adding a small handful of salt, she stirred the pot. The

pink pieces of rabbit meat were just starting to turn grey and bits of thyme and chopped onions swirled around the wooden spoon. The water came to a boil and she pushed the iron cook-arm to the edge of the fire to reduce it to a simmer.

"Riah! Come forth."

She froze. The words resounded in her head as clearly as if they had been spoken aloud: Kyra, the thought-language of the falconforms. Tossing the spoon onto the table, she ran into the vegetable garden. The giant creature landed in a whirlwind of feathers and wings. It towered over her, and the tip of its dagger-sharp beak, with a frown built into its base, hovered an arm's length above her head.

Breathless, she tilted her head back and met the fierce, golden gaze. "Where is Drapak?" she cried. "And who are you?"

"I am Yarahe, son of king Drapak."

"For twelve *years* I've looked for him! How could your people abandon me?"

"Enmity sprung up between our people and yours. I would have come, but my father forbade me to leave Shunder. Now one of our eyries has been grievously attacked, and an alliance has been made between us against the Spider-king."

"What of my son?" she cried. "What of my mother?"

The wind ruffled the white feathers above the falconform's hooded, far-seeing eyes. "Se Mena grieves for you, and for both her grandsons."

"'Both?'" A lump formed in her chest. "What do you mean? Teller should be safe in the Seani." All that they'd done, all these years of separation, was supposed to ensure that.

"I am sorry. Your son has passed away from us."

A long chill slipped down her spine. "Oh Rulve!" she breathed. "Oh God, how could that happen?"

"It was twelve years ago, on a day in Acorn. Se Celume foretold it, but we"—his gaze shifted aside, as if with a pang of memory, then returned—"I could not prevent it. The Seah—"

He continued to speak, but she no longer heard him. Her child, her dark little boy, was dead. Twelve *years* ago! He would have been only six years old. Why didn't she feel his dying? Why didn't she know?

A cold feeling passed over her. Sheft had known. That nightmare he'd had in Acorn, when he was only six years old—a dream of wings and a bell. He had felt it, felt the same wrenching loss that she was feeling now, and she had paid no attention. Oh God, it was the synchronicity of twins. It must have affected Sheft his entire childhood, and she had never noticed. The sunny day around her drained away, and the darkness she fought so hard began to bleed through everything. Her son was dead.

"—many summers the Seani was immersed in grief. But now the compound has recovered, and Sheft will soon be summoned home. Rulve has need of him. With Teller gone, he is Shunder's last hope. He must be educated in the Seani, and his power discerned. Have you told him who he is?"

Still stunned, Riah could concentrate only on the last question. "No! How could I tell him anything? For years I waited for some word, for some guidance. I needed to see the toltyr. I needed to know everything was real, and not some dream!"

The falconform raised his huge claw, and it held a leather pouch. She took it and spilled the contents into her hand. Round, made of grey pewter, and attached to a black, tightly braided leather cord, it was the Toltyr Arulve. The medallion was engraved on both sides with what appeared to be the same symbol, but was not. She had not seen the medallion since she left the Seani, eighteen years ago.

She rubbed the smooth metal with her thumb, and its image blurred with her tears. There were, she remembered, two medallions, one for each boy. Oh Rulve, was Teller wearing his when he—

Yarahe, his unblinking eyes upon her, interrupted the terrible thought. "You must give this to Sheft. You must tell him who he is. Do this soon, before the season turns. I will come again in Hawk with further instructions." The falcon-form spread its formidable wings, which cast a shadow over Riah, and swiftly departed.

He disappeared into the blue sky, trailing unanswered, hopeless questions that no longer mattered. Only one son now. Oh God Rulve, she had only one son left.

When Sheft arrived at Moro's house, Etane was just leaving in the wagon. He was off to a horse-farm in Ferce, on some business of his father's, but it was clear that the main object of his journey was a young woman he had met during the summer: the horseman's daughter, Leeza. Sheft wished him luck, and Etane drove away grinning.

Mariat's eyes lit up at the sight of the bee he'd carved, and she set it on the shelf next to the jar of honey, "where it would feel at home." After informing Mariat that she was invited for dinner, he made himself useful to Ane in the kitchen garden. She asked him to pick the squash before the borers got to them, and then insisted that they take a basket of them back to Riah. Mariat took one handle, Sheft the other, and they walked back through the hayfield.

When he pushed open the door to his house, he

stopped in dismay. Riah sat on the bench at the table exactly as he had left her and looked as if she had been crying. He glanced at the hearth and was relieved to see a pot bubbling there.

They put the basket of squashes on the floor. "These are for you," Mariat said to Riah. "Can I help you cut one up for dinner?"

Riah made a visible effort to focus on them. She rose and indicated that Mariat sit down. "You are the guest here. I'll do it."

She took a squash to the side counter and began to peel it. Sheft sat next to Mariat on the bench as she chatted about the gossip in her aunt's village of Okrup, but the shadow over Riah seemed to deepen.

"Is everything all right?" The question came out before he realized how futile it would be. The dark moods that prompted him to ask seemed always to prevent her from answering.

Her back to him, Riah continued cutting the squash into small pieces. His heart sank at her silence, but then she spoke. "I suppose I was thinking of your aunt, Mariat. How alone she'd have been without you."

A look of regret passed over Mariat's face. "She had many friends, but they all had their own lives. Their own family troubles. I kept her company, cooked and cleaned, but couldn't take away the pain. It just got worse. Those last few weeks… I don't think she even knew I was there."

Mariat looked so despondent that he longed to take her hand and look deep into her eyes.

But he must not do that. Instead, with his gaze averted, he leaned toward her. "I'm sorry. You must have felt very lonely."

She turned her head away and nodded, her eyes

moist. Then she looked up at him and produced a smile. "Well, I'm home now—and so is auntie."

"In the end," Riah said in a low voice, "we must all die alone." She moved past them, her face set, and scraped the diced squash off the cutting board and into the stew.

The early twilight of autumn crept into the room as they wiped off the rest of the squashes, stored them in the root cellar, and cut the bread for dinner. He was helping Mariat set out spoons and bowls when he suddenly remembered what he'd seen earlier. "On the way to Mariat's house," he said to Riah, "I spotted an enormous falcon heading this way. Did you see it too?"

His mother plunked mugs on the table and didn't look up. "How could I? I was in the house most of the day."

Just then the door banged open, and Tarn came in late, asking about dinner. It was soon served, but they would have to eat quickly if Sheft were to get Mariat home before dark. Their hasty meal suited him, for neither his mother nor father had much to say. After they'd finished, he went out to hitch Padiky to the wagon, for the night would overtake them if they walked.

A huge yellow moon hung low in the deepening twilight as Padiky plodded down the track. Mariat sat next to him, not touching, but so close the space between them seemed to vibrate. He ached to put his arm around her, but kept his wrists bound in the reins. They said little, but when they arrived at Moro's house, and he jumped down to help her from the seat, their hands touched. A shiver went through him. Once on the ground, she did not let go of him, and he lowered his gaze.

"Sheft, you don't have to do that anymore."

He had looked at her many times, but always askance, always dropping his eyes when she turned to him.

"Look at me," she whispered.

He would do anything for her, even this, but fear kept his gaze on the ground.

"Please."

Knowing what she would see, hoping it would be his heart, he raised his eyes.

She searched them, with something like wonder, then reached up and very gently, so gently that he felt it throughout his whole body, touched his eyelid with the tip of her finger.

He drew her close and she came gladly, as if to the warmth. Her temple felt warm under his cheek; he brushed his lips against her hair. His need grew and swelled as he held her in his arms, and she leaned against him in trust. He bent his head to kiss her, and her mouth and the feel of her body tight against his pulsed through his abdomen and down. It was difficult finally to set her apart, to whisper good-night, to watch her enter her house and close the door. He drove away, still connected to her in a tether of breathless joy.

That autumn seemed magical to Sheft. The harvested fields lay in spent satisfaction, framed by empty milkweed pods and tall bluecurls that smelled like mint. Sometimes Moro brought out a chair for Ane so she could sit in the sun with a blanket over her lap, and she watched their comings and goings with a wan smile. Sheft brushed past her while he carried baskets of apples or potatoes to their root cellar and sometimes he bent down to speak to her, and she squeezed his hand and called him wheat-head. By the middle of Acorn, however, Ane could no longer leave her bed, and Sheft came as often as he could to visit.

One day, after he had read to her from the book of tales, she smiled up at him from her pillow. "I'm getting ready to leave this world, but I'm not afraid. Rulve is right here beside me."

"I'm glad for that, Ane."

Her old eyes twinkled at him. "I mean you, Sheft. Those who love wear Rulve's body."

"I don't understand."

"The Creator of the world is a spirit. With no hands or heart but ours. So if Rulve's work is to be done, if his love is to be poured out, then our bodies will have to do it."

Her words overwhelmed him, and he didn't know what to say.

She breathed out a laugh and glanced at Moro, who was taking his boots off at the kitchen door. "And at night I have a bulky Rulve snoring next to me, and sometimes he rolls over and takes all the covers."

One warm afternoon, Sheft persuaded Mariat to come with him to their old spot where the Wysher Creek met the Meera. Mariat spread out a blanket and sat close to him as the burbling of the water mingled with the hum of late-ranging bees.

"This will probably be our last trip here before the cold weather sets in," he said. Autumn brought endings, and he didn't want anything to end. A thought edged into his mind—*you might never come here with her again.*

She took his hand. "Don't be sad. When winter comes we can sit together by the fire."

He put his arm around her and they sat, quietly holding each other, until she curled up with her head on his lap and fell asleep. The river slid by, sun-lit clouds reflecting on its surface, but in the current beneath, old leaves turned slowly, like unasked questions. The sky hazed over and a light breeze sprang up, heavy with the smell of rain. A few strands of her hair wisped across her cheek. He tenderly brushed her hair back and covered her legs with a corner of the blanket.

She trusted him completely, but did not know him. She did not know how wrong things were inside him.

Leaves swirled down from the trees and were caught in the river's current. They formed loose mats of maroon and yellow and bright green that circled and drifted apart. The hazy ball of the sun was touching the Riftwood's tallest trees when Sheft woke her. "It's time to go home."

They stood and embraced, length to sweet length. "I love you, Sheft," she murmured.

"Oh God, I love you too." The words poured out before he could stop them. He had all he ever wanted in his arms, but the pain of an inevitable future loss kept his eyes tight shut against her blowing hair.

CHAPTER 8

MIRAMAKAMEN

At the end of Acorn, when the fields had been harvested and a few golden leaves still dangled from the ash trees and the rest pooled like sunlight beneath them, the big market-fair was held in Ferce. It was a social event for young and old alike; and not only did the neighboring farmers come, but also peddlers from as far away as Ullar-Sent. Mariat had sewn a new skirt for the occasion, and after setting aside a store for both Tarn's and Moro's families, announced she had all her honey pots filled and sealed. Sheft packed his woodware in a box, ready to be taken to the fair.

The paper sheets dried at last; but then, two days before the fair, Etane was invited to spend a few days with the family of Leeza, the young lady he'd met in Ferce. Moro would not leave Ane, so Mariat was left without an escort. Since no respectable young woman ever traveled alone, Sheft knew she faced bitter disappointment. Pushing away the thought of confronting a gauntlet of suspicion and hostility in a strange town, he offered to take her. Moro gave his solemn permission.

Most of Sheft's thoughts now revolved around Mariat. It was as if the night clouds under which he lived had thinned, and he glimpsed a high and lovely star. She could have had her choice of several young men in At-

Wysher, yet she had chosen him. This wonder had come upon him as a gift unbelievably great.

But it was a gift he should never accept.

The morning of the fair dawned cold, although there had not yet been a frost, so he put on his sheepskin jacket and, full of both joy and dread, loaded the box of woodwares and toys into the wagon.

When he arrived at Moro's house, smoke was rising out of the chimney into the chilly air, and Mariat was waiting for him, wearing her brown wool cloak. She whisked it aside to show him her skirt. It was a chestnut color, with thin strips of burnt orange, yellow, and scarlet woven in.

"What do you think? Do you like it?"

She was so beautiful that he hardly ever noticed what she wore. "I do. But I like the person who's wearing it better."

She laughed, and they loaded the wagon with three boxes of her honey jars, each one sealed with wax, covered with leather, and wound with a cord.

They set out, the sun came up pink and gold, and it looked to be a fine autumn day. It may as well have been drizzling, however; because, sitting so close to one he needed so badly, he knew that the very love he felt for her demanded he stay far away from her.

He cleared his throat. "Mariat, I've been thinking."

"Thinking what?"

"Well, that we might be somewhat—somewhat mismatched." He groaned inwardly at the inadequacy of the word, at the blunt way he had begun this conversation.

"What do you mean?"

"Well, you're the prettiest girl in the village, and the kindest. You have so much to offer, but that's not—not the case with me. I can't give you much of a future." He could give her no future. He wanted to enfold her in his love, lay his strength at her feet; but life with a hated foreigner would be a life of misery and humiliation.

"Oh, Sheft." She took his arm and rested her head against his shoulder. "Of course we have a future together. You've worked a successful fieldhold all your life, and you know paper craft. My beehives and knowledge of herbs will help too. Our future will be just fine."

"It's not that. You know I'm not—not accepted around here."

"*I* accept you. My father and mother and brother accept you."

But none of them knew the deeper truth. None of them knew what was drawn to his blood. Mariat looked up at him with a slight frown. "All this talk about being mismatched. Are you trying to get rid of me, and I'm too stupid to notice?"

"*Rid* of you! Mariat, that's just—"

She put a finger over his lips. "All right then. We love each other, and that's what counts." She snuggled beside him until other vehicles appeared and forced her to sit up more properly. "You worry too much, sweetheart. Always so serious. I'll make it my duty to cheer you up."

The wagon creaked along, and in the face of her smile, he couldn't bring himself to continue telling her their relationship would only hurt her.

They arrived at mid-morning. The market was set up in a large field between the Village House and the Meera and the entrance fee made a fine profit for the Town of Ferce. There were two wagons ahead of them, and by now his hands were sweating. What if they wouldn't let him in? He winced away from the thought, a blunt example of what he had tried to explain to Mariat. They drew up to the man collecting the toll, and he gave Sheft a sharp look.

"Where are you from?"

"Ullar-Sent," he answered truthfully. He held out ten coppers, double what was needed.

The man looked around quickly, took the coins, and pocketed half. "Find any place you want," he said, motioning for the next wagon to approach.

With a sigh of relief, Sheft drove slowly through the crowd. Open wagons, carts, and tents were lined up in rows, and the paths between them were already crowded with customers. Mariat soon gave up her idea of finding a place in the shade, and they pulled into a spot between a large wagon full of crates of squawking chickens and a cart laden with baskets of purple onions. Behind them were the sheep pens. Sheft unhitched Padiky and led her to the pasture fenced in for the occasion, where he had to pay yet more coppers to yet another sharp-eyed and frowning Fercian.

When he returned, he set up their wooden trestle tables and stacked them with the honey pots and woodware. Mariat discovered the wooden toys and, delighted, put all of them out. They would, she declared, attract children— followed by mothers with coin-filled pouches. On every side farmwives bustled by, clutching large bags and holding toddlers by the hand, young men flirted with pretty girls, and excited children ran between the stalls. Sellers shouted out praise for their goods and men led bleating sheep or cows with clanging bells around their necks.

Soon Mariat's first customer appeared. Sheft sat in the back of the wagon, facing the sheep pens, where most people would not see him. He glanced over his shoulder from time to time, keeping an eye on Mariat, who conducted a fairly brisk business. Twice he came forward to help, but after one look at him, mothers pulled their children away and moved on. So he returned to his seat, brought out his carving knife, and began working on another wooden hay-mouse. A few children who had come to look at the sheep noticed him and gathered to watch. One small boy wanted a carving lesson, so Sheft sat him on his lap and, guiding his right hand with his own, showed him how to hold the knife. The boy lost interest when he discovered carving was harder than it looked and ran off.

As Mariat had predicted, the toys did indeed draw the attention of children. She had to rescue a carved fish as it disappeared over the edge of the table and into a child's grasp. There were several whining requests for purchases, and one temper tantrum from a young girl whose mother wouldn't buy anything. Within a few hours, much of the woodware, all but three carved toys, and most of the honey pots were gone. The day grew warm, and Mariat tucked her cloak and Sheft's jacket into a corner of the wagon.

When they smelled meat grilling and pan-bread frying, and when customers drifted towards the booths selling food and ale, Mariat brought out their lunch. They sat in the front of the wagon, eating their boiled eggs and bread and sharing the water jug.

Mariat nudged him. "A drama in the making," she said, nodding toward a group of shoppers across from them.

A small boy, about three years old, sat by his mother's feet while she haggled over some unbleached cloth. Next to him stood the pot of honey she'd just purchased. Holding one of Sheft's wooden ducks under his arm, the boy uncovered the pot. He dipped the duck's bill deep into it, made gobbling sounds, then pulled the duck out and slurped the honey off. Sticky liquid ran down his chin. They watched, holding back their laughter, until the mother looked down with a horrified squeal.

"It looks like all our customers are eating lunch," Mariat said. "Including your duck there. Now's our chance to visit some of the other stalls."

That would not, he knew, be a good idea; but she looked so disappointed he decided that if they didn't go far and he kept his eyes lowered, he could risk it. "All right."

Her eyes sparkling, Mariat quickly made arrangements with the onion lady to watch their booth, scooped the coppers they had earned into her pocket, and took his hand. They threaded past the poultry, pigs, and vegetables and headed toward the center of the fair. There they marveled at the great choice of candles, medicinals, furs, mugs, and pots of all kinds. Sheft discovered a display of woodcarving tools and, at Mariat's urging, used several coppers from his morning's profits to purchase a short curved blade, perfect for etching. They stopped to admire a pile of wool blankets dyed in unusual colors. Mariat bargained hard with the seller, using a talent that surprised Sheft, and purchased a pale yellow blanket for Ane. It looked like the morning sun, she said, and would cheer her mother up.

Carrying the blanket over his shoulder, Sheft wandered with her to another stall. He studied a jar full of long sticks, each one topped with a miniature claw-like hand. "Look at these creepy things. What could they be for?"

"Observe." Mariat selected one, stuck it down her boot, and scratched. "I would think it also works on backs."

The stall owner popped up from where he had been napping behind the table. "That'll be one ducat."

"One ducat!" Mariat exclaimed. "I could just use a stick."

"Yeh, and have it crack off in yer boot or leave splinters. This here's solid ash."

"My friend here makes carvings far better and sells them for less."

The man looked at him, squinting. "He'd have to, wouldn't he?"

"Let's move on." Sheft pulled Mariat away.

About halfway down the row, she stopped again and pointed at a green and white striped tent at the far end, set up under a tree. "Look there. Miramakamen the Marvelous."

"Who's he?"

"I don't know. But the sign says 'marvelous,' so we must see!"

The flap was closed, but a large sign outside proclaimed: MIRAMAKAMEN THE MARVELOUS. FORTUNES TOLD. PALMS READ. KNOW THE FUTURE. ONLY THREE COPPERS.

The tent stood quietly under the sun. No sound came from within. As he watched, one of the fabric walls rippled in a breeze, then all was still again.

"I don't want to know my future," he said.

"Well, then wait here for me. I'm going in." With that, she opened the tent flap and disappeared inside. Sheft stood under the tree and waited. Soon he noticed glances shooting his way, and he hoped Mariat would hurry. A farm wife at a nearby booth peered out from between the harnesses and bridles she was selling to stare at him. He moved back into the shadows.

At last Mariat emerged. Her cheeks were flushed, and she looked thoughtful. "Go in, Sheft. It's—well, you've got to try it."

The farm wife had gotten her husband, and now both were craning their necks toward him.

He thought it might be prudent to disappear for a while, so he gave Mariat the blanket, pushed the tent flap aside, and ducked in.

The warm, canvas-filtered light threw sun-washed green stripes over the grass floor. Ragged blankets strung on a sagging rope served as a wall between two rooms. A short, well-worn path led toward a bench, which faced a rough-hewn table. There, with his back to him, sat an old man with long grey hair. He was wearing an extraordinary dark blue robe embroidered with gold stars and quarter-moons, and he seemed to be rummaging through a pouch on his lap.

"With the tinkling of the coins," he said, indicating with one knobby finger a bowl on the table behind him, "Miramakamen commences."

Sheft dropped three coppers into the bowl, making sure they tinkled.

Not turning around, the old man apparently found what he was looking for in the pouch and popped it into his mouth. "Be seated," he said, leaning back against his chair and cracking his knuckles. "Now then. You will be going on a long journey. In a far-off village you will meet the"—he glanced over his shoulder and Sheft saw that his beard was as long as his hair—"the girl of your dre—" He stopped, and without getting up or taking his eyes off Sheft, hitched his chair completely around. "Oh my," he said.

Sheft lowered his head.

"No, no," the man said impatiently. "It's not about what you look like, only who you are. We must talk." He drew the small pouch from his lap and placed it on the table in front of him. "But first, care for some cheese?

Bread? An apple perhaps?" As he spoke he withdrew these objects from the bag that seemed too small to contain them. "No? A mouse? Oh, there you are, Pippit." He placed a small grey mouse on the table and looked up at Sheft apologetically. "Of course you would not like a mouse. Now, you were saying, S'eft?"

His smile fell away. "What did you call me?"

The old man looked at him with eyes that glistened on the surface but reached down to unknowable, brown depths. "I have called you by your name, my son. Surely there is nothing to fear in that."

But there was everything to fear. With that name came bad memories, the suspicious looks of his own mother, and the dread of finding that a dark door, best kept locked, now stood ajar.

The old man gazed at him—with no revulsion, no judgment, and no rejection. The deep eyes saw everything: the root-ridden blood, the isolation of ice, the shame and the fear. Compassion welled up from the bottomless gaze. As it had in the wheat field, time seemed to slow.

Something was coming, something always longed for, but now—suddenly feared. Sheft flung out his hand to block it.

But it came anyway, for he wanted it desperately. He lowered his hand, and what felt like gentle warmth shone upon him. It seeped through his skin and settled with deep tenderness into the recesses of his spirikai. It broke open inside him, like a jar of golden oil, and penetrated his entire body.

It was love—unconditional and extravagant. It came from no human heart, but from a heart that encompassed the world and shared all its pain. It pulled him into itself, caressed him, enfolded him in joy, and in that sweet mingling he was blessedly lost. For several trembling moments it stayed with him; and then, with a sigh, it dissipated into the bright dust motes that floated around him.

He was back in his own skin, never before realizing he could be out of it, and knowing now how heavy was the burden of constant self-awareness.

The experience left him soaked in gratitude. Because of mercy or mad generosity, it had been given to him—the foreigner, the hayseed, the one whose very blood was corrupt—the immeasurably great gift of feeling divine love.

Oh God Rulve, why me? Why should I be loved so much?

The old man's deep eyes gazed at him, and to his surprise, he heard a clear answer inside his head. "So you would know how all people are loved, whether they feel it or not."

Even as he looked at the old man, and his heart said over and over *thank you, thank you*, he knew that there would be a price. Not one imposed on him, but one he somehow yearned to pay. The cost would be great, like the love itself, but never its match.

Miramakamen held the mouse in his hand, gently petting it with the back of one finger. His colorful garment had faded away, and now he was only an old man, wearing a brown, patched robe and sitting inside a dingy tent. "Much will be expected of you, lad," he said. "Beyond your choosing, you bear a great burden. The great escritors have written about you, for you are a beloved son of Rulve, the s'eft of his precious coin."

Like a sudden, demanding wind, the words took his breath away. "What are you *saying*?"

"I am telling you who you are."

Fear darted through Sheft, followed by an inexplicable bitterness. "I know who I am!" he cried. "I'm a farmer and the son of a farmer, and never will I amount to anything more."

Miramakamen rose from his chair and came to sit beside him on the bench. "I'm afraid not, S'eft. None of those things are true, and you must know the truth. You have the power to restore a poisoned land, and redeem many who have been snatched away."

"I don't know what you're talking about!" But he remembered the distant cries, the vision in the common field, and how he had rejected it.

The old man put his hand on Sheft's shoulder, and such was the strength of his kindness that he could not pull away. "Do you want to know?"

"No! I didn't come here for that."

"I'm sorry, son, but this is how the tree of the world continues to grow and unfold. You can accept or reject it, but this burden is yours."

"My only burden is the one you see in my face, in my veins! You know exactly what I am, and it's not this—this redeemer."

"As you say, lad, I know exactly who you are." He reached out and touched, very gently, the place beneath Sheft's ribs. "And deep in there, you also know."

Sheft dashed the man's hand aside. "I know about hate, about being a foreigner. I know about blood so dirty it attracts night-beetles. I know about roots and ice and fear. That's what I know."

"There's more to you than that."

"I can't be what you said!"

Untroubled, the old man gazed into his eyes, and for a moment the memory of that incredible love brushed over Sheft. "I hear your words," Miramakamen said, "but I will keep listening for your heart to speak. I trust you, S'eft, and you must also trust me."

The old man stood, and so did Sheft. He felt as if some crisis had passed, but then realized it had merely moved into a future time and place. His face, he discovered, was wet with tears. He didn't know why they were there, and wiped them away on his sleeve. "Miramakamen, what should I do regarding Mariat?"

"The young lady I just spoke to?"

He nodded.

"You must act with courage, my son, and with compassion. But most of all, you must do what love demands."

The old man scooped Sheft's coins out of the bowl. "I will not take these from you, for you will be asked to pay a far greater price. I am sorry, S'eft, but because you love, you will be wounded." He placed the three coins in Sheft's hand, one by one, as he spoke. "By a child, by your brother, and by the dark."

Emotions he could not understand raked through him. "I have no brother!"

Miramakamen turned him around, held open the tent flap, and gently pushed him through.

CHAPTER 9

IN THE HORSE FIELD

It seemed to Sheft that he came back to a different world. Clouds had gathered while he was in the tent, and the colorful crowd now had become faded and sparse. Many people were packing up their wares and leaving. But Mariat, waiting under the tree and holding the pale yellow blanket, seemed as dear and compelling as ever, though somehow far away. It felt as if he walked a long distance until he could take her into his arms.

She looked up at him in concern. "You're as pale as a mushroom! What did Miramakamen say to you in there?"

Arm in arm, he led her back toward the wagon. What could he tell her? Where to begin? He needed to go off alone, to make some sense out of what he had just experienced, but Mariat was looking at him expectantly. He chose the most truthful answer he could manage. "A journey. He said I was about to go on a journey."

"The same was predicted for me! And I am to meet a tall, dark, and handsome stranger." She smiled teasingly. "Just like you, Sheft, except you're not dark." She was silent a moment. "But you said 'he.' Miramakamen is an old lady."

"An old lady! With a grey beard?"

"You saw an old *man?*"

"I did."

Mariat chuckled. "The rascals. Probably a husband and wife team, relieving each other from time to time." Her arm went around his waist. "Perhaps that's something we can do one day. Abandon dull farm work! Travel the countryside! Work the market-fairs and make a living off gullible villagers."

He drew her closer to him, but his spirikai squirmed with vulnerability and denial, his mind spun with questions, and what was it exactly that love demanded? What he saw after they got settled behind their trestle table, however, put an end to such thoughts.

A broad-shouldered man stopped a short distance away, and his eyes darted from Mariat to Sheft and then back again. Gwin, his lips pressed tightly together, strode over to them and glared at Mariat. "What are you doing here with him?"

She coldly returned his look. "Selling honey. Do you want to buy?"

"Selling honey. Is that what you call it?"

"That's what she calls it because that's what it is," Sheft grated.

Gwin cast a burning glance at him, then looked down at the few pots of honey that were left. He pointed to the biggest one. "How much?"

"One ducat," Mariat answered. She held out her hand.

Gwin fished the coin from his pocket and, staring fixedly at her, pressed it into her palm. He held her hand while slowly rubbing the coin with his thumb. "I can pay as much as he does, and more."

Sheft seized Gwin by the wrist, and Mariat pulled away. She held the coin in an upraised fist and her eyes flashed. Still staring at her, Gwin twisted from Sheft's grasp. "Not as sweet as what you sell?"

Anger made Sheft's voice low and flat. "Get out of here, Gwin."

Gwin lifted a corner of his lip. "Is that how you do business, by ordering customers away? I've got more right to be here than you do." He indicated the toy animals with his chin. "What are these things supposed to be?"

"They're toys," Mariat said. "Sheft made them."

Gwin's eyebrows shot up. "Toys! Something he wants to sell to our *children*? Something from his hands our *children* will hold?"

"What's the matter with you?" Mariat exclaimed. "If you want something else here, buy it. Otherwise, move on."

Gwin leaned toward her. "What's the matter with *me*? You saunter about in full view of everyone here, fawning over this foreigner, making a spectacle of yourself, and you ask what's the matter with *me*?" He threw a look of loathing at Sheft. "This freak is an insult to our traditions, cursed by Ele, and you can walk arm in arm with him? Look at him! He's disfigured, seized by demons, and you hold his hand in public? What's the matter with *you*?"

In a blaze of anger, Sheft lunged across the trestle table and snatched at the man's shirt. But Gwin jumped out of his reach and stood his ground. Sheft stared at him, feeling the blood drain from his face as his anger gave way to a devastating realization. Gwin had done nothing but expose the same agonizing concerns he himself had tried, and failed, to discuss with Mariat in private.

"There's no freak here," Mariat exclaimed, "unless it's you, Gwin! My family and I have known Sheft for years, and he is kind and gentle and brave. And as for seizures, perhaps you're having one now, for indeed I don't know what's come over you."

"Gwin! Gwin!" a voice piped. It was Oris, Gwin's little half-brother, who had come up without anyone noticing. "Buy me one of these." With one hand he pulled on Gwin's sleeve and with the other he rolled a carved wooden hay-mouse back and forth on the trestle table. "I want *this* one."

"Put that thing down!" Gwin pried the toy out of his hand and banged it on the table. He turned back to Mariat, and his demeanor changed, into something that to Sheft felt far more dangerous.

"Mariat," he said, bowing slightly, "please forgive me. I shouldn't have spoken to you in that insulting way. But I lose my head when I see a beautiful young lady choosing the company of a person like this. I have more experience than you, and will one day take my father's place on the council. And I say to you, if you stay by his side, this foreigner will bring you nothing but grief. There are those in At-Wysher who could give you a life of honor and respect, who could offer you standing in the community, and prosperity. But this one never could. I ask only that you think carefully about what you're doing."

"She needs no advice from you," Sheft said.

Gwin picked up the honey he had purchased and turned to him, his face wrinkled with disgust. "She's young and soft-hearted, and feels only pity for you. If you don't see it, you're truly blind." His look changed to one of warning. "For her sake, and for yours: leave—her—alone."

He pulled Oris away from the table, nodded once to Mariat, and walked off. He didn't seem to notice that his brother, at the last minute, had snatched the toy mouse and stuffed it into his pocket.

Anger and humiliation trembled deep in his throat as

Sheft watched Gwin's retreating back. The wind picked up, heavy with a coming rain, and Mariat shivered. He pulled her cloak out of the wagon but stopped himself from draping it over her shoulders. Instead, eyes askance, he held it out to her. She took the cloak, and his hand as well.

"Look at me, Sheft. Such words can't be erased. But it's up to us to decide how important they will be between us. As for my part, I've already decided."

He turned away from her, for her decision had been made without her knowing the truth. "Gwin was telling you exactly as it is," he said. *But there's more, so much more, and I can never ask you to share the weight of it.*

"No. It's not as he said. Gwin spoke about prosperity and pity, but he never touched upon what we feel for each other. He never mentioned love."

Love. The word struck him hard. He'd accepted her love and professed his own, and that was the worst kind of selfishness. *"Do what love demands,"* the old man had said. But what *was* that? To pour out to Mariat that he thought of her constantly, that he wanted to spend the rest of his life with her? Or to do the much harder thing: spare her and walk away forever? It was obvious what was best for her, so the fact that he felt torn between these two courses proved he was as despicable as Gwin thought him.

"It's getting late," he said. "And it looks like rain. It's time we went home." Shoulders bowed, he went off to get Padiky.

When he arrived at the field, he could not at first find the horse in the midst of so many others, but at last spotted her at the farthest edge. She was not loose, as he had left her, but tethered against the fence. Gwin and Voy sat on the top rail, their coats draped over it. As he approached, they eased off the fence and faced him. Sheft's stomach tightened at the sight of Gwin's bulging arms and thick neck.

The man outweighed him, but might not be as quick on his feet. Etane had engaged Sheft in a few sparring contests over the years and taught him a thing or two, but in a bout with Gwin, there would be inevitable consequences. He thought he had enough ice control to stop these consequences from bleeding, but he could do it only as long as he kept his head—and stayed conscious. Voy joining the fray was another matter.

Taking a deep breath and flinging a call to Rulve for help, he walked toward Padiky. She was their only way home.

The two men stood solidly, watching him. If only he was wearing his well-padded jacket, or better yet, one of those suits of armor he'd seen in the red book of tales.

He reached out to untie his horse, but Gwin grabbed his arm. "When I told you to leave Mariat alone, I meant it. And I meant now. After I've finished here, I'll drive her home myself."

Voy leered at him. "With a few little stops along the way, I'll bet."

All Sheft's doubts about facing the two of them flashed into total commitment. "Get out of my way."

"You don't want to tangle with me, hayseed."

"Because you've made it two against one?"

Gwin glanced at Voy, who grinned and backed off, waving his hands in the air. Gwin thrust his face into Sheft's. "Turn and walk away. Or else I'll make you wish you'd never been born."

"Try it."

Murderous intent leaped into Gwin's eyes an instant before Sheft blocked his punch. The way Gwin's thumb had slid around in Mariat's hand, his disgusting insinuations, the brutal truth he had spewed—all boiled up in Sheft and exploded. He smashed his fist against the square jaw. Gwin tottered back, tripped over a weed-clump, and landed in a sitting position on the grass. A look of shock spread over his face. Padiky nervously sidled away.

Sheft barely had time to register his own astonishment when Voy slammed into his legs. He went down, the other man on top of him. They pummeled each other, too close to do much damage, until Sheft managed to shove Voy away and scramble to his feet. Out of nowhere, Gwin's big fist rammed into his cheek, which erupted in pain. Sheft reeled, constricting with ice, but just as he regained his balance, Voy pulled his arms behind his back.

Regarding him with hate in his eyes, Gwin wiped blood off his chin with the back of his hand. "I should've done this a long time ago." He lunged.

Sheft kicked out with both feet and hit Gwin in the legs. It was like hitting the side of a cow. The bigger man merely staggered back with a curse, but the recoil sent Sheft and Voy sprawling. Voy spun into position above his head, pinned down Sheft's flailing right arm, then pounced on the left. Gwin leaped onto him, straddling him between his knees. Sheft's spirikai screamed a warning, but the rank unfairness of the fight and Voy's leering supposition flamed into a hard and angry determination. *There would be*—he jerked an arm free—*no stops*—he got one leg under Gwin's knee—*along the way!* He strained to overturn him, but Gwin, red in the face, drew back his beefy fist.

The blow never came. Someone stayed Gwin's arm and pulled him roughly away.

"No fightin' in the horse field!" a man shouted. Two

angry Fercians dragged Sheft and Voy, both breathing heavily, to their feet. A third, the tallest, held a stout club under Gwin's nose.

"Yer scaring' the horses," the tall man said. "Payin' customers don't like their horses all riled up."

"It's them bumpkins from down At-Wysher," the one holding Voy added. "Don't know how to behave when they get into a real town."

The man who had pulled up Sheft peered into his face. "What's wrong with you?"

He was getting tired of people asking him that, but before he could answer, Gwin spoke up.

"Can't you see? He's demon-seized and cursed by Ele. We were taking care of it. I'm the son of Rom, an elder on the Council of At-Wysher, and you have no right to interfere with my business."

"Demon-seized?" the second man said with a laugh. "As are many of them Wysher-ites, I've heard."

"Don't matter who you are, or who he is," the tall man said. "This is Ferce, not At-Wysher, and there's no fightin' in the horse field. You all get movin' right now or pay a big fine."

Voy turned away. "He's not worth any fine," he said to Gwin. "We can take care of him for free back home."

"Not free," Sheft muttered. "It'll cost you." But he knew who'd be the one to pay the price.

Gwin glared at him. "This isn't over. The line is crossed when you put your filthy hands all over our women. I warned you before, and you didn't listen." A hard gleam came into his eyes. "See you at the Rites, piss-head."

Gwin stalked off, massaging his fist, with Voy behind him. Two of the Fercians followed, threading their way through the milling horses.

The tall man prodded him in the shoulder with his club. "Get out of our town," he said. "Right now."

Sheft nodded, and the man moved off.

His cheek felt wet. With clumsy fingers, Sheft fished a cloth out of his pocket and wiped his face with it; but the ice had done its work and nothing came off but dirt. His cheek throbbed though, and he could hardly untie the horse with a right hand that felt as if it were a bag of crushed bones. But it wasn't bleeding either.

Leading Padiky, he trudged toward the gate. He felt light-headed and foggy, and the ground seemed to shift under his feet. A full ice reaction was beginning and he didn't want Mariat to see it. There was no secluded place, so he stopped in the midst of several grazing horses and positioned Padiky between him and the entrance gate. Quivering, he leaned his forehead against the horse's neck, twined his good hand in her mane, and stood there until the worst had passed, and he could go on.

By the time he got back to the wagon, a few drops of rain were falling. Mariat had already packed up their remaining wares, and she and the onion-lady were shoving the last trestle table boards into the wagon. Sheft winced as he got into his jacket, then harnessed the horse to the wagon while Mariat gave the woman a pot of honey for her trouble. Within minutes they were on the road home, and the drops increased to a drizzle.

Mariat reached behind her and pulled out the pale yellow blanket, and moving close to Sheft, threw it over their heads. Then she asked him the dreaded question. "What happened to you?"

Perhaps he could bluff her. "What do you mean?"

"Sheft, it's obvious. There's a big bruise on your cheek and your hand is all swollen. You were in a fight, weren't you?"

He nodded.

"With…?"

The anger he felt earlier flooded back. "With Gwin and Voy. Gwin decided to take Padiky and drive you home himself." His voice became hard. "With stops along the way. I didn't think you would care for it."

Her eyes filled with tender dismay. "I wouldn't." She put her arm around him and rested her head on his shoulder. "But he'd never get me to leave without you."

"Mariat, he was right in what he said about me. Any man in the village can give you a better life. For weeks I've wanted to speak to you about that, but I—didn't have the courage."

The rain pattered on the road and glistened on Padiky's haunches, but the blanket was keeping them dry. "Why," Mariat murmured from beside him, "would it take courage?"

He glanced down at the top of her head, then out at the wet and stony road. "Because I don't want to lose you."

"Then let's not talk anymore about it. I won't be lost, but will stay right beside you." He held the reins in his left hand, and she gently took the right and cradled it in her lap.

Ashamed of the dishonesty that hid things from her, but glad of what truth he had managed to speak, he laid down for a moment a great burden. On the rainy way home, the air was full of the smell of fallen leaves, and they sat under their private pale sun, as close to each other as love demanded.

CHAPTER 10

DRONE-FLIES

Sitting with her two friends at the table, Ubela glanced out the open window in the back of the alehouse scullery. Nothing but muggy air came through. The unseasonable combination of yesterday's rain with today's hot sun left puddles in the street and humidity in the air. Drone-fly weather. A good, hard frost—already overdue —would get rid of them, but now they swarmed everywhere. Just like the small, persistent rumors she was itching to pass on.

The alehouse hadn't opened yet; so Cloor, busy in the brew-shed out back, had set them to making bunches of flybane to hang from the rafters.

She sat back in her chair, stretched luxuriously, then glanced around the table. "So we all agree Temo's a bore. Who's next?"

Wena giggled. "I wonder if the guys talk about us like we talk about them."

Melis looked up from the pile of herbs she was sorting. Her long, thick lashes never failed to elicit a stab of envy in Ubela. "Of course they do. Only they say coarser things. So what's your opinion of Delo's boys, Ubela?"

"Well, the younger son isn't bad looking, except of course he's so *short*. And the older one, Gede, has that tickly mustache."

"How do you know it tickles?" Wena asked, her eyes as wide as a puppy dog's.

Ubela made a face at her. "For Ele's sake, girl. Take a guess."

"I found out about Gede's mustache the same way you did," Melis remarked, examining her nails.

"What!" Ubela exclaimed.

"Don't get your nose out of joint. It was before you and he got together."

Ubela bit off a piece of string and tied a bunch of flybane together. "That's over, anyway. Now I'm looking at Gwin. All those muscles under that tight shirt." She spoke as casually as she could, but with a thrill of excitement at the risk. Gwin's late-night visits to Cloor's, after she was left alone to clean up, were a secret even from her friends. If her stepfather ever found out—but he wouldn't.

"What about the hayseed?" Wena asked. "He's tall, with broad shoulders. And those seductive, unreadable eyes!" Her dreamy smile disappeared at Ubela's snort. "Well, he's tall, that's all I'm saying."

"Wena loves the hayseed," Melis chanted, throwing flybane at her. "Wena loves the hayseed."

"I do not!" Wena brushed the leaves off her blouse. "He's so strange I'd never want to be alone with him. Not really." She blinked furiously, a habit, Ubela noticed, when something upset her—like getting caught in a lie.

"Well you better not," Ubela said, lowering her voice, "because I have a story to tell about him."

The girls leaned forward.

"Yesterday, at the market-fair in Ferce, he and Mariat were *seen* together. With no brother or father *anywhere* around. I'm told he had his filthy hands all over her."

"She *let* him?" Wena, looking shocked, dropped her hands in her lap.

"I heard it wasn't a matter of *let*. I heard Mariat looked very scared."

"That's not like Mariat to go off with someone like him," Wena objected. "She used to be pretty sensible." A terrible thought seemed to come to her, and she started blinking again. "Maybe she couldn't help it. Maybe those eyes of his cast a spell on her, and took away her free will."

"I think that's exactly what happened," Ubela said. "Just listen to this. Someone I know has a friend up in Ferce, and this friend's brother was one of the toll-takers at the fair. He actually remembers this wagon coming in from the south, which would be from here. A strange-looking man was driving, he said, and a young girl positively *cowered* next to him. The toll-taker said he wasn't going to let them in, but this strange man gave him the evil eye, and the poor toll man found himself admitting them. There's your proof that Wena is right."

"That's hardly proof," Melis scoffed.

"Don't be so naïve! The hayseed's mother was a street-walker in a heathen city, a place crawling with sorcerers and wizards. Who knows what her son is?"

"Tarn's his father though," Wena mused. "That makes the foreigner—"

"A half-breed," Ubela said. "Some kind of mongrel."

Melis pulled flybane twigs out of the pile in the center of the table and wound them with a string. "Everyone knows he's demon-seized. We all saw one of those seizures at the harvest, right there in the common field. People like that don't have any self-control."

"Every time he comes into town," Ubela said, "he stares at me like a lecher." She shivered daintily. "I swear his eyes take off every *stitch* of my clothes."

"Men seem to do that to you quite often," Melis remarked.

Ubela frowned at her, but Melis only lifted her eyebrows innocently.

Wena, who seemed to have missed this exchange, wore a worried expression. "First you, Ubela, and now this business with Mariat. Why doesn't the council step in?"

"They never stepped in after Dorik's son-in-law was killed," Melis pointed out.

"Well," Ubela said, laying down the bunch of flybane she was working on. "That's another whole story. It's a scandal what went on in the Holdman's house. People say Dorik's daughter died having *twins*. They're all denying it of course—two babies by two different men." She raised her eyebrow again. "And with all of them living there together, with Dorik a widower, it isn't hard to guess who the second man was."

Wena put her hands to her cheeks. "You're terrible! Dorik with his own daughter? How can you *say* such things?"

"It's not just me. Everyone's talking. And that's not all." She looked around and lowered her voice. "For sure there was two murders! The son-in-law has a convenient 'accident,' and the second twin is quietly disposed of. All to avoid scandal. Then the other baby died, so now there's four deaths there, not three."

"Oh no!" Wena exclaimed.

"Murder shmurder," Melis said. "The foreigner is the real problem. He's what you call a corrupting influence. Parduka always said so. Women used to feel safe here, and now look: we're all in danger." She pursed her lips, leaned back in her chair, and stared into the mid-distance. "Him and those dangerous silver eyes. That hard, lean body. He needs a strong woman to tame him."

Ubela shot a glance at her. "Your father would have a fit if he knew what you were thinking."

Melis pulled a sprig of lavender that had gotten into the pile and brushed it reflectively under her nose. "I'm not thinking anything, Ubela. What are *you* thinking?"

"If Mariat got taken in," Wena said in a small voice, "then none of us are safe. The council is supposed to do something. It's their job to protect the women of our village."

"He's strong, and he's quiet," Melis said. "You'd never hear him coming. Once he got you alone in some barn, just imagine what he could do to you."

Silence fell upon the group, and Ubela *did* imagine it, her heart pounding with forbidden scenarios. Scenarios shared, by the look of them, with the other two: Wena with a blush creeping up her cheeks, and Melis with the hint of a half-smile playing over her lips.

Ubela glanced into the alehouse. Cloor would open up soon, and Gwin would surely come in later. She pulled the neckline of her blouse down over her shoulders, spit on her fingers, and twirled her hair into ringlets over her ears.

The warm drizzle started up again just after Gwin joined his father at Cloor's. He had two reasons for going there, one of them named Ubela. Last time, she'd let him get his hands under her blouse. This time, she might be even more accommodating. Voy was sitting at the table, already in his cups, along with Vehoke, Delo the cattleman, and Cloor himself. Pogreb was there too, but the old man sat facing the hearth and ignored the others.

"No customers in the general store either?" Gwin remarked to Vehoke.

The thin, earnest-eyed man wiped his long nose in a handkerchief and shook his head mournfully. "It's the rain. More days like these will make a pauper out of me."

"I hear you," Rom said. "The road gets so bad in that hollow north of here the farmers can't make it down to my shop." He turned to Delo. "So how are those two boys of yours?"

Delo folded his hands over his ample stomach. "They work too hard, especially Gede. Poor boy lives like a monk, devoted to the cattle, you know. Just like in your smithy, Rom. What would you do without Gwin here?"

Gwin smiled sourly as his father clapped him on the shoulder. He'd had another run-in with Rom's second wife, and his father—again—had taken her side.

A drone-fly buzzed past Vehoke, and he tried to snatch it from the air, but missed.

"Now you've knocked it into my ale," Voy said, peering into his mug. "Ubela," he shouted. "Bring me another round!"

"Just fish it out," Vehoke said. "It surely hasn't drunk as much as you have." He chuckled at his own joke, but no one else did.

Ubela sashayed in to refill their cups, and Gwin exchanged a glance with her—*I'll see you later tonight.* He noticed with disapproval that his father stared appreciatively as the little flirt left the room. When he turned back to the others, Delo was peering at his face.

"That's a big bruise you've got there," he said.

Gwin rubbed his jaw, which was still sore. "It happened at the market-fair yesterday. You didn't hear about it?"

Nobody had, and all looked as if they wanted to. It was what he had counted on. "Well, the whole thing bothers me, bothers me quite a bit." Gwin waved a fly away and looked around the table at the expectant faces. "Here's the story. Voy and I took Oris up there for the day. The other two were getting something to eat, and I was buying some honey for my stepmother, when I looked up and almost dropped the jar. Not two strides away from me was the foreigner. He had Mariat with him, you know, Moro's daughter? She was alone, no brother or anything. His hands were all over her and he was dragging her toward his wagon."

"He *abducted* her?" Delo asked in a shocked tone.

Gwin spread out his hands. "I'm not accusing anyone. All I'm saying is she looked small and scared, and he just loomed over her."

"He musht've seen her on the road and lured her into coming with him," Voy said.

"Probably through sorcery and the evil eye," Delo muttered. "We've all heard the rumors."

Pogreb turned away from his contemplation of the fire to listen. Outside, rain spattered down in another brief shower.

"There's no doubt in my mind that Mariat was coerced," Gwin said, "and I'm sure the foreigner managed to control himself at first. But then Mariat found herself in trouble, far from home and surrounded by strangers. I tell you she looked downright desperate."

Delo sat back, shaking his head. "I have to say it. No one here ever really cared for that boy. Remember how he reacted to that knife Blinor had, the one with the swirls on the hilt? It was years ago, and the whelp was only six or seven years old, but I can't forget the way he pounced on that blade. The greedy look on his face, it wasn't normal."

"Tarn had to actually pry it out of his hand."

"I remember that," Delo said, scratching one of his chins.

"The foreigner never made friends with any of the lads," Vehoke added. "Thinks he's better than everyone else."

Rom nodded. "When he was just a boy, we could

overlook things for his father's sake. But now he's grown, and Tarn can't seem to control him anymore."

"Now," Voy said, "he thinks he can help 'imshelf to our women."

Gwin let the words hang in the air, then continued his story. "I was worried about Mariat. I told the foreigner I was going to take her home myself."

"To make sure there would be no shtops along the way," Voy explained carefully to Delo.

"But as I went to get my wagon," Gwin went on, "I got this." He pointed to his jaw. "Never saw it coming. Think he used a tree branch or something and knocked me flat. By the time I could get up, he'd run away."

Vehoke plunked down his cup, splashing ale on the table. "By Ele! What a cowardly thing to do! You could've been badly hurt."

"We can't have people like him running amok," Delo stated, his voice high-pitched with indignation. "Frightening our young girls, flashing the evil eye, ambushing people. Something has to be done!"

"I don't want to cause the man any more trouble, but I'm beginning to think the same way." Gwin waved off a fly that buzzed around the spilled ale.

"What did you do then?" Cloor asked.

"We saw him leaving the fair with Mariat and followed as fast as we could. But we never did catch up with them, did we, Voy?"

They all turned to Gwin's friend, but he was snoring with his head on the table.

Something apparently occurred to Vehoke, for worried wrinkles creased his forehead. "Maybe you didn't see them because they weren't there. On the road, I mean. Maybe he drove *off* the road, for a—oh Ele!—'a stop along the way.'"

Gwin shot him a black look. He intended to marry Mariat one day and didn't want to imply she might be used goods. "We saw no evidence of that."

"I just hope to Ele," Delo said, "that nothing happened that could have been prevented."

"What happened or didn't happen," Rom said, reaching out to grasp his son's arm, "don't blame yourself, Gwin. You did all you could."

Gwin used the same arm to reach for his ale, and thereby dislodged his father's hand.

"Such goings-on might be allowed in Ullar-Sent," Vehoke said, "but not here in our own village." He stood up so suddenly that his chair fell over. "I have an innocent daughter to protect!" The noise woke Voy, who sat up, blinking.

"My two boys would never act in such a manner!" Delo exclaimed. "Gede in particular has the utmost respect for women." He glared around the table. "We've got three council elders here. Do something!"

"You forget," Rom said in a low voice, "Tarn and Dorik have their supporters." He glanced significantly at Cloor, but the man was busy helping Vehoke back into his chair.

Delo banged a pudgy fist on the table. His mug tipped but he hastily righted it. "We need a new Holdman, an upright, moral man. A man who recognizes the Groper's work when he sees it."

"We need a Holdman who'll enforce the law," Vehoke agreed. "Even Moro's son is keeping company with a girl from Ferce. We need to put a stop to that kind of thing."

"There's no law against foreigners," Cloor said mildly, taking his seat once more.

"It's our tradition! We can't tolerate any more

outsiders. Especially when there are many young ladies right here in the village to choose from. My own Melis for instance. A quiet respectable girl."

Using his cane, Pogreb got to his feet and dragged his chair to their table. "You are devout, Vehoke, and you are right. Our goddess Ele does not want outsiders among us. But—hee, hee, hee—one is already here, stalking our maidens like a wolf." The old man sat down and a fly settled on his balding head, but he did not seem to notice. "All of you should have listened to our priestess in Redstar. She begged the council to restore the ancient Rites. But no, nothing was done." The fly crawled down the old man's face, and he waved it away. "Now one reeking with sin will be part of our holiest circle at the Rites!"

The resulting silence gave Gwin the opportunity he'd been waiting for. "I'm not sure if I should bring this up," he said, "but Pogreb has a point. Something else happened yesterday. Even more troubling."

Every pair of eyes swiveled toward him, "When we first got to the fair, we saw this table full of carved animals for sale. They were all crudely done, but I noticed that children, even Oris, were oddly attracted to them. You noticed that too, didn't you, Voy?"

Voy managed to nod with his cup tilted to his lips, and Gwin continued.

"Apparently the foreigner had carved them. He was sitting in the back of the wagon, in the shadows. With that hair, you can't mistake him." He clasped his hands around his mug and stared at it. "Anyway, I went round back and—well, I saw what he was doing." He paused, then looked up at them. "He was too busy to notice me. The piss-head was restraining a little boy, holding him tight between his legs. In one hand the foreigner clutched one of his so-called *toys*. In the other"—he took a breath —"he held a carving knife."

"What!" Vehoke exclaimed in horror. "He was molesting a little boy?"

"I think he had been," Gwin said with a grimace. "The child was whimpering. But what I actually witnessed was something even worse." He chewed his lip, as if reluctant to continue.

"Speak up, son," Rom murmured.

Gwin leaned back and crossed his arms over his chest. He told how, in the shadows behind the wagon, the foreigner had committed an act so vile that he could only stand there in shock.

Dead silence descended. The rain had stopped, and the mewlet bones hanging outside the open door clattered softly.

"What you just described is a sacrilege!" Pogreb cried in a tremulous voice. "A filthy abomination!"

Cloor stared at Gwin. "You've made a serious allegation here. Can you prove it?"

Gwin spread out his arms. "You have only my word. But by Ele, I'm telling you the truth. When the foreigner finally turned and saw me, he had this grin on his face. Like an animal's. And his eyes! They were glowing with —there's no other way to describe it—with a kind of demonic glee."

"My god!" Vehoke exclaimed.

"In the old days," Pogreb hissed, "those eyes would be taken care of. In the days of the ancient Rites, they would be put to good use."

Cloor put both hands on the table and looked at each man. "That's enough. As the owner here, I listen to a lot of crap. But as a council elder, I draw the line at this kind of talk. Molesting a child is one thing, Gwin, but what you're saying is another. I'm not spreading that around, and I advise none of you do either." He stood up. "It's getting dark and I'm closing up."

Some of the men muttered, but they all left. Gwin, steadying Voy in a firm grasp, was the last out the door. The rain had let up for the moment, but there was a damp wind coming off the deadlands, which would surely bring another downpour. No one was out on the street.

"Where'd you get that shtuff about the grin?" Voy said, stumbling and bleary-eyed.

"Shut up." That detail had slipped out, and Gwin didn't want to talk about it. He put no truck in dreams, but a recent one haunted him. In his dream he was staring at a figure with its back to him. The figure turned, and it was the foreigner. An inhuman grin spread over its face, the expression sly and—somehow—horribly intimate. *Come closer*, it seemed to say. *Embrace me.* Even days later, the sickness of it stuck in his throat.

Gwin deposited Voy on his doorstep and walked on alone. Maybe he should have kept his mouth shut in front of Cloor, and talked to the others later. But he'd had no idea the man was so close-minded. In any case, he'd been forthcoming with everyone. Not in every superficial detail, but in what he knew in his very bones to be the truth. A fundamental truth upon which their village had been founded and by which the goddess kept them safe. For the good of all, the Council of Elders must understand that the piss-head was the greatest threat their village had ever faced.

Gwin stepped around a puddle in the street. He would not think about that idiot Vehoke, with his disgusting allusions regarding Mariat and the foreigner. But if it were true, or even if a tithe of it were true, he would make sure the hayseed would never be able to trouble any woman in that way again.

When he got home, Oris was still up, playing with his wooden soldiers on the floor. The child should have eaten his dinner and been in bed already, as Rom had always insisted he be at that age. But now Rom acted the indulgent father with his stepson and didn't use enough discipline on him. Instead he sat at the fire with his boots off, wiggling his toes.

Gwin was further irritated to see his father's wife—he could never think of her as his stepmother—was just now setting out plates when dinner should have been already on the table. What did she do all day? He was about to speak to her, for Rom certainly would not, when he noticed Oris had suddenly gone quiet. The child looked guiltily up at him and held something behind his back.

"What are you hiding?"

"Nothing. Mama said I could play with it."

"You should be in bed, not playing with toys. Give it to me."

Oris looked up at him, his chin set. Gwin made a move towards him, and the boy quickly handed him a toy wooden mouse with painted eyes.

Gwin stared at it in horror. "You stole this, didn't you?"

Oris ran to his mother and hid behind her skirt. "You wouldn't buy it for me!"

"The foreigner made this," Gwin shouted. "It's fit only for kindling!" He turned to throw the vile object into the hearth.

But Rom stayed his hand. "Just a minute, Gwin." He turned to Oris. "Did you take this without paying for it?"

The boy hesitated, but his mother poked him in the arm, and he nodded.

"Stealing is a serious matter, Oris, and one I won't tolerate. But since you've admitted it, this time I will overlook what you've done. Gwin will return this to the man who made it. Don't speak about this to anyone— ever. I don't want the whole village to think my stepson is a thief."

Round-eyed, the boy nodded again.

Motioning to Gwin to bring the toy and follow him, Rom stepped into the bedroom and closed the door. "Keep that safe, and out of sight," he said in a low voice. "I have the feeling that one day it may prove useful."

Rom grinned, and from the knowing look in his eyes Gwin realized that for once he and his father were on the same side.

Chapter 11

Allegations

On the day after the fair, Sheft avoided the intermittent rain showers by working in the barn. He hadn't slept well. Used to the slow procession of seasons and crops, yesterday's barrage of events swirled in his head.

He should never have fallen in love with Mariat, never allowed her to fall in love with him. Given what he was, both were despicable acts. Even Gwin could see that. But if he parted from her, he would have to face the inevitable consequence: to watch her being courted by some other man. And that other man would be Gwin. Both at the common harvest and yesterday at the fair, he'd made his feelings for Mariat clear.

Seizing the hand brush, he reached into the deep shelf at the back of the barn and jabbed at the cobwebs and dead leaves. The fabric screens would be stored here for the winter and the shelf had to be kept clean and dry. He stepped back to check for leaks in the roof. The face of Miramakamen sprang into his mind.

The old man had intimated that he, Sheft, was chosen by Rulve, that he had some kind of destiny. He couldn't accept that. What better way to make up for a lifetime of rejection than imagining oneself to be special? To believe that the Creator of the world chose him for anything at all could only arise from pathetic need. Or from something even worse: a monumental pride, a deep-seated belief he was better than everyone else. He groaned at the thought.

The only thing of which he was certain, the only thing he could not deny, was that experience of divine love. It was a love he could never deserve and never repay, but its source was undeniably the compassion and providence of Rulve.

But if Rulve was the God who calls, why had he heard only cries on the wind, the ghost of a bell, the ravings of a crazy old man? Sheft clenched his fists, wincing at the pain the right one caused him.

If you want something, Rulve, shout it out. Be loud like your thunder, speak through your whirlwind. Anything less I can't hear, I can't understand!

The barn rang with silence. With a despairing sigh, he stacked the screens and piled them onto the shelf.

Then another thought jumped into his mind like a grinning specter: the Rites of the Dark Circle were only five nights away.

At dawn the next morning, someone pounded on the door. Sheft moved past Riah, who was frying eggs, to open it. Etane stood there. He looked ragged, as if he, too, had spent a wakeful night. "Mama's dead." he said.

Something twisted in Sheft's throat; but before he could really feel it, numbness, almost like the ice, spread through him. Behind him, Riah uttered a soft exclamation.

"She—she just slipped away." Etane glanced at the shovel he held and then, as if apologizing for its presence, at Sheft. "I need help to dig the grave."

A grave? For Ane? In his mind she was still alive; the wan smile she gave him only days ago still lingered in his heart.

A short time later he stood in the deadlands with Etane, digging in the muddy ground. In only a few hours, this dark hole would claim the gentle woman who was like a mother to him. Neither spoke. Yesterday's showers had ended, leaving behind a high fog and humidity. Sheft's shirt clung to his back and drone-flies swarmed around them. After they finished gathering a pile of rocks for a cairn, Etane trudged home to prepare for the wake. Sheft followed him as far as his own house, where he scraped the mud from his boots on the doorstep. But the reality of the grave still clung to them.

The house was empty. Riah had gone to help Mariat with preparations for the wake, and Tarn had ridden into the village to tell the news of Ane's death to those who might want to pay their respects. Sheft peeled off his clothes, washed at the basin, and put on his best outfit—a collared tunic and trousers passed down to him by his father.

He had to give Ane something—something she loved that she could take with her. He found a quill, and copied on a sheet of his father's paper a passage from Ane's favorite story from the book of tales: "You can only save your life if you lose it." When the ink was dry, he folded the paper, put it in his pocket and set out for Moro's house.

Mariat opened the door and immediately fell into his arms. Wordless, she clung to him.

She needed him, he realized with a pang, as no one else ever had. In spite of what Gwin had spewed at the fair, what if courage and compassion demanded he stay by her side? What if love demanded he never let her go? They drew apart. Her eyes were awash with grief, but they also held a kind of aching wisdom, as if she had gazed upon a darkly shining mystery that had forever deepened her. She had witnessed two deaths in less than half a year.

With her hand tightly in his, Sheft sat down beside Moro. A row of chairs and makeshift benches faced the bier. It was only the trestle table, which two days ago had held their wares in Ferce. Now it was pushed against the wall and draped with a cloth. Ane lay there in her best dress, her head resting on a pillow and covered to the waist with the pale yellow blanket they had purchased at the fair. Her grey hair was neatly combed, and her blue-veined hands lay folded over the blanket. Plates holding beeswax candles were arranged on the floor around the bier. Four candles were burning already, and with a glance at Sheft, Etane lit another. A muggy air wafted through the open door, swaying the bunches of flybane that hung from the ceiling and making the candle-flames gutter.

"It happened so quietly," Moro said, staring at the bier. "She took a breath, and I waited—holding my own breath, I think—but then…nothing." Faint puzzlement creased his forehead.

Riah, who was bending over a pot at the hearth, took a fork out and tapped it on the rim. "The potatoes are done," she said in a low voice.

The rattle of an incoming wagon came through the door, followed shortly after by Tarn. His lips formed a tight, white line. He avoided looking at Sheft and spoke only to Moro. "When I broke the news to Dorik, he told me there might be trouble if Sheft were seen at this wake. After speaking with him, I agreed. Therefore, only I will represent our family here today. I am sure you understand."

Never taking his eyes from the bier, Moro nodded, but seemed not to hear. Sheft, however, got to his feet, a cold knot forming inside him. "Trouble? What kind of trouble?"

Mariat also stood. "Why can't Sheft stay?"

Tarn turned to her. "I was told there are certain allegations being made in the village. I will consider them later. For now, Sheft must leave."

"What allegations?" Sheft asked. "From who?"

His father finally looked at him. "You tell me. Rumor has it you were quite busy at the market-fair in Ferce. Now is not the time to discuss it." But his demeanor clearly stated: *when this burial is over, there will be hell to pay.*

Riah took off her apron. "Take us both home. The villagers have no particular liking for me either, nor I for them. When everyone has gone, come get us on the way to the gravesite."

"But I don't understand!" Mariat exclaimed, turning to Sheft.

"Neither do I. But my father is right: we'll settle this later." He glanced at Tarn, then back to her. "I won't go home, Mariat. I'll wait in the barn."

"But you were closer to Ane than any villager," Mariat objected. "You should have a place right here with her." And with me, her eyes said.

"I won't be far."

"Better get out there then," Etane urged him, looking out the back window. "A wagon is coming."

"If you insist on this," Tarn said to Sheft, "have the decency to stay out of sight." He and Riah left the house, and a moment later their wagon rattled off.

Sheft found a place in the barn where he could not be seen, but where he could look out through the open doors. Had Dorik found out about the fight with Gwin and Voy? Why would the Holdman care about that? He'd done nothing but defend himself, nothing but make sure Mariat got home safe.

A wagon rumbled up and Delo and his wife climbed out, the wife carrying a covered dish. Soon other carts pulled in and other families brought food. Sheft settled back into a pile of hay and some of the tension in his shoulders and neck, which he had not realized was there, began to ease. The toll from two restless nights crept over him and images of Ane wafted through his mind.

Smiling, she wiped her hands on her apron; frowning, she parted leaves in the squash patch, looking for borers. She sat by the hearth, the pale yellow blanket over her lap, while he sat at her feet and read to her from the book of tales. Her frail hand caressed his hair. "Wheat-head," she murmured, "will you wear Rulve's body and save the land?"

With a start, he woke.

"Agh!" Etane cried. "You almost made me drop this." He held out a steaming plate.

Sheft looked terrible, Etane thought, and it wasn't all because of Ane's death. There were shadows under his eyes and a bruise on his cheek. "I figured you didn't have anything to eat all day, so I snuck this out." Fishing a fork out of his pocket, he handed it to Sheft along with a plate of chicken, boiled potatoes, and rhubarb preserves.

"Thanks." He looked down. "I'm sorry, Etane. Sorry about your mom."

"Yeah." Etane lowered himself beside him in the hay, and they sat in silence for a while.

"Do you know what's bothering my father?" Sheft asked him.

Etane shrugged. "People in the village don't say much to me because they know we're friends." This wasn't quite true. When he stopped at Cloor's on the way home from Ferce yesterday, he discovered the village was buzzing with wild rumors about the one they called—still, after all these years—the foreigner.

"You know something, Etane. I can tell."

"Well, a few of the village girls have been talking, mainly Ubela."

"Delo's daughter?"

"For Ele's sake, Sheft. You've lived here all your life and still don't know who's who? She's the butcher's step-daughter." Etane sighed. Sheft's standoffish reserve sometimes made him impatient, even though he certainly understood the reason for it.

"Sorry. You're right. But what were these girls talking about?"

"Just some gossip. It's not worth even getting into."

"What kind of gossip?" In his obvious dismay Sheft looked full at him. At the sight of those silver eyes, Etane felt himself stiffen. Sheft must have seen it, because immediately he winced away.

I'm sorry, Etane thought, *but I just can't help it*. He looked at his friend's lowered eyes, his bruised face, and with a surge of sympathy put a hand on his shoulder. "It's all rumor and foolish talk. But there's gossip about something else that happened at the market-fair, and I want to get your version of it. People are claiming you jumped out and attacked Gwin."

"What!"

"They say you whacked him when he wasn't looking, with a tree limb or a cudgel. Someone—get this, Sheft—someone actually said you used a wooden leg. Supposedly you wrested it off a poor beggar sunning himself in the horse-field."

They looked at each other for a second, then burst out laughing. Sheft fell back against the haystack. "That old man," he gasped, "put up a ferocious resistance!"

"I can see by looking at you that he did. Your cheek is a mess and so is your right hand."

Sheft straightened up. "You and your sister. Neither of you miss a thing."

"So what really happened?"

Various troubled expressions passed over Sheft's face. "A—a problem arose," he said at last. "When Gwin decided he'd take your sister home from the fair. Instead of me taking her home."

"I see. And then?"

"Well, there was a disagreement about that."

He finally got the whole story out of Sheft, and at the end felt a kind of wry admiration for him. "It certainly was no fair fight. But I also heard you got thrown out of town."

The side of Sheft's mouth went up in a rueful quirk. "It was more like I was asked to leave."

Etane blew a breath from his puffed-out cheeks. This all seemed so ironic for his quiet and self-effacing friend. But Sheft now had a deadly enemy and could have been badly hurt. He resolved to keep an eye out for him. "Actually, I was at the fair the same day you were, but we went early in the morning when it just opened. I was staying the night with Leeza's family."

"Sounds like things are getting serious between you two."

"I guess they are." As far as things getting serious, he'd noticed for some time how Sheft and his sister looked at each other. He'd been anticipating that Sheft would speak to Moro, to ask for Mariat in troth, but so far it hadn't happened. Apparently his friend moved rather slowly in these matters and needed a subtle hint. "You know, I've been hoping one day you'd clear a fieldhold nearby. Marry my sister and settle down on it. Mama would have liked that too."

For some reason, Sheft's face clouded. He put his plate on the hay beside him.

"I've even told Leeza about you," Etane went on. "Don't worry: I mentioned your mother comes from Ullar-Sent and therefore you look a little odd. See, I was thinking that come late winter, maybe as early as the middle of Herb-Bearer, I'd have a field-burn to clear out my land. Build a little place on it and settle down."

"With Leeza?"

"Yeah. I asked her to marry me, and she said yes."

Sheft leaned over and clapped him on the shoulder. "That's wonderful news, Etane. I'm glad for you."

He spoke sincerely, but also a little sadly. Etane got the distinct impression of someone out in the cold, gazing into fire lit windows. But that was Sheft's fault. He'd be cold only until he got the courage to ask for Mariat, who would then keep him warm for the rest of his days. "Can I count on you to help at the field-burn? I wanted you to be firstman at our wedding, but…well, it might be better if I ask Leeza's brother instead."

"I understand."

"I'll still need you as my field manager. When everyone's gone, you come in and make sure the work's been done right. What do you say?"

Sheft hesitated, but then said, "Of course I'll do it. You're my friend."

Etane nodded, and for a while they talked about his new field. Moro had originally cleared it when Etane was born and for years kept a cow on it. Except for one beautiful grove, most of the big trees had been cut down, but a lot of brush still remained. They agreed that if the weather allowed, he and Sheft would do some preliminary cutting in the next few weeks.

Activity in the yard caused Etane to turn. Tarn came back alone in the wagon and went into the house, and then another wagon rattled in. It was Gwin, who drove the finest horse in At-Wysher, a brown gelding with two white forefeet. He wore a coat fitted at the waist and what looked like new boots. With a confident set to his shoulders, he entered the house.

Etane glanced at Sheft, whose face had hardened at the sight of Gwin. "Don't let him bother you. Just finish your dinner." He waved away a drone-fly that was hovering over Sheft's plate.

Sheft took a bite of chicken, then began pushing a piece of potato around with his fork. "Did your father," he asked without looking up, "ever tell you anything about—about the Rites?"

The Rites. Neither he nor Moro had to take part this year, so Etane had forgotten about them. The moon was shrinking away; and two nights from now, the first of Hawk, it would fall into its dark circle. That's when the Rites were traditionally held—and they would be Sheft's first. He shifted uneasily on the hay. "All I know is there are twenty men in the circle, including the Holdman, the elders, and their first-born sons eighteen or over."

"That's only eighteen people."

"Yeah. To make it twenty, Parduka appoints a different man and his son on a rotating basis.

Thank Ele she hasn't chosen us this year. With the funeral and all, it would kill my dad—plus I'm not that anxious to go ever. Maybe she forgot I'm eighteen."

"I know it's all supposed to be kept secret, but"—his friend shot a pleading glance at him and looked quickly down again—"but Moro must've said *something* more."

And Tarn, he thought with a pang of sympathy for Sheft, apparently hadn't said anything at all. "Well, no one's allowed to talk about what goes on, but he did mention that men have a duty to appease Wask."

Sheft stiffened. "Appease? How?"

"I'm not sure. But don't worry about going out that

night. The whole Circle is under the protection of Ele."

For a moment Sheft said nothing. "But I don't believe in Ele."

He shrugged. "You'll get through it. Everyone does."

Easy for you to say, Sheft thought. He put his plate aside and rubbed the back of his neck. He couldn't seem to blot out the mental picture of what he feared regarding the Rites: a sharp blade, sharp eyes watching, blood dripping toward the waiting ground.

The sound of a door closing made him turn. Gwin was leaving the house. Voy, who had apparently been sleeping in his wagon, poked his head up. The two spoke in low tones, Voy laughed, and Gwin drove away. Tarn's wagon stood alone now in front of the house.

Moro peered toward the barn, looking for them. "Come on, Sheft," Etane said. "Help me harness the horse. It's time." His eyes were sad.

Back in the house, Sheft put his unfinished dinner on the table and saw that only fifteen or so additional candles had been lighted.

"Most of the villagers stayed home," Tarn reported. "They didn't think Ane was getting a proper funeral. Don't take this amiss, Moro, but Parduka complained that a ceremony should have been conducted in the House of Ele, with the cremation out back. Graves in the deadlands insult the goddess, she says. The one who is really insulted, I suspect, is the priestess, who will receive no funeral offering. Dorik sends his respects, but doesn't want to quarrel with Parduka over this."

"Ane put her faith in Rulve," Moro said with a hint of stubbornness. "She'll be buried according to her wishes."

One by one, Mariat blew out the candles. In the dim light, Sheft leaned over the bier and looked at the quiet face he'd never see again. He tucked beside her body the paper with the quote from the book of tales. *How I'll miss you, Ane. How I'll miss you.* He still felt numb, even as Mariat wrapped Ane in her new blanket and he helped carry her out to Moro's wagon. She was so light he could have done it himself. He could have cradled her in his arms like a child.

The two wagons headed east, picking up Riah on the way. The sky had become so overcast that Sheft couldn't tell where the sun was. At the gravesite, he watched Moro and Etane remove the frail body from Moro's wagon and lower it into the earth. At the bottom of the hole, the pale yellow blanket shone faintly, as if with its own light.

Tarn's shovel scraped. Clods of dirt scattered over the blanket.

No! He clenched his shovel with both hands, his chest tight.

"She's not down there, Sheft," a gentle voice beside him whispered. Mariat touched his arm. "She's in Rulve's hands."

He looked at her, into her lovely eyes full of both grief and faith, and felt ashamed. He was supposed to be comforting her, not the other way around. He nodded and turned to the work at hand, but the tightness inside him intensified as the yellow blanket gradually disappeared under shovelfuls of dirt. Soon all the light was obliterated from the hole where Ane lay.

On top of the mound they placed in a circle the rocks he and Etane had gathered earlier. In the center Moro planted the torch, and struck the flint. The torch had become so damp it took him a while to light it. Finally it flared, and everyone stood silent, gazing down on the grave. Mariat took his hand, and it was the only human touch between the stony ground and the dead sky.

The light changed, and he looked up. Clouds streamed past, thinning the veil over the diffuse disk of the sun in the west, until all around them the mist-filled air suddenly glowed gold. For a moment the flame of the little torch was engulfed by a greater light. A bittersweet emotion ached in his chest.

Too soon the glory passed: the overcast closed in once more and Ane had gone forever.

The small group rode away in the wagons. Sheft watched the lonely torch flame grow smaller, until it finally dipped out of sight behind a rise in the land.

CHAPTER 12

ON FIRE

Sitting in the back of the rattling wagon, Sheft looked at Mariat, riding ahead. How could she endure this grief? She'd been home barely three months, been reunited with her family for only one short season, and now her mother had been snatched away. He turned his head to where he had last seen the sun. The grey sky had swallowed it.

But in its place rose an ominous black plume. Dread washed through him. "Something's burning," he said to his father. "In our fieldhold."

Tarn squinted where Sheft pointed, then shouted up to Moro. "There's smoke coming from our place!" The men jumped out, leaving Riah and Mariat to bring the vehicles in by the road, and ran over the muddy fields. Sheft caught the sharp tang of cinders. He and Etane reached the fieldhold before the older men. "Thank Ele it's not your house!" Etane cried.

But Sheft had known that already and ran around the corner. Dirt-brown wisps curled around the edges of the closed door of the chicken shed. Tendrils rose from chinks in the steaming roof. Only one frantic hen clucked and flapped in the farthest corner of the chicken yard. Where were the others? He rushed to the door of the shed and, knowing what would happen, darted to the side as he pulled it open. A thick cloud of smoke rolled out. He bent down to look under the worst of it and glimpsed a smoldering pile of straw and old nests in the center of the shed. The recent rain had so far kept the shed from bursting into flames, but the pile seethed with burning embers.

"We need rakes," Sheft cried. They each grabbed one out of the barn, almost colliding with the two older men as they rushed up. "Get water!" he called to them.

He and Etane, bending low to avoid the roiling smoke, fought their way into the shed and began raking the pile toward the door. Heat beat against his face, and smoke stung his eyes and throat. Tarn appeared, threw a bucket of water on the pile, which hissed out another cloud of smoke, and then dashed out. "The roof!" Sheft cried after him. "Douse the roof!"

Coughing and blinking, he raked, glimpsed the bodies of two charred hens, smelled burnt feathers. Whoever had done this made sure most of the fowl were trapped inside. A gush of soot-filled water from the ceiling soaked his shirt, followed soon after by another. No wind was blowing through the lattice window in the back of the shed, but the humid air wafting down from the Riftwood sent smoke and fumes directly into his eyes. He could hardly see the shadowy form of Etane beside him.

His boots squished over the muddy ground, his face stung from the heat, and his shoulders ached as he raked as fast as he could. He finally got most of the debris out the door and staggered to the side, wiping his eyes on his sleeve and taking gulps of clean air. Etane was out too, bent over and coughing.

Tarn and Moro shouldered past them, armed with hoes. Soon the remains of the debris lay spread out in the chicken yard for the women to pour water over. The last embers winked out, leaving a caustic smell and pall of smoke. Breathing heavily, leaning on their rakes, their faces and hair streaked with soot, they all rested for a moment, then surveyed the damage.

Inside the shed, the charred roof sagged open in the center and the remains of four hens, their bones poking out of ashes, lay on the floor. More ominous, eggshells crunched underfoot, and trails of yolks and whites were cooked onto the smoke-blackened walls. They found the rooster near the back window, its neck twisted. Whoever started the fire had killed the rooster and hurled eggs against the wood.

"Who in Ele's name would do this?" Moro cried.

Sheft remembered the odd way Gwin and Voy had acted at Moro's house earlier that day. He knew exactly who had done this, and why.

Under the soot, Tarn's face was white. "Whoever started this fire could have torched our house and barn. This was merely a warning." He turned on Sheft. "This happened because of what you did at the market-fair. Admit it!"

It was as if he had been hit by a board. His own anger flared. "Why do you believe every village gossip, but not your own son? What I say isn't good enough for you, is it? Nothing I've ever *done* was good enough!"

Tarn thrust his face into his. "So you're blaming me for this?" he shouted.

Sheft kept his gaze averted, but the father who rarely looked at him now glared into his soul. Tarn demanded the truth. And the truth, he realized with a cold wash of insight, was that he himself bore the ultimate responsibility. This destruction happened because of what he was. Those who had done it hated him, and he alone should have borne the burden of that hatred.

He raised his eyes to meet his father's gaze. He laid bare the alien silver, the cursed blood that crawled in his veins. He'd always been a devastating disappointment to his father and his only hope for forgiveness lay in this difficult confession. "I know what I am," he rasped. "I don't deny my part in this." His throat tightened so much he couldn't continue, but an instinct urged him—an instinct deep in his spirikai and reaching as far back as he could remember—to speak from the heart. "I was never the son you wanted. Please forgive me. Help me— somehow—to get it right."

Red suffused Tarn's cheeks and he grabbed the front of Sheft's shirt. "How dare you glare at me in shameless defiance!"

Stunned, Sheft felt ice rush to his heart, as if his father's words had been a slashing blade. Too late, he lowered his eyes. "I'm sorry," he choked out. "Sorry you see it like that."

Tarn's grip trembled with intensity. "How else should I see it? What are you sorry for? For what exactly do you take responsibility?" He pushed him away. "For nothing!" He turned to Moro. "Is this what you want for your daughter, Moro?"

"This is not the time for family quarrels," Riah said.

"This goes far beyond family quarrels! What if tomorrow I'm summoned like some criminal before the council, to answer for Sheft's behavior?"

"He did nothing but defend himself at the fair," Etane objected. "Some fathers may have been proud of him."

"Proud of a man who attacks from ambush? Who takes up a weapon against one who has none?"

"That's not how it happened!" Sheft cried.

Mariat stepped to his side. "I was with Sheft at the

market-fair. He did nothing wrong. I will swear so, under any oath, to the council."

"The council would never accept your word," Tarn retorted. "If you went to the fair with Sheft willingly, you would be too involved to tell the truth. If you went unwillingly, then you were under his influence and had to lie."

"Under my influence!" Sheft turned to Moro. "What is he *saying*?"

Moro put his hand on his shoulder. "Some are spreading a tale that you abducted Mariat at the fair and forced yourself on her. It's only silly girls gossiping in the village, lad. Pay it no mind."

"Pay it no *mind*?" Sheft looked at Moro in horror. So this is what Etane wouldn't tell him. "Moro, I would never do anything that would hurt your daughter! That would be the *last*—"

"I know, lad. I know."

"This is all madness!" Mariat cried.

"Madness or not," Tarn said, "someone wrung the neck of that rooster, trapped our hens, and set fire to our property. Something instigated that. Such actions don't arise from pure air."

Etane extended his hands as if to show him the obvious. "They arise from cowardly prejudice!"

Moro wiped his soot-stained forehead on his sleeve. He looked deeply tired. "Dorik is a sensible fellow," he said to Tarn. "He won't summon you in front of the council without better ground than rumors. If anything, you should demand an inquiry into who started this fire."

Riah had been looking around uneasily and now spoke. "It's getting dark, Moro."

They had been too distracted to notice, but their faces were beginning to blur in the last of the twilight.

"I think we can make it home," Etane said, "if we hurry."

"No," Riah said firmly. "All of you will all stay the night. Etane, bring in the leftover food your sister packed for us. It will be enough for our dinner." She left the ruined yard and headed toward the house. The others, too tired to argue, followed while Sheft took care of the horses. By the time he finished and went inside, the lanterns had been lit and water heated. He looked down at his best clothes, which were wet and streaked with soot. His hands were covered with greasy ash, which must be all over his face and hair.

He joined the men and washed at basins set up on the kitchen table. Riah and Mariat emerged newly scrubbed from the bedroom, carrying bowls of soot-colored water which they dumped outside. Clothing that reeked of smoke was thrown on the doorstep until it could be laundered, and Riah found clean shirts and pants to more or less fit everyone except Moro, who made do with a blanket while his trousers dried by the fire. Wearing one of Riah's dresses, loose but belted at the waist, Mariat placed a pan of leftover chicken and potatoes over the hearth and set out a jar of preserves.

While they were waiting for dinner to heat, the two older men sat at the table. Tarn spoke ostensibly to Moro, but loud enough for Sheft, who was sitting on the rug in his customary corner near the hearth, to hear.

"At council meetings, Moro, time and again, I have listened to certain fathers hotly deny accusations made against their wayward sons. They claim lies were being told against them, or that someone else did the deed. I always vowed I'd never excuse any wrong-doer merely because he lived under my roof. It's only just to treat an accusation against my house as seriously as I would any other."

Moro sighed. "Of course we must have justice. But the older I get, the more I value mercy."

Sheft sat with his damp head in his hands. He was what he was, but had never intended to endanger his father's position as a council elder. Tarn was a proud man, and earning his respect, much less his love, would never happen now. Without his conscious decision, his spirikai tensed as if he were being cut. Since when did it act on its own? He made an effort to unloose the inner knot.

The food was finally set out, and he ate what he could of it. Everyone was too tired and disheartened to talk much, so after the plates were cleared away, Riah passed out blankets. She and Tarn withdrew, closing the door to their bedroom, while Moro and Etane stretched out on the floor in front of the hearth, leaving a place for Sheft. Soon, soft snores came from the large mound that was Moro.

Mariat, who had been looking pale and strained, had fallen asleep on the nodding chair. After putting a clean blanket on his mattress in the loft, Sheft reluctantly shook her awake. "Sleep upstairs," he whispered.

"I don't want to take your bed."

"But I want you to."

She glanced around to make sure no one was looking, gave him a quick peck on the cheek, and disappeared up the ladder.

Sheft lay down, but even though he was bone-weary, could not sleep. This morning he had imagined that Mariat needed him, but the events of this day proved he was the last person she needed. He couldn't be seen at her mother's funeral or take part in her brother's wedding. And because of him, her name had been dragged through the mud. *"Is this what you want for your daughter, Moro?"*

No. He must let her go. It was what love demanded.

With a deep breath, he turned onto his back and stared at the reflections from the low hearth-fire flickering on the ceiling. Above him in the loft, Mariat was lying on his mattress. His blanket covered her. In a manner, she shared his bed.

But it would be the only time, and the only way, he could ever let that happen.

Everyone except Sheft left for Moro's house at dawn. Riah went to help Mariat clean up after the wake and the others to collect odd-sized boards that had been sitting in Moro's barn for years. Sheft worked inside the chicken shed, scraping cooked egg and char off the walls and then helped unload the wagon when the other men returned. They fixed the roof; but even when Sheft and his father worked shoulder to shoulder, Tarn said nothing to him the entire time.

Moro and Etane returned home in the early afternoon, and Tarn drove off to purchase another rooster and a few hens. It occurred to Sheft that no one had checked on the barn after the fire, so he went inside and looked around. Nothing seemed amiss. No damage had been done and the box holding the few unsold carved items brought back from Ferce lay under the stored paper-drying tables, just where he'd left it.

So why did he feel so uneasy?

With no answer to that, he went back to replacing the nest-shelves in the shed. Thoughts about the Rites—only a little more than twenty-four hours away—crept into his mind. He was aware when his parents came home, but quit his work only when twilight began slipping out of the Riftwood.

Dinner was eaten in grim silence. After it was over, Tarn took his seat by the fire while Riah rearranged the clothes she had washed on the drying rack. Sheft was putting away the last of the plates when his father spoke. "No one in the village would sell me any hens. Therefore, tomorrow morning, I must go all the way to Greak's." He cast a cold glance at Sheft.

He knew it would be ill-advised to offer to go to Greak's himself, so he shut the cabinet door, climbed the ladder to his loft, and flung himself onto his mattress. He stared into the shadows. Tomorrow night he would be out in the dark, trying to deal with the bloody Rites.

He turned onto his stomach. Last night Mariat had lain exactly here, beneath him. His body ached for her, his groin swelled at the thought of her. But he'd made the right decision to let her go.

The mattress held too much of her, and he could bear it no longer. He rolled onto the floorboards, and there he spent the long, hard night.

Chapter 13

Rites of the Dark Circle

A thorny vine dragged him down. Like a sensate needle and thread, it whipstitched him onto the dirt, and out of the cuts emerged a myriad of root-like worms. A cry stuck in his throat and Sheft awoke, sitting bolt upright on the floor. He tried to rub away the crawling sensation in his arms, tried to calm himself, while the black rectangle of his window gradually faded to grey. The reality was as bad as the nightmare: it was the first day of Hawk, the dark of the moon, and only hours remained until the time of the Rites.

Etane had said something about the Rites "appeasing" Wask, which posed ominous questions that crept up the back of his spine. He crawled onto his mat and tried to pray to Rulve. But the presence and the love had disappeared as if they had never existed.

At first light, feeling as if he hadn't slept at all, he dressed and went in search of his mother. He shouldn't go to her; he knew that. She'd been despondent even before Ane died and was in no shape to give comfort. But he didn't know where else to go.

The weather had turned cooler, and low grey clouds rolled over his head toward the deadlands. He found Riah at a place by the river where a willow tree had washed down from some long-forgotten flood. Soil had built up in a hollow, and in the midst of decay, a few dwarf plants grew. His mother sat there under her hooded cloak, staring at the river.

He stood beside her, tense with questions, and waited for her to acknowledge him.

Her low voice came out of the hood. "What do you want?"

He took a quavering breath. "How do you pray? How do you pray to Rulve?"

She continued staring straight ahead. "How indeed, S'eft."

The name she used should have warned him, should have told him not to expect any answers, but he was desperate. "You said Rulve cared about us."

"Perhaps. In his own way." Her hands lay in her lap, and she opened one in a brief gesture of futility. "But not in any way I understand."

"You used to understand."

As, he once thought, did he. Even though this God had no face and this Goddess no form, he had still sensed her in different dawns: sometimes veiled in lavender clouds edged with gold, sometimes as a sun-disk that laid long ribbons of light across the furrows. In the month of Sky-path, when the winged seeds spiraled down on his head like a blessing, he felt his touch. In the old man's tent, regardless of whatever else had happened there, he experienced the permeating love.

But today he felt afraid and abandoned. "You told me I was placed into his hands, but I can't feel them. I can't feel Rulve at all now. The Rites are tonight and I don't know what to do!"

The cold murmur of the river was his only answer. Blindly, he turned to leave, but her voice stopped him.

"There is a verse, written long ago. From the *Tajemnika*,

the red book of tales. It's in Widjar, and a poor transla-
tion is all I can offer you." She paused, then recited:

"Under a wide and icy sheet, the waters sleep.
Looking for a seed, the wind fingers the hard ground.
The earth lies in frost, waiting for the low command:
'Rise up now.'"

The words meant nothing to him, and he trudged
back to the barn.

For the rest of the day, what little he had gleaned
about the Rites followed him around like a grotesque
shadow. He forked straw into Padiky's stall, remembering
the broad hints Gwin and Voy had dropped about a self-
inflicted wound. Dealing with accidents was hard
enough, but the thought of cutting his own skin, in front
of the priestess and the council of elders, made his
stomach twist. He hauled water into the house crock, and
his breath came short at the remembered image of a
sickle spinning toward him. If Gwin had done that in
broad daylight, what might transpire in the dark of the
moon? He cut back the stems of the paper-plants, and his
throat closed at the image of drops of root-ridden blood
falling into the earth. Bleeding by day in village's
common field had already summoned the Groper. What
would happen if he bled by night in the creature's very
domain? He ran a hand through his hair in agitation.
He'd have to control the ice more tightly than he ever
had, and control it in front of the priestess and twenty
men. Some of whom may have accused him of crimes he
didn't commit.

Tarn came home just before dinner, his face like
stone. "Greak sold me some hens, but wouldn't part with
a rooster. That means a trip to Ferce tomorrow, where I'll
have to spend at least fifteen ducats to stay the night." He
sat down at his place at the table. "I stopped at the

Council House on my way home," he said to Riah. He turned to glare at Sheft. "There is a matter we have to discuss, and we will discuss it tonight."

"The Rites are tonight."

"I know well when they are. Our discussion will take place afterward."

All three ate in silence, the only sound being the clink of Tarn's spoon against his bowl. A part of Sheft wanted to insist on having his father's discussion immediately, but the larger part was too agitated about the ordeal ahead to risk what was sure to be another argument. His stomach was so knotted up it rebelled at the sight of his lentil soup. Under Tarn's disapproving gaze, he pushed it away. Twilight faded into darkness as they put on two black cloaks that Tarn took out of the clothes chest and shook out. They pulled the deep hoods over their heads and left the warm house for the dampness of a heavy autumn fog that had crept into the Meera Valley.

Sheft hitched up Padiky, hung the lantern on its pole in front of the wagon, and they rode off. Soon the smell of smoke from their chimney gave way to the tang of old, wet leaves. The small circle of light from the lantern passed over skeletal trees and twig-fingered bushes that reached out of the darkness on either side of the Mill Road.

"On this night," his father said, "we can travel safely after dark. On this night, Wask doesn't have to cross the Meera."

"What do you mean?"

"Tonight *we* cross, and go to him."

What felt like a leech dropped onto his hand and Sheft almost cried out. But it was only a sodden leaf, which he quickly peeled away. "What—" the word came out as a croak, and he tried again. "What else happens?"

Tarn stared straight ahead. "Just don't shame me in front of the others."

The words screwed into his heart. He could never redeem himself in Tarn's eyes, but tonight at all costs he must not add to his humiliation.

They reached the Council House, across the road from the House of Ele, where they tethered their horse next to the other wagons. A group of silent figures waited in back. Several of them held torches, which seemed to be smothering in the foggy night.

"They're tense," Tarn muttered. "More than usual." He disappeared into the murk, leaving Sheft left alone with a group of cloaked and hooded men. One of them would be Gwin, a resourceful and intelligent enemy who'd already made an attempt to get rid of him. Others were no doubt convinced he was a lecher who molested women and a coward who attacked from ambush.

He tried to keep his eyes and face out of the torchlight and his hair well covered. In only a few hours, he told himself, it would be over. Then he would go home, to face what was sure to be an unpleasant confrontation with his father. Even worse, he'd have to tell Mariat their relationship had ended.

He soon realized no one was paying him any attention. The hoods all faced the Meera, as if the eyes within sought to penetrate the wall of fog. He found his own gaze drawn there, but could see nothing. Yet, across the river, he felt a diffuse awareness, slowly separating itself from the gauzy blanket of the night.

He turned away, trying to think of something else. Etane and Moro, son and father who loved each other, were probably sitting warm by their fireplace at home. Perhaps Mariat had made tea, and they were reminiscing about Ane, their faces half in shadow, half in hearth light.

The men stirred as Parduka, wearing a red cloak, emerged from the fog. Six hooded figures marched behind her. Four carried a live sheep tied by its legs to a pole and two bore a ceremonial drum suspended from a wooden stand. Was one of the figures Tarn? Was that tall one Gwin? He couldn't tell. His eyes cut back to Parduka. She carried two objects at her belt: a narrow leather pouch and a knife. The blade of the knife, finely honed, flashed out of the dark and into torchlight as she walked.

A sharp rattle startled him. It was a pebble-gourd, which began to shake out a slow and measured rhythm. As if for protection, everyone gathered closely around Parduka, who moved toward the river. They followed her like blind men, marching to the rattled cadence and crunching stones underfoot, while the sound of the gourd ran up and down his arms like shivers. Fog hemmed them in on all sides. Torches glimmered inside pearlescent spheres and illuminated nothing. They marched on, and the Meera seemed much farther away than it did in daylight. At last, with a long shake, the gourd fell silent, and Sheft heard the riffling of the invisible river.

Parduka turned toward them, in the direction of the House of Ele, and raised her arms. "Come, O Ele," she chanted. "Red Mother, All-Mother, hear me! We come to do your will and to obey your command. We come to keep your covenant with Meerghast and your bargain with Wask. Protect our circle this night, and for another year deliver us from the grasp of Rûk." Uttering the three solemn names by which Wask was known, her voice quavered so badly that Sheft, standing in the back, could hardly make out the words. The damp seeped through his cloak while she repeated the prayer twice more.

The priestess turned and led them forward. They

trudged slightly downhill, the weedy terrain giving over to stones. The gurgling of the river grew louder, and black water appeared suddenly at his feet.

He, along with most of the people in At-Wysher, had never learned to swim. The river was usually too shallow, except during the rare spring floods when it was swift and dangerous. The Meera was a boundary they were never meant to cross. Except for tonight.

Fear roiled in his stomach as he waded in after the others. Cold water crept up to his ankles and then to his calves. Keeping close to the nearest man with a torch, he pushed his way through the gliding water. The fog was even thicker here. All he could see ahead of him were pearlescent spheres of light moving like will-o'-the-wisps, and vague, backlit shapes.

The black-clad man in front of him dissolved into the gloom and Sheft hastened to keep up. But it was as if he struggled against the stream of time, as if he were traversing an underground river in the land of the dead.

He had no idea how far they had come. The current spun past his feet, coming out of nowhere and disappearing; the sideways rush of water tugged at his legs; light-reflections spattered through the dark. All this confused and unsteadied him, and he feared stepping into a pothole or tripping over a rock.

Just as the water lapped against his knees, just as he pictured the river rising to his waist and sweeping him away into the night, he found himself climbing up a slight incline. The last to emerge, he stood on a gravel bank with the others, his cloak dripping and his pants sticking to his legs. He waited, shivering, an intruder in the land of Wask.

Parduka seized a torch from the figure behind her and peered ahead. Nothing moved.

But behind the veil of fog, he sensed a presence. A warning, sharp as a thin blade, keened inside him.

"We come under the protection of Ele!" the priestess cried.

Her voice was swallowed by the fog. With a shaking arm, she lifted the torch higher. "The Red Mother sends us!"

Cold air crept down from the direction of the Windgate, heavy with the smell of earth, as if from an open grave. The torch-flames wavered. Sheft's chest thickened with so much fear that he could hardly breathe.

Slowly, reluctantly, the presence backed away.

Parduka led them forward, then stopped to face them. The hooded figures carrying the bound sheep laid it on the ground in front of the priestess, and the two bearing the suspended drum placed it near the animal's head. The rattle shook, unexpected and loud. This was apparently a signal, for they all formed a circle with the priestess facing them and her back to the woods. She raised her arms, and this time she held the knife. Starting with the man directly opposite her, the circle began unwinding into a line in front of her.

Sheft watched, his shoulders tense, as the first man took the knife, shook back the sleeve of his cloak, and with careful deliberation, made a long cut on his forearm. The sight screeched inside him all the way, as if the blade were cutting across his spirikai.

Blood flowed. Avid interest sparked behind the curtain of fog.

The man knelt on one knee, wiped the knife on the back of the sheep's neck, and rubbed his bloody arm into its fleece. He stood, passed the knife to the figure behind him, and moved to stand beside Parduka. The line of hooded cloaks edged forward. As each man finished, he turned alternately either right or left, forming the circle once more.

Sheft tried to concentrate on the rough fabric of the hood in front of him, tried to use the man as a shield against what waited ahead; but the line kept advancing, kept reeling him into a black tunnel that ended at a sharp blade. He pulled his hood down as far as it would go, but the hungry gaze still crawled over his body like a swarm of ants.

The distance dwindled between him and the knife. The inner warning shrilled, scraping against the back of his throat. Just as it had when the sickle spun toward his chest. Just as it had all those years ago, when the black mist hovered within inches of his bare feet.

The man directly in front of him turned aside, and Sheft forced himself to step into his place. The monstrous presence behind the priestess leaned forward. The knife, warm and sticky, was pressed into his hand.

He tightened his spirikai into an icy knot, shook back his sleeve, and placed the tip of the knife where the others had: midway between wrist and elbow. It was as if he pressed it against his own throat. The inner warning rose to a shriek, and at its crescendo he pushed down on the blade.

His numb attempt didn't even pierce the skin.

Acutely conscious of Parduka watching him, of the entire circle watching his every move, he pressed harder.

Too hard! Panic gripped him; he fought it down. Letting up on the pressure, he dragged the sharp point up his arm. Blood welled and chased the point. Ice surged in the coils of his spirikai, but he held it back. He had to bleed long enough for the priestess to see, long enough to make a smear on the sheep. Red trickled down his arm, and the ground seemed to spring up at him. Just in time, he swooped down on one knee and thrust his oozing arm into the wool. It was slick with other men's blood.

He wiped his arm and released the pent-up ice. It raced up his chest, through his shoulder and down past his elbow. He felt it freeze the cut. Pulling down his sleeve, he climbed to his feet. Had Parduka noticed the tremor in his hands? Had she sensed his terror? Ice was spreading into his wrist and fingers, and more of it was rushing out of his spirikai. He let up on the constriction, but the biting cold raced through his other shoulder before he could control it. Stiffly, he turned away.

A hand grabbed his arm. In the torchlight Parduka's face crawled with shadow-deepened wrinkles, and two points glinted from the pits of her eyes.

"The knife, you fool!" she growled. "Give me the knife!"

He was the last man, still clutching the weapon. Blindly he passed it to her and stumbled back to his place, into the now intact circle.

He breathed. He was just another black-cloaked figure, hidden among the others. The ice was taking its time to retreat, longer than it ever had, but finally only his left forearm was heavy with cold. He shook with relief—and the beginning of reaction. It was over. Thank God Rulve, he had done what he had to do, and now it was over.

But it wasn't.

The men crowded closer and watched Parduka, who was now kneeling beside the sheep. From her pouch she removed an object and held it up in the torchlight. It was a metal spoon with serrated edges and a sharp point.

She gestured, and three of the hooded figures came forward. Two grasped the animal's bound legs, and one held its head firmly by the ears. Parduka spread open the sheep's eyelid to reveal the staring white ball. She placed the point of the spoon at its corner. With a quick, hard thrust she dug in, scooped out the eye, and flicked it onto the ground. Black liquid spurted.

The animal squealed and thrashed. Sheft squeezed his eyes shut, twisted his head into the hood. The sounds sawed through his stomach. He smelled the reek of blood, the feces of a terrified animal. He swallowed again and again, struggling not to be sick.

A thump told him when they turned the animal over. Oh God, she was going to cut out the other eye too. He steeled himself.

The sheep bellowed, and the man next to him gasped. Sheft jerked his eyes open. The sharp spoon was shining in the firelight—hacking, glinting, coming down again and again.

"It's butchery!" the man whispered in horror.

Gouts of blood spurted over Parduka's hands. Splotches of white writhed on the ground as the blood-streaked animal squealed and kicked against the ropes.

At last she scooped out the eye, a pathetic, dripping thing, and flicked it away. The sheep lay twitching on the ground.

Shaking, Parduka got to her feet. She took a breath, then turned and faced the Riftwood. She raised her arms, the right hand gloved with blood. "Come, Wask!" she cried. "Accept our sacrifice."

Boom. A single beat of the drum sent a wild chill down Sheft's back.

"Come, Meerghast! Accept our blood."

Boom.

"Come, Rûk! Take away our sin."

Boom.

The torch-flames sputtered, precarious and vulnerable

in the immense darkness. It was madness to summon a creature that was already too close. He fought an urgent need to hide, to huddle on the ground under his cloak.

The sheep, unbound now, tottered to its feet, blood streaming from its eye sockets. The hooded figures funneled it mercilessly forward with swipes of the torch against its hindquarters.

The drum beat faster—*boom boom-boom*—but it was his own heart pounding in his ears and resonating in his chest. It was beating down the barrier between him and Wask, between his will, his veins, and the thing in the dark. His blood drew it. His very pulse jerked it closer.

Like a vortex, its presence funneled toward him. It whirled into his mind, two urgent whispers twined as one.

"Come—come to me—to me."

The dual command rushed through his spirikai; with equal strength it repelled and compelled him.

"Bring to me—bring—the sweet blood—bring."

It summoned him like a drumbeat, like a great, tolling bell. It caressed him like a lover's touch, and he yearned to respond. A muscle in his thigh tensed, about to move him forward.

With a deep chill, the vortex passed through him. It wound around the circle, then spun into the dark.

The vision cracked, splintered all around him, and he realized what he had almost done. Wask didn't know who he was. It didn't know his name. It had issued a general call, and he had almost left the circle to answer.

In petrified silence, the men holding the drum stared into the Riftwood, the instrument forgotten. The priestess held the torch high. The night rose up like a wall, and it squirmed with images his straining vision produced. There was no wind, but old leaves rustled. His arms erupted in pinpricks.

Parduka stood absolutely still. Then, staring fixedly at something just outside the torchlight, she backed away.

The fog stirred. A shadowed hump rose slowly, stretching up and up, until it reared over their heads. A hollow intake of air sucked at his cloak, as if into a cavern. He crouched to keep his balance as dead leaves and stones streamed toward it, followed by the sheep. It fell, kicked feebly, and its blood-soaked body disappeared into the maw of darkness. It left a long black smear.

Under its length, the ground quivered. Antennae sprouted like obscene plants, followed by hundreds of shiny brown carapaces scrabbling out of the soil. The night shrilled with the sound of night-beetles.

As one, every person turned and fled.

He stumbled among them, the soaked edge of his cloak flapping against his pant legs, his hood falling back. A stiff wind sprang up, sending shreds of fog sailing through their midst. Two men snatched up the drum, which twisted wildly on its crosspiece as they ran. Hooded figures splashed into the Meera, a few running backward and holding out their wind-whipped torches like defensive swords. Men fought to stay close to a halo of torchlight, and those left behind cried out and redoubled their efforts. A man grabbed for another man's torch, and it fell into the river and winked out.

Sheft churned through the water, panic clawing at his back, the chittering of night-beetles and the howling of the wind rising like a black tide behind him. A man next to him slipped, windmilled his arms, and fell with a splash. Screaming, he fought his own cloak as it billowed around him. Sheft yanked the man to his feet. He glimpsed a long nose and wide, frightened eyes before the man pushed past him, almost knocking him down. Another man roiled by, moaning in fear.

An inimical gaze raked down Sheft's back, but he dared not turn. He concentrated on the lights of the village, too far away, while the huge dark breathed down his neck. The warning clamored inside his head, mingling with the manic clattering of pebble-gourds tied to someone's belt. He plowed on, dizzy with reaction, terrified of losing his balance, slowed by limbs numb with ice.

Jerking his hood back over his head, he was among the last to stagger out of the river. The figures in front of him shouldered past each other, gasping for breath, their wet cloaks swirling in the wind. Glancing behind them, they rushed to their wagons or down the village street. Those who had lanterns held them high, but their lights soon disappeared as they drove or ran off, as fast as they could, to their homes. The farmer Greak barely waited long enough for his son Temo to swing onto their wagon. In a panic he whipped up the horse, and they careened off to their fieldhold to the north.

Sheft stood shivering by their wagon until one of the figures approached him, swung up onto the seat, and tossed back its hood. It was Tarn. His lips were white in the light of the lantern.

"It's never been like this before," he said in a strained voice. "Parduka is losing control."

With numb hands, Sheft pulled himself onto the seat and they rode off. The wind died down and soon the few lights of village were left behind. The wooden wheels creaked in the still, cold night. He realized that the cut on his arm was stinging fiercely and had been for quite some time.

From the cave of his hood, he looked out at a world completely different from what it had been only a short time ago. The mild weather of Acorn had slipped away, and Hawk gripped the valley. The fog was gone and the silent threat of frost hovered over the fields. Too many stars glared down, too close and glittering with sharp, crystalline points. On his right, the Riftwood kept pace with the wagon, like a constant stalking presence.

The beauty around him, his intimations of Rulve, the love he'd felt in the tent—all these had led him down a naïve and childish path. He had believed creation was permeated by a divine presence, but now he saw the truth of it. Malice threaded through his world like a mold. Evil waited on one side of the Meera, evil on the other side sought to placate it, and evil from his own veins fed it.

He had crossed a forbidden river, and he himself was the bridge.

CHAPTER 14

"BUT THE BOY LIVED."

When they got home, Sheft toed off his damp shoes, threw his cloak on the chest, and headed toward the ladder to his loft.

"Sit down," Tarn ordered. He removed his cloak and draped it over the back of the nodding chair. Riah, wearing a shawl over her winter nightgown, had waited up for them. She sat in the circle of light cast by the oil lantern on the table, where she'd been stripping leaves off a pile of thamar stems for tea.

Sheft had forgotten about the discussion Tarn wanted. Reluctantly, he crossed the room and lowered himself into his usual place on the floor near the hearth. It was banked for the night, with only a few coals glowering in the ashes.

Riah took one look at him. "Are you all right?" she asked in a low tone.

"No," Tarn answered for him. "Nothing is all right with him. And this is the point of what I have to say." He took seat and, ignoring Sheft, spoke only to Riah. "On my way home from Greak's this afternoon, I stopped at the Council House. I wanted to learn more about the allegations against Sheft. Dorik, Pogreb, and Rom were there. It was not a pleasant conversation." He sat on his chair by the hearth, pulled off his shoes, and flung them down. "I was informed if I did not keep my son under control, the elders could not answer for what the council might have to do. Pogreb even brought up that old matter of restoring the Rites."

Sheft's arm throbbed, his pant legs were still damp and cold, and ice-reaction filled his head with wool. "Father, this isn't—"

Tarn went on as if he did not hear him. "Dorik reminded those present that two residents were needed to bring any formal charges to the council for investigation."

"Formal charges? Did it come to that?"

Again he was ignored. "Pogreb suggested Voy and Gwin, but Rom was reluctant for the son of one elder to bring accusation against the son of another."

"He didn't want Gwin involved," Riah said, "because no proof was involved either. Rom must be careful if he hopes to be Holdman one day."

"At one time he would have entertained no such hopes," Tarn retorted, "for I would have taken that position. But now it appears I cannot manage my own household, much less village affairs."

"What were the actual charges?" Riah asked, leaning forward. "Or is everyone still dealing in rumors and gossip?"

"Dorik said five accusations were made, none formal—at this point. Three I had already heard: assault, public brawling, and accosting a woman."

Although Etane and Moro had warned him, the list was still devastating. "But we went through all that," Sheft said. "Father, I didn't assault anyone. It was exactly the opposite. And Mariat herself said—"

"Another accusation was bribery."

Bribery! Who in Ele's name did they think he bribed?

Suddenly he remembered the toll-taker. "But Father, I only—"

"There was a fifth allegation."

Sheft took a breath, as if he were about to be submerged.

"Dorik said there was no proof as yet, and therefore no charges, but he had a duty to inform me." Tarn's whole visage hardened. "The attempted molestation of a child."

Of a *child*? The words stunned him. What could he have possibly done to warrant—?

"I was told Sheft lured a small boy onto his lap, where he threatened him with a knife. Rom hinted you had done something even worse than that, but refused to talk about it."

Worse? The charge of molestation was so monstrous that for a moment he couldn't speak. "That's not true!" he choked out. "There *was* a little boy—he wanted to learn how to carve wood—but I only—"

"I had to sit there," Tarn said, "and hear from men I have known all my life, that my son—the first time he showed his face in another town—ran completely amok." He cast an icy glance at Sheft. "If you had planned this for a dozen years, you couldn't have done anything worse to my reputation."

"It's all lies!" he exclaimed. "How can you believe any one of them?"

"What I believe is not the problem. What the villagers believe is."

Riah slapped her hand on the table and stared at Tarn. "Those men would find any excuse to attack you. You should know that. You've been to Ullar-Sent and have seen the world. But these villagers are worse than dumb animals. They grub about in this little backwater, in this trash-heap of a town, and spew venom out of their ignorance. Why in God's name do you listen?"

Tarn jerked his head toward her. "I listen because I must! This 'trash-heap' is my home. You may come from some fine realm in the north, but I live *here*. I was to become Holdman *here*. My dream was to drag this backwater out of darkness and into the light of law and justice. I listen because gossip and rumor have power, the power to ruin us. Every day we who believe in the light battle against those like Pogreb and Parduka, who would cast us into the darkness of ages past. That is why I listen!"

"But you're listening to lies!" Sheft cried. "Father, none of those things are true."

The minute the words left his mouth, he remembered exactly what had been itching at the back of his mind ever since the events in Miramakamen's tent. He had protested that he was a farmer, and the son of a farmer, and the old man told him "none of those things are true."

A sudden cold enveloped him.

Tarn sighed deeply, pinching the bridge of his nose. "Don't call me that, Sheft. I was never your father, and you were never my son. I thought that would be plain to you by now."

Sheft stared at him. Surely his father had spoken in anger, in terrible disappointment, using rash words meant only to hurt. He looked at Tarn's lined face, but now it held no anger, only weariness. For a long moment, Sheft forgot to breathe.

Tarn shook his head. "I'm not surprised you never saw it. You always chose to remain aloof, to draw your strangeness about you like some distinctive cloak. You are too wrapped up in yourself to notice anyone or anything else."

The words hit him like an icy wave. He had to swallow, hard, before he could speak. Even now his question seemed absurd. "Whose son am I?"

Tarn got up from his chair, and suddenly he seemed like a stiff old man. He went to the cupboard for a mug. "Explain it to him, Riah."

"I? You have decided on this course, so now finish it. We agreed I would tell him when the time was right."

"And when was that going to be? On your death-bed? It has already been too long." He spooned thamar-leaves from the jar into the cup and poured hot water from the kettle into it. At first Sheft thought he would not answer his question, but then he turned.

"My first wife died, giving birth to a stillborn son." The slight tremble in his lower lip lasted but a blink of an eye. "I did not want to live. My father urged me to forget the past, to travel to Ullar-Sent and learn the paper-craft there. So I went, but the city teemed with strangers, and I could find no healing for my grief. I petitioned Ul in the Great Temple, but received no answer."

Tarn lowered himself into his chair, careful not to spill his tea. "Nevertheless, I persisted in my studies. Less than a year later, in the hall of the paper-crafters, I met a young foreign woman, a widow. She had been put into the care of the old scholar who taught us. At that time, she seemed very beautiful to me and in need of protection, for she had with her an infant boy, barely two months old. Riah told me she was the wife of—what was the man's name?"

Riah gazed at the table. "Neal. His name was Neal."

"This Neal," Tarn continued, "was a ruler who lived far to the north. He was killed in some quarrel with his younger brother, who then took the holding as his own.

When Riah was delivered of a son—who was, I suppose, the true heir—the brother and his faction sought to eliminate this danger to his succession. A few Neal loyalists filled a pouch with coins for Riah and helped her and her infant escape to a family friend in Ullar-Sent. This friend was the scholar who taught the paper-craft."

His eyes on the past, Tarn sipped his tea. "I learned of Riah's story and began to see her as the gift of Ul, the answer to my prayers. With a mother's loving smile, she held up her son to me and proclaimed he was destined from birth to do great things. Even though the infant appeared sickly to me, and with those eyes of his perhaps even blind, I raised no dispute, for I hoped Riah would fill the gap in my heart. We became held-fast, and I brought her to my house. By then my father had passed on. Riah's baby, however, did not thrive. He cried incessantly, and I was certain he would die."

Tarn placed his cup on the small table beside his chair. "Caring for him seemed to impose an emotional burden on Riah. She changed; became anxious and distant. But the boy"—not a muscle moved in his face—"lived. As time went on, I began to realize that taking on a second family had not been a good idea."

He didn't have to say why. The piss-head, the eel-eyes, had lived.

Tarn sighed and rubbed his eyes. "But the coins paid for the paper plants, the drying screens, and the glass panes in our windows. I learned a valuable lesson, which I used to the good in my deliberations with the council: never allow heart to rule instead of mind."

Riah scooped the thamar leaves into the jar and quietly withdrew. Tarn arranged his shoes in front of the hearth, then he too crossed to their bedroom and closed the door.

Sheft squeezed his eyes shut and rested his forehead on his drawn-up knees. Nothing had really changed. His father—*Tarn* he corrected himself angrily—Tarn was still the same man. He would still react to him in the cold way he always had. Why shouldn't he? He himself was still the same—still the foreigner, still accused, still hurting anyone who came too close.

He opened his eyes. Why was he lying to himself? Everything had changed. Who was he? Who was this Neal? Was it Neal's ghostly voice he heard on the wind, calling him to vengeance? Was it Neal's legacy he carried in his veins?

To answer these questions he must go—home. He must go back to where he had been born, to a place ruled by an uncle who murdered his brother, stole his holding, and tried to kill his own infant nephew. An uncle who might share his own dark blood.

In the north, he had a heritage. All he had to do was claim it.

Was this the great mission Miramakamen had predicted for him? Gather a band of hardened warriors loyal to him, equip them with swords and armor which Rom no doubt kept in the back of the smithy and would give to him at no cost, and ride off on a horse he did not possess to a holding somewhere in the north? There he would do battle with an ensconced ruler who'd probably engendered several heirs by now. These would be his cousins, and they would hate him.

A bitter laugh rose up inside him, but soon trickled away. He had to go. Even if he went alone and on foot. He had to find out who he was and where he belonged. He'd promised Etane to help with the field-burn, but after that he'd be gone. Even though his leaving town would surely be seen as an admission of guilt, Tarn the council elder would be better off without him.

And he wouldn't have to watch Mariat find happiness with someone else.

He heart lifted when he considered there might be a chance he could outrun the black mist and leave behind his blood's curse. But the brief hope winked out; there was an equal chance he would only drag it with him.

He raised his head. The house he had lived in all his life now seemed alien, and the people who dwelled here he no longer knew.

CHAPTER 15

TENDRILS

In the dark of his loft, Sheft lay rigid on his mattress. He managed to put aside Tarn's revelation, put aside the new accusations; but now, like a flock of persistent crows, thoughts of the Rites flapped and pecked.

Not only had his blood summoned Wask, but Wask had also summoned him.

Along with another voice.

It had called him like the bell in his dream, a mighty bell hidden under the ground, reverberating through the earth and into his bones and heart. It called him as Mira-makamen said he had been called. It was as if good and evil had uttered the same command, had thrust questing tendrils out of the same seed.

Ice reaction gripped him and he couldn't think clearly. What was happening to him? His life was breaking apart. The villagers twisted everything he did, believed him capable of the most cowardly of crimes. The only reality was the gash on his arm, which burned and throbbed. It seemed the last cut from the sickle had barely healed, and now here was another.

But in all his darkness, there was one bleak light. For him there would be no more Rites. In the early spring, right after Etane's wedding, he would be gone.

*

The moonless night lay silent over the stony bank. With its curved brown nails, Wask ripped open the wool-covered skin and tore out the warm meat. After the last shred of flesh had been devoured and the last bone sucked dry, it chewed on the blood-soaked wool. With a final lick across its sticky fingers, it savored the last of the wild, sweet flavor.

Now it was certain. It had tasted the unique blood long ago, then lately in a wheat field, and again this night. The human it sought must have been among the others, within its grasp. Now it would find him.

Wask stalked into the river, melted into a black mist, and crossed. On the other side, the mist changed into a skin as dry and thin as a cloak made of old leaves. Wask hissed out a summons, and the night-beetles responded. Swarming like a turbid creek, they poured into its skin. Legs swelled, a torso formed, arms bulged. The beetle-man stood on the deserted road.

He swiveled his lumpy body to the south and put forth his senses. He detected nothing but a faint, repellent chill. The face turned north. There! The warmth of humans. Two of them, out on the open road and not far away.

The beetle-man stumped after them.

The next morning, the red sun still low over the deadlands, Parduka gathered her cloak around her and made her way over the frost-touched grass to the ceremonial site. She stood at the riverbank and scanned the other side. A chill rushed through her.

Across the Meera, almost at the water's edge, lay the scattered bones of the sheep. They'd been picked clean, and the ribs curved like sly grins. She had never seen that before—never. Always the carcass had been dragged off somewhere, not left in plain sight.

The Rites had been a disaster. Even at the beginning, her voice had quavered. On the dark side of the Meera, Wask had prowled back and forth just outside her vision, like a predator that smelled raw meat. She was barely able to keep it in check. Then that poor sheep. She swallowed and put her hand to her mouth, remembering how, all the while, the presence behind her back had become heavier, more impatient, and hungrier. Parduka rubbed her arms. They crawled with the image she could not get out of her mind: the ground alive with night-beetles.

The Rites were sliding away from her control. They had slipped from prevention, to placation, to some kind of grisly attraction. She had dreamed of appalling things in the night.

A discreet cough behind her made her whirl. Rom and Gwin stood there.

"Forgive us," the blacksmith said. "We didn't mean to startle you. But there is something you ought to know, priestess."

"Yes?"

"It's about the foreigner," Gwin said. "And what he did at the market-fair in Ferce."

"Five allegations came forward," Rom said, "but all were summarily dismissed by Dorik. So we come to you, because we knew he wouldn't listen to the sixth."

"And why should I?"

"Because it is directly related to the goddess," Gwin said.

So she listened in growing horror and could barely believe what she was hearing. The foreigner had committed a brazen sacrilege against Ele. He had committed the ultimate sin. Her only relief came with the realization that what had happened at the Rites was not her fault, but his. Because of what the foreigner had done, the goddess was beginning to exact her retribution, was beginning to withdraw her protection of the village from Wask.

"I'm sorry to burden you with this," Gwin finished, "but something must be done."

Before she could even think of how to respond, someone shouted her name. She turned to see the young farmer Temo and his mother frantically pounding on the doors of the House of Ele. They all hurried over.

"My father Greak is dead!" Temo cried. "Taken by the beetle-man."

CHAPTER 16

THE PRIESTESS

After comforting Greak's family as best she could and after making arrangements for the cremation, Parduka escorted the poor man's stricken wife and son out of Ele's house. She shoved the thick oak doors shut, doors that seemed to get heavier every year, then drew the bolt. The goddess had not spoken to her for almost three months, ever since her failure regarding Dorik's son-in-law, but now she must try again. The foreigner had committed an appalling crime, and Wask had killed again. The first action had led directly to the second, and she desperately needed Ele's guidance.

Shivering, she walked through the empty hall of worship. The windowless stone walls harbored the cold, and her robe was too threadbare to keep off the chill. Parduka unlocked the small, high-ceilinged room at the back—the sacred Chamber of Ele. Like the hall, the room had no windows, only a smoke-hole in the roof. The few coals glowing in the fire pit cast only enough light to hint at the drawings of pregnant animals on the walls and barely touched the massive stone form that filled the room.

Her knees protested, but she knelt on the hard-packed earth, touched it with palms and forehead, then reached into a small bowl beside her for a handful of dried herbs and incense. The mixture was expensive, but would convince the goddess of her need.

Parduka rubbed the offering between her hands and threw it on the remains of the fire. The coals hissed and released wisps of smoke into the gloom. She leaned over and breathed deeply. The smell seeped into her brain like a heady wine. It numbed her lips and the tips of her fingers. Her body relaxed, and the room took on a dreamy cast. Sitting back on her heels, she looked up at the goddess to whom she had given her life.

Shadows veiled Ele's face and body. Only her pedestal and big, square toes, carved from pink marble veined with darker red, were visible.

A joint creaked behind her. Parduka turned to see a scrawny old woman standing in the shadows. The wall showed through her filmy form, but her eyes stood out black and intense. It was her mother Basa, leaning on a staff and wearing a once-fine cloak that was now spotted with mold. The left side of her face drooped and her lips were twisted by the numbing stroke which had eventually killed her.

"You have failed," she accused. "Ele is displeased and will not speak to you. You have failed to comply with her specific command, and now you come groveling for her help."

"Yess, displeased," hissed a voice behind her, where the faint image of an even older crone sat against the wall. She munched toothless gums, and her claw-like fingers picked at her ragged robe. The two drifted forward, to stand on either side of Parduka.

"You failed to convince the council in Redstar," Basa informed her, "even after Wask attacked. Now another man is dead. Another wife is widowed. Another child has no father."

"Now a foreigner walks free, unpunished for his crimes, and Wask walks in your streets."

"I did what I could," Parduka murmured. Her lips felt so thick it was hard to pronounce the words. "The council refused to—"

"The council! The council!" her mother screeched. "You have allowed it to leech power from this House. Ignore the council and form another!"

"Yess," the crone intoned. "You must obey Ele. Only she can solve your problems. You must raise up a council that will restore the Rites."

"When I was priestess here," Basa said, "the Rites were powerful."

"When I was priestess here," the crone echoed, "they were rich with earth, dark with blood."

"The sacred Rites are being held at the wrong time, in the wrong place, in the wrong way! No wonder they are failing."

The crone stirred, her robe rustling like a spider in dead leaves. "The old ways," she insisted. "The village will be made clean, but you must go back to the old ways."

"The Rites of the Dark Circle must be restored!" Basa struck her staff against a hearthstone, causing a trail of sparks to shoot up like fire-wraiths. "It has been too long. Too long since they were performed correctly. And now Ele's people are paying the price."

The room seemed to spin slowly and the two faces blurred. "Sacrificing a sheep is one thing," Parduka muttered. "Doing what you ask is another."

"It is not we who ask. It is Ele! She knows who Wask seeks."

"It is one who mocks our traditions."

"Who ambushes our men."

"Who attacks our women."

"Who molests our children."

"Send the straw-head!" the crone cried. "Send the foreign straw-head!"

Parduka shrank away from their anger. "You live down there in the dark. Up here, I must contend with powerful men."

"Tell them they must act like men. Tell them they must put aside womanish qualms. Tell them they must do their duty. Tell them!"

Parduka licked her lips. "What about Tarn? He won't stand idly by."

"Are you feeble-minded as well as cowardly?" Basa demanded. "Neither Tarn nor Dorik need know your plans. There are others to help you. Far more pious. Just as influential. This very day Rom handed you the hammer you need to forge change."

"And don't forget Gwin. He has always suspected, now he *knows*. For years he comes with offerings to Ele, yess. How often has the foreigner come?"

"Not once," Parduka said. "Nor has the mother. She spreads heresy about some other god. At the Rites the foreigner hung back, made the shortest cut, tried brazenly to walk away with the sacred knife."

Basa leaned closer. "He is anathema to Ele. You let the evil take root, and now it is full grown."

Their voices went on, becoming whispers that wound around each other like braids of smoke, brushing across her cheeks, blaming, urging, becoming fainter and fainter until they were indistinguishable from the simmering of the coals.

Parduka pulled herself up from her sore knees and stumbled out of the chamber. Why was it left to her, an old woman, to save the village? Why couldn't Ele choose one of the elders for this hard task? Her head was beginning to clear, and suddenly the answer came to her: Ele had done this very thing. Ele had chosen Rom.

An inner trembling told her she must eat. She turned to the left and pushed open the door to her cramped and chilly kitchen. A pot of thin chicken broth, dotted with circles of grease, hung from the cook-arm. As she bent to ladle the broth into a bowl, she thought she still heard their whispers, seething in the hearth.

"I hear you, Mother. I understand, Grandmother. This very night I will meet with Rom."

That afternoon, Mariat made her way to Tarn's house, her heart troubled. She hadn't seen Sheft since he helped bury her mother. Riah stood over steaming tubs at the table, washing shirts. She glanced up as Mariat entered and then went back to her work. "Tarn went to Ferce to buy a rooster," she said. "He may have to spend the night."

"Where's Sheft?"

Riah removed a shirt from the rinse water, wrung it out, and placed it on a towel. "I advise you to stay away from him."

Mariat stared in disbelief. "Why? Because of village gossip?"

"I don't want you to be hurt. I don't want him to be hurt. No more hearts must be broken."

"Sheft would never break my heart!"

"Not intentionally perhaps. But eventually. If you stay with him, it will happen. Your mother is gone, and I give you a mother's advice. Find someone else." She plunged a second shirt into the wash water.

"But Ane loved Sheft! And so do I."

Riah looked up at that and assayed her for a long moment. "I see. But I know what will happen, Mariat."

"No one can see the future," she protested. "It's in Rulve's hands. I think you're letting foolish gossip worry you far too much. It will soon be forgotten. None of it was true in the first place, and truth always wins out in the end."

Riah returned to scrubbing a sleeve between her rough, red knuckles. "Truth is a hard, sharp thing," she muttered, "with many cutting edges. It isn't easily grasped."

Mariat remembered that her aunt, as well as some of her older visitors, were often anxious and seemed to look for things to worry about. She had also noticed that many mothers feared to lose their only sons and wanted to keep them near throughout their old age. If marriage lay in the future, Riah should have no concern, for it was exactly as the adage had it: she would be gaining a daughter, not losing a son.

"Thank you for caring about me," Mariat said gently, "but not long ago a wise woman"—an old wise woman in a green and white tent—"advised me regarding your son. One of the things she said was to have courage and follow my heart. You did this exact thing, Riah, when you came all the way from Ullar-Sent to this foreign land. People in love do such things, no matter what the cost. So don't worry about my heart. It will be fine."

Riah's shoulders sagged. She wrung out the second shirt and dropped it into the rinse water. "Sheft is in the barn."

Mariat walked through the yard, her breath visible in the cold air. The old woman in Ferce had given her other advice regarding Sheft: "Leave whole the heart, or break it." In other words, accept him the way he was and don't try to change him. Easy enough to do, since she loved him.

Or, came the unbidden thought, did the old lady mean something else, not quite so easy?

It was quiet inside the barn. Sheft was on his knees, tightening the wheel of an old cart. He glanced up, quickly pulled down his rolled-up sleeve, and continued working.

She settled onto the straw beside him. "You're going to *use* this old thing?" The cart had only a single central shaft that hitched it to the horse.

"For the chickens. During bitter cold spells, when we bring them into the barn."

He wasn't looking at her, and she sensed something was wrong. "The shaft is starting to crack, there in the middle."

"My fa—Tarn says leave it alone."

Mariat studied the side of his face, the tension in his jaw. "What is it, Sheft?"

For a moment he didn't answer, but then sat back on his heels and looked at her. She was caught again by his eyes. They had become beautiful to her, but now they were brimming with so much pain they almost seemed to bleed. A muscle twitched in his throat, and he averted his gaze.

Something had happened to him. She remembered what she had glimpsed moments ago—a raw red cut on his arm.

The Rites. With her mother's death, she had forgotten about them. Her father and brother were not required to attend this year, and they all spent the evening quietly together. But Sheft had been out last night. He had endured something she did not know, and was wounded. Very gently, she put her hand over his arm.

He stiffened, but did not pull away. He just knelt there, staring at the ground and trembling under her touch.

He was in need, and she loved him. She drew him close and pushed his pale head into the curve of her neck and shoulder.

Something in him cracked. His arms came tightly around her, and he shook with emotion.

"It's all right, Sheft," she murmured. "It's all right, my darling."

He didn't answer. As if he were desperate, he clutched a handful of her hair.

A chill entered her heart. It was almost as if he were trying to say good-bye.

CHAPTER 17

TOLTYR

The next morning, Sheft stood at the sideboard and, at his mother's behest, scraped at the stubborn, burned-on clumps at the bottom of her cast iron stew pot. The Rite-wound, even after three days, still stung, as if Wask's deadly mind-summons had somehow affected it. Dredging up ice left him so drained the odious job was taking far too long.

He should have spoken to Mariat yesterday. He should have told her everything was over between them. But Riah kept calling him for more firewood, more water, with such insistence that Mariat had finally gone home.

Tarn banged through the door. He'd evidently had to spend the night in Ferce and looked to be in a bad mood. Ignoring Sheft, Tarn hung up his cloak and, sounding slightly hoarse, spoke to Riah. "I had to spend twenty ducats at the inn and an outrageous price for the rooster. Out and out robbery." He swallowed. "And now I seem to have gotten a sore throat."

Sheft didn't want to deal with Tarn's bad mood. He wiped his greasy hands on a rag and headed toward the door.

"Where are you going?" Tarn asked harshly.

"To unharness Padiky."

"Leave it. I have to haul mulch to the paper-plants." He turned back to Riah, who was mending socks on the nodding chair. "On the way through the village I spoke to Dorik. He said Olan had fallen ill just after Ane's funeral, and now his daughter is sick. His wife as well. He's afraid it's the fluenza, and that it will spread. Better make me some tea with wine, Riah. I have too much to do to get sick."

She put down her mending and went into the cupboard. "The healers in Ullar-Sent," she remarked, "would say the drone-flies brought it on."

"Well, the cold weather has killed them now." He took his seat on the bench at the table. "That wasn't all Dorik had to say."

Sheft folded his arms and leaned against the wall. "I'm sure it wasn't. I'm probably accused of something else now. Arson maybe—that I started our own chicken shed on fire."

The man he had known as Father glared up at him. "How typical of you. A man has been found dead, the priestess wants to disband the council, and all you can think of is yourself."

The words ripped through Sheft's foggy head like a knife, followed by a stab of guilt. Another death? Dread curled in his stomach.

"Who died?" Riah asked. She put a steaming mug of tea in front of Tarn.

"Greak. He left the Rites, driving too fast. Apparently he veered off the road and a wheel sank into the ditch."

It was more than driving too fast, Sheft knew. Panic had been at everyone's back that night. He sank down on the bench across from Tarn.

"Temo is saying," Tarn went on, "that he and his father were down by the hollow, trying to get the wagon out, when their horse started getting restive. It pricked up its ears and kept turning its head to look back the way they had come. Temo couldn't see around the bend there, but he heard something dragging itself up the road. Something big and powerful."

He took a sip of his tea, grimaced slightly, and then continued. "They had just pulled the wagon free when their horse bolted and left them behind. Temo claims he saw a man-shape emerging out of the dark and heard the sound of night-beetles. He ran. He swears Greak was right behind him, swears he heard his labored breathing. But his father wasn't behind him when Temo got home."

Tarn glanced at the hearth. "Is there any oatmeal left? I didn't want to spend the ridiculous price they wanted for breakfast at the inn."

Riah brought him a bowl, and Tarn spooned a chunk of butter into it. "The wife and son," he said, "supposedly cowered in their house all night, but Greak never appeared. In the morning they found the body. The cloak and hood were intact. But not the rest of him."

Sheft sat numb. He had bled at the Rites, and another man died. He couldn't tell himself it was a coincidence this time. Hidden under his sleeve, the unhealing Rite-wound writhed on his arm, and he once more bore down on his spirikai for ice.

Tarn took a spoonful of oatmeal and swallowed it. "Greak was getting on in years and was shaken by the Rites. Exertion caused by panic no doubt proved too much for him. As for the state of the body when it was found, any corpse left out in the night would certainly fall prey to scavengers, including night-beetles." He took another spoonful. "This seems to be helping," he said to Riah.

"Is the council going to conduct another inquiry, like it did in Redstar?"

Tarn frowned, as if troubled by the question. "No one seems to have asked for one."

Which was odd, Sheft thought. The priestess was eager enough to demand an inquiry when Dorik's son-in-law died.

Riah sat down on the nodding chair and picked up her mending. "So what's this about Parduka wanting to disband the council?"

Tarn reached for the honey, stirred some into his tea, and turned to face her. "Dorik warned me that something is going on in the village. People are complaining about criminals running free, about foreigners taking over." He chewed his lip. "Some are saying Greak would be alive if the council had made another decision in Redstar. A few loudmouths are actually calling our faction murderers."

Riah said nothing, but her face seemed to pale.

"Parduka's behind all this. She'd like nothing better than to form a new council, one more open to her obsession with reviving the old ways." He pushed his empty bowl away and clutched the mug. "Things aren't looking good, Riah. All I've worked for is in danger of crumbling away. I stopped in at the alehouse. Cloor was friendly enough, but not many others. I could cut the hostility with a knife."

Tarn took a sip of his tea, put the mug down, and turned to Sheft. "Based on what I heard today, I've been forced to make a decision. I've done all I can for you. For your own safety, if nothing else, you must leave the area. That's the easiest way—perhaps the only way now—to protect the council and stabilize the situation in the village." He turned his head, thoughtfully rapped his knuckles on the table, then looked back at him. "But you can't leave yet; it will look as if you're running away, as if my enemies are right. Dorik, Rom, and Cloor can handle

Parduka until after the spring plowing. I expect you to stay confined to my fieldhold until then. After that, I will get hirelings to help me."

Sheft stood, anger flaring. "I've already decided to leave." Not for his own safety—far from it. "But it'll be *before* the spring planting and after Etane's wedding."

Riah looked up, her forehead wrinkled with concern. "But where will you go?"

"It's obvious," he answered. "I'll go home."

He stormed out of the house, but made it only as far as the well. Still shaky from ice-reaction, he slumped down with his back against it, bright sunlight cutting into his eyes. Tree branches, almost leafless now, cast sharp-edged shadows over the yard.

He had no home. And, in spite of what Tarn said, he was responsible for two deaths. If he had been quicker with the ice back in Redstar, Greak would still be alive. If he had refused to attend the Rites, Temo would still have a father. But he hadn't.

Nor had he told Mariat it was over between them. Instead—and the thought brought on a wave of self-loathing—he had allowed her to touch him, embrace him, yesterday in the barn.

He picked up a stone and threw it as hard as he could at the star-nut tree. His root-ridden blood itched inside him. An urgent desire seized him: to slash his veins with the carving knife and let the malignancy inside him rush out. But even at the thought, his spirikai constricted. Ice rushed through him, seeking a wound that didn't exist. It was denying him any easy escape. His own spirikai had decreed his fate: to bear the guilt for two murders for the rest of his life.

Nausea rose in his throat, and he lowered his head between his knees. The gravelly soil between his boots came slowly into focus. It brought a harrowing question. What if it happened again? What if some accident between now and Etane's wedding proved too much for the ice?

Horror jerked him upright. He should leave immediately. He should get up and start walking.

But, he suddenly remembered, the Groper rarely stirred in the dead of winter. It hated frost, snow, and the frozen ground. He had time to fulfill a promise to his only friend, who stood by him when most of the villagers turned against him. Time to say good-bye to the woman he loved with all his heart.

Then he'd do what he must: begin the long journey to his homeland. Bearing the shame of who he was, and what he had done, all the way.

He got to his feet and spent the rest of the morning raking the now dry hay into ricks. He did this chore methodically, stifling all thoughts and feelings. Tarn took a wagonload and headed toward the field. Soon after, Riah called him in for lunch.

He stared at the soup in front of him, a spoon in his hand, vaguely aware that his mother, who had been pacing in front of the hearth, now stood with her arms folded at the head of the table.

"You cannot go to the holding in the north," she said.

"I'm going," he said curtly.

"You cannot go there because it does not exist."

What? He looked up at her.

"Tarn believes the story he told you is the truth. It's not. You were born in some other place altogether."

"What other place?"

"You were born in Shunder, across the Riftwood. You must go back there, and soon. That is why I am telling you this now, S'eft."

The spoon slipped out of his hand and clattered against the table. Her use of the dreaded name, for the second time in three days, shocked him. And there was nothing beyond the Riftwood. It went on forever.

"Are you hearing me?" Riah asked him sharply, but now she was someone else, the mother who was a stranger.

"You said the holding does not exist. What about this Neal? Does he not exist as well?"

"He was my husband. That is true enough."

"Therefore Neal was my father, right?"

Staring evenly at him, she waited a heartbeat too long to respond. "We hope he was."

A warning clamored inside him, like the one that had saved his life in the wheat field. Out of the unknown, something sharp and lethal was spinning toward him, and somehow he must seize the handle and live. "What do you mean you *hope* Neal was my father? Was he or wasn't he?"

Riah lowered herself onto the bench across from him. "Please sit."

He discovered he was standing and reluctantly sat down.

"You and I were born in Shunder, a land that lies between the Riftwood and the Eeron River. Our home is a beautiful place, S'eft, yet our people suffer greatly. They are oppressed by a malevolent lord, who seizes their children and ravages their land. Only morue relieves their pain. This is an addictive herb hybridized by this lord, and he alone controls who sells it. Those entrapped by it would die for its purple leaves and cannot live without them."

Her gaze was level, her voice composed. Only the tense lines around her mouth revealed any emotion. "Neal and I were wed one month. We lived in a small

174

community called the Seani, which has long opposed the evil that looms over Shunder. In the course of a spy-mission into the lord's stronghold, my husband and I were taken and separately held captive."

She transferred her gaze to the hearth. "They questioned me, then locked me in a cell and left me alone in the dark. I was young and afraid, but still held about me the confidence of the Seani-born. Until someone entered." Lines deepened around her mouth. "He made use of me, and I could not prevent it."

Even though the hearth fire crackled only a few strides away, a dank chill settled on him.

Riah went on, calm and distant, as if she were telling him about some long-ago dream. "Afterward, he asked my name. He repeated it—so strangely, like a long breath: 'Ree-aahh.' Sometimes I hear it, at the edge of my nightmares, the whisper of my own name."

So she had nightmares too, as bad as his.

"Then he went away. I found the door of my cell was no longer locked, and I was allowed to escape. We do not know why. I never saw Neal again. In the course of time, you were born."

A black current was rushing against his knees and if he couldn't find something solid to hold onto, he would be swept off his feet and drown. "So this man, this rapist, is my father?" The origin of his cursed blood?

With a deep sigh, Riah rose to stand above him. "I never believed it, and I told everyone so. In any case, this is yours." She withdrew from her pocket a pendant Sheft had never seen before. It lay, grey and faintly lustrous, in her palm. "This is the Toltyr Arulve. It was brought here for you by the falconform Yarahe. Your brother had one exactly like it."

He stared at her. Like the old man in the tent, she was

using words he didn't understand, flinging huge revelations at him, one after another. He grasped the one word that meant something to him. "Brother?" The old man had mentioned a brother.

"You were both born on the same day, the sixth of Seed. You are twins, but not identical. Don't look so horrified. We of Shunder have long known that twins indeed have the same father. Only among the ignorant—as here—is it thought otherwise. Now take this." She thrust the pendant at him.

It hung by a braided cord of black leather. As it turned slowly before his eyes, he saw engravings on both sides, now gleaming in sunlight, now dark in shadow.

"No," he said. "It's just another lie." He pushed back from the table so abruptly that some of his soup slopped out of the bowl.

"Everything I told you is the truth."

"As you told the truth about a holding in the north, and some uncle, and now this brother? How many relatives is this now? How many fathers? Are there any more waiting at the door?" He leaped to his feet and stood face to face with her. "Keep your toltyr and keep your stories. I want none of them." He turned to get out of the house, into the sun and air, but she grabbed his arm.

"What you want is of no concern here. You can't run away from this. Look at me, and don't be such a damned coward."

He stared into eyes of iron. He did not know her, did not know her past or her strength or what she had endured. He did not know her, but she wasn't lying to him. She never had and wasn't now.

Riah let go of him and held up the pendant. "This is a sign of your calling. This belongs to you because you are niyalahn-rista."

He'd never heard that word, yet it crawled up his back like a cold-footed mouse. He saw she had more to say and sank down onto the bench. An incipient dread filled him, a desire to block out her words, so her lips would move, but he would hear nothing.

She paced, speaking like some dispassionate scholar. "'Niyalahn-rista' is a Widjar word in the ancient language of the escritors. It is used to describe something exceedingly rare in Shunder: fraternal twins. These are children born of the same womb, but because they are free of the morue taint, they do not look alike. 'Niyalahn' is the word for identical twins, which morue has made common among us. These children endure much anguish, for they are cruelly separated at a young age. One of the twins stays with its family, and that one is the niyal." Her eyes clouded. "But the other is taken by the lord, into a life of slavery. That one is the ahn."

A log shifted in the fire. It sounded loud in the silence. He didn't want to know any more, yet heard his voice far off. "And what about the rest of the word? The rista part."

"A rista is a first-born single child. Such children are free from the morue that runs in the blood of almost all in Shunder. Sometimes ristas possess special powers, and these children also are taken to serve the lord."

She looked down at him. "But the niyalahn-ristas are all these things, and bear all this pain. They are called by Rulve, to redeem. The Creator placed seeds of power inside you and your brother, and marked you as her own. This Toltyr Arulve was made, in hope, for you." Once again she extended the pendant to him.

It reminded him of a coin, of how Miramakamen had placed three coins in his hand. *You will be wounded—by a child, by your brother, and by the dark.*

No. He had a choice. Just as in Miramakamen's tent, he could choose. "Prophecies and pendants have nothing to do with me." He pushed it away. "Give it to my brother."

The iron gaze never faltered. "Your brother is dead. Shunder's redemption lies in you alone."

A cold feeling swept through him. In a sudden vision, he was back at the Rites, the knife opening his arm, but what emerged was a mass of tiny black root hairs. Tightly packed, they slowly mounded out. The vision rose like bile in his throat. "I can bring no redemption," he cried, "only damnation! There are things about me you don't know."

Her eyes never left his face, and she sat down next to him on the bench. "You are the niyalahn-rista. Of that there is no doubt. With this title comes both pain and power, for that is how you were born. The pain has only begun. It made you cry as an infant, because the bond between you and your brother was strained. It continues, because you are not accepted here. The power may bloom only under the Seani's care. At one time,"—she looked briefly away, anguish creasing her face—"we believed it would flash forth in reunion with your brother. That will not happen now. But power you do have, recognized or not, claimed or not. Whether you use it for good or for evil is to be discovered, for your will is free."

The Rite-wound was burning, worse than before, burning through layers of guilt and shame. Again, as he had over and over the last two days, he had to reach into the center of his being and freeze everything he was. He tensed with the effort, dizzy from the icy constriction that would, once more, quench the flow of blood.

"There is something in me, but it isn't power. It's a curse. I've hidden it from you. From everyone. Since childhood." He took a breath, then forced out the words. "Any—any drop of my blood that touches the ground draws evil out of the Riftwood."

For several heartbeats she said nothing. "What evil?" she asked at last.

"The mist. Beetles. Nothing of Rulve's."

She pondered this for a moment. "All things are Rulve's."

His throat was stretched so tight he could hardly speak. "Not the Groper."

She stared at him. "As you were growing up, I watched you, very carefully. I saw nothing."

"But it happened! Three times. Once when I was six and bled under the star-nut tree. That night, I went outside, and the Groper came to the spot. Then there was an accident at the harvest, just this Redstar, and the next morning the place where my blood fell had been eaten to the ground by night-beetles." He took a shuddering breath. "And then at the Rites. Even worse."

She shifted her gaze to the hearth. "Night-beetles are scavengers, S'eft."

"But that's not all! I can stop any bleeding, with ice from my spirikai. I'm doing it now." He hesitated, then plunged on. "But I didn't do it good enough in Redstar, or at the Rites, and two people in the village died."

She glanced sharply at him. "You mean those deaths the council investigated? You had nothing to do with them."

"Oh God. I think Wask was looking for me, and found them."

Riah studied his face for a moment, then turned back to the fire. "After I left the Seani," she said, "I was alone, with no one to guide me. I struggled against despair and emptiness, and these settle often upon my shoulders. I watched you growing up and told myself I saw Neal in you. Another part doubted and searched for the dark in you." Her eyes met his, cool and level. "And if I had found it, I would have rid the earth of you."

A chill went through him and then a shaft of pain. His death would have been justice, and it would have been mercy.

"But now I know the dark cannot be separated from the light. It's all grey, S'eft. More and more, it's all grey. I wasn't always a good mother to you. I carried many burdens. But that cannot be undone. What I am, what you are—these things lie in the hands of Rulve."

"Two men died, and I'm responsible!"

"If you believe that, you will atone. Soon you will have to leave everything, S'eft. You will have to travel through the Riftwood and into Shunder. It is your part to follow Rulve's call, bearing what you must. In turn, it is said that Rulve brings salvation to all things, through all things—no matter how terrible they may seem to us."

He couldn't answer her, couldn't speak.

"I could have prevented your births," she went on, "but children are rare in the Seani, and always a source of hope. We decided to trust that Rulve is present in all events and can redeem all things, even the most destructive. And we were right. For born to us were the niyalahnristas."

Her face swam before him, and he realized there were tears in his eyes. "There's an end to hope," he choked out, "and a limit to redemption."

"Perhaps for us humans. But not for Rulve, who is completely free, even of gender. You are as she made you, and you never intended to hurt anyone. That must not be scorned. Will you take Rulve's pendant?"

Finely-wrought, it lay there in her hand—too holy, too clean for his pollution. It came with a title too high, a responsibility too deep, and the gap between what lived in his veins and Rulve's call was far too wide. He pushed her hand away.

Her gaze hardened. She placed the cord over her neck and hid the toltyr under her shirt. "Accepting who you are takes courage and humility, S'eft. You have neither. I will bear this burden for you, until you are man enough to relieve me of it."

CHAPTER 18

A CLOAK FOLDED AND PUT AWAY

Simmering with resentment, Sheft left the house and returned to his work in the hayfield. Riah's demands stood in his mind as hard and hostile as a stone wall. He who'd been despised most of his life was now expected, easily and unquestioningly, to believe he was some kind of redeemer. He was supposed to wear a pendant that completely negated everything he was and march into an ancient forest riddled with danger. And if he didn't do all that, he'd earn his mother's scorn. He raked angrily at the hay. Riah had sounded just like that charlatan at the fair.

By the time his work was done, it was too late to walk over the fields and face Mariat. It was just as well. He'd need most of the night to piece together what he would say.

Early the next morning, just as he was about to trudge out to Mariat's house, Tarn informed him that, because he was feeling much better, they must go out and replenish their store of coal for the winter. Tarn's grandfather had discovered a seam of it out in the dead-lands, and since the coal came at no cost except the heavy one of digging it out and hauling it home, he had kept his valuable discovery a family secret.

Sheft retreated into the loft and wound a bandage

around his arm, but after a short time in the coal-field, he found that swinging the pick-ax threatened to re-open the cut, which resulted in a constant, exhausting demand for ice.

"What in Ele's name is wrong with you?" Tarn cried as the pick-ax slipped for the second time from Sheft's grasp. "Load all this loose coal in the wagon, and then work over there, lest you skewer me!"

The next morning Riah made them breakfast, but said she felt tired and achy. When they returned from another exhausting day in the coalfield, they found a cold house and no supper. Riah lay in the dark bedroom, hollow-eyed and coughing. She was shivering under her blanket, so Sheft put on another. As Tarn heated up the remains of yesterday's dinner, Sheft tried to follow his mother's directions to make a medicine, but ice-reaction kept driving the ingredients out of his head. Ashamed, he had to ask again and again. The coal fire was burning brightly when he crawled up the ladder to the loft, but he felt none of its warmth, only ice.

The next morning his swollen forearm pulsed against the now tight bandage, and the loft seemed to tilt as he made his way under the low roof to the ladder. When he reached the bottom, the planked floor spun slowly under his feet. It was, he realized, very late, and Tarn was nowhere to be seen.

Riah was taken by a bad coughing fit, and he rushed to her side. Her face was flushed, etched with long grooves on either side of her mouth. He helped her sit up, and her shoulders were thin and hot. When the worst of her coughing seemed to be over, he eased her back onto the pillow. She didn't look at him, but her hand fumbled for the braided cord around her neck. He turned away and left the room.

Intending to make tea for her, he filled a pot with water from the crock and swung the cook-arm over the flame. It was so cold under the ice that he took his sheepskin jacket down from its hook and eased into it. He sagged onto the clothes chest against the back wall, next to the bedroom, where he could both watch the pot and hear if his mother needed anything.

When Tarn ushered Mariat into his house, she immediately rescued a pot that had almost boiled dry and then spied Sheft sitting on the clothes chest. Even though it was warm enough inside, he wore his heavy jacket and cradled his left arm as if it were broken. She was shocked to see lines of pain around his eyes. It seemed to take a moment for him to recognize her, but when he did, his face lit up.

Her heart leaped across the room in response. But, as if he remembered some troubling dream, the light in his silver eyes faded and he looked away.

Mariat put her basket full of jars and vials on the table, removed her cloak, and addressed Tarn. "I thought you said it was Riah who was ill."

"She is. Come this way." He guided her past Sheft and into the bedroom. Riah was coughing from deep in her chest, and Mariat didn't like the sound of it, nor the flush on her face. She felt Riah's forehead, put her ear close to her chest, but a part of her was outside the door with Sheft.

"Father came down with something like this soon after Mama's burial," she told Tarn, "but he recovered fairly quickly." She turned to him and lowered her voice. "We'll have to watch Riah, though. My aunt said foreigners sometimes fare worse with certain illnesses than local people do."

When she came out to get her medicines, Sheft was gathering himself to stand. "I have to talk to you, Mariat." His silver eyes looked bleak, and his voice sounded frayed.

"In a moment," she whispered to him. "You don't look so good either." She pressed him firmly back onto the clothes chest. "Now let me attend to Riah."

At that, he didn't argue, and sank down.

Through a haze of ice-reaction, he watched Mariat come and go. She made broth, prepared a potion, and disappeared into the bedroom with it. He must have dozed off, because the next thing he knew Mariat was sitting with Tarn at the table.

"Just do as I've told you," she was saying to him, "and make sure she gets her medicine. For the next few days I'll be in Ferce with Etane and Father, to stay with Leeza's family. If you need help before I get back, fetch Blinor's wife from the village."

She turned toward Sheft, and under the warmth in her eyes he melted. "Are you sick too?" she asked gently.

His blood lured the dark and was packed with roots. He had refused to lift a heavy burden from around his ailing mother's neck and two deaths lay at his door. Yes he was sick.

"It's that arm," Tarn answered her, "still, after all this time! The cut is nothing, barely this long, but he's worse than useless with it. You should take a look at it if he is ever going to get any work done. Come here, Sheft, into the light."

He longed to go to her and be healed. But he should not, he knew he should not. He had decided to leave her. He couldn't allow her to touch him again.

"What in Ele's name is wrong with you?" Tarn demanded. "Get this taken care of and be done with it."

185

After the Rites, he had hidden the wound from her, hidden everything. How could he let Mariat see what he himself did not want to look at? But he needed to be near her, just this one last time. He got to his feet, his arm falling heavily to his side, and sat down at the table across from them. Mariat helped him pull off his jacket and roll up his sleeve, and then her warm, sure fingers unwound the bandage.

He steeled himself for her reaction. She must know it was a Rite-wound.

She took a deep breath, but her hands on him did not draw back. "Not good," she muttered.

"What can you do about it?" Tarn asked.

She met Tarn's eyes—with an expression that seemed to say exactly what she'd like to do about the Rites—and then went back to her examination. "It's a fairly deep cut. But didn't seem to bleed much. Strange. That's probably why it got infected. Bleeding actually cleanses a wound, you know." She raised her beautiful eyes to his. "This needs to be washed out, Sheft, and then stitched."

The cut did not repel her. She saw it as something she could repair.

Mariat laid out a cloth and a basin and came to sit at his side. "With all this swelling, I'm afraid this is going to hurt. Tarn, please pour a little of that wine I brought."

Tarn did so and pushed a small cup across the table. Sheft was about to refuse it, because the glow of wine interfered with ice, but Mariat took the cup and downed it.

"Just to steady my nerves," she explained.

That made him smile. She was always surprising him. How much he loved her.

Mariat placed his arm over the basin and trickled a clear liquid—eferven, she said it was—onto the cut. It fizzed, then burned. "Ouch," she said for him, but kept on cleaning the wound. She patted it dry with the cloth, then rummaged in the basket to find a needle and black thread. The needle she passed through the lamp flame, and the thread she coated with the green, moldy-smelling salve called burvena. "Now. Just rest your arm here and look out the window or something, and I apologize in advance, all right?"

"All right." Obediently, he looked away.

Muttering something about Padiky, Tarn left the house.

Sheft soon found that he needed the ice again and had to dredge up yet more. Mariat must not see a single drop. The needle pricked in and out of the throbbing already present and caused him to stiffen, but she only murmured "Sorry," and went on.

At last she was finished and slathered on more of the burvena salve. Sheft glanced at a neat line of stitches on his arm. He slumped in relief, not because the pain was gone, for indeed it seemed worse, but now he could finally withdraw the ice and clear his head. He was stitched together, spared for now the threat of emerging roots, and nothing would spill out of him to cry out from the ground. "Thank you, Mariat," he breathed. "Thank you."

"Glad to be of service," she said, and smiled into his eyes.

Her gaze held him and he could not look away. He wanted to reach out to her, touch her cheek, her hair. But he did not.

As if she knew what he longed to do, Mariat picked up his good hand and held it.

Only a thin layer of skin lay between her fingers and his root-filled veins, between her warmth and the numbing ice. He knew he must pull away, but couldn't do it. He ached to put both arms around her tightly and stay like that, but he couldn't do that either. All he could manage was to look at her without hope.

Her smile faded, replaced with a kind of puzzled tenderness. "You said earlier you wanted to talk to me. What is it, my dear?"

The beautiful word she called him twisted into his heart, and would lodge there forever.

He didn't know how to begin. Tarn might reappear at any time and there was no way he could tell her in only a few minutes about the terrible accusations that had emerged, and the deaths, and his shadowed parentage. In spite of himself, his right hand clung tightly to hers, but his left arm, stitched against roots, he kept under the table. She waited for an answer, and it occurred to him that he could at least tell her part of the truth, a part that might be enough. "Mariat, it's much worse than what you heard after the fire. Now the villagers are saying that—that I molested a child. A little boy, at the market-fair." He felt as ashamed of saying it as if he had in truth done it, and could hardly meet her gaze.

She took his hand in both of hers and her eyes filled with hurt for him. "I know, Sheft. Etane heard all kinds of rumors in the village and tried to keep them from me, but I heard him tell Father. At the fair you didn't notice me looking, but I saw you with that little boy. He wanted to learn carving, and you were gentle with him and patient. You never tried to hurt anyone."

"But that's not the point, Mariat. An entire faction in the village believes it." Nor was that all they believed, nor all that was wrong with him, but he couldn't get into that now. "I—have to go away. Right after your brother's wedding in Herb-Bearer."

"Go away! Why?"

"There's trouble on the council over me. If I don't leave, it will only get worse. For everyone."

She was silent for a moment, still holding his hand. "But you said 'I', that 'I' must go. Where is the 'we' in this?"

For her sake, there should have never been a "we." He spoke as gently as he could. "I have to go alone."

She took her hands away, and left his empty. "I think I understand. We've spoken of this before, on the way home from the market-fair. You said you had nothing to offer me, that any man in the village could give me a better life."

He nodded miserably.

"But what if I don't want this so-called 'better life'? What if I don't want a life without you?

Sheft, I love you and want to go where you go. No matter where, and gladly."

She had no idea about what he was, yet looked at him in utter simplicity and handed him her whole life. She tore his heart in two.

"Mariat, you don't under—"

Tarn came through the door. "Padiky has lost a shoe. If I'm to get you home, Mariat, and then take her to the smith's and be back before dark, we must go immediately." He held up her cloak.

"I'll take her home and go on to Rom's," Sheft said. He jumped to his feet, but the room spun around him and he had to grab the edge of the table for support.

Two "no's" rang out. One was Mariat's, out of concern for him, and the other was Tarn's. "I told you to stay out of the village," he growled, and left the house.

Behind him, Sheft heard his mother coughing again.

"Give her more of this now." Mariat handed him

Riah's medicine, then the small jar of green salve. "Put this on your cut in the morning and at night. After I get back from Ferce, I'll come to check on Riah and also take out those stitches. We'll talk then." She gave Sheft a swift kiss on the cheek and went out the door. The light left with her.

He had told her parts of the truth, which amounted to a monstrous lie, and now he'd have to begin all over again.

Sick at heart, he gave his mother the medicine, then offered a cup of broth which she barely tasted. Mariat had left a loaf of bread and a wheel of cheese, which was their dinner when Tarn returned. Soon after, Tarn climbed up to the loft, saying Riah's coughing kept him awake and he needed a good night's sleep.

Lying on a blanket in front of the hearth, Sheft allowed himself to linger for a while with the dream of a life with Mariat. He let her love soak into him like a golden healing oil and her choice to be with him brush over his skin. His need for her swelled painfully and he longed to pull her body tight against his.

But he forced himself to acknowledge that Mariat's dream—his dream—like some precious cloak woven for someone else, had already been folded and put away.

Oh God Rulve, he could never atone for how he would have to hurt her.

CHAPTER 19

YARAHE

The next day, Tarn drove off to the village to help with the annual hog butchering. By noon, in spite of Mariat's medicines, Riah took a turn for the worse. Her breathing came in wheezing gasps between fits of coughing, and the rag she held to her mouth was stained a bright red.

Tarn returned late in the afternoon, his hands raw from salting pork. After they roasted part of his share of the meat for dinner, Tarn climbed up to the loft. "She will get over this," he said, "just as Moro did."

During the night Sheft doubled the strength of Mariat's elever tea, made a tisane of salicy as she had directed, and tried to rest on the nodding chair between going back and forth to his mother. By dawn her coughing was shaking the bed frame. Tarn came down, took one look at her, and after a quick breakfast, set out to the village for the miller's wife.

Sheft brought in more wood and heated up a little of Mariat's leftover broth. He tried to get his mother to eat it, but she turned away from the spoon he held to her lips. Her eyes were only half open as he eased her back onto the pillow.

At last she drifted off. Haggard and barely able to keep his eyes open, he settled on the floor with his back against the side of the bed. It occurred to him that he forgot to put the green salve on his arm, but—he'd do that in a minute. He closed his eyes and listened to Riah's shallow breathing, underlined by a persistent rattle in her chest.

Sleep overcame him, and he slipped into a dream. He was driving the wagon on a deserted road, Mariat close beside him. He looked into the soft sky of early spring, into the smiling, wind-washed blue. The old T-scar above his knee itched, and he idly scratched it. Far above, a falcon wheeled in a lazy spiral, its banded tail spread open. Suddenly it folded its wings and dived toward him, uttering a series of high, urgent calls.

He jerked awake. His mother moved restlessly on the bed, her eyes fluttering open, but it wasn't she who had called out.

"Riah! Riah, daughter of Mena!" With a start, he realized he was hearing the words inside his head, but that they were coming from outside the house.

He jumped up and rushed out the door. After the dimness of the bedroom, the bright sunlight smacked against his eyes. Half-blind, he stumbled around the corner and into the kitchen garden, then stopped dead.

An impossibility towered there: an enormous falcon, half again the height of a man.

Standing in its cold shadow, he gaped up at it. It was real. Wind ruffled its feathers and the afternoon sun shone through their delicate edges. The lethal yellow beak gleamed above him as sharp as a dagger. It could bite his head off.

Its eyes glared down on him and mind-words seemed to travel down their golden beams. "Y'rulve, emjadi. Honor to you, niyalahn-rista."

Stunned, he could only stand there.

"I am Yarahe, son of Drapak the Claw, lord of the falcon-forms. I bear a message concerning you." As if listening, the creature tilted its great head, more massive in proportion to its size than any bird's. "I hear from your thoughts that Riah is dying."

He was facing a being that could read his mind.

"The toltyr lies heavy upon her. Why do you allow another to bear your burden?"

His mute astonishment disappeared in a sudden need to defend himself. "It isn't mine! It has nothing to do with me."

"Then why do you fear it so much?"

"I don't fear it!" But as soon as the denial jumped out of his mouth, he realized it was a lie.

"Without fear, there can be no courage."

"It's not a matter of courage! The toltyr isn't mine. I'm not worthy of it. I caused the death of two people."

"Did you kill them, emjadi?"

The uncompromising integrity in the falcon's gaze seemed to slice into his ability to think. "Not—not directly. But they died because of what I am."

The unblinking eyes bored deep. "Blaming yourself is an evasion. Do not use it to hide from what you must do."

The statement clutched him in its claw, and like a pinned-down rabbit, he struggled to escape. "It would be pride to take the toltyr. Pride to imagine myself someone I'm not."

"You have been called: by the wind, by the bell, and by the cries of the land. Why do you deny the summons? It is humility, not pride, to accept it."

His mother had said something similar, and it stung that now another was judging him. "I am not this niyalahn-rista! I'm no better than anybody else."

Suddenly he realized what he'd just said. Of course

he—of all people—was no better than anybody else. Why would he deny something so patently obvious, if he did not, deep in his core, think the opposite? Why else hadn't he made more friends, not bothered to learn the names of people in the village, looked down at their beliefs as much as his mother did? The realization doused him like a bucket of icy water.

"You are correct when you say you are no better. No one created by Rulve is better than another. But you are niyal'arist, as I am falconform. Why is this so hard for you to accept?"

The resentment he'd felt earlier flooded back. "The villagers accuse me of a long list of crimes, my own blood haunts me, even my best friend can't look me in the eye, and suddenly I'm supposed to forget all that? Accept some grandiose title and march off to the tune of voices and bells to a place I know nothing about?"

"Your shortcomings are irrelevant, emjadi. You are summoned. You have been given the power to save a dying land and redeem those who live in darkness. Twice you have been told this, and twice you rejected it. Now you must cast off the cloak you have clutched to yourself and stand before Rulve as she made you."

He remembered Tarn's angry words to him the night before the Rites, the accusation that he drew his strangeness about himself "like some distinctive cloak." His chest tightened with chaotic emotions that had been rising ever since the fair, and suddenly they all became too much. "Look at me!" he cried bitterly. "I'm not good enough for Rulve's toltyr, not clean enough. In all these years, who redeemed *me*?"

The words fell into a pool of silence. Out of it crawled another memory of what Tarn had once said: "All you can think of is yourself." Something inside him cracked.

"You are angry and hurt," Yarahe said, "yet ashamed. You know you are betraying what you sense inside: a call to something greater than yourself."

It was true. He had felt the longing, heard the voices calling, felt the response rise up in his soul. But— "I don't know what I'm supposed to do, Yarahe. I don't know what Rulve wants." Again he heard himself, and groaned inwardly. Was even this a denial? He remembered the tale about the desert and the creek, words he thought he had buried deep with Ane: *There the cloud emptied itself in joy, and fell over the land as rain, and under it the desert bloomed.* He remembered his odd reaction to Ane's green cloak. Dread shot through him like sleet through a winter's night.

Yarahe cocked his head in a quizzical gesture that seemed almost human. "It seems you demand to see every outcome before setting your foot on the road."

He stood drenched in his own inadequacy, knowing Yarahe would tolerate no more excuses and no more denials. He had to face what he most feared. "The toltyr is too great for me," he choked out. "If I take it up, I will fail. And I've failed enough as it is."

The great falcon ruffled his feathers, apparently unconcerned by this cowardly admission. "Perhaps. But fear of failure is rooted in the pride you fear so much. Rulve calls. You are required to answer, not to succeed."

His throat was too tight to speak. He could only nod. The sudden thought of Mariat's lovely face slashed across his heart, as sharp and bright as a blade.

"Your leaving her is a wound you must endure. You must take up the toltyr and journey through the Riftwood, bearing your love and your doubts and your pull toward pride. You must go now, before winter sets in."

He longed to leave everything behind and start a new

life. But he had promised to help Etane with the field-burn. It was the last gift he could give in return for a lifetime of friendship, one small way his sweat could atone for his blood. Because of the pollution inside him, he must never have a wife, never have children; but he could clear a field, and on it Etane's wife would plant a kitchen garden, and Etane's children would play. "I need more time," he said in a ragged voice, "to repay a great debt."

"You must leave now."

"I have given my word, Yarahe. To stay until Herb-Bearer."

The falconform's gaze never wavered, but it shifted from one foot to the other as if in hesitation. "Once given, the emjadi's word should not be taken lightly. It shall be as you have said, niyal'arist. But hear me: two days after the dark of the moon, as it begins to wax in Seed, you must come at dawn to the Wind-gate. Rift-riders will meet you there and take you to the Seani. Beware the waning moon, and especially the night of its fall."

He knew the Wind-gate, a gully that came down from the Riftwood across the river from the Council House. Yarahe spread out the great wings, and Sheft stepped back.

"Will you be there?" the creature asked.

He bowed his head. "I seem to have a destiny, Yarahe. But no real hope."

"Your eyrie has failed you, niyal'arist. A community must provide support and safety for its members, so that they may find the true identity within. This has not been done. Neither for you nor for your brother. The consequences, I fear, will be grave. Yet we must trust. Will you be there?"

He looked up, allowing his silver gaze to meet the creature's penetrating gold. "I will." The words were like a gust of wind moving through a long-locked room. He took a deep breath, and for a moment the burden of past denials was lifted, and he soared.

But almost immediately the fear of what the future might bring dragged him down.

"Y'rulve, emjadi." The falconform stretched out its great neck and leaped into the wind. Its wings whipped up fallen leaves as it swept over the fields.

He watched it fly over the Riftwood until it dwindled into the autumn sky. He hadn't even thought to ask what "emjadi" meant.

The wind had picked up, and he was shaking. He stumbled through the cold sunshine back into the house. Gusts rattled the windows in the kitchen and moaned through chinks in the walls, but his mother's room was still. He went directly to her bed and knelt beside it. She turned her head on the pillow, and her eyes, bright with fever, met his. There was no doubt she had heard the entire conversation. She plucked feebly at the cord around her neck. Trying not to touch her hot skin with his cold hands, he helped her take it off.

For the first time, he looked closely at the toltyr. It reminded him of the tale his mother had once told him when he was small and ached for help, a tale about a green disk set into the wall of a great, tree-supported hall. The medallion was punctured with three star-shaped holes in a triangular pattern at the top, and two curved hands were carved at the bottom. They were Rulve's hands, filled with power, yet open in need. At first it seemed both sides depicted the hands holding the same object—the wavy blade of a knife. But as he looked closer, he saw that what he had thought a blade was on one side a tongue of flame and on the other a faintly veined leaf.

He didn't know what it meant, nor did it tell him what he must do. But he looped the toltyr over his head and dropped it under his shirt. It felt heavy, cold, and alien against his chest, but he could no longer deny it belonged to him.

"I'm sorry," his mother whispered, "so sorry."

All these years she had been alone. Even sleeping beside Tarn, she had been even more alone than he. "Forgive me, Mother. Please forgive me."

"My son," she breathed, "there is no need." She lifted her hand and, in tears, he took it between both of his.

Head bowed, he stayed kneeling by her side, until her hand grew cold and she was gone.

When Tarn came through the door, he was alone. "No one was willing to come and help Riah," he said. "Blinor told me to 'get my ass out of his house.' In years past, no one would have spoken to me that way."

"Riah's dead," Sheft said.

Tarn stared at him a moment, then hung up his cloak and walked into the bedroom. After a short time he came back to the kitchen. "Tomorrow I'll take her body to the House of Ele. She will be cremated there according to our local tradition."

Sheft stiffened. "No. She belonged to Rulve. She cared nothing for Ele, and neither do you."

Tarn turned away and opened and closed cupboard doors, apparently looking for something. He removed the egg basket and slammed it on the table. "It is you who have made this cremation necessary. Because of you, I must do everything under Parduka's watchful eye."

"No matter what you think I've done, you can't do this to her."

"You muddied these waters, so don't whine to me now. In the spring you will be gone, but I must live here and begin another life." He jerked his head toward the door. "Get out to the coop. I'm going to check the rabbit traps." He took his cloak off the peg and left.

Anger surged through Sheft and he rushed toward the door. But he stopped before opening it. What was he going to do? Shout at him? Strike him? Argue with him while his mother's body stiffened in her bed? Riah deserved better than that.

He collected the eggs, then went to her side. She lay like an empty seed-pod, her hair askew on the pillow, her hands open. At the very least, he could sit watch with her in the tradition of Moro's family. He washed her face, combed her hair, and wrapped her in her cloak. He spread a blanket before the hearth, laid her body there, and then placed two lit candles beside her.

Tarn returned empty-handed and glanced at the arrangement. Making no comment, he boiled the eggs for dinner, changed the sheets on his bed, and withdrew, quietly shutting the door. Sheft sank into the nodding chair. He stared at the serene candle flames until grief blurred them.

In the middle of the night, he woke from a vivid dream. Riah was gazing into a grey, winter sky. While he watched, her body fell away and her spirit moved into the lowering clouds. A whisper of words trailed behind her, like a sparkling drift of snow: *The earth lies in frost, waiting for the low command: 'Rise up now.'*

In the morning it was indeed snowing, but only lightly, and the yard was barely white when they carried Riah's body to the wagon. He watched Tarn drive away. Then, carrying the flint box and an unlit torch, he trudged out to the deadlands. Ane's grave was still a raw rectangle in the ground, and what was left of her scorched burial torch protruded from the cairn. He lit the torch he had brought and placed it beside Ane's.

The torch flared as a solitary light against the snow-flecked grey, and its smoke curled into the leaden sky. He returned home, following his own melting footprints, black against the white filigreed ground.

CHAPTER 20

WHAT LOVE DEMANDS

Sheft had been watching for it, dreading it, until two days later he saw it—a coil of smoke rising from the direction of Moro's house. His heart sank. Mariat had come home from Ferce. For what he knew would be the last time, he took the familiar path through the fields.

In contrast to his own cold house, Moro's cottage was warm and lamp-lit when he stepped inside. He'd always felt at home there, with people who were like family to him. But what he had to do would change all that.

They sat at the kitchen table and he told them of Riah's death. He needed an iron will, but when Mariat came from her seat to embrace him, he found himself melting like wax. Moro reached over to grasp his shoulder when he heard of the cremation, and Sheft looked down at his hands while they gave him their sympathy and their memories. After a while, Mariat said it was time to take out the stitches from his arm. Sheft cast a meaningful look at Etane, who reminded his father of work that had to be done, immediately, in the barn. They left the two of them alone.

"Roll up your sleeve," she said, setting down a scissors and a bowl for the threads.

He did, then steeled himself for the first brush of her fingers. Her touches on his arm were gentle, but ice fled to them as if each were a wound. He sat rigidly as she clipped at the stitches, her head bent, her hands deft and warm.

He filled the time with looking at her. The subtle, gleaming colors in her brown hair, the practical set of her chin, her soft mouth, slightly pursed now in concentration. He took a deep breath of her, and she smelled like apples and clean, wind-dried sheets. She pulled out stitch after stitch, but the only pain was that of her nearness.

At length she sighed. "All done."

His arm, though marked, was clean. She laid her hand lightly on the place, and it was like a brief blessing, too soon removed.

He had to speak.

"Mariat, thank you. It—it seems I'm always thanking you." *You were the only one who ever needed me, who could look into my eyes without flinching. You trusted me from the start. I could never thank you enough for that.*

"And much deserved thanks it is."

Her eyes shone with that teasing look he would hold in his heart and never forget. She took both his hands and everything welled up in him again. He could only move his thumbs over her fingers and stare helplessly as her look turned tender, at the gaze that did not turn away from him but waited upon him.

"You've been thinking about the spring," she said.

He had to swallow the constriction in his throat before he could speak. "Very much," he said. "All the time."

"So we will leave right after the field-burn?"

He had gone over the words in his mind, many times over many hours, and now he wrenched them out. "Mariat, I must go alone."

She only looked at him; but something, something alive and joyous, drained out of her face.

Oh God, what took the most courage? To admit his pollution and have her turn from him in horror, or free her for a normal life? What was compassionate? To let her believe they had a future together, or to kill the hope for it right now? He had to do what love demanded. He had to make an end. "From now on," he said, "there can be no 'we.'"

Her eyes slowly filled with liquid hurt. "Are you certain?"

So he wouldn't see what he was doing to her, he lowered his head. "Yes."

Her hands slipped out of his. "You tried to tell me this before I left for Ferce, didn't you?"

"Yes."

"So was there never this 'we' between us? For you, I mean? For me it was—very real."

He hadn't planned for her questions, hadn't planned for the almost imperceptible quaver in her voice, didn't know he would be hacking at something beautiful, each word an ax-blow. "It wasn't real," he said woodenly.

"You said you loved me. That day by the creek."

The pain in her voice moved like a knife-point across his spirikai. He couldn't do this. He couldn't hurt her any more. His resolve was slipping away. "Oh, Mariat—" he began, leaning toward her. But then his eyes fell upon the bowl. It held the stitches she had taken out of him. The black threads lay there like obscene roots. What ran in his veins could never be denied, and he was finished with denials. With all his courage, with all his compassion for her, he dragged out the only answer he had left—a blatant lie. "I made a mistake," he said.

Her sleeves rustled as she drew back. "Look at me and say you don't love me."

"Please, Mariat," he begged. After going over and

over it, after putting it off for too long, after finally assuring himself it was for her good, he had made his decision. But it had been made when her arm on the table wasn't a hairsbreadth away from his, when he couldn't feel the warmth from her skin.

"Say it—if you can."

Rulve, help me! Say it!

But he couldn't find the strength, couldn't look at her again or deny his love for her anymore. Blindly he stood up, made his way to the door, and grabbed his jacket from the peg. "Good-bye," he said in a strangled voice. He hesitated for an instant, took a long, heavy breath, and walked out.

The door banged shut against the warmth, and everything he had ever needed was left behind.

In the days that followed, he rose, ate, and worked like a carved figure. He refused to think about anything except what was directly in front of him and thrust aside split-second images of her warm eyes or the curve of her throat, over and over, many times in a day, before they could form the entire picture of one he must forget.

Now that Riah was gone, it took him and Tarn an inordinate amount of time to accomplish what had been taken for granted before. Dirty clothes had to be scrubbed, rinsed, and hung on the rack, where there never seemed to be enough room. No hot stew waited when they came in hungry and cold from outdoor chores. Neither of them knew where Riah had stored things, so they had to search for the salt, the paring knife, the needle and thread when a button popped off Tarn's coat. With much less cooking going on, a chill crept into the walls, and honey congealed in the jar. They engaged in terse arguments about whose turn it was to feed the chickens, wash the dishes, sweep the floor, bring in water from the well.

At other times there was little to do. They would sit, not speaking, before the fire, and go early to bed. Or Sheft would work on the wooden bowl he was making as Etane and Leeza's wedding gift. He sanded it as smooth as a river stone, carved an intricate row of wheat-stalks along the outer edge, and rubbed it with oil until it gleamed. But that was all he carved, and the box left from the market-fair lay abandoned in the barn.

The past he had known and the future he had once hoped for had slipped away. In exchange he had accepted an alien identity, a medallion engraved with enigmatic symbols, and a title in a foreign tongue. The toltyr hung heavy from his neck, an icy brand that marked him for failure, but he did not remove it. It belonged to him, and in reality he possessed nothing else.

Mariat's bouts of testiness had been giving Etane no peace, so he came one day over the frost-touched fields to speak to Sheft. He found him hauling bags of feed off the wagon and piling them in the barn.

Sheft had changed in the short time since he'd seen him last. Two lines were engraved between his eyebrows now, and the metallic eyes were like lead. He wore his sheepskin jacket, and there was a cord around his neck which Etane had never noticed before. Whatever hung from it was hidden inside his shirt. Etane noticed that Sheft stiffened when he saw him, his breath a cloud in the cold air of the barn.

"Don't worry," Etane said. "I haven't come to beat the hell out of you. Although it may not be a bad idea, now that I think of it."

Sheft dropped the bag he was carrying and sank down

on it. He stared at the floor, looking utterly bereft. "I had to do it. Rulve help me, I had no other choice."

Etane brought up one of the stools stored next to the paper-making screens and sat down in front of him. "I know you, Sheft. I know you believe you're doing what's best for my sister, and I respect you for it. But have you thought it all through?"

Sheft looked at him with a kind of tortured disbelief, and Etane winced. Of course he had thought about it. Knowing him, probably for weeks.

"So your father finally told you to leave, eh?"

Sheft sighed and rubbed the back of his neck. "I'd already decided that. And he's not my father." One foot scuffed at the bedraggled straw at his feet. "He told me just before the Rites. I don't know who my father is."

Etane remembered the rumors about Riah and her supposed activities in Ullar-Sent, but decided that was none of his business. "You're not the only one around here like that. And your being somebody else's son wouldn't matter to Mariat."

"Etane, you don't understand." Sheft was almost pleading with him. "I can't explain it to you. There was no other way!"

"I guess it all really hinges on whether you love her or not."

"Oh God!" Sheft groaned.

Etane saw the open anguish in his face and grasped him by the shoulder. "You don't have to leave us."

Sheft swallowed hard. "I'll stay until after the field-burn. I want to do that for you and Leeza. You were my only friend, and I want to help you at your wedding."

That was weeks away, and Etane saw in Sheft's eyes what it would cost him to stay until then. He couldn't bring himself to mention that Gwin had already come to call on Mariat, and that his father was encouraging his visits. "I'll have the burn as soon as possible in Herb-Bearer, as soon as the fields dry out enough. Maybe you'll come to your senses by then."

Sheft's whole body sagged, and it was obvious to Etane he wouldn't change his mind. "How fares—your sister?" he asked in a dead voice.

Poor man, he couldn't even say her name. He wanted to say, "She's sad. What do you expect?" but he had already made too many hurtful blunders. "Mariat doesn't talk much, just buries herself in work. Suddenly everything has to be scoured, or swept, or washed. She says it's for the field-burn celebration and the wedding afterward. It's driving me crazy, but that's how she deals with it."

He wanted to talk about Leeza and his stay with her family, about the games they played at their table, how Leeza's cheeks turned pink when he teased her—but that definitely wouldn't cheer up Sheft. "You know, in a perfect world, you and Mariat would have...well, anyway. Leeza's oldest brother agreed to be my firstman, but believe me, Sheft, I wish it could be you."

"I know. I do too. But whenever I can, I'll get out to your field and do some brush cutting. And I'm glad for you. Soon you'll be a happily married man."

Although Sheft tried to smile, he looked so miserable that Etane felt a wave of compassion for him. It was, however, mingled with exasperation. He didn't know where this streak of stubborn nobility came from in Sheft—probably from those tales of knights his mother read to him long ago—but it would be his undoing. Such an attitude was causing suffering for both his sister and himself, and it was completely unnecessary. "I'll join you out there when I can. Anyway, I've got to get back. It smells like snow is coming."

He stopped at the barn door. "I've been in the village, and there's something going on there. Lots of dark looks. But the odd thing is there's no gossip. Nothing at Cloor's, everyone suddenly busy when I stop at Rom's, Blinor tight-lipped at the mill. No one's saying much, but there are ugly rumors about people gathering in Ele's house after the doors are shut for the night. It might mean nothing, but I'd stay clear of the village if I were you."

And if I were you, he thought as he headed home, *I'd also quit worrying about who wasn't my father, and make up as fast as I could with the girl who still loves you.*

That led him to think of Leeza, and other, much more pleasant, thoughts.

It was Candle, the month of the longest nights. Tarn disappeared for days at a time, going to Ferce and staying at the inn. A widow managed the place, the mother of two strong boys. Sheft pictured him in the bright warmth, surrounded by people and pipe smoke and noise. Tarn would no doubt marry again after he was gone, and the boys would help him run the fieldhold.

He missed Riah, the quiet presence he had taken for granted. Too late, he realized there were a host of questions he should have asked her. Should have asked Yarahe. The book of tales sat dusty on the mantle, and the only sounds at night were the forlorn wind in the chimney and the simmer of dying coals. It was then he felt the weight of the decision he had made, and the cost of what love demanded.

Candle crept into Hearth, and after splitting logs or shoveling ash out of the hearth, he took long walks in the deadlands, stopping to tend the two cairns. Several times he worked alone in Etane's field, cutting brush and piling it away from where the firebreak furrows would be dug.

One cold day, he finished work and headed home, knowing that Tarn was gone again and the house would be empty. He walked with a bent head, seeing only his boots as they crunched methodically over the inch of snow on the ground. There was no wind, but he thought he heard again the far-off cries, the bereft voices raised in anguish.

He knew now they were real and where they came from, but not what he would be asked to do about them. They ached inside him, and he put his hand over his spirikai. He didn't know if it was their pain he felt or his, or if it mattered. He walked.

Suddenly he smelled wood smoke and looked up. To his dismay, he saw he had veered away from his house and come upon Moro's. He stopped, meaning to turn and stride off, but his eyes were drawn to the fine horse tethered outside the house. It was brown, with two white forefeet.

He knew this would happen. He knew that someone would surely seek out Mariat. But did it have to be Gwin?

He stood there, his hands clenched, until the bitterness ebbed away. It left behind a soul-soaking grief. He had made his choice and given Mariat the freedom to choose as well.

Riah had told him there was no limit to redemption, but it was atonement that had no end.

The toltyr heavy upon him, he turned away. It was hard to see on the way back.

That night in the loft, he reached out to Rulve, seeking the all-encompassing love that he had once experienced. His mind told him it was there, all around him in the dark, but he couldn't feel it. Even if he did, how would that change things or make anything easier? His losses lay behind him and couldn't be retrieved, and an unknown destiny awaited him and couldn't be avoided.

He climbed down the ladder, put on his sheepskin jacket, and trudged a short way into the dark. The glittering sky of winter arched over him, and the icy night settled onto his upturned face. Embedded stars pulsed with half-perceived blues and reds and golds, and the vast power of creation thrummed behind them. The constellation of the Owl was rising over the deadlands, a lonely Walker glowing in its heart. He longed for a warm presence, but instead this distant immensity hung over him. The night was cold, but not cold enough to freeze what ached inside him.

A sense of unease gradually crept over him. He swept his eyes around the horizon. It surrounded him, and he stood alone in the center of its dark circle.

CHAPTER 21

THE MOUSE AND THE RAT

In the middle of Herb-Bearer, just days before Etane had hoped his field-burn and wedding would take place, a sudden blizzard struck. Sheft and Tarn hustled Padiky and the chickens into the barn, but all day the wind rattled the door and whistled down the chimney, and snow filtered through tiny chinks in the north wall. When Sheft peered through the window of his loft, he could barely see the barn beyond the thick, swirling snowflakes.

On the second morning the storm momentarily let up. A huge drift blocked the door, so Sheft had to climb out the kitchen window. The whole fieldhold had changed into a vast whiteness, and everything lay under a strange, moist silence. From the look of the sky, there was more bad weather to come. They spent the rest of the day clearing a way to the barn, distributing feed, and filling the water trough. From time to time, a few flakes filtered down.

When all was done and Sheft was trudging toward the house, a sudden awareness of the Riftwood prickled across the back of his neck. He turned to look at it. The trees stood bone-silent and aware.

He had promised Yarahe that he would soon go there. As he watched, the Riftwood seemed to inhale the light from the snow-covered fields and exhale a twilight that crept across the river. Uneasy, he entered the house.

That evening the wind picked up again and soon sharpened with needles of ice. He lay on his mattress as the roof crackled with every gust, as the window thumped and rattled and the dried herbs hanging in the eaves twisted in the cold air.

When he ventured out in the morning, everything was covered with a veneer of ice. The sunrise had glazed the tops of the trees with gold, and dazzling crystal sheathed every hard bud or withered leaf. The slightest breeze filled the air with creaking sounds, like straining ropes, and caused bits of ice to rattle down from branches onto the hard-crusted snow. The storm had swept past, leaving behind a catastrophe.

Fruit and nut trees all over the valley would be damaged, heavily-burdened roofs would collapse, and the toll would be high for any livestock caught in the open. With the roads impassable, some families in the more isolated fieldholds might be marooned in their houses for days.

At least, he thought, Tarn would not be going to the inn at Ferce for a while.

After Cloor had extinguished the lanterns out front and gone home, Ubela was left to put the last of the mugs away. There was a tap on the back door and, as she had known he would, Gwin came in. He stamped the snow off his boots, flung his cloak onto the work-table, and looked at her hungrily.

She rushed into his arms. "I can't stay long," Ubela murmured. "My stepfather—"

"You've been out late before," he whispered in her ear. "And you only have to go next door."

With a low chuckle, she stood on tip-toe to nibble his ear. "I'm persuaded, my sweet."

So they lingered, and finally Gwin slipped out.

Holding her cloak tight about her, Ubela hurried down the cleared path between Cloor's and her house behind the butcher shop. Surely her stepfather would be in bed by now.

He wasn't. He began railing at her the minute she wiped her feet on the mat. "Where were you?" he demanded, his small eyes narrowed in suspicion. He put down a tankard and stood, swaying slightly, to face her. "Who were you with?"

Sokol was a powerful man, whose big hands were accustomed to heaving sides of meat and hacking through gristle, and Ubela was terrified of him. She hung up her cloak and turned to him, trying to keep a quaver out of her voice. "I was just finishing up at the ale-house. And I wasn't with anybody. Just ask Cloor." She licked dry lips. "Did you eat? Do you want me to make you something?"

He grabbed her with a hairy arm. "Was it Gede?"

"No! Let me go! It wasn't anybody."

"You know what I'd do to him, don't you?"

Twice he had dragged her into the shop out front and showed her his big, carefully sharpened knives. "Yes, you told me. But I was alone."

"No man in this village must touch you. Damned if any of them are good enough for you."

Ubela smelled the beer on his breath and pulled away from him. "They don't come near me. I make sure of it. I'm always with Wena or Melis. Just ask them."

"I will," he muttered, staring hard at her. "I will ask them." A different light crept into his eyes, and his gaze moved slowly down her body.

"I'm going to bed now," Ubela said quickly. "I'm very tired and it's—it's my moon-time." She felt his look on her as she entered her sleeping room and drew the curtain behind her.

Since her mother's death, she had pleaded over and over for a real door, but he had never found the time to install one. So far, the flimsy curtain kept him out. She had her back to it, and began undressing for bed when the curtain was suddenly whisked aside. She whirled to face him, clutching her blouse in front of her.

He reached for her, then stopped. "What's that on your shoulder?"

"What? Where?"

He spun her sideways, into the light coming from the other room. "This, right here. By Ele, it's a love-bite!"

Ubela almost blacked out from fear. She didn't think Gwin had marked her. Sokol jerked her around to face him. "Who did this to you?"

"No one! It's a spider bite."

"I'm no fool! I know what I see."

"It fell from the rafters while I was cleaning at Cloor's!"

He slapped her. She staggered back, her cheek stinging, barely holding onto her blouse.

"Tell me, or you'll regret it." He took a step forward, his big hand clenched into a fist.

"It was the foreigner! Tarn's son. He was there at the back door, just as I turned to leave Cloor's. I tried to stop him, Sokol, but I couldn't."

"You're lying to me!"

"No! Who else would do such a thing? You've heard the rumors. They're true. They're all true, and here, right here on my shoulder, is the proof."

"Why didn't you scream? I would've heard."

"He said he would kill me if I did. He had a knife."

"He took a *knife* to you?"

She nodded, fear thumping in her chest. "A—a carving knife. But I threw a pan at him and got away."

"By Ele's eyes," he shouted, whirling about and stumbling out of the room. "He wants to play with knives? Well, I've got plenty right here!"

Ubela flung on her blouse and ran to stop him. "He's gone. You'll never find him in the dark. Tell Parduka in the morning."

"Eh? Why her?"

"She knows the truth about the foreigner. Lots of the men do. I heard them talking at Cloor's, about how they meet in the House of Ele at night. Join them, Sokol. They're making plans about what should be done."

"I don't need any plans," he muttered. "My knives are my plans." Breathing heavily, he sank down at the table again. He muttered curses against the demon-spawned foreigner, the council that let him live, and their weak-kneed Holdman. At last he noticed his cup was empty. "All this talk," he grumbled, "makes me thirsty. Fill up my cup, Ubela. That's a good girl."

She obeyed, shaking with relief. Now he would drink himself into a stupor, and no more curtains would be wrenched aside this night.

The next morning, Parduka closed the door on the butcher's retreating back, her heart full of praise for the goddess. Nine men were needed to form the new council, and she had just been granted the seventh. All her persuading and cajoling these past weeks—at cremations, during worship, at secret meetings in the night—were bearing fruit.

As the snow melted and the damage in the surrounding

fieldholds was revealed, farmers and villagers came to the House of Ele to bemoan their losses. To these also she preached her message. "Dorik and his cronies have forsaken the righteous path, and now Ele punishes us all! Our goddess will relent—but only when we face our responsibilities, take up our courage, and reclaim our ancient heritage. She will take us to her bosom again, like a mother who comforts her children, but only when we form a new council and restore her sacred Rites. But we must act quickly, for the dark moon of Seed is approaching."

Her words helped them place blame where it belonged, fueled the anger needed for change, and added urgency to their task. By the end of the month, she judged it was time for another meeting and sent word out through Gwin.

It was the first day of Seed. Although there was a chill in the air, the sun shone brightly, a few red-winged blackbirds were calling their *conk-a-rees* near the river, and the air smelled strongly of earth. The blizzard of two weeks ago lingered only in a few patches of snow under the long-skirted fir trees. Out in the yard, Sheft scooped up a handful of soil. It stuck together in a ball, too wet for planting, but just right for a field-burn.

Etane must have thought so too, because his face was flushed with excitement when he appeared at Sheft's door a short time later. "Tomorrow, Sheft! We'll start digging the perimeter tomorrow, and the burn will take place the next morning. Thanks to you, I'll be a married man that very afternoon."

Field-burns were much anticipated celebrations, especially if they preceded a wedding. Guests from neighboring villages traveled to the prospective groom's house to feast, catch up on gossip, and help clear a field for the young couple. The actual wedding ceremony, a simple exchange of vows in the presence of the Holdman, usually took place on the third day after the burn. But, because Sheft had spent so much time during the winter cutting brush and raking it into piles, Etane would have his bride at the end of only two.

"That's what I hoped for," Sheft said. "I know you did too."

Etane nodded, and his eyes shone with so much happiness that Sheft had to look away.

"I'm in a rush," Etane went on. "A lot of Leeza's relatives will be spending the night, so my dad will need help spreading straw in the barn for those who can't fit in the house. Ask Tarn if he can come over today to give us a hand setting up and all."

A thought dawned on Sheft. "All these people will have to be fed. It sounds like a lot of work for—" He found he couldn't say her name, so ended with a lame-sounding "for everyone."

"Leeza's mother and sister are already here, helping Mariat peel and bake and whatnot. And—I'm sorry, Sheft—Dad invited Gwin to the field-burn. Gwin's got my father convinced he's a 'fine lad,' and there wasn't anything I could do about it. I'll make sure he and the others will be working on the other end of the field from you."

"I understand. I'll be leaving, but you have to live with these people."

At this reminder of his departure, Etane's face fell. "I'll be sorry to see you go. Maybe—maybe me and Leeza can come up to Ullar-Sent someday and visit you."

Sheft squirmed inwardly at the assumption he'd allowed his friend to make. But the truth was just too complicated. "Maybe. But first I want to give you something." He went into the house and emerged with the bowl he had carved. "This is for you and Leeza."

With a half-smile, Etane ran his finger over the wheat design. "This will always remind us of you. Thank you." He grabbed Sheft in a thumping hug, then hurried home over the fields.

That night Parduka held her lantern high as seven cloaked figures darted through the back door of the House of Ele. Their cast-back hoods revealed the angry, indignant, or determined faces that belonged to Pogreb, Blinor the miller, Gwin, young Temo, two of Greak's neighbors, and the newcomer to their group, the butcher Sokol.

Carrying a lantern, Parduka led them to a shadowy corner of the hall, swept aside a weaving that hid a door, and ushered them into the low, narrow room in which they had been meeting. She placed the lantern on a small table, then rubbed her hands to warm them as the others found places on the two short rows of benches. They all seemed distraught.

Asher, one of Greak's neighbors, was practically moaning. "Most of my fruit trees—oh Ele, even my beautiful peaches—they're all ruined. Blasted by ice. How will I feed my family?"

"Every one of our chickens is gone," the other neighbor said bleakly. "Blizzard took the fence, and wolves got 'em. They were supposed to feed us for the rest of the winter."

Temo grabbed her arm. "Mama broke her leg," he cried, "slipping on the ice! She's an old woman, priestess, still grieving Father's loss."

"I feel for you," Parduka told them. "My heart breaks

over all these disasters." She raised her clenched fists in frustration. "But every one of them could have been avoided! Even the deaths from the fluenza. Ele would never have sent these punishments if the council had listened to reason."

Asher spread out his big, calloused hands. "How can the elders look at all these catastrophes and still protect the foreigner? Can't they see he's at the very root of them?"

"He took a knife to my Ubela," Sokol spat out. "I won't be satisfied until I take a knife to *him*."

In the midst of their talk, Rom and Gwin came through the door. Parduka's heart leaped when she saw that two others followed them: the cattleman Delo and Olan, who had barely survived the fluenza. She had tried to convince both of them to come, but Rom apparently had had better luck. The blacksmith threw back his hood and gave her a worried look, as if to say, "I'm not sure about these two."

They both knew they were running out of time. The moon of Seed would fall into darkness in only four nights. She waited until they all sat down, then welcomed the newcomers.

"So you finally got off your asses and joined us," Blinor growled at them.

"I haven't joined you," Delo said in a tremulous voice. "Rom said just come for more information."

"Tell them what happened to you during the blizzard," Rom prompted.

A bitter look hardened the man's round face. "Two of my prize cows died. Including one serviced by Ferce's best bull. Every ducat I paid to breed her was wasted! My sons say this would never have happened if—" He sniffed, looked uncomfortable, and waved the rest of the thought away.

Everyone turned to Olan, who still looked gaunt from the fluenza. "My daughter was badly injured, priestess. She was in the barn, getting the milk bucket, when"—his voice cracked, and he took a moment to compose himself—"when the roof caved in under the heavy snow. If I join you, will Ele heal her?"

"I'm sure the goddess will be compassionate, my son. She has a mother's heart. But it all depends on your faith. And on your courage, Olan. Even Ele can do nothing without that."

"Looks to me," Asher said, "there's nine men in this room right now, all eligible to form a new council." As a former Holdman, Pogreb was the exception.

"And they"—Blinor grinned, nodding in the direction of the Council House across the road—"are only eight."

Rom held up his hand. "But they don't know that yet. They believe I'm still with them."

"Moro should be here," Blinor said. "He got taken in by the foreigner's lies to the point where his wife wasn't even decently buried. Now her bones are out in the dead-lands somewhere, being gnawed at by mewlets and wolves."

His remark opened a floodgate, and everyone began talking at once.

"He sits there with that carving knife, molesting babies, and our witless council does nothing."

"Mama suffers in her chair, and he walks free to jump out and attack us."

"What he did to Ubela, to Mariat, he can do to the daughter of any man here!"

"The worst of his crimes remains unpunished, and every one of us pays the price!"

Sokol jumped to his feet. "No more talk! It's time to act. What about the rest of you?"

It was the moment Parduka had been waiting for, praying for. The moment when they heard, loud and clear, Ele's call. She looked at Rom, seated in the back, and every head turned to him. The smith was the one they most respected, the one who could call forth their strength and ignite their resolve.

He got to his feet and looked each man in the eye, one by one in the wavering light. "Sokol is right. It's time to decide. Who stands with us?"

Gwin jumped up, followed by Blinor and Greak's two neighbors. Temo stood next. They all looked down at the two remaining men: the newcomers, Olan and Delo.

"What's the matter with you?" Gwin asked Olan. "You almost died from the fluenza the foreigner brought upon us. And what happened to your daughter demands justice."

Olan bit his lip. "Justice, yes. But these restored Rites —are they the only way to save my little girl?"

"Saving this one or that one," Blinor retorted, "isn't the point. We must do what we must do, for the good of all. We may not like it or feel easy about it, but the protection of the entire village is laid upon us."

Olan still hesitated, and Parduka's heart began to pound. "What about proof?" he asked. "Of all his crimes, only the one deserves death. Do we have proof that he did it?"

"We have two witnesses!" Blinor cried. "What more proof do you need, man!"

Parduka put her hands on Olan's shoulders. "Rest easy, my son. There is no doubt. Not one of us would have come to this point if there were. Come now, step out in faith, and join us."

"Only faith will save your daughter, Olan," Rom said gently.

The others murmured agreement.

His face pale, Olan nodded and rose to his feet.

They all turned to Delo, the only one still sitting.

"Did you come here just to talk, Delo?" Sokol snarled. "Or are you going to stand up like a man?"

The corpulent cattleman flushed and climbed to his feet. "It just takes me longer to get up," he muttered.

They stood in the candlelight and regarded each other.

"We are nine!" Parduka cried. "At last we are nine! Our goddess has performed a miracle, just in time for her dark moon." She raised her arms to Ele. "Thank you, All-Mother. Thank you for the faith and courage that you have bestowed on all of us here. Thank you making us a righteous instrument in your hands."

"We have just formed the new Council of At-Wysher," Rom said to them, "a new governance that will root out evil and make our village safe for our families again. Together we will foster piety and restore important values that have been hacked away. Things will be different from now on."

Faith glowed in Olan's eyes. "The goddess will heal my daughter. I know it. The very night we perform the new Rites, my little one will rise from her bed and walk to me."

Parduka grasped his arm and spoke gently. "Those who trust in Ele will never be forsaken."

She turned to face the others. "In four days we will meet in this room. We will formally pronounce our vows to Ele and elect a new Holdman. Then we will go forth after midnight, into the dark moon of Seed, and for the first time in decades, perform the ancient Rites at their traditional time and rightful place."

Pogreb leaned forward, his one eye gleaming. "A new

council has formed, yes; but also a new Dark Circle. A circle—hee, hee, hee!—that will become a noose around the foreigner's neck!"

After everyone left, Rom stayed behind. "Did you bring it?" Parduka asked.

He withdrew from his pocket one of the foreigner's carvings: a wooden hay-mouse. It was the one, she knew, he had taken from Oris, his younger son.

Parduka shuddered when she saw what Rom had done to it. "I can barely look at this," she muttered. "Yet it is excellent work. This is a true symbol of the evil that lies in the foreigner's black heart." She looked up at him. "You are Ele's chosen, Rom. You are truly a warrior in her service."

He took the carving from her. "Voy already went through the foreigner's barn," he said. "The sneaky little rat will know just where to put this."

CHAPTER 22

THE FIELD-BURN

Sheft spent the next day alone at the south end of Etane's field, digging the furrow that tomorrow would contain the fire there. In the distance, at the north end, men were doing the same thing. Sheft glimpsed Oris running around with a smaller boy who was probably one of the Fercian relatives. By late afternoon, everyone had finished their work and gone to their pre-wedding merriment, and Sheft trudged home. Tarn was staying overnight at Moro's house, so Sheft fed the chickens, washed up, and ate a solitary supper.

Afterward he went out to stand on the doorstep. Deep purple suffused the sky in the east, but in the west the great trees of the Riftwood stood silhouetted against a fading band of gold, set with the sparkling jewel of the Twilight Star. Etane's celebration was probably in full swing by now. Torches would be set outside, and guests would not fear the night because it was said Ele especially protected weddings. He thought he heard bursts of distant laughter on the still air.

In five days, when the moon was a new crescent, he would go to the Wind-gate. There would be very little to pack: a blanket, his carving knives, a few articles of clothing. He'd also take the book of tales; Riah would've wanted him to have it.

At times his conversation with Yarahe seemed like an improbable dream. Soon he would be leaving home, and going home, but he had no idea what he might face there. At night he held the Toltyr Arulve in a tight fist and prayed for courage.

Early the next morning, he answered the knock on his door to find Etane on the doorstep. It looked to be a cool, clear day with no wind—perfect weather for both the burn and the wedding.

Etane, however, looked harried. "Leeza's father broke a wagon wheel last night, wouldn't you know it? He feels terrible about it, but now we'll need Tarn's wagon to get the trestle tables from Vehoke, and my father's wagon to fetch the casks from Cloor, and that means we'll have to use Leeza's *brother's* wagon for the aunts who are still waiting for a ride—and as angry as stirred-up wasps, I'm told—and *that* means he can't get the kunta-kart from his uncle's house." He looked at Sheft in horror. "Oh Ele, I'm babbling, aren't I?"

"No, no. Grooms are supposed to get nervous before—"

"What I'm trying to say is we'll need your old cart as kunta." This was a cart used to store the men's tools after a burn. They had to be kept safely out of sight because the presence of any earth-plunging object at a wedding ceremony was considered bad luck—symbols of competition, the old men chortled, for the groom.

"That cart has a crack in the shaft."

"It'll be fine. Nobody will be riding in it."

"But what if—"

"It won't. When the burn's over, I'll make sure all our rakes and hoes get put into the cart. Oris will bring Padiky out to you when we're through with her, and then after the ceremony you can just leave the cart behind our barn."

"All right."

"Be on the lookout for greensnakes; they're just emerging from their holes. And watch for flare-ups! Everyone will be in a rush to get cleaned up for the ceremony, so a brush pile may be left smoldering." He glanced anxiously toward his father's house. "Ele's eyes, I don't want a major fire on my wedding day. Oh, make sure there's a good, deep ditch around that grove of trees I showed you. I don't want the burn going through there. Leeza thinks it's so pretty with those wildflowers and all."

"I'll see to it."

Etane hesitated. "Leeza and I will be going up to Ferce for a few days after the wedding, so...I guess this is good-bye." He grasped Sheft's shoulder and shook it gently. "Take care of yourself."

Sheft had been so preoccupied that he forgot this moment would be coming. Regret that he'd never see Etane again rushed over him. "You too." He was near tears, but what he'd told the falconform remained true: even now, his best friend couldn't look him in the eyes.

Etane, near tears himself, squeezed his shoulder. He turned and rushed off toward a thin line of smoke rising into the sunlit air. The burn had begun.

With a heavy sigh, Sheft went into the barn and assayed the cart. The chickens had left their droppings on it during the blizzard, but no one would care about that. The crack had not gotten any worse since the fall, and it looked like the shaft could withstand a load of light tools.

He pulled the cart to Etane's field. Even though it carried nothing but his rake, shovel, and ax, the cumbersome thing was built high off the ground, seemed to weigh as much as a full-size wagon, and tended to seesaw between its big wheels. He was glad to drop it just outside the shallow ditch. After drinking water from his flagon, he inspected the entire length of the perimeter dug the day before, making sure the ditch was deep enough to contain the burn.

All was well, so he crossed over the fire-break and threaded his way past the piles of brush toward Etane's grove. Several fine trees grew there, including a large star-nut just beginning to bud. A carpet of yellow crocus lay at its feet, and airy, pink-veined harbingers nodded in the sun. No wonder Etane wanted to protect this place for Leeza. He would probably build their house here, maybe make a swing for their children and hang it from a tree.

Whoever had dug the ditch that protected all this, however, had done a poor job. The fire-break was too close to the trees in one place and non-existent in another, where several boar-bushes grew. It was noon by the time he finished axing out their tough roots, and he was tired and sweaty. By now the line of low flames was advancing toward him, as well as the men who were raking debris into it.

He ducked out of sight into the woods behind the field and took the long way home. There he ate a bowl of groats leftover from breakfast, planted a row of peas in the kitchen garden, and when he judged the burn was over, returned to the blackened field for a final check. All the workers had gone to clean up for the wedding, leaving behind a haze of smoke. The grove was untouched, an island of greenery in the midst of the ash.

Just beyond the cart, however, two brush-heaps hadn't burned completely. An occasional tongue of flame licked out of the twigs that poked from their charred circles. Not good, but soon remedied.

He propped up the shaft to keep the cart level and unhooked the back. The workers had carelessly tossed spades, hoes, rakes, and axes into a sharp and dangerous heap; and everything had gotten tangled in a coil of rope. Even worse, the cart was overloaded, for they had thrown in an old hand-plough as well. Irritated—Etane knew how cautious he was with metal tools—Sheft carefully extricated a rake, stepped over the furrow, and began to break up the farther brush heap.

The sun was hot, the cord of the toltyr rubbed against the back of his sunburned neck, and the smoke rasping against his throat reminded him he'd forgotten to refill the water flagon. In spite of all this, he smiled to himself at one point, thinking that soon Etane would be saying his wedding vows. But, with a twist in his heart, the smile disappeared. He'd never exchange such vows himself.

The first brush fire was out by the time Oris arrived with Padiky. For once doing what he'd been told, the boy hitched her to the cart and kicked away the prop. Wiping his forehead on his sleeve, Sheft began working on the other brush heap, in which a few low flames crackled.

Oris didn't immediately run off and Sheft turned to see what he was doing. On the other side of the furrow, almost hidden in the grass, he lay on his stomach in the meager shade just behind the cart, apparently watching for small creatures that always emerged from a burn.

He didn't like to see the boy lying so close to an open cart filled with sharp tools. Uneasy, he walked out of the perimeter with his rake. "You should get back to Moro's house. The party will be starting soon."

The boy rolled partly on his side and squinted up at him. He wore a light spring shirt and his face was smudged. "I was waiting for you."

"What for?"

"For a toy. The kind you brought to the market-fair. Remember?"

"I remember."

"Well, Gwin was mean. He took mine away. Can I have another one?"

"I think there's one or two left. But right now get away from that cart."

"First get the toy. I'll wait here while—"

Padiky started and tossed her head. The cart shuddered. The mass of tools creaked, shifted toward the opening. The mare's eye rolled back, staring at something that moved toward her in the grass. A greensnake.

Sheft dropped his rake and ran forward. "Oris, get away!"

The snake swirled around Padiky's hooves and she bucked in terror. With a loud crack, the shaft splintered partway through, the cart tipped, and its sharp-edged contents began sliding toward Oris.

The boy screamed, buried his face in his arms, and there was nothing between him and the cart's jagged cargo except a thin shirt. Sheft dived over him an instant before the shaft gave way. An avalanche of edges slammed onto his back. It bit down as Padiky squealed in terror and bolted, dragging the tangled pile of iron and steel. Metal clanged and screeched. He cringed as sharp prongs caught on his shoulder blade, tore free. With eyes squeezed shut, he held on to Oris as rakes and hoes plowed over his back, as something heavy cracked into his ribs, as wooden handles bounced over his legs. In seconds, everything was dragged away.

Then silence. The jingle of harness. Padiky must have stopped, shaken herself. Feeling oddly numb, he opened his eyes. Inches from his face, a greensnake slid away into the grass.

Beneath him, Oris whimpered.

Sheft pushed a hoe off himself and got onto his hands

and knees. "Are you hurt?" He turned the child over and peered into his face. "Oris, are you *hurt?*"

The boy's mouth contorted. "My leg's all twisted! You broke it!"

Sheft felt Oris's leg. "It's—it's all right. No b-broken bones." He climbed unsteadily to his feet. His back felt wet and cold, and he couldn't seem to take a deep breath.

Padiky stood, shivering, a short distance away, but now inside the perimeter. A trail of implements led to a pile of hoes and rakes still entangled in the rope.

He felt strangely unbalanced, as if he carried a sodden pack.

"You don't look so good." Oris was standing now, staring at him.

Sudden pain seared down his back and stabbed into his ribs. Hot and heavy, it pushed him to his knees. He turned his head, to see a bright red stain spreading over his left sleeve.

"Oris," he croaked. "Unhitch the horse. Be careful of the broken shaft. Ride to Moro's house and get Tarn." He swallowed, his throat dry. "Hurry."

Oris rode off, and Sheft bore down on the spirikai knot. He constricted it as tightly as he could, while pain lashed across his back. The ice took a long time coming, and then it rushed up and numbed his brain and froze his hands into clumsy blocks. The red stain slowed but did not stop, and the thirsty ground wheeled under him. Panting for air, he lifted his head. The house was too far away. He'd never make it.

The cart. He had to get into the cart. The planks would soak up the blood until he could summon enough ice.

Using the hoe to support himself, he got to his feet, lost the hoe when he stumbled over the furrow, and reached the wooden platform. Part of the broken shaft had been driven into the ground, anchoring the cart and propping it almost level. The vehicle shook as he pulled himself onto it, but it didn't tilt. He groaned under the red-hot gashes and collapsed face down on the surface.

But he had found no refuge. There were gaps between the boards. He could see the ground beneath him. The toltyr still hung from his neck, but the medallion had fallen through a crack. It dangled beneath him, blood oozing down the length of the cord, coalescing on the medallion, falling drop by drop onto the ashy ground.

Shuddering with effort, he constricted the inner knot even tighter. It wasn't enough. Blood was oozing out from under him, staining the planks.

The smell of smoke penetrated the pain, and he twisted his head to the left. The second debris pile. It was only a foot away and burning brightly. Flames danced near the dry wood of the cart wheel.

He jerked at the cord, but the medallion was stuck between the planks. He couldn't raise his head more than an inch or two above the boards to get it off his neck. As if in a nightmare, the earth beneath him darkened. It stirred, formed bubbles, then seeds. They wriggled into the ground and erupted into a mass of tiny plants.

He fumbled with icy hands to free the toltyr, but the crack was too narrow to get his fingers through. A wave of pain squeezed his eyes shut. When he opened them, flames were licking at the cart wheel, crackling and hissing.

He raised his head as far as he could and strained at the cord. Its braided thickness bit into the back of his neck but held, and he couldn't get it over his head, couldn't think through the pain and smoke and ice. Gasping for air, choking on acrid fumes, he jerked at the toltyr until his strength gave way and his cheek thudded against the rough wood. He was tethered to the cart, and oh God Rulve, there was nothing he could do about it.

Except burn.

Relax the inner constriction. Allow himself to bleed. Fire would save him.

Fire would destroy the plants beneath him, would lick the blood off his skin, would sear his veins into a charred and twiggy heap. It would devour the red-stained cart and leave nothing to attract the black mist. The roots and the pain and the far-off anguished voices would be swept away in a blaze of merciful immolation. The long struggle would be over.

It would be justice, and it would be mercy.

Mariat's face leaped into his thought, the sweet curve of her cheek, the soft glow in her eyes, but he had pushed her out of his life. Pain slashed through him, followed by waves of blistering heat. He ground his forehead against the boards, clutched the edge of the cart.

Burn it all, Rulve. Burn it all away and make me clean at last.

CHAPTER 23

WHEN DEITIES CONTEND

Etane extricated himself from one of Leeza's aunts—Gerta? Greta?—and threaded his way through the crowd of guests in the yard. Gwin and Voy were supposed to have set up the ale-table in the barn, but he'd better make sure they did it.

He noticed Oris carelessly looping the reins of Tarn's horse over the fence. The child filched a small cake from the trestle table, turned, and ran directly into his legs.

"Whoa, boy," Etane said, grabbing his arm. "What's Padiky doing back here?"

Oris struggled in his grasp. "I don't know."

"Didn't you hitch her to the kunta-kart like I told you?"

Oris stopped struggling and studied his feet. "I did just what you said."

"So what's she doing here?" A feeling of unease came over him. "Is something wrong?"

"*He's* the one that did something wrong! *He's* the one that broke the cart. Everything spilled out, but it wasn't me."

"The cart broke?"

"Yes, over there. But don't tell my father. I'm not hurt." Oris took a bite of his cake. "I think the foreigner is, though."

"Sheft is hurt?"

"Who?"

"The foreigner! Is he hurt?"

"Rakes fell on him and there was blood all over."

The boy darted away. Etane caught sight of Moro atop their wagon, helping Tarn unload the last of the ale-kegs. "We've got to get over to Sheft!" he shouted at him. "I think there's been an accident!"

He quickly tied Padiky to their wagon, jumped in the back, and the three men rattled over the track and down to his newly charred field. A fire had broken out near the perimeter. Smoke roiled around Tarn's cart and one of the wheels was burning. A trail of farm implements, a few of the wood handles also burning, led to a tangled pile nearby. Sheft was nowhere in sight.

Etane jumped out of the wagon and spotted him, lying face down in the cart. Blood covered his back and pooled on the boards around him. He wasn't moving, and the wheel burned only two feet away from his pale, soot-streaked hair.

He's dead, Etane thought. *Oh God, my best friend died in a terrible accident on my wedding day.*

But then he saw fresh blood welling up from a wound over his left shoulder. "We've got to get him out of there!"

"Watch out for that burning wheel," Tarn warned.

Noting that a slight breeze directed the flames toward the field and away from Sheft—at least for now—Etane clambered onto the cart. It shook ominously under his weight, and he had a vision of the wheel collapsing and the two of them sliding into the fire. Sheft moaned in protest as Etane pried his friend's blood-stained hands from where they clutched the edge of the cart. Through a billow of smoke, he spied a cord around Sheft's neck, a pendant that dangled below the narrow crack. He tried to pull it free. "Dad, his head's caught!"

None of them had a knife, and the braided leather cord was too strong to break. Skirting the flames, Moro ran to the other side of the cart and bent to look under it. His body appeared to waver in the rising heat as he shielded his face with his arm. "I can't get any closer!"

"Tarn!" Etane cried. "Use that spade. Throw dirt on the flames here!"

Tarn snatched up the spade and began heaving soil. Coughing from the smoke, Moro crawled under the cart. On the second try he managed to push the medallion through the crack, and Etane pulled it free. "Get his legs!"

The three of them maneuvered Sheft off the cart and onto the wagon. Etane knelt beside him as it lurched quickly off. His friend lay on his stomach, his red-streaked hands tightly clenched beside his head. "Yell if you want to, Sheft. There's no shame in it."

"Blood," Sheft groaned. "On the boards."

"God, Sheft! Don't worry about the damn wagon. You've stopped bleeding and there's nothing on the boards here."

But there had been plenty on the cart, even dripping through the cracks. Etane's stomach was knotted with worry. The ride seemed to take forever and consisted of hard bumps that he'd never paid any attention to before, but which now made him wince in sympathy for what his friend must be feeling. Finally they got to Tarn's house. Sheft was shaking with pain as they pulled him off the wagon and carried him through the door.

Etane ran up to the loft, dragged Sheft's mattress down the ladder, and placed it near the hearth. The men laid him on it, face down, with his feet toward the fire.

"Go back to your wedding, Etane," Tarn said. "I'll take care of him."

"We need water! Get that bloody shirt off him." Etane turned toward the house crock.

Tarn pulled him back. "Listen to me! I know what to do. You have guests from two villages and a bride waiting for you. Get back to them. He'll be fine."

He looked down at Sheft, who did not look fine at all, then back up at Tarn.

Tarn squeezed his arm. "Your father has spent much of what he has on this wedding."

"That's not important!" Moro protested, but Tarn ignored him.

"You can't leave Leeza waiting there, in front of her whole family. You can't leave Dorik wondering what's happened. Go! I'm an elder of the council. I'll take care of this. Moro, tie Padiky in the yard and get your wagon back to your house. Stand witness to your son's wedding."

"I can't leave him like this!" Etane cried. "He would've been my firstman."

"Then he of all people would urge you to go."

Etane winced; Tarn was right. "I'll check up on him later, right after the wedding." With a worried backward glance, he and his father hurried out.

Tarn looked down at the rigid, blood-soaked figure on the mattress and thought about the impenetrable will of Ul.

He had hoped for a boy who would help him fight the dark, but Ul had sent one who was enmeshed in it. The god in his wisdom had seen fit that Sheft should not only live and bring ostracism upon the house of Tarn, but also ruin the very mission against Parduka that Ul should have blessed.

Why? He was a religious man. Why didn't Ul support his servant's tireless efforts to bring the light of law into this far corner of his realm?

Tarn bent over Sheft. He had lost a lot of blood, and his wounds—now that he had a chance to consider them—were beyond his repair. Beyond anyone's repair, by the look of it.

Troubled, Tarn sat down at the kitchen table. It would be mercy to let him die. His death would clear the way for justice to rule at last. With Sheft no longer a factor, Parduka's fight against the council would be cut off at the knees. Even the devout in the village would be satisfied. He would point out that Ele, no longer angered by foreigners in her sight, would now resume protecting them from the Groper. He could say the goddess had taken care of matters herself, and there was no need for the council to act.

He drummed his fingers thoughtfully on the table. Objections to foreign marriages—Dorik's, Etane's, or even, one day, his own—would be forgotten. The Rites would remain unchanged and not revert to the monstrous rituals they once were.

The sweet smell of a spring afternoon wafted in, causing Tarn to notice that the door was still open. A breeze, thankfully, was blowing the smoke of the burn away from his house.

The thought gave him pause. Perhaps Ul had a hand in these events after all. Perhaps the great god's power was indeed blowing the winds of suspicion away from his house. It could even be argued that it was Ul, not Ele at all, who had acted. With growing wonder, Tarn saw that whatever had happened to Sheft could be the god's way of redeeming the entire village.

The revelation stunned him with its intelligence, its

logic. He felt as if he stood upon a mountain and saw from on high a great pattern, one not visible from lower elevations. As an elder, as Ul's faithful servant who worked so tirelessly for the light, he had a sacred duty to make this pattern plain to all.

The village would recognize him as Ul's humble prophet, for he alone had discerned how the deities contended with each other, and which one got the upper hand. Under Ul's blazing light, the power of Ele would fade away. Even the ridiculous belief in Rulve—which could potentially spread—would be nipped in the bud, because this he-she abomination seemed to have no interest at all in its followers. The council would reign supreme, and in due course he would take his rightful place as Holdman.

Tarn smiled grimly. What at first appeared to be Ele's revenge would be her own undoing—and at the hands of Ul himself.

The god was even merciful to Sheft, sparing him the hard journey to the north, with its likely fatal outcome. The lad had no future, and his death would be for the greater good.

Tarn got up from the chair and stood over Sheft once more. It would be wrong for him to interfere with the will of Ul. Puny human beings had no business meddling in weighty matters of life and death, for in these things the gods of heaven ruled.

A glance out the door told him the afternoon was waning. He felt a sudden strong aversion to being alone in the house when Sheft passed on, and night fell. It would be best to leave immediately. Going back to the wedding would arouse too many questions, so he'd pay a visit to the widow in Ferce.

Tarn pulled his cloak off the peg, but stopped. He

found a blanket and threw it over Sheft's mangled back, then scooped the last of the water from the crock into a cup and placed it on the floor beside Sheft's head. Ul might will his death, but neither the god nor he himself was devoid of compassion.

On his way out, it occurred to him that the cart would have to be replaced. He would see about purchasing another, perhaps used, in Ferce. When he came back, he would tell Moro the truth: no one could be found to help Sheft in time, and he had died in the night.

Parduka would insist on displaying the body in the village and then on disposing of it in her own way. In the meanwhile, however, since his vehicle was being used at Moro's house, he would have to ride Padiky all the way to Ferce, and the wagon-horse did not particularly like being ridden.

CHAPTER 24

THE FORGE

Heat beat against his skin. He was going to burn, *needed* to burn. Sheft stiffened, steeled himself to endure it. But someone shouted and hands pulled at him. *Leave me*, he cried, but all that came out was a groan. He was lifted and carried off the cart, the cracked rib jolted, wounds tore open. He fought to close them, shaking with the effort, until the constant jarring stopped and the voices around him faded into echoes, then silence. He lay face down on a sticky mattress. Level with his eyes, flames flickered over an expanse of floorboards. They drifted sideways in a haze of ice reaction.

The fire must have followed him out of the field-burn, and now it squirmed in long lines down his back. Why was it taking so long to kill him? He willed the flames higher, willed a cremation that would roar through him and destroy everything.

Instead, the flames licked at the toltyr pressed against his chest. The medallion grew warm, then hot. It melted under him, spread to the edge of his outstretched arms, then hardened. He was sprawled face down on its iron circle.

Miramakamen, the old man from the green and white tent, leaned over him, but he was wearing the face of Rom the smith. "Do you trust me, niyal'arist? Will you let me answer your deepest prayer?"

Oh God, do what you must.
Pain hammered down, melded him into metal. He burned on the toltyr's hard surface and its strength was pounded into his bones. Writhing in anguish, he yet opened his back to it, for he could no longer stay the way he was. Something new had to be forged.

In the midst of the inferno great hands upheld him, staying firm while charred chunks of himself fell away. What remained he had once feared the most.

He was summoned. He was niyalahn-rista. He would be wounded: by a child, by his brother, and by the dark.

The first had already happened, and two more awaited him.

A thick snake swirled through the underground passage, his pale green eyes glowing in the dark. He made his way through tunnels beneath the ancient forest, a living root sliding through the earth. Time and distance meant nothing to him, for he was Rûk the shadow-king, Rûk the devisor, and under his rule the Riftwood lay. He emerged from the passage into the cold night. Somewhere beneath the rim of the world, the moon was slowly draining into its full dark circle.

Wask awaited him. Its face was as rough and deeply lined as tree bark, and it wore a thin cloak made of old veined leaves. Bowing low, it spoke in the mind-speech.
"Greetings, great thakur."
"Why have you called me?"
"Long ago I savored sweet blood. I searched for years, but found no more. Until lately: in the wheat field and then in the wool. Now I sense it again, very strong. It is the blood that makes the earth dance."

Rûk's head darted down to Wask's level. The green eyes glittered. "You have seen this?"

"Yes, thakur. Two times."

"Describe to me exactly what you saw."

"Root-hairs ground under, seedlings trampled. A strong memory in the earth, of itself teeming with life."

Rûk's body rose up and he hissed. "Why have you not reported this sooner?"

"There was only a little blood. I was not certain. Now there is much more."

Rûk flicked out his tongue and turned to taste the air. Suddenly he thrust his flat head forward and focused on a certain direction. "Go. Find the human vessel that contains this blood, and bring it to me."

"I want to drink my fill of it."

"No. I have long sought this blood. It has an important purpose."

"You have decreed me Meerghast. Everything that comes to me, you have allowed me to keep."

Rûk swayed his head from side to side in warning. "In the past and in the future, but not this time."

Craftiness crept over the tree-bark face. "Perhaps I will do what I like, in a place where you cannot go."

As if to strike, Rûk pulled back his head. The reptilian eyes hardened. "Of your own you have nothing. Even your shapes are but shadowy imitations of mine. Disobey me, displease me, and I will ban you forever from my Riftwood. You will diminish, and the sun will burn away your power like a lingering mist. Is that worth one drink, no matter how sweet?"

Wask hesitated. "It is not."

"Then bring this vessel to me."

Wask glanced toward the east. "Dawn is not far off. As soon as the day is over, I will do as you command."

"Listen now to what you must say to him."

"Yes, thakur."

CHAPTER 25

MARIAT'S NIGHTMARE

The accident clouded his wedding ceremony, but out of love for Leeza, Etane tried not to ruin it for her as well. Tarn would look after Sheft, and he'd get back to his friend as soon as he could.

It wasn't until the next morning, after the wedding night was over and he had found delight with his new wife, that he saw he wouldn't be able to get away. Cloor wanted his empty casks back at his ale-house, and the trestle tables had to be returned, or Vehoke the grocer would charge another day's rent. He intended to ask Mariat to go help Tarn in his place, but between the coming and going he couldn't speak to his sister until well after the noon meal. She was washing yet another big stack of plates.

"I didn't have a chance to tell you yesterday," he said in a low voice, "but Sheft got hurt at the field-burn. I think Tarn could use some help with him."

"Am I to run over there every time someone stubs a toe?" Mariat asked irritably. "Let his father take care of it. Good-bye was good-bye."

Etane saw Leeza's mother bearing down on him. "Oh god. What does she want now? But listen, Mariat. Go over there if you can. Sheft told me Tarn isn't really his father, and maybe that's what he was trying to protect you from."

Startled, she turned to him. "What?"

Before he could say another word, his new mother-in-law snatched him away.

Mariat returned to the pan of soapy water and plunged a pile of plates into it. Sheft was trying to protect her? Where had her brother gotten *that* idea? Sheft was gone from her life. He'd said he loved her, then got rid of her, and that was that.

But if he was hurt… Mother always liked Sheft. For her sake, at least, she should go and see what was wrong. She finished her task, sourly gathered up her basket of herbs and salves, and took the familiar—and now quite desolate—path over the fields. The smell of smoke still lingered in the afternoon air. This visit was an act of charity, nothing more.

But her heart leaned toward where Sheft was, and her feet hurried after. When she got to the house, the place looked deserted. There was no sign of Padiky, which was odd, because Tarn's wagon was still at their house.

"Is anybody here?" She knocked. No one answered, so she opened the door. The fire had gone out, leaving a chill inside.

Sheft was sleeping on a mattress on the floor, covered with a brown blanket. A bright shaft of sunlight coming from the window illuminated his pale hair. At the sight of him, once so dear, a pang went through her heart. But why was he sleeping down here? And where was Tarn?

Placing the basket on the table, she noticed a cup at Sheft's head had been knocked over and water spilled. She leaned over him. "Sheft?"

He wasn't asleep. His eyes were squeezed shut, and his forehead was creased in pain. Fear jumped into her. "Sheft!"

He seemed unaware of her. The blanket covering his back was dark with a large stain. She bent closer and detected the unmistakable smell of blood. She sank to her knees beside him, but when she tried to pull back a corner of the blanket, he gasped. The blanket had been soaked with blood, which had dried and stuck to his back.

Oh God Rulve. Mariat flung off her cloak and ran to get water, but the house crock was empty. The fire was out. Where were the kitchen cloths? Where had Tarn gone? He just threw a blanket over his son and left him? But then he wasn't his son, was he? Thoughts tumbled, and for a moment she panicked, then forced herself to be calm. With deliberate motions she got the fire going, drew water from the well and set it over the flames, found a mug in the cupboard. She knelt next to Sheft and carefully poured water on the blanket to loosen it.

The creaking of the door broke into her absorption. Oris stood tentatively in the opening. "I came for my toy," he said. "The foreigner said I could."

"Toy?" She sat back on her heels. "What are you talking about?"

Oris indicated Sheft with his chin. "The ones he makes." He stepped in and peered at the mattress. "Is he dead?"

The word was like a cold hand wrapping itself around her heart. "No," she answered firmly. She would not allow the question, not even the possibility, to shake her. She returned to her work, dreading what she would find under the blanket. "Go home, Oris. I'll bring you a toy later."

"He promised me the same thing, and never did it. Instead he broke my leg."

Startled, she looked up. "Broke your leg! When?"

"Yesterday. At the field-burn. See, I can hardly walk on it." He took a few steps with an exaggerated limp.

"You got hurt at the field-burn?"

"All the rakes and things were spilling out of the cart. So he fell over me, and then all the tools fell on *him*. That's when my leg got broken."

For a moment she could not speak. "Why did the tools spill?"

"A greensnake scared the horse, and the shaft broke. It wasn't my fault." He glanced around curiously. "Where are the toys?"

She looked down at Sheft, who was quivering in pain, and a lump formed in her throat. She swallowed it. "Did you ever say thank you?"

He looked at her, surprised. "I didn't get my toy yet."

She wanted to shake him. She wanted to scream at all the gossips and rumor-mongers and hate-filled people who had made this boy the way he was. "He saved your life, Oris! This"—she indicated Sheft's rigid body on the mattress—"could've been you, only you'd be dead."

Oris shrugged. "I don't think so. My dad says I'm strong. Are the toys in here someplace?"

They stared at each other, and she recognized in his matter-of-fact gaze an innocence already corrupted. Sheft was right to leave this accursed place, for they had accused him of doing to their children what they themselves had already done. "I don't know where the toys are. Go back to my father and tell him—" He still had a house full of wedding guests, and there was nothing he could do here. "Tell him I'll be staying here tonight. Tell him I said you could have one of those leftover raspberry jam tarts."

"All right!" He whirled and ran to the door, where he stopped to look back. "Um, Gwin would be mad at you

if you said I was here. And then, um, I'd just say I wasn't."
With that, he was gone.

Mariat turned to Sheft, and all she had ever felt for
him came rushing back. She wanted to lean over and kiss
his flushed cheek, brush a tangle of wheat-colored hair
off his forehead but—good-bye was good-bye. Her
throat tightened. "You did a brave thing," she managed to
whisper to him. "Oris and his family will never thank
you, but I do."

She poured more water on the blanket, then began
carefully peeling it away. He stiffened,
and with an indrawn hiss of pain, slumped into the
mattress and was still. Biting her lip, fearing what she
would see, Mariat removed the blanket.

"Oh, Rulve!"

In the common field she'd watched him work, shirtless
and sweaty. She admired his straight back, the muscles in
his shoulders, and had imagined running her hand down
the smooth groove of his spine. But what she saw now
scraped across her stomach. Deep gashes in his left
shoulder raked down his back to the right side of his
waist. Scarlet strips of his shirt were embedded in the
wounds, and sickening glimpses of rib-bone and torn
muscle showed through the skin. As she watched, bright
red welled up in places where blood had already dried.

Oh Sheft! How can you bear this?

He inhaled, making a long ragged sound like a sob.
He seemed to fight his way into consciousness, and his
whole body clenched with some kind of concentrated
effort.

She watched in disbelief as blood receded into the
open gashes. Some instinct told her they would ooze
once more if he passed out again.

With wounds like these, he should have already bled

to death. Incredibly, he seemed to be doing something to prevent that. A memory snapped into her mind: when she'd stitched up his arm in Hawk, that wound hadn't bled either. She leaned back and studied his face. Whatever he was doing, the lines of strain there told her the cost must be terrible. Her heart poured out to him and tears stung the back of her eyes.

But she had no time for them now. She quickly gathered as many clean cloths as she could find and brought them, her medicines, and a bowl of warm water to his side. The cord around his neck was in the way, so she lifted his head and gently took it off. He moaned in protest, his eyes half-open.

"It's all right, Sheft. I'll put it back when I'm done." Her aunt always told her to speak to the sick as if they could hear and understand. She took a deep breath. "Now I have to get your shirt off. I'll be as quick and careful as I can."

She soaked the whole shredded area of his back with herb-water, then carefully peeled off the bloody strips of his shirt. In addition to everything else, a large, ugly bruise had formed midway down his right side. Something heavy must have cracked a rib. No wonder he couldn't seem to take a deep breath. But there was little she could do about it, so she concentrated on the jagged wounds. The worst gaped at his left shoulder, then scored diagonally down. She dabbed away every speck of dirt she could see "Sheft, I'm going to pour some efervcn on you. Remember this is the medicine"—oh God—"that stings." She dribbled the clear liquid on his back, a little at a time.

He gasped and dug his forehead into the mattress as the medicine bubbled in the deep cuts and punctures.

She wiped away tears with her sleeve and forced herself to continue. When she was finished, she sat back and allowed them both to rest for a while. "You did good, sweetheart," she murmured. To her dismay, the last word just slipped out.

Without turning his head, he stretched his right hand toward her. It trembled, and she couldn't help but catch it up, warm and dear and calloused from work, and kissed the palm. He didn't open his eyes, but she could see him swallow. She wanted to bend down and nuzzle under the curve of his jaw.

But enough of that. Now they both had to endure the needle and thread. "Sheft, I have to do some stitching here. But I'll go as easy as I can." He winced at the first prick. She did too, for it was as if she felt it on her own skin. She thrust the sensation away, kept her voice low, her hand steady. "It'll help if you grip the sides of the mattress. Yes, like that."

Mid-way through her efforts, he shuddered and passed out. Immediately, as she had somehow known it would, red welled up again. It took all her attention to dab it away so she could see to stitch. After only moments, he stiffened and again the bleeding stopped. He must have spent the entire night doing that, all alone and in agony.

Don't think about it. Concentrate on what you're doing.

The mattress was drenched and her hands sticky when the job was finally finished. She leaned back and wiped her forehead on her sleeve. "We're done, sweetheart. The worst is over now."

Either he heard her or realized the needle had stopped tormenting him, for the muscles in his shoulders slowly relaxed.

Her hands had been steady, but now they shook. She scrubbed them until they stopped, then carefully dribbled healoil over every inch of the gashes and scrapes on

Sheft's back. She folded several kitchen cloths, tore another into strips, and spread green burvena thickly over the bandage.

"Sheft, I'm going to put a cloth on your back. The salve might feel cold." He flinched when she laid it over him, and his eyes fluttered open. "Now can you raise your chest a little?"

He did the best he could while she got the cloth strips under him and tied them over his shoulder and across his back to keep the bandage in place. He eased down with a sigh when she finished.

She suddenly remembered the spilled water. He must have tried to reach it in the night. "Oh, Rulve!" she exclaimed, jumping up in dismay. "With all that blood loss, you must be raging with thirst. I'm so sorry!"

Having had plenty of practice with her aunt, she got him to turn to the side as far as he could and raised his head. He gulped the water down, spilling only a little onto the towel she held beneath his chin, then sank down and closed his eyes.

She watched him breathing, this man she still, in spite of everything, loved so much. Gently, she slid her hand over his uninjured shoulder. His arm twitched, but his eyes stayed closed. "This part of your back is still beautiful," she whispered. "Still beautiful."

But never again would the rest of it be.

She took a deep breath. "You can't spend the night on that bloody mattress." She pulled one of the two straw mattresses off Tarn's bed, positioned it beside Sheft, and helped him edge onto its surface. The other mattress she wrestled out the door and threw the stained blanket on top of it. "I'll take care of all that in the morning."

He cried out, startling her. She rushed to him and his eyes were glazed, but lit with urgency. "No! Burn."

"Everything's all right. The field-burn is over. Etane says you did a fine job."

"Burn it!" He grabbed her hand.

"It is, Sheft," she soothed him. "It's all burned. Don't worry about it, sweetheart."

He continued insisting and trying to get up until she got a sleeping potion into him. When he finally quieted down, she washed the blood and soot off his face and hands and hair. Even though he didn't seem to see her, gratitude spilled over the pain in his eyes. His hand fumbled at his neck, looking for the pendant. Riah must have left it to him.

"Just a minute," she told him. "I'll have to clean it up." She swished the medallion in water and washed away the blood. After drying it in a towel, she inspected it closely, marveling at the three perfect star-shaped holes. "Both sides are the same. No, I see now they aren't. But here are Rulve's great hands." She looked at him and emotion tightened in her throat. *Dear God, hold him safe. Rulve, please heal him.*

As soon as she looped the pendant over his head, his right hand found and clutched it. After a while the potion took its deeper effect, and he lay still, his silver eyes blank, until they finally closed.

His thirst was gone. Cool touches eased his back. Strips of cloth held him together, restrained the roots. The bloody mattress was burned, wouldn't attract Wask.

Mariat was here, the sweet fruit of all the pain. In spite of all he'd said, of all he'd done, she had come to him. Surrounded by her presence, he slipped away. In one hand he held her kiss, in the other the warm toltyr.

Mariat covered him to the waist with his blanket from

the loft, pried the medallion out of his hand, and placed it close to his head on the mattress. "I'll make some soup," she whispered, smoothing back his damp hair, "and maybe later you can eat some of it."

She pulled the rug from over the trap-door to the root cellar, descended the short ladder, and gathered carrots, a cabbage, and a few slices of salted pork. After the soup was simmering, she sank onto Tarn's nodding chair.

It was twilight now, and quiet. She rocked—*creak-crick, creak*-crick—and slowly her energy drained away, leaving an aching void.

Oh God Rulve, please help him. Those terrible wounds! He got them trying to save a little boy, so please don't let them fester. Please don't let a fever come. Oh God, don't let him die. She soon found she was praying not only for Sheft's healing, but also for that of the painful rent that had pulled them apart, for reasons she never fully understood.

I don't know what's wrong, or what went wrong. Mother God, we need you. Father God, we need your strength. Help us. Help *us!*

Following secret paths out of the Riftwood, Wask crossed the Meera. An old hunger made it stop at the K'meen Arûk, the sacrificial stone on which the wet white eyeballs used to be set out for him. They had thin skins that popped when its teeth bit down, and they filled its mouth with a salty juice.

But none had been left here for a long time, and it found only a dead bird. Wask sucked at it, but it was dry and bloodless, so it threw the body aside and moved on. Collapsing into a black mist, the creature that was now the Groper slipped along the riverbank, intent on its surroundings. To the right, it sensed the place where many people had gathered in merriment the night before.

The torches were gone now, and the fieldhold lay in darkness.

A slight breeze brought a whiff of smoke, but underneath, it detected the lingering sweet scent it had detected earlier. The Groper turned and rushed along a newly dug ditch to the far side of a field. Here the blood had fallen, not long ago, full and strong.

Extending a tendril, the Groper fingered the blackened remains of what once had been a cart. But the dry wood—and what had flowed so freely into it—had been consumed by fire. Angry red flickers darted through the mist. It withdrew the tendril and sniffed the ground. A short distance away it found what it sought: a faint trail that smelled of blood.

Darkness pressed against the window, but the hearth glowed brightly. Sitting in the nodding chair, staring at the fire, Mariat felt again the desolation of Sheft's leaving her. Her father insisted that a strapping husband like Gwin, and then a child, would eventually fill the empty spot. She couldn't imagine that ever happening—and certainly not with Gwin.

The chair creaked and a log in the fire settled. "Maybe it will be easier for me after you go away, Sheft. Then I can work on forgetting you. God knows, I'll have a lifetime to do it." In the years ahead would he remember her, ever think of her? She didn't even know where he was going.

He lay with his eyes closed, the side of his face pale in the flickering light, the bandage barely moving with his shallow breaths.

She was so tired and dejected that tears sprang up again, and she dashed them away impatiently. "Gwin's been coming around. Once he brought Oris with him.

Etane said it was because Gwin thinks women are attracted to a man who holds a child on his lap." She grimaced. "In this case, it didn't work. Oris isn't one to sit quietly while the adults talk."

The fire radiated its warmth, the soup simmered gently, and the clean, cold smell of an early spring night wafted through the open kitchen window. These were cozy, everyday things, precious things that couples shared for a lifetime—but which she and Sheft never would.

Tears threatened again, and she leaned out from her chair to look down at him. "You could have told me Tarn wasn't your father. That wouldn't have mattered to me. You really didn't know me very well to think it would."

But at their parting he had given another reason altogether. He said he didn't love her.

Low at first, merely troubling at first, an insistent inner warning brought him floating to the surface. Foggy memories came together, then congealed into horror. The mattress. She'd pulled the blood-soaked mattress outside, into the night, and it would act like a beacon to Wask. It seemed he threw off the blanket to take a torch to it, over and over, but never got through the door.

His eyes jerked open. He must've been dreaming. "Go!" he said thickly. "Go!"

Worried brown eyes looked into his. "What is it, Sheft? Do you need something?"

"Blood's…everywhere. Go 'fore dark." He heard his own words, garbled and far off.

"It's all right. Everything is cleaned up now."

He plucked at the mattress. "Burn it!" he pleaded. "Get torches…root-cellar. Torches!"

She disappeared from view, and the next thing he saw

was her leaning two torches on the wall near the door. He pushed the blanket aside and tried to raise himself. She pressed him back down. "Lie still, Sheft. Please lie still. I think you had a nightmare, but all is well."

"Yes! A nightmare!" It was moving through the Riftwood. Crossing the Meera. Groping its way over the fields. Black and inevitable, it was following the trail of his blood. He tried desperately to warn her, but the words got muffled in the fog.

She stroked his hair, his cheek. "It's all right, dear. Everything's all right. What happened to you is all over now." She gave him water, which he swallowed eagerly until he realized it was more of the sleeping potion and pushed it away.

A nail through his ribs held him down, and the potion swirled through his head, but he had to protect her. It hurt to breathe, but he had to place himself between her and the door. The reason for that was slipping away. She said everything was all right. It was all over now. She was close to him, and he loved her. He reached out and touched her hand. *Lie down behind me, Mariat. Sleep with me. Stay by me, and never leave again.*

She smiled at him through her tears. He was the one who had left.

"You don't know me very well, Sheft."

He wasn't sure if he was asleep or awake, but he held her beautiful face in his hands. "I always wanted to."

He lay quiet, so Mariat took the soup off the fire. After forcing herself to eat a small bowl of it, she turned her attention to the state of the kitchen. The lantern revealed what looked like a week's worth of dirty dishes waiting on the sideboard. She washed and dried them, then scrubbed the table. With the hearth fire stoked so high, it had gotten quite warm in the room and the smell of blood and medicines still lingered. Fresh air, her aunt always said, chased sickness away. As she headed toward the door, however, a lifelong fear scrabbled a warning in her stomach. *I'll just stand on the doorstep,* she told herself, *and let a little air in.*

Brushing her hair behind her ears, she opened the door. A crooked rectangle of light fell onto the stony yard. All was still, but something was wrong. Something was out there that shouldn't be.

Her gaze cut to the left. Caught at the edge of the light, a low shadow humped. Chills erupted all over her skin, and she stood transfixed.

Nothing moved. She blinked, and then let out a breath of relief. It was only the blanket and the bloody mattress, folded over on itself. How silly—she'd forgotten they were out there. Yet, for some reason the pile made her feel uneasy, so she stepped back and shut the door. She made sure it was barred, and closed the window as well. *You were right to be afraid of that stained bedding,* she thought, *because it will be the devil's own mess to clean in the morning.* She rubbed her tired eyes, then knelt down beside Sheft to check on him.

To her surprise, he was awake and looking at her, this time with full recognition. The pain had crept back into his face, pain she could not take away, but his eyes shone with tenderness. "You're real," he said.

Blinking back tears, she smiled at him. "Always was."

"Sleep here with me."

"I thought you'd never ask."

A rueful grin tugged at his mouth, followed by a wince of pain. With the wound on his left shoulder and a broken rib on the right, they both knew he could barely turn to her in the night.

She pulled out Tarn's other mattress and a blanket and placed them where Sheft indicated, close behind him. Leaning over, she kissed his shoulder, then settled down with a sigh.

He reached out behind him, and she held his hand until he fell asleep. Only then did she tuck it under his blanket, close her eyes, and fall softly into the warmth. Sometime later, dimly aware the fire had died down, she pulled the covers up to her chin.

Sniffing the earth, the Groper followed the ruts of a wagon through the moonless night. Suddenly it reared up. There! Not far off. The mist coalesced into an inky rivulet and rushed forward. Unerringly the smell drew it, with ever-greater strength, until at last the Groper burst into a stony yard. The blood-smell lay directly before it, pulsing red in the dark, only hours old.

The Groper fell upon the straw mattress like a wave. The mist became a flat, peat-colored skin, and it summoned the night-beetles. Hundreds of them churned out of the ground. They swarmed over the blood-soaked mattress, digging and burrowing and devouring, their avaricious mouth-parts clicking.

"Enough! Now come to me."

They surged into the skin, filling it like a swelling corpse, and slowly Wask the beetle-man rose into full strength. It pulled the skin close around the tightly-packed mass.

He surfaced, opened his eyes. What had awakened him? She breathed softly behind him, a healing presence he could not turn to embrace. An inner warning scraped across his spirikai. He raised his head. The fire burned low. Everything was still. The door, a black rectangle darker than the shadow-filled room, was barred. He stared at it, and all his senses scanned the night beyond.

The beetle-man half-saw, half-sensed the bulk of a house, and stumped to the door. Glittering filaments winked around the frame. Wards, put there by the woman now dead. They were weak, and its lumpy hands pulled them down like cobwebs. Staring at the door, the beetle-man willed it to open. With a faint groan, the bar inside lifted, and the heavy door turned inward. Warm air wafted out, as well as the rush of the heady, sweet smell.

This was the house. What it sought lived within. The beetle-eyes discerned only shadows.

One with bright hair stood in its way.

A chill was seeping into the room. Into her dream.

She was cold, even though, for some reason, she was wearing Sheft's sheepskin jacket. Tense, listening for what she knew was out there, she sat against a great tree, her arms wrapped around her knees. The darkness of the Riftwood hemmed her in on every side and the presence of ancient trees bent over her. Light from the meager campfire in front of her shuddered over the ground. Roots lay over the soil like fat snakes—unmoving when she glanced at them, but creeping toward her the moment she looked away. She leaned forward, her eyes straining to penetrate the blackness beyond the fire.

Chills ran like centipedes down her arms. Something was approaching. It was crunching toward her, coming out of the dark.

Mariat jerked awake. Every instinct within her cried out. Something rustled beside her, and she rolled over. Incredibly, Sheft had gotten to his feet.

★

He stood there, eyes fixed on the door. Of its own, the bar began to rise. The door creaked open, to the sound of chittering beetle wings. Cold air poured in from the night beyond.

Something large filled the opening—a stiff and lumpy form.

CHAPTER 26

DARKNESS AT THE DOOR

A swampy odor emanated from the earth-brown thing that filled the entrance. It wore a robe of leaves so rotted it was nothing but a thin net of veins. The face and hands crawled with what looked like slowly-moving cysts under the skin. They contorted the lump that was its face into a series of expressions—avid, tortured, triumphant. Chitinous wings whirred in one of the eye sockets, and as Sheft watched in horrified fascination, a beetle crawled out. It left an empty hole.

Behind him, Mariat uttered a strangled sound. Her terror beat against his back, and he moved to block the creature's view of her. Its gaze was fixed so hungrily on his face it did not seem aware of anything else.

Wask the beetle-man heaved itself into the room, and only the kitchen table stood between them. The lipless mouth flopped open and a tentacle—felt more than seen—flicked out.

Sheft jerked aside, but not in time. Like a fat night-crawler, the moist, ribbed power of Wask slipped inside him. Sickened, he clutched the edge of the table as, with a kind of slimy tenderness, Wask exuded words into his mind.

"Come. I will take you home."

Home. In spite of the nausea that filled him, the word

resonated. Home was a place where he belonged. A place where he would not be despised or accused, where his people would look him in the eye and accept him with a smile. Hadn't Yarahe called him to go there? Hadn't the voices, all his life? And now this creature called him too.

Except. Except, for him, home would be a place not of comfort but of challenge, a place where he would face failure. He struggled to break free from the beetle-man's tether. "I will go home," he got out, "but you won't take me there."

The beetle-man's power inside him rapidly changed form—into something dry and many-legged. It picked its way over his veins as delicately as a spider over its web. "Be rid of these roots inside you. Let me suck out of you this cursed black blood."

It promised what he longed for: an end to self-disgust, an end to the filth that ran in his veins. He had once imagined how a knife would do the job, but ice had intervened. Now this creature offered him release.

"Yes!" the beetle-man hissed. "Come and be drained. Let me make you clean at last." Eager, it took another step toward him.

It was what he had prayed for. Now he could fall into the beetle-man, let it paralyze his will, roll him in silky threads of oblivion. Let it suck out his blood and do what the fire had not.

But even as his body leaned toward it, an inner instinct screamed in protest. Wask was offering, not cleansing, but beetles swarming over his skin, burrowing and gnawing—making of him what this thing was. He tried to twist away, but Wask's power held him fast, and its awareness probed deeper.

It came upon his spirikai, and reaching out with one tentative spider-leg, touched it. "Ahh," it breathed. It scuttled over the tensely-coiled strands, over the sensitive, looping nerves. It unearthed his deepest desire, and stroked it.

Sheft shuddered with a horrible mix of repulsion and pleasure.

"How you long to bleed," the beetle-man crooned. "How you yearn to give your life! Beyond the land of Rûk, the soil is dying of thirst. It cries out for your sweet, black blood."

The words shivered over him like an obscene caress. He felt the shame of it, but could no longer deny it: to bleed into the ground was his heart's desire, and for this utter emptying he knew he had been born.

The creature opened its arms for him, and it was the personification of the far-off voices he had heard all his life. It was the pull of the bell in his long-ago dream, the whisper of a wind that tousled his hair: "*Come, S'eft.*"

His very veins responded. He moved forward.

And bumped into the kitchen table. Its mundane solidity brought him up short. It wasn't suffering people that called him, but the voice that had almost ensnared him at the Rites. "Leave me alone!" he tried to shout, but only a strangled sound came out.

A look of pity rippled over the lumpy face. "For most humans there is only one end: the mold and the worms. For you there is a choice. Follow me into your destiny."

A vision flashed. A yellow blanket disappearing under shovelfuls of dirt. Ane being buried under soil that writhed with blind and probing mouths. Even now, they were eating at her face. His gorge was rising and he couldn't breathe, couldn't swallow.

"She's not down there, Sheft. She's in Rulve's hands."

Rulve's hands. Hands that had held him up in the forge, kept him alive while he burned. Hands carved into the pendant he wore, its cord rough around his neck.

With an effort of will, he pushed words past the repulsion in his throat. "I've already died. I've walked through clean fire, and will not now be commanded by bugs!"

The beetle-man lowered its arms, then grinned horribly. One leg stumped forward. The kitchen table between the creature and Sheft began to slide away.

He grasped the toltyr, at the thin disk that was his only strength, and held it up. "I call on this Toltyr Arulve," he choked out. "I claim the power of niyalahn-rista!" He hardly knew what he was saying, using words he didn't understand and could barely pronounce. But the table abruptly stopped moving.

The beetle-man stared at him. Its grin disappeared. "Ah, niyalahn-rista. Now I see. Listen, for I speak to your soul. Come. Pour out your life. Bleed freely and water the earth. Release your power and be transformed, and from a great height you will look down upon those who despise you."

Oh God, it was a seduction more powerful than he had ever known. It promised everything he wanted, everything he desperately needed: expiation, transformation, a final and glorious justification. The villagers would have to look up to see him. Gwin would shrink beneath his gaze. Every cruel remark, every untruth, every dark, hard look would be ground into their faces like a rotten potato. The creature stood only two arm-lengths away. Its hands were extended, full of power and the pull of truth. All he had to do was step around the table and walk into them.

"Sheft?" It was Mariat's voice, small and tremulous.

The beetle-man's head swiveled toward her, and Sheft's heart sank. Its gaze turned back to him, and its power twined around his spirikai. "Come, emjadi. She is nothing. Your destiny is beyond her. You are intended for sacrifice and redemption, and she cannot understand what you must do."

It was true. Beyond his choosing, the burden was his. How could she understand what he did not? How could she bear what his own heart flinched from, yet burned to do?

He felt her at his back. Her kiss had anointed his shoulder and her eyes had looked upon him with grace. She had touched his wounds and was not repelled. Now he alone stood between her and this thing of the outer dark.

"You know you must leave her. You have already chosen it." The beetle-man took another step forward. Its hand snaked out, impossibly long, and grasped his wrist.

At the instant of physical contact, Sheft constricted his spirikai. Ice crackled, and with an abruptness that made him gasp, Wask's power whipped out of him and back into the creature's mouth.

But its hand tightened. "You will come," it growled. "You have no choice. One way or another, you will come."

"No!" With a wrenching effort, Sheft thrust ice down his arm and slammed it into the creature's hand. The beetle-man let go of him so suddenly Sheft sprawled onto the table. The cracked rib stabbed into his side.

"If you do not come, I will take the woman instead." The creature turned stiffly toward Mariat, its expression crawling into a leer.

Sheft pulled himself upright. "If you want my blood," he said through his raw throat, "ice comes with it." He constricted, shoved the table aside, and with hands that felt like frozen, impervious blocks, advanced upon Wask. Grinning, it wagged the worm of power at him. With an icy fist, Sheft hit it in the mouth.

The beetle-man reeled back, its lips rimmed with frost, but still the mind-words gloated, "The Riftwood awaits you. Death will swallow you." It locked its hands together and smashed them into Sheft's broken rib.

Hot pain shattered the ice. With a gasp, he dredged up more; but now the snake-like arms were grabbing at his throat, swiping at his eyes, trying to encircle his wrists. He fended them off, but fire streaked down his back and the fractured rib ground into him with every thrust.

The creature's eyes whirred in glee. "You are a fool to fight me, for I am part of your deepest self. There is no way to win."

The beetle-man's fist hit his cheek like a pouch packed with stones, but Sheft managed to block the next blow. Step by step, twisting out ice, he drove it back. The creature never stopped grinning, as if it were merely toying with him. But was it death or the truth that he fought?

"You contend with both, for in this speech I cannot lie." Abruptly, it stepped backward through the door and disappeared into the dark.

Sheft grabbed a torch, lit it with a thrust in the hearth, and stumbled after Wask into the yard. Panting, half blind with fire and ice, he looked wildly around. Shadows jittered in the torch-flame, and the folded-over mattress seemed to quiver.

A blow from behind knocked him to the stony ground. Pain ripped through his back and the torch fell. The beetle-man stood over him, its face crawling. "You will fail, niyal'arist."

"Not yet," he shouted. "Not here."

On his knees, he lunged out and chopped at Wask's shin with the side of his icy hand. Its skin tore open and the creature lurched back. Beetles poured out of its leg. A flood of them rushed at Sheft. He scrambled to his feet, snatched up the still-burning torch, and swept the insects back.

Fixed on Sheft, the beetle-man's eyes spun and glittered. It began dissolving its other leg and more insects churned out, boiling over the ones that had fled from the torch. They swarmed toward him like a brown, chittering tide, surging in closer after each sweep of fire. Every movement sent pain clawing through his shoulder, he couldn't fill his lungs with air, and still they came.

Bleeding, failing, he sank down to one knee, the creature's voice thrumming in his head. "The dark will take your blood, niyal'arist, down to the last dregs."

Chapter 27

Niyalahn~Rista

A second torch flared. Its flame swept the beetles back, and Mariat stood there, facing Wask.

The creature, now up to its calves in insects, sputtered with laughter. "There is too much of me," it said, "and not enough of you." It chittered a command, and a low wall of night-beetles, multi-legs churning and antennae waving, turned and roiled toward her.

Sheft groped over the dark ground and seized a good-sized rock. He grasped it tightly in both hands and bore down hard on his spirikai. Ice crystallized, ran down his arms and into the rock. He could hear Mariat frantically sweeping the torch, hear the squeals of terror in her throat, but he didn't dare look up, didn't dare break his concentration. He squeezed the rock until frost glittered on the rough surface, then hurled it into the beetle-man's chest.

It hit hard. A hole tore open, bleeding beetles. Unbalanced on its dissolving legs, the creature fell onto its back. It opened its rictus mouth and issued a high, thin call. The tide of insects, now barely an inch away from Mariat's feet, swerved and rushed to the creature's aid. They carried the disintegrating remains of its upper body onto what was left of the mattress and burrowed into the pile of bloody straw and fabric. There they sought new sustenance, new strength.

Sheft got to his feet and propped himself up with his hands on his knees. "The lantern, Mariat," he gasped. "Get the oil lantern!"

Topped with the grotesque head and neck, most of Wask's torso had collapsed into a living, churning heap; but the insects were refilling it, swelling into a thick chest, bulging shoulders, and stumps of what would soon be arms. The head turned to look at him, beetles swirling in its eye sockets. "You will fail, niyal'arist. Redemption always involves failure."

Mariat shoved the lantern into his hands. He flung it onto the beetle-infested mattress, grabbed her torch, and thrust it into the spilled oil. The straw burst into flames.

With an inhuman cry, Wask tried to twist its torso out of the fire as beetles fled wildly from its body. Like an exhaling lung, the skin emptied and flattened. Abruptly, Wask changed into an inky rivulet. It abandoned the mattress and rushed toward the barn. Sheft careened after it, wielding the torch with an icy hand. His boots crunched over the spot where a terrified little boy had first encountered the Groper, but now he bore the toltyr and a flame held high, and the night-time horror fled from him.

The rivulet rolled into the shadow of the barn. It tossed last words back to him. "Because of you, she also will be taken."

His breath coming in painful gasps, Sheft stopped and watched the Groper disappear into the night. It left behind a dead silence. The Riftwood, black against the starlit sky, stretched unmapped over the curve of the world, and the flame of his torch was nothing but a brief spark. His victory was a hollow gourd, and fear for Mariat rattled inside it. A deep instinct told him that the beetle-man had spoken the truth, that its every threat was a prophecy.

Sheft made his way back to her, the torch suddenly so heavy it was an effort to hold it upright. Mariat, one hand clutching her skirt, was sweeping beetles into the flaming straw with the torch he had dropped earlier. But now the insects had lost their animating force and were running about in mindless panic, so he pulled her aside and allowed the beetles to scuttle off.

The blazing pile soon settled into ash, and the last of the sparks sailed like glowing orange crystals into the dark. It must be after midnight. Shivering inside, Sheft turned to Mariat. Her eyes were enormous, her face white.

"Are you," they both asked in breathless unison, "all right?"

Together, they nodded.

He guided her toward the house, extinguishing the torches on the way. Just inside the door, Mariat looked down and yelped. A lone beetle had scurried in, and she ground it furiously under her boot. With a grimace, she wiped it on the doorstep, then shut the door. They looked at each other and swallowed.

Mariat lowered herself onto the bench at the table. "Wine," she said. "Wine would be good now."

Wine? Tarn had no wine. But then Sheft remembered: Mariat had brought some when she had stitched up his arm in Hawk. It was far back in the cupboard. He set the bottle and two cups on the table, sank down across from Mariat, and poured a glass for her, his hand shaking so much the bottle clattered against the cup rim. She took two big gulps while he managed to pour some for himself.

"Wait," she said when he brought the cup to his lips.

"Wait. You shouldn't drink that on an empty stomach. When was the last time you had something to eat?"

"I d-don't know," he stammered. "Groats. I had a bowl of groats just after the field-burn."

"That's too long!" She jumped up. "I made soup. You've got to eat."

He put the cup down, too hard, and wine splashed out. "No, wait a minute, Mariat. Please, sit down." All unknowing, she had come to heal him and wound up fighting the darkness at his side. She was innocent, and he had involved her, endangered her, yet again. He owed her everything—including the truth.

"Mariat, I have to talk to you. But I don't have much time. I think pretty soon I'm going to wind up on that mattress again." The pain in his back, which his battle with the beetle-man had largely driven from his head, was beginning to reassert itself with a vengeance. His wounds felt swollen and hot, and the room blurred under an ice-reaction daze.

"I don't know how you ever got off it!" she exclaimed. "What happened? Why did that—that creature—why did it *come* here? How did you drive it away?" She pointed at the toltyr. "With magery?"

Magery? He stared at her. "N-no. No magery. This is called a toltyr. The Toltyr Arulve."

"Toltyr Arulve?"

"I don't know what that means. Something about Rulve."

"Riah left it to you?"

"Yes. No. It belongs to me." He held the medallion out, as if it could explain itself to her.

Without taking her eyes off him, she sat down again. "You screamed out something. 'Ni—nilan-rista'. What is that?"

"It's me. I'm niyalahn-rista."

"Is that—is that your family name?"

"No, no. Please let me explain. My brother and I together—I had a brother, Mariat. We're doubles. *Were* doubles. I'm sorry. But it's not what you think." He took a breath. "Actually—actually it's worse." The ice reaction made it hard to form coherent thoughts, but the returning pain told him he must speak quickly. "Riah told me before she died. We—I—am apparently this niyalahn-rista. But I don't know what that means. I didn't want to take the toltyr, Mariat, but now, since the—the accident, it's become part of me."

Seeing the look on her face, he felt hopelessly unable to explain. He rubbed his face. "So much happened to me. I don't know where to start."

"Wait. You have to eat something first. You're not making any sense."

She brought him a bowl of soup, and to please her he ate some of it. But after a few mouthfuls he put the spoon down. Mariat looked at him with wide eyes and clutched her cup of wine with both hands. "Just start anywhere."

He began to speak—clumsily, hesitating, ashamed. He told her everything, from the beginning: about his root-ridden blood and the ice, about what happened in Miramakamen's tent, and Riah's rape, and his conversation with the great falconform. Partway through, he took a swallow of wine, but it tasted like vinegar and he put it aside. He kept nothing hidden from her.

She listened without interruption, occasionally motioning for him to take a spoonful of soup. It and her wine gradually dwindled away.

Near the end of the telling he was exhausted, aware that his battle with the beetle-man had taken an enormous toll. Taut with pain and humiliation, he slumped with his elbows on the table, holding his bowed head in his hands. "That's why I had to let you go, Mariat."

Now that she knew the ugly truth, she would leave for home as soon as it was light. Two days later he would leave too, but in an entirely different direction.

She reached over the table and took both of his hands. "You spoke to me with courage, Sheft, and humility. You are more dear to me than my own heart."

Not sure he had heard her correctly, he lifted his head to look into her eyes. They shone with love and tears, and they were both for him. She knew everything, and still looked at him like this. Mariat stood and came around the table to him. He reached up to embrace her, and pressed his cheek against her waist. Her arms came around him, and she leaned down to spread kisses in his hair, down the back of his neck.

After a moment she drew back. "I have to replace your bandage. It's all red, dear heart."

Panic twisted in his stomach. He was bleeding, and had no ice left. What if the beetle-man should return? Return as the Groper, seeping under the door, or as Wask, tearing it from its hinges? Some instinct told him he would encounter the creature again, in a form even more powerful, and that it would happen soon.

"You saved us, Sheft, and now this is the price. But you won't pay it alone." She helped him back to the mattress, untied the bandage, and carefully removed it.

Tense, he waited while she examined the cuts.

"The stitches held, dear heart. They bled a little, but held."

He sagged in relief.

"Now just relax, and I'll clean your back again." She dabbed at the wounds with a cloth wrung in warm water, prepared another salve-spread bandage, and tied it securely around him. With a glance at the door, she threw the bloody cloths into the fire.

He settled gratefully onto his stomach, his face turned toward her, and they lay side by side on their separate, narrow mattresses. Tiredness lined her face, there were dark smudges under her eyes, and her hair was askew. She was so beautiful.

"What are you going to do now?" she asked, her gaze soft with concern.

The pain made it hard to talk. "As Yarahe said. One day after the dark of the moon—that's the day after tomorrow—I'll go to the Wind-gate. Then through the Riftwood." The way he felt now, it seemed like an impossible journey.

"I'll come with you."

They were dream-words, ice-reaction words. Cruel in their seeming reality.

"Sheft, did you hear me? I want to come with you."

They were real words. But he could never allow her to come with him through the Riftwood. "No. You can't."

She laid her hand over his arm, and the thrill of her touch fled over his skin. "I want to."

"I could never ask it."

"You didn't ask. I volunteered."

"You can't come, Mariat."

"You must allow me my choice. Don't make that mistake again."

"I *couldn't* allow you to choose. You didn't know what you were choosing. Now you do. That thing in the doorway—" He stopped to gather his strength. The ice-reaction was worse than he had ever experienced, and it felt as if a hot rake were scoring his back. "It came

looking for me. It will come again. It wants my blood
and now it wants you."

"Me!"

"It told me, it *predicted*, that because of me, you also
would be taken."

She raised her eyebrows. "And you believed it?"

Her question stopped him, but only for a moment.
"The—the mind-words, Mariat. They can't lie."
Somehow, with a knowledge he must have been born
with, he knew they came from a deep well of truth.

"But if I come with you, I *will* be taken—in a manner
of speaking."

"No, no," he groaned. "It wasn't like that."

"You drove the creature away, Sheft."

"But can I do it the next time?" He covered his eyes
with his hand. "I don't know what I can do. I don't know
who I am."

She drew his hand down. "Niyalahn-rista. That's
who you are."

"But what is that? The *beetle-man* seemed to know
more about it than I do."

With a tender smile, she caressed his cheek. "We'll
learn together who you are. All I know is I fell in love
with Sheft, and that's you."

"But what about those deaths, Mariat? Those people
who died in the village. I'm responsible for them."

She was silent a moment, searching his face. "I think,"
she said, "you'll have to get over that. Even if that creature
was looking for you and found them instead, how can
that be your fault? If you let guilt eat away at you, then
the beetle-man has won."

"It's my blood," he groaned. "It's cursed, packed with
roots."

She hesitated, and he thought at last the enormous

truth he had told her was beginning to sink in. "I stitched you up, Sheft, twice already. I saw no roots."

Her remark stunned him. How could she not understand? "Of course you can't see them. They're a— a symbol of what's inside me. Of the thing inside me that draws the Groper."

"I realize that, but I don't see anything evil inside you. It's just not there. Perhaps this power in your blood is somehow a good thing, a gift from Rulve."

"A gift! Mariat, how can you say that? You saw with your own eyes what it summoned!"

"Sheft." Gently, she shook his right shoulder, bare above the bandage, and this time the touch rushed down to his groin. "Be at peace, sweetheart. Perhaps the wise people of the Seani can advise you, heal you. It's surely Rulve's providence that summons you there. In any case, I'm coming with you."

"No, Mariat. Absolutely n—"

She put a finger on his lips. "The Rift-riders will protect us. You seem to have forgotten all about them."

She was looking at him with such love that for a moment he couldn't speak. A hope too big to acknowledge was beginning to dawn on him, but he quickly thrust it away. "I can't let you do this. Oh God, I want to! But I can't."

Her face clouded. "You pushed me away once before —out of fear for me, you said. Don't let fear separate us again."

He remembered the terrible winter without her, how precious she was to him, what his life would be like if she wasn't part of it. How could she have such faith in him? Such miracles didn't happen in his world, and he was having a hard time comprehending they might. "For how long would you stay with me?"

She reared back slightly in surprise. "What do you mean, how long will I stay? I'll stay always, like any other wife."

The pain must be making him hear things. He could hardly believe the word she used so casually: *wife*. Everything he thought he could never possess—commitment he could never deserve, intimacy he never dared hope for—resided in that word. "You would hold-fast to me as—as your husband? In spite of all you know about me?"

Her eyes danced as she looked at him. "Yes." She wriggled closer to him, tucked her head under his chin, and placed her hand lightly over his waist. "This I choose. This I would hold fast."

He put his arm around her, but had to continue. He had to make certain she understood—that *he* understood. Taking a deep breath, he plunged on. "What about—about children?" Another word, beyond belief.

She answered him sleepily, her voice muffled against his chest. "Babies are very nice," she said. "You would make a good father."

The word stunned him, another simple word, and sudden elation leaped up in him. *Husband, father*—such words he had always dismissed, quickly, before they could hurt him. But now she offered them to him as if they were not some impossible resurrection.

"Mariat, I don't even know who my father is. What if it wasn't Neal, but someone who attacked a helpless woman in the dark?"

She nuzzled him. "I'm holding fast to you, Sheft, not your father."

"But what would our children be?"

"I don't know. Parents never know." Her eyes were closing. The wine, the long hours she spent caring for him, the encounter with the beetle-man—all must be taking their toll. "But I think they would be like usual—part me, part you."

"But I'm—"

"You're kind and brave and strong."

She was beyond his imagining, and always had been. But still he had to be certain. "Because of me, the darkness came tonight. Would you face such a nightmare again?"

With her eyes closed, she murmured against him: "Isn't that the grace given to husband and wife? That they can face anything if they're together?"

She had faith, and courage—enough for them both. She knew everything about him and accepted him, exactly as he was, and loved him. His heart swelled with wild joy and he pulled her tightly against him. "Oh, Mariat! I will love you forever, no matter what, with everything in me."

"I love you too, Sheft," she breathed. "So now we are betrothed." With a sigh she fell asleep against him.

For hours it was not pain that kept him awake, but the need to make sure she was still there. And she always was.

CHAPTER 28

TARN'S UNEASE

Mariat stirred in the half-dark, dimly aware of a robin singing far off, its lone, clear voice echoing in the distant halls of dawn. With a dreamy smile, she moved closer to the warmth of her beloved's body.

It was broad day when she next awoke. The blanket that she had used to cover Sheft last night was now tucked around her. Mariat propped herself up on one elbow and gazed at her betrothed. He lay asleep on his stomach, his head turned toward her, with only a corner of the blanket covering his waist. The crook of his right arm covered his eyes and partially shielded the strands of his wheat-colored hair. It was as if he tried to hide his appearance even in sleep.

Her eyes caressed him, and ran over the muscles of his bare shoulders and arms. He was so beautiful. He had endured so much, had opened his heart so completely to her. In their darkest hour, grace had come to them, and their lives had become inextricably intertwined.

She sighed in pleasure and stretched to her toes, a woman pledged in troth. Inextricably intertwined. A delicious concept. Soon, after they were married, they would in truth become inextricably intertwined. Softly, so as not to wake him, she leaned over and kissed his wrist. It felt hot against her lips.

He sighed and moved his arm, and Mariat laid her hand over his forehead. "You have a fever!" she cried. "I was afraid of this. Of this exact thing."

His silver eyes flickered open and rested on her. "Sorry," he mumbled. "Sorry, Mariat."

"It's not your fault, dear heart. Of course you can't help it." She got up, wrung a cloth in cold water, and placed it around his neck. The bandage covering his back was clean, but now he faced another danger.

"You used up so much ice last night!" she exclaimed. "Is there any left?" She shook him gently. "Ice, dear heart. We need ice, for the fever."

Eyes closed, he licked his lips. "Working... I'm working on it."

She brought water, but soon after he drank it, he began shivering. Then he got hot again and threw off the blanket. Trying to keep him still and the bandage intact, she fought the fever, rinsing and replacing the cloth, bathing his face and arms in cool water, and putting another blanket on him when he began shivering again. She prayed to Rulve and made the sign of his circle on Sheft's forehead with healoil. They were supposed to leave on their journey the day after tomorrow. After this relapse, would he have the strength? If they arrived late, would the Rift-riders wait for them?

In the early afternoon the door burst open, and she was so concerned for Sheft that it startled her not at all. It was her father, who gave her a big hug. "I got Oris's message. How is Sheft?"

"He was getting better, but now he's got a fever!"

She led him to stand over Sheft, whose face looked flushed against the pillow. Moro got down on one knee and inspected the bandage, gently touching it here and there. "Poor lad. Tarn did a fine job, though." He looked around. "Where is he? I've brought back his wagon."

Mariat decided not to mention that Tarn had nothing to do with Sheft's bandage, and that as far as she could tell, had heartlessly abandoned him. The news would only fill her father with recriminations. Instead she mumbled something about needing more burvena from the apothecary in Ferce, which she did, and let Moro assume Tarn had gone to get it, which he certainly had not.

"I'm sure you were a great help here, Mariat. You did well to spend the night."

You don't know the half of it, she thought.

"You don't know," Sheft mumbled from his mattress, "the half of it. She's…a very brave woman."

Moro looked puzzled. "Eh?"

"He's feverish," Mariat said quickly. "He doesn't know what he's saying."

Sheft groaned a disagreement and pushed the cloth off his neck. "Very brave." He opened his eyes, which were like pools of melted silver, and found her face. "Fever. I think from ice-reaction, Mariat, not—" He gestured feebly toward his back.

"Icy action?" Moro asked. "What's that?"

"It's the fever talking." Hastily Mariat knelt beside Sheft and gave him a poke in the arm. "Moro's here, Sheft. Don't speak. Just save your strength."

He blinked at her, seemed to remember what he had just said, then nodded sheepishly.

Mariat lifted an edge of the bandage and sniffed at it. Sheft was right: the wounds were not infected. The fever must be a reaction to the great drain of ice, perhaps his body's way of trying to balance the humors after an overwhelming effort. But he had a fever nonetheless, and maybe a potion would help.

She got her father to bring in water and firewood. He clomped in and out, talking about the wedding, while she made a medicine and helped Sheft drink it. After she had settled him down again, her father invited her outside. "Looks like you need a little fresh air."

As they went through the door, Mariat felt a momentary chill as she passed through the ghostly memory of the beetle-man who had stood there only hours ago. Now a square of sunlight tried to purify the spot.

They sat on the doorstep. It was a hazy afternoon, and an east wind blew from the deadlands, bringing the rich smell of earth. Later on, there would be rain.

Moro cleared his throat. "You still care for him, don't you?"

Her heart full, she nodded.

"Daughter, marriage is hard enough for a man and wife who are more or less alike, but if they're different— well, all kinds of things can crop up. As young as he is, Sheft knows this, and he's already said his good-byes. It's for the best that you part." He patted her knee. "Take another look at Gwin, now. You ignored him at the wedding, and he came around again yesterday, asking about you. He's a fine lad, and one day will take over his father's smithy. He's good with children—we've seen that for ourselves—and treats you and our family with respect. You can't ask for much more in a husband."

It took all her restraint to keep from blurting out the truth: *Forget Gwin! I'm already espoused. To one I love so much.* But as she looked at her father's lined face, she realized that he had just spent his first night completely alone since Mama died, with no son or daughter to keep him company. He missed his wife terribly, and hinted that he looked forward to the time when both his children would settle nearby and raise grandchildren. She must prepare him gently for the news of her departure. She began by telling him what Sheft had done for Oris.

"Daddy, everyone in the village should know he saved the boy's life. Then they would see Sheft as I do, and change their minds about him."

Her father shook his head sadly. "They wouldn't believe it, Mariat. They're too far gone in hate. Your mother—and Riah too—always said this hatred came from fear. But I think it's much worse than that. In order to thrive, evil must be fed, and that's not done out of fear. For his own good, Sheft is better off in Ullar-Sent."

She had no answer to that, and Moro stood up. "Come home as soon as Tarn returns."

She reached up to hug him. "I love you, Daddy." He smiled back at her as he rode away.

Leaving him was going to hurt, both him and herself, more than she had thought.

It was mid-afternoon, and she had just scrubbed the carrots she was going to use for dinner, when Sheft woke. His forehead was still warmer than it should be, but at least he could sit up, cross-legged on the mattress. He looked around and sniffed the spring air that came through the open door. "I feel like a man pulled out of the grave."

She smiled at him fondly. "And that's exactly what you look like. You should see your hair."

With a wry smile he ran his fingers through it, with little effect.

"Here, let me do that." She pulled a comb out of her pack and sat on the mattress beside him. "Bend your head down a little." He did, and she worked the comb through his tousled, pale hair.

"Ow."

"Sorry." She worked in silence for a moment, then

drew back to view him. "I think I liked you better the other way."

Obligingly, he messed his hair up.

"Stop that! I was only teasing." She plied the comb again. "There, that's better." They faced each other, and she was acutely aware that only the crack between the mattresses separated them. She looked away.

"There's soot and dried blood all over your pants," she said. "Lie back. I washed the top half of you yesterday, now I should do the bottom half." She brought a cloth and a basin of warm water and knelt beside him.

"I'll do it," he murmured, fumbling one-handedly at the tie at his waistband. "Just go and finish making dinner."

"Sweetheart, you'll pull on those stitches. Let me."

For a moment he resisted, but then took a position partly on his left side, an elbow crooked under his head. A flush crept up his neck as she removed his pants and small-cloth.

At the sight of him her throat swelled, as did the warm place between her legs.

He slid the elbow under his head over his eyes. "Sorry, Mariat," he said in a low voice. "I guess it's obvious what I want to do."

It was. Very. A little breathless, a little shaken by how much she loved him, she cupped her hand over that part of him. "After we're wed, sweetheart," she whispered. "After those stitches come out."

Under the shadow of his arm, he swallowed and nodded.

Knowing what she was doing to him and trying not to, she washed him as matter-of-factly as she could, but her hands were heavy with tenderness. She attempted to concentrate on cleaning off the blood, on rinsing out the washcloth, on commenting to herself that his hair down here was as pale as that on his head, but she was failing. The muscles of his legs felt solid as she rubbed soap over them, and her whole body wanted to press against his.

The hand at his waist tightened into a fist. *When we're wed, beloved. When we're wed.* For both their sakes she finished quickly, and he was soon wearing a clean small-cloth and pants. When she came back to his side after emptying the basin, he turned and gazed at her with his heart in his eyes.

She caressed the side of his face. "You covered me up in the night." She smiled at the thought of him leaning over her and tucking the blanket around her. "That was nice."

He sat up, took her hand, and with lowered eyes traced the outline with one finger, moving it slowly between each of hers. She felt what he was doing all over her skin. "I hope it won't be long," he said, "until I can do other nice things for you in the night." His voice was light and teasing, but when he raised that silver gaze to her, she knew what troubled him.

"I've never—been with anyone—either," she admitted.

His diffidence drained away, and he was seeing only her. He pulled her close. His arms were strong, his kiss urgent and deep. The feel of his chest against hers, of his bare shoulders under her hands, sent a hot stroke of desire through her.

They drew back and he simply looked at her. But lines of pain between his eyebrows seemed to express a love so strong and so vulnerable it hurt. Tears stung, for her longing for him was almost more than she could bear. "Beloved," she whispered.

He squeezed her hand, and not taking his eyes from her, sank back. They both knew if they were to go anywhere the day after tomorrow, he'd have to regain his strength. She covered him with the blanket, and with a sigh he closed his eyes.

My dearest love, she thought to him.

Now it was her turn to wash. She climbed to her feet and emptied and refilled the basin. After making herself presentable, she hauled Tarn's mattress back into his room.

A good thing too, because in the middle of preparing supper, she heard the creak and rumble of a cart, and Tarn came through the door. He seemed taken aback to see her. Then his eyes fastened on Sheft—clean, bandaged, and asleep on the floor.

So he had lived. Again the boy had lived.

Apparently it was more important to Ul, Tarn thought bitterly, that one foreigner survive than an entire village be saved. But if he had learned anything in his life, it was to avoid rushing into judgment, especially of the gods. Perhaps events were still unfolding, and he should wait and watch.

"You may go home now, Mariat," he said. "Thank you for what you've done here."

Instead of murmuring some modest response, she lifted her chin at him and her eyes flashed. "Where were you?"

Her attitude first startled, then angered him. She had no business questioning him, and he answered curtly. "In Ferce. Replacing the cart."

This explanation plainly did not suit her, but because she was Moro's daughter, he summoned up the patience to keep matters within the grasp of her experience. "Mariat, you are young and probably can't understand why I left him. No doubt it seemed heartless to you, but you're not aware how grave the situation has gotten in At-Wysher. Because of this, I've asked Sheft to leave. It's best for everyone."

She stood there stiffly. "He saved Oris. He took the brunt of the field tools spilling out of the kunta-kart."

He sighed. "Whatever he says happened, Sheft still should have died. It was the will of Ul, and you pulled him back. Now he'll be a cripple and a burden on his family up north."

"He won't be a cripple! He'll be scarred, and might not have full use of his shoulder, but that's all."

"I know you meant well, Mariat, but I saw the injuries. Think on what have you done. Who will hire someone like him, afflicted and now maimed? How will he make his way in the world? It would have been better to leave him in the hands of the god."

"Your god. Not mine."

He shook his head. She would never understand the great vision. It was beyond her comprehension what he had been trying to do, how he and the council had struggled to take the small but constant steps toward the light, to keep the flame of reason burning in the face of stubborn ignorance. Her god or goddess—whatever—was a small deity. Her Rulve was a god fit only for women, a god concerned with family matters, with individual happiness, with the well-being of girls who confused pity for love. Ul was a different matter altogether.

"Mariat, I'm sorry you can't grasp what I tried to do. Now you had best be off, before dark."

Her face hardened into an unbecoming stubbornness. "I would like to stay."

"We're short a mattress. I saw you burned one in the yard, rather than clean it."

She looked at Sheft, then back at him, and her face

softened into a more suitable expression for a young unmarried woman. "Tarn, please. I can sleep on the chair. My father has given me permission to stay. It will do no harm, and I can finish making supper. Then in the morning I'll prepare a hot breakfast."

Whatever she was cooking smelled quite good. He had lingered too long with Wyla, and in his haste to get home before dark, had missed lunch. If he didn't allow her to stay, Moro and Etane might not understand. As a council elder already none too popular, he could ill afford to alienate what was left of his friends. "All right, Mariat. As you say, it can do no harm."

After dinner Mariat served him a glass of wine, which was welcome indeed, and which he savored in front of the fire. Meanwhile she tidied up the kitchen. A good girl, but he must speak to Moro about that streak of impertinence.

He watched her check Sheft's bandage and feel his forehead, while the boy slept on. The wine made him pleasantly drowsy, and soon after finishing it, he retired. He lay on his cool, plumped up pillow and thought about the spring plowing. It could come as early as next week. Wyla's two boys would help out. They could bring their own blankets and sleep in the loft. If Sheft wasn't in any shape to leave by then, he could finish recuperating in the barn. He should get used to that in any case, since he was unlikely to find better lodgings during his journey up north.

A vague unease brushed against him as he remembered his ride through the village that afternoon. The unusually quiet street. Sokol in front of the butcher's shed, arms crossed over his stained leather apron, watching him. Rom glancing up from the forge, unsmiling, holding his eyes just a little too long.

No matter. The cause of their ire would soon be gone. The curtain at the partly open window stirred in a damp, intermittent breeze. A storm gathering... When was the roof due to be re-thatched?

The sky over the Riftwood flickered. Far off, thunder muttered. The wind died down and left the tight-budded branches still. Clouds swelled at the edge of the storm and crept with deadly purpose over the stars.

Sweet tension pulsed through Sheft's dreams, the vivid touch of her hands on his body. They faded, replaced by a distant but growing warning. His back simmering, Sheft stirred in a hot and troubled sleep. It vied with pain and fever and, exhausted, he groped for ice.

CHAPTER 29

THE BLACK MOON OF SEED

Gusts of wind from the coming storm tugged at Parduka's red robe as she stood in the doorway of the House of Ele. It was the night of Seed's dark moon. The moon that month after month was never seen, its existence never suspected in the day-lit sky, until the rare occasions when its silent, shocking power emerged to gnaw at the noonday sun. The priestess remembered the eclipse from years ago, when Ele's black circle swallowed Ul's insipid face, and made of it a tunnel into the night.

The last man entered, and Parduka pushed the heavy doors shut against the stiffening wind. No need to use the back door any longer, no need to hide. Ele was about to give them her official blessing. After the men shook the raindrops off their waxed wool cloaks, she called them to attention. "Are you ready," she asked them, "to make your solemn pledge to the goddess?"

Their answers growled in the shadows. "We are."

She led them through the dim hall and into the Chamber of Ele. Flashes of light from the fire pit leaped over the stone walls, illuminating the charcoal drawings of spiraled moons and big-bellied animals with staring eyes. The men gathered in front of the goddess and looked up at her while shadows jumped in and out of the hollows of their faces.

Towering over their heads, the Red Mother squatted on her pedestal, her arms crossed under pendulous breasts. Her square body, carved from pale red marble, crawled with maroon veins. She stared straight ahead, obsidian stones glittering in her eye-pits. A ladder leaned against the pedestal, ending directly beneath the long, pursed mouth. Above her head, wind rushed over the black smoke-hole in the roof.

Silent, they all knelt before the goddess while Parduka touched the ground with palms and forehead. From the pot beside her, she withdrew a handful of the gritty mixture of holy herbs and incense and threw it onto the fire. The flames leaped, then sent out a cloud of pungent smoke. She did this twice more, until the fire drooped low and a red, twisting haze enveloped them all.

"Breathe in now, all you servants of Ele. Purify yourselves while I call to our goddess." The smell spiraled into her head and seemed to make the room throb like the inside of a hot, beating heart. "Come, O Ele." She heard herself pronounce the familiar words, but they seemed to come from some other source. "Red Mother, All-Mother, hear me. We come to do your will. We come to obey your command."

Ele's veins pulsed in the light. The obsidian eye-stones seemed to shift their blank gaze and look down at them.

A chill of awe skittered down Parduka's back. At last. After all this time, at last the goddess heard her. Her voice cut through the incense haze. "We stand ready to pledge our oaths, to restore your sacred Rites. Form us this night into your holy circle."

Rapt, she raised open hands to her, and it seemed the Red Mother nodded. As if in a dream, Parduka climbed the ladder. The distance between her dry lips and Ele's tubular mouth lessened, until Parduka found the narrow opening to the will of the Mother. She thrust her tongue deeply inside, and a thrill of power slipped up its length. Lightning flashed over the smoke-hole, and Ele's eyes flickered. Parduka drew back, her mouth tasting of ancient stone, and laid both hands on Ele's planed cheeks. The crack and rumble of thunder almost drowned out her words.

"Great Goddess, on this sacred night, I pledge myself to your true Rites. I do this for your glory, that your full power might be restored." Now she must pronounce the rest of the vow, the curse that Ele would throw down upon her if she did not fulfill her promise. A vision of her mother's last days flashed before her—the paralyzed body, the horrible contortion in the left side of her face, the smoldering eyes completely aware to the end. "I take this vow, Ele, under pain of the numbing stroke." Her palms sweaty, she turned away and descended.

The figure of Rom rose up in the haze. Like a man in a trance, he climbed to the mouth of Ele. He performed the ritual kiss, and then, in a low but steady voice, he too vowed.

"I pledge myself to the restored Rites, under pain of public disgrace. I do this out of my duty to protect all those who live in At-Wysher Village." Lightning flashed, and his form leaped into clarity. A roll of thunder followed him, now a faceless shadow, back to his place.

Blinor was next. "May my mill burn to the ground," he growled, "my entire livelihood destroyed, if I do not lift my hand against abomination and filth."

His voice catching, young Temo cried out, "Because my father was pulled down by the evil one, I commit myself to perform these Rites. If I do not, may I never engender a son!"

Rain cascaded down. It drummed on the roof and spilled through the smoke-hole as each man climbed up to express the reason for his vow and the curse that would ensure his faithfulness to it. On this holy night, they kissed the mouth of the goddess, while her stone eyes flashed and her great body seemed to shudder with cracks of thunder.

"Under pain of madness," Sokol the butcher shouted against the noise of the storm, "I pledge myself. No longer will the foreigner paw at our women."

Olan's voice shook, and unshed tears stood in his eyes. "I vow to obey you, Ele, and you may take my daughter if I don't. I beg—oh great goddess, hear me!—that you will help her walk again."

Delo managed to climb the ladder, but seemed so agitated he almost missed a rung. "I will return to the old ways," he quavered, "for the good of all the villagers. Or, or let"—Parduka felt a stab of panic at his hesitation—"let my cattle perish, down to the last animal."

Greak's neighbors came next, then Gwin as the last. "I call down upon myself the wasting disease," he cried in a loud voice, "if I don't expel the foreigner who corrupts innocent children."

Finally all stood before Ele, vowed and committed. With a mutter of thunder, the storm rolled into the deadlands, and a few drops of water fell from the smoke-hole, hissing as they hit the dying flames.

They quickly elected Rom as Holdman. "Let us go, then," Parduka said, "and may Ele's blessing, or Ele's curse, fall upon us."

In silence, everyone threw on their black cloaks, processed through the great doors, and slipped into a dripping night. Lightning glittered over the Riftwood, signaling another storm to come. Two wagons, each with its lantern, awaited them. Delo's son Gede sat at one and Voy at the other. Oiled leather covered several unlit torches, the sacred drum and the pebble-gourd.

Parduka glanced up at Voy. With a grin, he patted the empty pouch at his side. Good. The carved hay-mouse had been set in place. In silence everyone climbed on the boards and pulled up their hoods, and the wagons headed down the Mill Road.

As they disappeared into the darkness, none looked behind them to see the sudden light of a lantern bloom in the house of the Holdman. The figure of Dorik appeared at the door, stared after the retreating wagons, then rushed across the road to Cloor's house. He was admitted just as the second storm descended upon the empty street.

A loud clap of thunder brought Moro half-awake, and he smiled into his pillow. Ane would surely snuggle close at that one! But then he remembered. Even now rain was muddying her grave in the deadlands.

He rolled over in his empty bed and stared at the ceiling, and the ache of her absence was more than he could bear. When the storm finally passed into the east, he wiped his eyes, got up, and looked out the rain-streaked window. Lights wavered at the end of the lane. What was this? He ran to the door and peered out. Two wagons, filled with hooded figures, were making their way down the overgrown track which was all that remained here of the Mill Road.

That wasn't right. Nothing lay in that direction except Tarn's house and—he realized with a drop of his heart—Mariat was spending the night there.

He threw on some clothes and ran to the barn for Surilla. The plow-horse was old, but big, and Moro thought he might need something that looked more intimidating than his small Skaileg pony. Without stopping to saddle her, he rode the mare out of the barn, tightly clutching her mane. "Ista!" He urged her forward, and the big horse plodded down the lane. "As!" he directed, and they turned right, down the dark road as fast as Surilla could move. Half-way toward his destination he realized he had forgotten a torch, and that this very night was the dark moon of Seed.

Sometime during the night, Mariat abandoned the nodding chair and lay on a blanket next to Sheft. Without a mattress, the floor was uncomfortable, but she was too tired to be more than dimly aware of a passing thunderstorm.

A groan, and Sheft moving beside her, brought her awake. Was he in pain? She lifted her head. A sudden banging on the door stopped her heart, and then set it pounding. Oh God, the beetle-man!

"Open!" a loud but human voice called out. "Tarn, open!"

Fear washed over her momentary relief. What was happening? She jumped to her feet as Tarn stumbled past her in the dark. The panels thudded again, and Sheft, with a sharp in-breath of pain, reached for his boots.

"What in Ele's name is this?" Tarn shouted.

"Council business. Unbar the door!"

Mariat recognized Rom's voice, but it was strained and hoarse.

Sheft climbed to his feet and looked at her over his shoulder. "Get up in the loft! Quick!"

But it was too late. Tarn was already lifting the bar as she darted into the shadows at the back of the house. A crowd of black-cloaked figures surged into the kitchen, bringing in a damp breeze and the glare of several torches. Parduka stood in their midst. Her gaze fastened on Sheft, and a triumphant gleam lit up her eyes. She flung aside her cloak, to reveal the ceremonial red robe.

Sheft's eyes must have been reflecting the light, because the crowd around her hesitated.

"What's the matter with all of you?" Parduka pushed forward, raised her torch to better illuminate him, then threw back her head and laughed. "Ele has delivered him up to us! See that bandage? See those feverish eyes? There'll be no sorcery out of him tonight."

"What nonsense is this?" Tarn demanded. "Who's in charge here?"

"Never you mind," a voice growled, and two men grabbed his arms.

"A demon has clawed him!" The figure next to Parduka sounded close to hysteria. "The foreigner's own demon turned on him, and now—now it's loose." He looked wildly around the room, which was alive with jumping shadows from the torches. "Loose in this house!"

"Don't be a fool." the priestess said. "He had some kind of accident at the field-burn."

"Yes!" Mariat screamed. "He saved—" Her voice ended in a gurgle as someone from behind clapped a hand over her mouth.

Amidst the clamor in the kitchen, the man dragged her backward, further into the shadows. She felt his lips moving close to her ear. "Be quiet! Don't say another word."

She tried to pull away from him, but his strong fingers dug into her upper arm.

Sheft had moved slightly to the side, and she knew he was trying to block the crowd's view of her. Everyone else seemed too intent to notice her in the shadows. One of the figures pointed a quavering finger at Sheft's toltyr. "Priestess! What's that around his neck?"

Parduka approached cautiously and peered at the pendant. "By all the gods," she hissed. "It's a sorcerer's amulet."

"No," Sheft cried. "It's nothing like that!"

She didn't even look at him, but called to someone in the crowd behind her. "Cut it off him!"

A man—Mariat recognized the burly form of the butcher Sokol—shouldered forward. He pulled out a large knife and held it in front of Sheft. With a sudden movement, he jabbed the blade toward his face. Sheft flinched and the butcher laughed. "Not so brave now, are you? Now that you're dealing with men, and not my helpless daughter."

"What are you talking about? I didn't do anything to your daughter."

Sokol grabbed the cord and pulled Sheft close to his face. "We don't need to hear your lies," he grated. In one rough move, he cut the braided leather and pushed Sheft away from him. The toltyr clattered to the floor and Sokol kicked it toward the hearth. Sheft's head turned to follow it.

"He's powerless now," the priestess pronounced. "Take him outside!"

A chill raced down Mariat's arms. Was that true? Did he have no way now to use ice in his defense? And even with it, what could he do against so many? There must be close to a dozen people in the room.

"Stop!" Tarn shouted, struggling against the men that held him. "I demand you—"

His words were drowned out as the others shoved the table and benches aside and rushed forward. They surged around Sheft, pale-haired and bandaged in the midst of the swirling black cloaks, and dragged him out the door.

One arm was held behind her, but with the other she clawed at the hand clamped over her mouth. The man pulled her into the darkness of Tarn's empty bedroom, where he jerked her around to face him.

It was Gwin. "Why in Ele's name are you here?" he asked.

"I came to help Sheft," she retorted, wiping her mouth on her sleeve. "He was wounded. He saved—"

"Forget him! After tonight you'll never see him again." He threw back his hood and grasped her upper arms. "Our village needs you, Mariat. It needs the healer you are. *I* need you!"

Her heart froze, for she heard only one thing. "What do mean I'll never see him again?"

"You weren't supposed to be here. You were supposed to be safe at home. But after this is all over, I promise you—"

"Where are they taking him? Gwin, what are they—?"

"It's for good of the village, Mariat. Please believe me."

She clutched the front of his black robe. "What do you mean? Stop them! Leave us alone!"

In the kitchen behind her Tarn was shouting. "I demand to know who's in charge! Where's Dorik?" The sound of a scuffle broke out, interspersed with oaths and grunts.

Gwin spoke over the noise. "Mariat, listen to me. I want you to be my wife. As Holdman, my father will appoint you our priestess, our healer. You will replace Parduka, and both the House of Ele and the Council House will be in our family's control. I'll build you a hospice for the sick. Together we'll restore Ele's full rule and return at last to our roots."

She barely heard him. "He's hurt, Gwin! Please, I beg for your help."

"Mariat, I love you. I know this isn't the right place or time to tell you that. God, I wanted this to be so different!"

His grip on her weakened and she twisted away, but he caught her just outside the doorway. In the kitchen, Tarn was grabbing at the men clustered at the door. She ignored them, her eyes searching frantically for a glimpse of Sheft as she struggled with Gwin. One of the black-cloaks who had gone outside pushed his way back into the house.

"Tarn!" the man called. "It's Rom. Stop fighting this. We've got custody of the foreigner, and no one else will be hurt."

Panting, Tarn stilled and the men let go of him. "What in Ul's name are you doing? Who *are* these people?" He looked at the hooded figures and the torches as if seeing them for the first time, then put his fist to his mouth. "Oh god Ul, it's the Rites. The restored Rites. Oh god, Rom, how could you do this?"

"We've all agreed." Rom flung out an arm to include the entire group. "It was our decision, and according to the will of Ele. We tried to warn you, but you wouldn't listen. Nothing can save your son now."

At these words, the fear that had been roiling in Mariat's stomach turned into an icy lump.

"But he's not—" Tarn began.

A cry came from outside. "A wagon's coming!"

Everyone in the kitchen rushed toward the door. One of the men shoved Tarn roughly out of his way. He stumbled and fell, hitting his head against the wooden bench. He sat there, dazed, as the others ran from the house. Gwin pulled Mariat into the kitchen and stopped in the shadow of the half-open front door.

Held tightly against him, she could see part of the yard through the narrow crack between the door and the frame. Men with torches rushed about, but she hardly saw them, for she caught sight of Sheft.

Delo's son Gede and Asher, one of Greak's neighbors, held him firmly between them. The night breeze ruffled his hair and stirred the ends of the bandage strips. He wore no shirt, and even though he stood erect, she could see he was shivering. Was it with fever, or with the cold, or with the same terror that squeezed her own heart?

Two empty wagons stood in the wet yard, and a third had just splashed through a puddle and came to a halt. Its oil lantern illuminated the grim faces of Dorik and Cloor. The crowd of black-cloaks, holding their torches high, confronted the new arrivals.

The two elders in the wagon stood up, commanding figures in the midst of chaos, and then, as a further reinforcement, the great hulk of Surilla pulled in beside them. Her father had come to help.

Three big men, atop a wagon and a great horse, towered over the crowd. Mariat slumped in relief. Surely they would stop this madness!

CHAPTER 30

EVIDENCE OF EVIL

"None of you have any business here," Dorik shouted. "In the name of the Council of At-Wysher, I order you back to your homes!"

"We take no orders from you!" Sokol bellowed, and he pulled the long knife from his belt.

Parduka clapped a restraining hand on his arm, and addressed the Holdman. "We are here at the command of Ele. We are vowed to her, and walk under her blessing, for on this night we restore her holy Rites."

"You have no authority to do that," Dorik retorted.

"Don't preach to me about authority! The council has thrown its authority away. It has allowed the Groper to crawl into our streets. It has done nothing about a foreigner who commits one crime after another. These men here are the new council, and Rom is our Holdman. That criminal"—she pointed at Sheft—"is under our jurisdiction now, and you have nothing to say about it!"

The crowd shouted agreement, but Dorik thundered over them. "By Ele's eyes! We told you—Gwin, Blinor, we told all of you. Show us proof of these crimes, proof of what you claim he's done, and then we'll take action. There was no proof. There *is* no proof. Without it, you will all be subject to arrest!" He turned to Rom. "You've proven yourself a traitor and a liar. But you were once a man of integrity. Disperse this new council of yours before it breaks the law."

Rom placed his hands on his hips. "We make the laws now."

"You don't. Get into that wagon and go home." Dorik raised his eyes and glared at the crowd. "Every last one of you!"

"No!" Sokol shouted. Raising his knife, he rushed forward, followed by several men.

Through the uproar her father's voice rang out. "Ista, Surilla!" The great horse plowed directly into the oncoming black-cloaks, sending them yelling and scrambling out of her way.

Except Sokol. He dodged aside, grabbed Moro's leg, and dragged him off the horse's back. Mariat watched in horror as her father fell heavily to the muddy ground. He lay there, groaning and holding his arm.

"Let me go to him!" She kicked at Gwin's ankles, but his grip on her only tightened.

"Stop it!" he ordered. "I'm trying to keep you from being hurt."

Outside, two of the black-cloaked figures restrained Dorik's horse, others stood threateningly around his wagon, and two more tied Surilla to the hitching post.

"For that attack, Moro," Rom said, "I take possession of your horse. From now on, it will be used for council business." He watched coldly while Mariat's father, in obvious pain, made his way to the Holdman's vehicle. Cloor helped him climb into the back.

Pushing men aside, the priestess strode up to Dorik. "All this time you refused to listen to us. You refused to acknowledge the bribery, the assault, the public brawling. Even when his atrocities escalated, even when they involved women and children, you did not listen. So on this night we take matters into our own hands." The men around her nodded, and some raised their fists. "On this night, we charge the foreigner with the ultimate crime."

"What ultimate crime?" Sheft cried out to her. "I didn't do any of those things!"

The priestess ignored him and continued to address Dorik. "Perhaps you think that even though his actions may be heinous, they affected only the man assaulted, the child molested, the woman raped." She raised her voice. "But sacrilege against the *goddess*, against the Red Mother who protects us all—that is a crime that strikes at the very root of our community. It deserves death!"

Stunned, Mariat stopped struggling against Gwin. Death? How could they— A sickening lump formed in her stomach as the crowd outside yelled its assent.

With the two men holding him fast, Sheft strained toward the priestess. "But I've never even *seen* the goddess! How could I commit a sacrilege against her?"

Parduka whirled to face him. "You admit your disdain of Ele! Not once have you entered her House. Not once bowed to her power. Out of your own mouth, you condemn yourself!"

"Now wait a—" Dorik began, but angry voices rang out:

"Because of what he did, we all have suffered!"

"Unless he's punished, Ele won't protect us!"

The crowd roiled around the Holdman's wagon, rocking it back and forth, until he was forced to sit down.

"The foreigner is guilty of sacrilege!" the priestess cried. "Sacrilege that arose from a lifetime of evil, of secret sins and corruption!"

"Prove it!" Dorik shouted.

"The proof stands in front of you! There, in the eyes of a foreigner you allowed to run amok. But you won't accept it. You have never accepted it. Yet Ele is merciful even to the stubbornly ignorant. She will provide clear evidence that even you can't refute."

"Then produce it," Dorik stated. "Here and now."

Rom pushed his way through the crowd. Hands at his hips, he looked up at the Holdman. "We all want to see justice done. So let's approach this logically. The priestess claims proof of sacrilege is present on this property. Half my men will search the house, with Tarn as witness. The other half will go to the barn with Cloor. You and I will stay here with the wagons to make sure all is done properly. If my men don't find anything that incriminates the foreigner, we'll leave."

Dorik glared down at the blacksmith, then at the figures that surrounded his horse and wagon. Clearly reluctant, he nodded.

Rom formed the men into two groups, and they rushed off in opposite directions. "Don't overlook the root cellar!" Parduka called after the ones heading toward the house.

Gwin pulled Mariat back into the shadows behind the door as black-cloaks clambered past them. One man banged cupboards open in the kitchen, another pounded up the ladder into the loft, and a third kicked the rug aside and hauled open the trap-door to the root cellar. Tarn, an ugly bruise on his forehead, sank into his nodding chair. He watched numbly while men he had grown up with ransacked his house.

Voy rushed in and spied them behind the door. "Ele's eyes!" he cried to Gwin. "What's *she* doing here?"

A plate shattered. Gwin turned, his grip loosened for an instant, and Mariat broke away. He snatched at her arm, but she twisted out of his reach, fled into the yard, and ran to Sheft. With Gede and Asher holding his upper arms, he stood with both hands clenched, and to her horror she saw that red had seeped through the bandage over his left shoulder. From the tautness in his body, she knew he was struggling to keep the stain from spreading. She grabbed his fist, which was ice-cold and trembling. "Oh, Sheft! They've hurt you! Oh God Rulve—"

Gwin wrenched her around to face him. Fury took hold of her. "Don't touch me, you filthy hypocrite!" She clawed at him, kicked and punched. "You make me sick! You filthy bastard! You come to my house with Oris while—"

"Stop!" Sheft cried. "Mariat, stop." The men were gripping his arms and he couldn't reach out to her, but she could see how much he wanted to. "Go to your father. Please. Go home with him right now."

"I won't!" She took a sobbing breath. "I won't leave you."

"You'll get hurt," he said in a voice ragged with strain. "I can't let that happen."

"I'm staying," she choked out.

His silver eyes gazed into hers. Liquid with anguish, they reflected a long and painful foreknowledge of their parting. "If you care for me," he pleaded, "if you care for me as I do for you, go now. It will be"—he swallowed—"easier for me, Mariat."

She heard what his whole body expressed: *I have to leave you, but will always love you.* She wanted to throw her arms around him, kiss the tender indentation at the base of his throat, but the tick in his jaw told her that would only make it worse for him.

Sheft tore his look away from her and transferred it to Gwin. Her own eyes were blurred with tears so she couldn't see what Gwin saw, but the man sucked in a breath and dug his fingers into her shoulders.

"Get her out of here," Sheft said. "Make sure she's safe. Then do what you came to do."

Possessively, Gwin pulled her against himself. "Her presence here was never part of my plan."

"I know."

His face flushed, Gwin addressed the two men holding Sheft. "She's under his influence right now and doesn't know what she's saying. But, thanks be to Ele, what we do here tonight will break that spell."

"There's no *spell!*" she screamed. "Gede, this is wrong. Asher, please listen—"

Gwin shoved her toward Gede, who dragged her away. She caught sight of Rom, standing with arms folded next to the priestess. "Rom! Listen to me! Sheft saved Oris. At the field-burn. Sheft is wounded because he saved your son."

The blacksmith's face turned red with anger. "How dare you bring an innocent child into this! How dare you bring my *son* into this!"

Gede pulled her through a world that had gone insane. She screamed out the truth, and no one heard it. Men with sense were shouted down by those who had lost every vestige of it. They were trying to make a criminal out of a man who'd risked his life to save a little boy.

Her guard thrust her onto the wagon seat beside tight-lipped Dorik just as a whoop of triumph came from the doorstep of the house. "A book of magery! A book of obscene magery!" Blinor threw the *Tajemnika* onto the ground in front of Dorik's wagon.

"It's only a book of tales!" Sheft cried. "One glance will tell you that."

One of the men whirled and punched him in the stomach. "Shut yer mouth!" He turned to the others. "Thinks he's better'n us 'cuz he can read."

Sheft, held by his two guards, bent over with a groan. Mariat flinched and grabbed Dorik's knee. "You've got to stop—!"

"Look at this, Dorik!" Delo waddled out of the house, gingerly holding the toltyr by its cord. "A sorcerer's amulet. We had to cut it off him." He flung it on top of the book.

"Here are poisons and evil potions," a third man bellowed. He dumped her basket of medicines and salves into the mud.

"No!" Mariat jumped up. "Those are mine!" But with all the noise, no one heard her except Dorik, who pushed her down onto the seat.

"Use your head!" he growled. "How will it help him if they turn on you?"

"See here, priestess," Olan called out excitedly. Holding his torch high, he pointed to the soggy remains of the mattress.

Parduka strode toward it and peered at it. "By Ele's sacred eyes. This was once a straw man. See, everyone, this bit of charred fabric? He formed an effigy, to curse and then burn!" She ran her dark eyes grimly over the crowd. "It was meant to be one of us."

Several men, aghast, poked through the mess with the toes of their boots, as if they searched for something of themselves in it.

"It's a mattress, for God's sake," Sheft cried. He swayed slightly, looking dazed.

"Sure it is," one of the men said with a sneer. "We all burn mattresses in the middle of the night."

"A box!" a man howled, rushing into the yard. "A locked wooden box! I found it under the bed." He pounded on it with a rock, then yelled when he mashed one of his fingers as well as the lock.

Another figure snatched the box away. It fell open, and a small mirror dropped to the ground. "Sorcery!" he exclaimed. He shattered the mirror under his heel. The first man grabbed Olan's torch and ignited the box. Hooting and waving his arms, he danced around it as it burned.

"Look!" Sokol stood triumphantly on the doorstep, holding up Sheft's jacket. "Made of sheepskin. By Ele, how appropriate! Let's put it on him."

Laughing, a group of men followed Sokol to where Sheft stood. They forced him to his knees, wrenched his arms back, and roughly stuffed them into the sleeves.

Oh God, his injuries! Across the distance between them, Mariat saw Sheft's face contort. She did not wince away, but felt what they did to him in her own body.

They walked away when they were done, leaving him on his hands and knees, taking shuddering breaths.

At least, she wailed to herself, he had a coat now. It would keep him warm. Oh God, at least it would protect the bandage and cushion his broken rib.

Anguish filled her throat, so thick she could hardly swallow. Her beloved was innocent. He bore wounds that would have fallen on someone else. Oh Rulve, he could barely stand, yet had to bear the weight of this immense, inconceivable hatred. She knew the men who were acting with such cruelty, had known them all her life. They were good men, husbands and fathers, hard workers; yet in the darkness of this night they had become demons.

A chill gathered in the small of her back. She looked into the dark beyond the torchlight. The leading edge of something she could not even begin to understand seemed to be stealing out of the night. An appalling evil, implacable and insidious, was creeping into their lives like—her arms prickled—the Groper itself.

Voy came running out of the house, waving a bundle in the air. "I found this, his cloak for the Rites. I claim it, and demand to join you tonight as your tenth man!"

Parduka looked up from the remains of the straw mattress. "Do you vow?"

"Sure do." He looked around with a grin. "And if I go back on my word, may I choke on my next gulp of ale." Voy donned the cloak, and the men around him chuckled and clapped him on the back.

A yell turned Mariat's head towards the barn. Gwin and several others, including a grim-looking Cloor, strode out. Gwin held a large wooden box in his hands, which rattled as he came forward. He threw its contents onto the ground in front of Sheft. "Are these your carvings?"

Beside her, Dorik stood to get a better view.

Still kneeling on the ground, Sheft lifted his head and glanced at the pile, a jumble of wood in the shadows. He nodded.

Parduka swooped onto the carvings, snatched one up, and stared at it, grimacing. "This was made for *children*!" she cried. "For innocent children!" She turned and threw the object to Dorik.

He caught it, and Mariat saw he held one of Sheft's toy mice. But it had been eerily altered. A black stone glittered in the eye socket.

"Turn it over," Parduka demanded.

He did so, stiffened, then sank onto the wagon seat.

The other side was even worse. The innocence of the toy's pink ears and painted nose was slashed by a chiseled-out hole.

"Sacrilege!" Parduka screamed. "Unspeakable abomination!"

Mariat looked up, confused. What were they talking about? Sheft would never disfigure one of his carvings like this, but how could the priestess think it had anything to do with sacrilege?

"What's going on?" Tarn asked from the doorstep. The crowd of men parted to let him make his way to the wagon. In the sudden silence, Dorik handed him the carving.

Tarn looked down at it. "Oh god. Oh god Ul." He dropped the figure and turned to clutch the wagon's sideboard.

Sheft climbed to his feet, his face lined with pain. As he got a better look at what lay on the ground, a flush burned on his cheekbones. "I never did that!" he exclaimed. "And if I did, why would I leave it lying around? Can't you see that someone planted it here?"

Parduka bent, seized the figure, and held it up in the torchlight. "This is proof of what Gwin saw. The foreigner used this object at the fair to lure a child into his clutches. A little boy not even from our village. He forced that child to watch while he gouged out the eye."

Someone in the crowd gasped.

"Such sacrilege deserves death!" the priestess shouted.

"I didn't," Sheft cried. "I didn't do—" His voice was drowned out by shouts.

"Blasphemer!"

"Filthy foreigner!"

Snarling and cursing, the crowd converged around Sheft.

But Parduka got there first. "Get back!" she cried, spreading her arms out in front of him. "We are restoring a sacred ceremony, not taking part in a slaughter!"

Rom joined her and shouted at the crowd. "We are the Council of At-Wysher and obedient servants of Ele. We must perform her Rites with proper procedure." He turned to Dorik. "Now leave us. We have our witness, and you have your proof. Leave us to do justice and the will of the goddess."

Cloor, his jaw tight, crossed the yard and climbed up beside Mariat. Dorik lowered himself onto the wagon seat. "None of you," he said heavily, "will ever forget what you've decided to do here. Your days and nights, and the days and nights of your children, will be cursed with it. When you've had your fill of blood and darkness, when you've returned to your senses, then come back to the council and we will try to repair this."

"We are the council now," Rom retorted, "and nothing we do here shames us or our children. We are upholding Ele's law and giving honor to the goddess who protects us. This is the beginning of a new time, a safer time, for everyone in our village."

Dorik ran his eyes over the group. Mariat knew what he saw: eleven determined men and one old woman, the recipient of ancient power. Stone-faced, they all met his gaze. He clicked to the horse and pulled the wagon around.

"No!" Mariat lunged over his legs to grab the reins. "He hasn't done anything wrong! Don't leave him here."

Cloor yanked her hands away. "Get in the back. Your father needs you." He pushed her off the bench, and she landed in a tangle of her skirt beside Moro on the wagon bed.

She scrambled to her knees and looked back. Torches illuminated the yard, where only last night she and her beloved had vanquished the beetle-man. His jacket open, Sheft struggled in the hands of his shadowy captors, while one of them waved the carving in front of his eyes. The figures shifted, a circle closed with terrible finality, and she could no longer see the side of his face or the gleam of his hair. A turn in the road hid the light.

This could not be happening. Their life together had

just begun. They were espoused. They were supposed to go on a journey together. She didn't realize tears were running down her face until she tasted them on her lips.

"Mariat," her father murmured, "don't look back. Let it be."

"Let it *be*?" she said in horror. "How can you even—"

"I know these people," Dorik said from the driver's seat. "In the morning they'll realize what they've done, and will come crawling back in regret." He shook his head slightly and sighed. "It could have been worse. What's one man, if the whole village is saved?"

A horrible apprehension clutched at her heart. "What do you mean? What are they going to do?"

Dorik stared steadily at the road ahead and did not answer. None of the men answered.

A sudden rattle, loud in the quiet night behind them, startled her. It became the rhythmic beat of a pebble-gourd. They drove on, and the sound behind her faded into the growing distance between her and her own heart.

CHAPTER 31

THE K'MEEN ARÛK

The wagon rattled away, and through a haze of pain, Sheft watched the pale oval of Mariat's face recede into the dark. The others crowded around him and blocked his view, but when he tried to see her once more, she was gone.

But she was safe, no thanks at all to his unforgivable lack of resolve. He should have sent her away two days ago, as soon as he realized she was in the house. He should have shouted at her until she left him. But he had not. He had clutched at a dream and forced her into a nightmare.

His guards held him as one of the black-cloaked figures kept thrusting the obscene toy in front of him. "Get that away from me," Sheft cried. "I had nothing to do with it."

The man backhanded him across the mouth, so hard Sheft's knees almost gave way. A realization hit him almost as harshly as the blow: it no longer mattered what he said or what he didn't do. A line had been crossed, and not one of his making. Shaking, he pulled up ice to keep his lip from bleeding.

"He can't walk far," one of them remarked.

"Put him on Moro's nag," Rom growled.

"Ele punished Moro by breaking his arm," someone

in the shadows said. "His family befriended this criminal, and now the son went and married a girl from Ferce."

"Moro isn't to blame," Gwin put in. "His whole family was bewitched. They are good, solid people at heart, and it's a shame what this foreigner did to them."

Gwin, Sheft realized, was trying to protect Mariat. In his own way, he cared about her, and that hurt. Or was it his own status he tried to protect? He didn't know, hadn't bothered to inform himself about what others wanted. Tarn's remembered face, creased with faint distaste, floated out of the dark: *"You are too wrapped up in yourself to notice anyone or anything else."*

The men pulled their hoods up and suddenly became unreal figures, chins and noses appearing and disappearing in the torch-light, casting crooked shadows that jumped from tall to short and back again. Two of the black-cloaks led Surilla forward. They shoved Sheft onto the big mare's back, a painful procedure that left him clutching the coarse mane with white-knuckled hands. The weather had changed and a cold wind fingered his hair. Shivering, he waited as the hooded figures took a position around him, their guttering torches level with his eyes. And then he saw it: the dark circle had been present all this time, and now it enclosed him.

Parduka pronounced the solemn invocation to Ele. The gourd rattled, shaking out its slow and deadly rhythm, and the group began their journey into the night. The restored Rites—and whatever they entailed—had begun.

High on the great horse, he rode completely exposed, with no hood to hide his hair, no crowd in which to lose himself. As the accused pervert who preyed on women, the monster who corrupted children, the heretic who trampled on their holiest rite, he was the sole prisoner of the torch-lit circle as it dragged him through the dark. Surilla plodded over the barren fields, every step jogging Sheft's broken rib. Ice reaction vied with dread, and at first he could not make out the terrain beyond the torchlight that dazzled his vision. The inner warning, which had been jangling for some time, suddenly shrilled loud and clear. With a jolt of terror, he knew exactly where they were going.

Oh God help me. Rulve, help me!

His plea went nowhere, only stayed on the surface of his fear like water pooling over rock-hard soil. He searched frantically for a means of escape. Surilla would respond to his vocal command, but not when the black-cloak had a firm hold on her lead. He envisioned himself sliding off her back and somehow dodging through the men who pressed closely around him. The thought of what that would do to his injuries rasped through his stomach like a thorny vine, but he had to try it.

He was gauging the distance to the ground when Blinor, close beside him, jammed his fist into his right side. Pain exploded, and he doubled over the horse's mane with a gasp.

"I'm watching you," the miller said. "Try something, filth, and I'll go after your lady-friend. Sort of like this, you know?" The big teeth shone in a leer as he ground his thumb into Sheft's side. "And I'll enjoy every minute of it."

Sheft swatted the hand away. "Leave her alone," he said through a now swollen lip. "She has nothing to do with any of this."

"Whether I leave her alone or not is entirely up to you."

They left the open field and wound through brush. Long, deep chills ran through him, like the sibilance of the gourd. He fumbled for the toltyr around his neck, but Sokol had cut it away. A sense of betrayal rose up like a bitter flood. Just as the toltyr was becoming part of him, just as he was beginning to think he might have a destiny, it had been wrenched away. He'd lost, not so much his mother's last gift or a pewter medallion that would give him courage, but the struggle to believe there was any meaning to his life.

The group came to a halt. Ice-reaction spun slowly inside his head, but he could make out, barely visible in the dark, the evil bulk of the K'meen Arûk. It crouched like a waiting predator. Two men dragged him off the horse and pulled his arms behind him, squeezing the gashes on his back into streaks of fire. They bound his wrists with a rope, hauled him toward the boulder where Parduka waited, then shoved him onto the ground and tied his ankles. He sat, each quick, short breath a stab of pain, and tried to his keep his back from rubbing against the rock. Silent figures gathered in a semi-circle in front of him, their dark eyes lit up like an encroaching pack of wolves. The fear that had been thrumming in his stomach climbed into his throat, swelling all the way.

Parduka stood over him, a hank of grey hair hanging over one cold eye. "Welcome, blasphemer, to the holy stone of Rûk." With her gesture, the crowd formed a line in front of him. She withdrew the ritual knife from her belt and handed it to the first cloaked figure.

His thumb testing the edge of the blade, the man looked down on him. With several swift moves, he pushed back his sleeve, cut his own arm, and smeared the blood in a rough swipe over Sheft's cheek and mouth. With a grim smile, he wiped the knife clean on the front of the sheepskin jacket and turned away.

The next black-cloak squatted in front of him and spit

in his face. He made the cut, rubbed the bloody wound into Sheft's hair, then pulled his jacket open and cleaned the knife on the cloth strips that held the bandage in place.

In turn the others came, black hoods looming above him, the knife glinting, red lines welling. Shadowed figures smeared their blood on his cheek, across his eyes, on his chest. He tasted it on his mouth, felt it drying cold in his hair, smelled it sickly-sweet all over him.

Sokol held the knife in front of Sheft's face, pulled his head back by the hair, then slowly wiped the blade along the side of his neck. Sheft stiffened, waiting for the sharp edge to turn, but instead the butcher kicked him, hard in the thigh.

"That's for my step-daughter Ubela," he said. "What Parduka will do is for me."

"Sokol," he croaked, "I never touched her."

Another vicious kick, this time in the ribs. He gasped, and bright dots scattered over his vision. When he could see again, the last man was handing the knife to Parduka.

"Position him over the rock," she commanded.

He bore down on his spirikai. Ice. He would need ice. More than he had, more than there was.

Hands jerked him upright, dragged him against the waist-high rock, and jammed his head sideways into the depression on top. A scummy film slimed against his cheek.

Someone behind him bent close to his ear, but spoke loudly enough for all to hear. "Lookey there, hayseed. Parduka's hands are shaking. Remember what happened at the Rites? Remember how the sheep screamed? How it kicked?"

Nervous laughter spattered through the crowd.

"You don't have to do this," Sheft said, his mouth

pressed against the rock. "Let me go, and you'll never see me again."

"You got that last part wrong," a voice growled. "It's you who'll never see again."

Their hands sought purchase against his stitched-up back as they pressed his chest and shoulders onto the rock. Every instinct screamed to slam ice into those that held him down, as he had with the beetle-man, but too much pain, too many vivid memories of the half-butchered sheep, shook his concentration.

The priestess raised her hand, and in it the sharp spoon glinted.

His heart skipped, then hammered. He called out in a shaking voice to the one who seemed closest to his own age. "Temo! Don't do this. It won't bring your father back."

"Shut your mouth," someone snarled, "or you'll lose your tongue as well."

Parduka leaned over him. He struggled to twist away, but many hands gripped him in an iron vise.

"Bring the light closer," Parduka directed. "Good. Steady now."

The serrated edge of the spoon filled his sight, growing larger as it approached, a lethal eclipse that would cut out all light. He strained to see something around it—a star, a flame, anything he could remember in the coming blackness.

Cold metal pressed at the corner of his right eye. Blind white terror seized him. He squeezed his eyes shut, tight and hard. *Rulve help me!* Clenching his jaw, tightening his bound hands into fists, he fought to constrict his spirikai.

Her strong fingers pried his eyelid open.

At the touch, his terror shattered. Ice splintered out

317

of his spirikai and he jammed it, hard, into Parduka's hand.

Sudden cold bit into her palm. Parduka jerked her hand away. It was numb. She couldn't feel her fingers. A memory flooded in: her mother's eyes widening, her face twisting. The old woman had emitted an animal cry and fell to the ground. She lay there stiffly, drool dribbling from the corner of her mouth.

Ele, no! Not the paralyzing stroke. Not now. Not here, in front of them all.

The icy chill crept up her wrist, and to her horror the spoon fell out of her useless fingers. Exclamations broke out around her.

"Again, priestess?" Sokol spat. "Another failure? Let me do it, if you can't." With his hand still pressed against the back of the foreigner's neck, he bent to sweep up the spoon.

It signified her power and he must not take it. With her left hand, Parduka snatched it away. "No, you fool! I have not failed. I will not." Under her cloak, she frantically rubbed her right hand against her thigh, and the warmth began flowing back.

It was not the paralyzing stroke. It was a sign. She had received a sign from Ele, who had stayed her hand. She looked at each of the faces, grotesque in the torchlight and surrounded by the dark. "At just this instant, Ele spoke to me! She spoke to me, and I trembled in her presence." Parduka brandished the holy instrument like a sword. "In the midst of her ancient Rites, she has issued a direct command."

Deep within, a crone's voice warned her: *"Do not touch him again."*

★

They held him down as an argument whirled over his head. Parduka's voice cut through it. "His eyes are diseased, as abhorrent to Ele as they are to us. On this night of all nights, they must not befoul the sacred bowl."

"What about our vows?" someone asked. "I don't want to lose all my cattle."

"What about the restored Rites?"

Parduka stepped forward, the edge of her sleeve sweeping over his hair. "They shall be made perfect, even more pleasing to Ele and more satisfying to Wask. The command of the goddess is this: allow Wask himself to pluck out the foreigner's eyes. At his leisure, throughout the night, let Wask feed on his flesh. It is Ele's justice. This sheep"—she prodded his shoulder with the spoon— "will be given completely into the beetle-man's will, for as long as it takes him to die."

"What about the tradition?" Sokol shouted. "It demands that we offer him, bound and blind, to Wask."

"But we can't wade across the river!" a frightened voice cried. "Look, it's risen from the storm. Oh, Ele, what are we going to do!"

"The Rites are failing!" someone wailed.

"They are not," Parduka stated firmly. "In her wisdom, in spite of storm and flood, Ele has provided the means to complete her Rites: Moro's horse. It will carry him across while we watch, safe on dry land."

Murmuring in relief, the men let go of him and stepped back. Awkward with hands and feet bound, Sheft dragged himself off the K'meen Arûk and slid to his knees. He pressed his forehead against the rock, hearing his own quick breaths, then seeing them in the cold air. Stones on the ground flashed bright in torch-flame, and he saw them too, focused on the way tiny crystals within them winked in the light. As booted feet milled around him, he stared at the stones, each different, each indescribably beautiful.

Only last night, the ice had been like a club he could wield, like a rock he could throw, but now it had been only a shard. Now the toltyr was gone, Mariat was gone, and he had no strength left. The pounding of his heart slowed, but the trembling went on as he slid into a red fog of pain and ice-reaction.

"No criminal should go seeing to the beetle-man," Sokol insisted. "It would be an insult."

"Let's get this over with!" Rom exclaimed. "Blindfold him, and that will fulfill the law."

"It is indeed Ele's express command," Parduka said.

The cloaked figures untied him, pulled him to his feet, and fastened a folded cloth tightly over his eyes. Hands dragged him stumbling back to Surilla. He was barely settled on her back when they jerked him into a prone position and tied his wrists under her neck. Someone fastened a rope around his ankles, then ran it under the mare's wide girth. When they were done, he was bound to the great horse, painfully stretched out and unable to lift his head more than a few inches off her mane. Boots scuffed as men gathered around him. Someone grabbed his hair and yanked his head up.

Parduka's strong voice addressed him. "With our blood upon you, go to Wask. With our curse upon you, go to the beetle-man. We give you to him so he may eat, and take away our transgressions before Ele."

His head was pulled so far back he could hardly swallow. Voices swelled around him, repeating the curse, naming his destiny; and their words struck like lashes.

The hand let go of his hair, and his forehead fell against the horse's neck. The gourd rattled, sudden and close. Someone grabbed the rope around his wrists and led Surilla forward. The big horse clopped along, and then hooves clattered over stones.

Everyone stopped. Surilla stamped nervously.

"Come, Wask." Parduka intoned.

Boom. He jumped at the sound of the drum, had not even realized it was present.

"Come, Meerghast."

Boom. Even expecting it, he still twitched.

"Come, Rûk."

Boom.

The drumbeat dissolved into the night. With a jerk, Surilla moved forward. The rustle of clothing and the creak of leather boots gave way to the sound of the Meera. It grew louder, sending dread running up his spine like a cold and bony finger. The circle dropped back, and the tension on the rope at his wrists fell away. The man leading Surilla must have let go. The big mare stood still, the rushing sound of water directly beneath him. The collective gaze of the crowd bored between his shoulder blades.

His heart thudded in his ears. The beetle-man's crawling face rose up in the darkness behind his eyes. *"The Riftwood awaits you. Death will swallow you."* Chill air from the massive cavern of the Riftwood directly ahead funneled down the back of his neck.

A torch whooshed behind him. Surilla screamed, jerked her head up, and lurched forward with a splash. The horse's thick neck dealt him a stunning blow to the left side of his face. Spears of light shot through his eye, his head spun, and he felt as if he were slipping sideways. He clung desperately to Surilla with his knees and forearms as the horse plowed into the river. Behind him, men shouted. Something hard hit his shoulder, a stone, then a hail of them. Surilla surged ahead. Her big muscles working, she plunged deeper into the Meera River.

He clung to Surilla as the water crept higher. The current swept past his fingers, wet the sleeves of his jacket. If the river was deeper here than it was upstream, if the mare was hit by a tumbling log, he would drown. Surilla churned ahead and images assailed him: of her falling, of water rushing over his head, of the sound of bubbles filling his ears. He couldn't breathe, couldn't see, couldn't get off her back.

The river began to fall away. He realized he'd been holding his breath and sucked in air. Stones dislodged under the big horse's hooves as she climbed into the shallows and heaved to the top of the embankment. She stood there a moment, shuddering.

His heart hammered. He was alone across the Meera River, in deepest night.

The mare shook herself, sending pain boring into his side, then trotted forward with a gait that threatened to rip open every stitch. He pulled his hands against her throat, hoping she would understand what he wanted. "Easy," he gasped. "Go easy, Surilla."

The horse slowed. Leaves crunched under her feet and branches brushed against his legs. With the blindfold tight across his eyes, all his senses funneled into the plodding gait, the fire on his back, the wet, rough rope biting into his wrists.

The bandage under his jacket clung wetly to him. Under the cloth, something trickled. Was it sweat—or blood? In a panic, he strained to constrict his spirikai yet again. The effort caused whatever blind, truncated reality he possessed to slide away.

He sat at Moro's table, clutching the green cloak in his sweaty hands. It was his burial shroud. Moro's voice floated back to him, full of regret. "Time you be leaving us, Sheft."

He forced himself to stand, to open the door, to leave Mariat behind. Out in the dark, a hollow wind moaned high overhead. It sucked up concepts that had once warmed his heart: of "wife," abandoned; of "husband," impossible; of "father," never. They rushed up like sparks from a bonfire into the night, whirling up and up, and out of the reach of his bound hands.

Pressure. He felt pressure under his right shoulder. Surilla seemed to be veering in a wide circle down the slope. He couldn't see, but remembered where he was. In the domain of Wask. Hardly daring to breathe, he molded himself against the horse's back, trying to blend into her silhouette. The blackness exuded a palpable presence that rose up behind him. Fear skittered over his skin.

But if the beetle-man were anywhere around, Surilla would surely know it. Instead, she was taking her time and picking her way. The realization overcame his sense of imminent malice. The feeling he was being watched dwindled into something he could shake off, could believe he was merely imagining, could try to ignore.

He focused on the horse. It soon became apparent she was trying to go home.

If left to herself, Surilla would instinctively find her way to Moro's barn, where these ropes would be cut away and the blindfold taken off. He would be saved. He had that choice.

But he could never take it.

He ground his forehead into the rough mane. He could never go back to the place that had cast him out, never go back to what he had already decided to leave behind. After the fair, he'd prayed to Rulve, begging for answers he could understand, for clarity in what he should do. He thought he'd gotten no reply, but now it seemed, in the inexorable working out of fate, the new village council had spelled it out for him. They had set him in the direction he must travel. No matter what awaited him, no matter how hopeless, this journey was his destiny.

His throat swelled with grief, and once more he wrenched out a mental prayer. *"Rulve help me!"* Invisible, androgynous, absent God—help me.

Like a tide, the past rushed up. His mother smiled down at his six-year-old self, telling him a story about great carved hands. *"Those who lie in them look up at the words inscribed far above: 'My life is in your hands'."* It was more than an expression of trust. It was a plea. But in an impossible reversal he never understood, a plea that was divine as well as human.

Ane nudged his elbow. *"Look here, Sheft."* She pointed to a line in the red book of tales. *'You can only save your life if you lose it.'* He'd buried those words with her, but she had kept them safe for him.

A breeze brushed over him, like a shimmer over dark water. It gently tousled his hair. *"S'eft,"* it whispered. *"Please come. Come as soon as you can."*

His shoulders slumped. But where? To do what? He'd lost everything.

The falconform opened its great beak and laughed at him. *"It seems you demand to see every outcome before setting your foot on the road. You are niyal'arist, as I am falconform. Why is this so hard for you to accept?"*

It had taken him a long time, but he *had* accepted it. He'd accepted the toltyr: the symbol, the summons, and the hope. Its physical presence was gone, but Rulve had forged its strength into his bones. He'd saved the village by leaving it, had set Mariat free, and had already paid the price. Now he had another choice, a harder one. He had to assent voluntarily to what others had thrust upon him. He had to choose this journey for himself.

With his forearms, he attempted to drag the big mare's head away from her homeward course, but didn't have the strength to do it. He remembered the words that would.

"Eechareeva, Surilla," he choked out. "Ista!"

She obeyed him, turning left and going forward, deeper into the Riftwood. It was a cold and bitter choice, and Rulve seemed nowhere around to validate it. He was alone.

They moved on. The riffling of the Meera faded away and the underbrush became sparse. The quality of the air changed, becoming heavy and still, full of the smell of humus and mold. Surilla's hooves no longer clattered on stones, but thumped with a hollow sound on thick loam. At times the horse picked up her feet as if she were stepping over fallen logs. The weighty presence of tree trunks towered over him. He was blind, couldn't feel his hands, and blood was draining from his head. All that existed was a dark circle that eclipsed both reason and faith.

From far away the voices called: the deeper tones of men, the screams of women, the sobs of children. They were the voices of the dying. His spirikai pulsed with their pleas, but all he could do was hurt with them, for he was one of them.

His despair shrank into the roughness of Surilla's mane against his forehead. His fear of the black mist congealed into unmitigated pain; and his helplessness sank into the empty ache of his heart. He was a man drowning in a well, glimpsing far stars above him, while waters of grief closed over his head. All he had left was one last prayer.

Ah, God, my life is in your hands.

CHAPTER 32

BIRTH-DAY

The cloud-wracked sky over the deadlands was just turning grey when Mariat, riding her father's Skaileg pony, pulled up at Tarn's house. Her mother's heavy green cloak covered the pants and belted tunic she normally wore for field work. Even though it was early spring, she could smell sleet in the air.

Late last night, after she set her father's broken arm and given him a potion against the pain, he had let slip the horrible significance of Sheft's altered carved mouse. He did not mention exactly what was done at the Rites, which had now somehow been restored, but his mumbled allusions and the way he covered his eyes, filled her with horror and a clawing urgency.

She made him as comfortable as she could, and if she made the potion a bit stronger than absolutely necessary, it was only because her father would try to prevent her from doing what she had to do. After propping his feet up by the hearth, she explained that she and Sheft were espoused, that she was going to find him, and that she would try to send a message if she could. Her father's only reaction was a puzzled, slightly vacant look.

But it was like a shaft through her heart. She told herself that Etane and his new wife would soon be settling nearby, then kissed her father's forehead and hugged him tightly. There was a lump in her throat when she rode away, but she didn't look back.

The pile of false evidence against Sheft lay in the yard. The wind riffled the open pages of the red book of tales and sent pieces of the charred mattress skimming over the ground like useless regrets. She slid off the pony and retrieved from the mud as many jars of her healing salves and herbs that were not broken. She stuffed them into saddlebags already packed with provisions and bandages. About to go into the house, she glimpsed something partly hidden under the shards of a broken jar. The toltyr.

She hesitated, then picked it up by its black, braided cord. Only two days ago—how could it have been only the day before yesterday?—she had washed the blood from it and gently looped it over his head.

Almost since she first laid eyes on it, she feared it had a claim on him even greater than the love he felt for her, that it would stand between them and a life together. But had that kind of life ever really existed for her and Sheft? Riah didn't think so, nor had Father. And neither did Sheft. He tried to say good-bye, but she hadn't accepted that.

A gust of wind chilled her. Was her beloved still alive? And if he was—oh God Rulve—could she repair whatever they had done to him? Once again, as it had since her father's drug-induced hints, the vision jumped before her: of Sheft's eyes, his beautiful silver eyes, changed into gaping bloody pools.

She bit her lip. *I will not*, she thought fiercely, *dwell on that. I'll concentrate on tracking him down, healing him, holding him close again.* She slipped the toltyr into her pocket and, without knocking, entered the house.

The door to Tarn's bedroom was closed, but she didn't care how much noise she made. He had abandoned Sheft, and she had no sympathy for him. She crunched over the broken crockery in the kitchen, climbed the ladder to the loft, and found clothes and blankets. The door to the bedroom was still shut when she left the house.

The day struggled to dawn behind her, but even in the dim light the tracks were, as she had hoped, plain. Many people and one large horse had gone toward the river.

At the grim rock of the K'meen Arûk, she slid off the horse's back. This was the closest she had ever been to the boulder, and just last night her father had told her its true name. The ground had been trampled all around it. Her heart pounding, she came closer, gripped the edges of the rock, then forced herself to look into the depression on top. Only a film of dirty water from last night's storm lay there. Tears of relief burned in her throat. Oh God, they hadn't taken his eyes.

At least not here. Apart from what little her father had said, she knew nothing about these terrible Rites, nothing about what Sheft might have suffered. She scanned the stony soil, found the trail heading west, and followed it to the banks of the river.

The ancient forest rose up ahead. It still held the night, still dwelt in the dark of winter. Wind sent low clouds fleeing over the trees, and a chill penetrated her heavy cloak. Sheft was in there, perhaps bleeding, shivering with ice reaction, with only his sheepskin jacket to keep him warm. He was wounded—oh Rulve, maybe blind!—in the realm of Wask. She couldn't wait for her brother's help or her father's permission, couldn't wait another entire day to meet the Rift-riders.

She took a deep and tremulous breath. With a whispered prayer to Rulve, she clicked to the pony and sent it splashing into the Meera River.

Today was her beloved's birth-day, this very day. It was the sixth of Seed, and he was nineteen years old.

End of Book One

QUESTIONS FOR DISCUSSION

1. Is *Blood Seed* a plot-driven book focused on events, or an unfolding story focused on character development? What do you think is the main theme?

2. How does Sheft change by the end of the book? What does he learn about himself?

3. Sheft is called three times to accept his vocation in life: by the old man in the green and white tent, by his mother Riah, and by the falconform Yarahe. Why do you think he refuses to listen at first? What finally convinces him?

4. Is there a deeper reason—other than his fear of the beetle-man—Sheft is so terrified of bleeding?

5. Do you think Sheft is totally committed to his calling as the book ends, or is it just the first step of his journey?

6. "A community," Yarahe said, "must provide support and safety for its members, that they may find the true identity within." How did this happen—or not happen—for Sheft?

7. There are several recurring symbolic elements in the book: like the dark circle, seeds, the beetle-man in his various forms, and the Toltyr Arulve. What meaning do they hold for you?

8. Tolkien, a linguist and a Catholic, coined the term "eucatastrophe," a terrible event that is redeemed. It's early in the series yet to see how it all works out for Sheft—and his twin brother—but can you detect ways that *Blood Seed* is a eucatastrophe?

9. Do you think Tarn is a one-dimensional character, or does he seem to be sincere in his beliefs? What about Parduka or Gwin?

10. The psychologist Carl Jung wrote about the shadow, the dark part of ourselves that we fear, are challenged by, or are ashamed of. But Jung maintained that, if rightly acknowledged, the shadow could reveal an inner light. What is Sheft's shadow, and how does he deal with it?

Thank you for taking the time to read *Blood Seed*. If you enjoyed it, please let your friends know that and consider posting a short review on Amazon and/or Goodreads. Word-of-mouth referrals are an author's best friend and much appreciated!

I invite you to sign up for my private email list for giveaways, sneak peeks, and notices about the next Coin of Rulve books. I won't spam you or share your address with anyone, and you can unsubscribe at any time. Sign up here: www.veronicadale.com

About the Author

With a background in pastoral ministry, Veronica Dale writes genre-bridging fiction that includes fantasy, romance, psychological intrigue, and spirituality. Her stories have received commendations from *Writer's Digest*, Writers of the Future, *Readers' Favorite Book Review*, *Midwest Book Review*, and the National League of American Pen Women. Much of her work has roots in the psychological concept of the Shadow, Tolkien's belief that even the worst catastrophe can be redeemed, and the insights of traditional and modern-day theologians. A member of Phi Beta Kappa, Vernie is a graduate of the Viable Paradise Science Fiction and Fantasy workshop, a Goodreads Author, and an established author with Detroit Working Writers. Visit her on at her website at www.veronicadale.com.

LOOK FOR DARK TWIN
BOOK TWO OF
THE POWERFUL NEW
FANTASY SERIES
COIN OF RULVE

Teller: damaged, driven, destined
Liasit: dares to confront him with his true name

Snatched as an innocent boy into the Spider-king's subterranean stronghold, Teller has no idea he is the emjadi, one of twin brothers called to walk the redeemer's path. Mind-probes twist his memories of home and he grows up as the dark rebel, simmering with hatred for the extended family he thinks abandoned him and the lord's acolytes who are ordered to corrupt him. A mysterious parchment hints of a chosen one with a name similar to his—and a connection to the twin brother he barely remembers. But when he discovers within himself the legendary power of fire, Teller must decide if he's the savior the beautiful slave Liasit needs him to be, or the lord's enforcer in a reign of bondage and addiction.

About the
Coin of Rulve
Series

Coin is the four-book story of lost innocence and tender love, of wounded healers struggling to accept their own power for good, of twin brothers who embark on a dark journey toward a distant light. Like the works of Tolkien, Lois McMaster Bujold, and Connie Willis, Coin is based on the belief that the truly great stories have at their core a moral premise that is inseparable from the human psyche. It describes the painful journey of self-discovery, the spiritual quest that often feels more like a forced march.

"A new approach to this genre"… "the story keeps getting better and better"… "a page-turner" … "wonderfully sympathetic characters and gifted prose"…"Wowza!"

ALSO BY VERONICA DALE
NIGHT CRUISER: SHORT
STORIES ABOUT
CREEPY, AMUSING OR
SPIRITUAL ENCOUNTERS
WITH THE SHADOW

If you're intrigued by the thing that takes shape at the foot of your bed at night, if you enjoy a little sly humor, if you crave tales that offer hope, and if you like stories that say a lot in a short space, take a ride on the *Night Cruiser*! Five star reviews on Amazon and Goodreads.

"Recommended reading, especially while the nights are long and dark!"… "fun, inventive, and thought provoking." … "'Advent' is an exceptional piece which is worth buying this collection for just to read it." … "I was fascinated, disturbed and haunted by 'Within Five Feet.'"… "flipped me from fantasy to horror to humor with a few skillful shakes." … "More please!"

www.veronicadale.com

Made in the USA
Lexington, KY
27 August 2017